DOC SAVAGE

The Wild Adventures of Doc Savage

Please visit www.adventuresinbronze.com for
more information on titles you may have missed.

(Don't miss another original Doc Savage adventure coming soon.)

SKULL ISLAND

A DOC SAVAGE ADVENTURE

BY WILL MURRAY

BASED ON A CONCEPT BY JOE DeVITO,
CREATOR OF KONG: KING OF SKULL ISLAND

COVER BY JOE DeVITO

DeVito Artworks, LLC

ALTUS PRESS • 2013

First Edition — March 2013

DESIGNED BY
Matthew Moring/Altus Press

Based on a Concept by Joe DeVito, creator of *KONG: King of Skull Island.*

SPECIAL THANKS TO
*James Bama, Jerry Birenz, John Bonness, Vicki Brown, Gary A. Buckingham, P.E.,
Nicholas Cain, Condé Nast, Col. Richard M. Cooper (Ret.), Jeff Deischer, Lester Dent,
Dafydd Neal Dyar, Theresa Henderson, Richard Kyle, Dave McDonnell, Randy Merritt,
Matthew Moring, Ray Riethmeier, Robert Seigel, Brad Strickland, Howard Wright.*

COVER ILLUSTRATION COMMISSIONED BY
Gary A. Buckingham, P.E.

Like us on Facebook: "The Wild Adventures of Doc Savage"

Printed in the United States of America

Set in Caslon.

Respectfully dedicated to Merian C. Cooper,

the visionary who conceived, co-produced and co-directed the original 1933 movie, *King Kong*.

Skull Island

Prologue

THREE PALE SEAGULLS circled the bald steel knob
that was the summit of the Empire State Building.

Where hours before, a squadron of Navy Curtiss O2C-2
warplanes had buzzed and swooped through clouds of burnt
cordite, now gulls ranged, emitting raucous cries, avid eyes
gazing down at the red flecks of animal flesh that bespattered
the skyscraper's austere Art Deco battlements.

Wheeling, one swooped down, its long beak gobbling up a
raw morsel.

Another attacked a gob of matter, carried it away trium-
phantly.

Lunging and pecking, they cleaned the carrion debris of
combat from every ledge and cranny, these ghostly buzzards of
the metropolis.

As morning continued its slow majestic breaking, they peeled
away, satiated, broad wings sun-burnished copper, never to
return.

In time, a warm rain began falling. What remained—red
fluid and sticky specks of fur—began to run and drain away.
Before the rain ceased, steel and granite had been washed off,
cleansed of all trace of that which was already falling into
legend....

FAR below, crowds clustered around the body of the vanquished.

Men in blue, their copper coat buttons afire, were busy unreeling kegs of barbed wire to cordon off the corpse. Press flashbulbs popped and were discarded, shattering on the wet pavement. Shoving bodies pressed closer, toppling the police sawhorses.

A police captain mounted a wooden keg. He lifted a megaphone to his face.

"Back, you men! Back!"

He might as well have been talking to a moving wall.

"You reporters have your stories," the captain exhorted. "Go home. The king is dead. And he won't be rising again."

A scribe called out, "Captain, what are you going to do with it?"

"That's for smarter men than me to decide, boyo."

"What does the Mayor say about this?"

"Why don't you ask him?" shot back the captain.

Another shouted, "What about the Governor? Is he in charge?"

"A bigger man than he is going to handle this. Don't you quote me, either!"

The questions kept flying. Brickbats would have been easier to fend off.

"Is the new President coming to New York?" demanded a reporter.

"I ain't heard that!" snapped the captain.

"What about—"

A shadow crossed the noon sky. A great aircraft, a tri-motor with wings as bronze as a Chinese gong, overflew the skyscraper. It circled twice, then droned off in the direction of North Beach airport.

The police captain gave out a windy sigh of relief.

"That's all!" he snapped, jumping off the keg. "No more comments. Be off with yez!"

AN hour later, a gunmetal gray roadster nosed its way through the congestion of packed humanity. There were no cars on Fifth Avenue, nor for many blocks around. Jostling pedestrians gave way reluctantly.

The man behind the wheel showed unusual patience as he tooled his quiet machine toward the skyscraper entrance. Animated eyes swept the way before him.

They were the color of golden flakes, ceaselessly swirling. Sunlight, touching his close-combed hair, made individual hairs smolder like thin wires of bronze and copper.

Busy bluecoats removed sawhorses to allow him to pass, replacing them swiftly to block all egress.

When the sedan drew up to the entrance, the police captain rushed to open the door.

"Thank Heaven you're here," he greeted.

The bronze-skinned individual who stepped out onto the running board seemed to unfold, until he stood erect, a colossus of a man. He moved forward, his face a mask of metal. Steady eyes fell on the great corpse that lay still on the cracked pavement, whereupon they hardened into gold nuggets.

Two mismatched men rushed out of the building entrance. One was a slim dandy who brandished a dark, elegant cane. The other, a red-haired human gorilla with a bullet head, whose long, dangling arms waved excitedly.

"Doc!" cried the first man. "You missed the entire bally spectacle."

"Yeah," growled the second. "After the thing broke loose, it terrorized the city, then climbed to the top of the skyscraper. The Navy sent warplanes to knock him off."

"They called the brute—"

The bronze giant waved their excited comments aside.

"Kong," he said softly, sadly.

"Oh, you heard the radio reports?"

The bronze giant shook his head slowly. "I know this creature."

The human gorilla's blocky jaw dropped open. "Blazes! You—

do?"

"Long ago, he saved my life," intoned the metallic man.

Ham Brooks and Monk Mayfair lost all power of speech.

"And I returned the favor in kind," said Doc Savage.

Book One:
THE *ORION*

Chapter I

CLARK SAVAGE, JUNIOR, the scientist and adventurer who was rapidly becoming a legend in the world as "Doc" Savage, dropped the telephone receiver into its bronze prong with a clank.

"That was the Mayor," he told Monk and Ham. "He has requested that we undertake the problem of removing the body."

"Good thing it's Sunday," grunted Monk—formerly Lieutenant Colonel Andrew Blodgett Mayfair. "The office buildings are deserted, so it'll be a snap to keep the streets clear."

Ham—he had been Brigadier General Theodore Marley Brooks during the World War—looked at his platinum wristwatch and remarked, "Renny should be here before long."

Monk nodded. "Between you and Renny, Doc, we'll get this problem fixed up quick."

Doc Savage said nothing. His golden eyes roved about the reception room of this topmost floor of the Empire State Building. He had only recently taken up residence here. The suite of rooms had belonged to his father, Clark Savage, Senior, whose recent passing remained fresh in their minds.

A model of a two-masted schooner stood on a pedestal as a reminder of the father's long career roving the world, doing good and accomplishing wonders. Now it was the son's turn to take up the family business—if business it could be called.

Doc's bronze hand moved along the ornate top of the great Oriental table that served as a desk. Inlays of ivory and rare woods had been cunningly set into the polished surface. In reality, some of these were electrical buttons, which triggered hidden mechanisms.

"You all knew that my father was an explorer in his way," Doc said quietly.

"Sure," said Monk. "He was a great man."

"Greater than any of us knew. He did much of his work quietly and without fanfare. He left his mark from New York to Chungking."

"He was a noted philanthropist," said Ham, eyeing the long slim barrel of his dark cane.

"He made and lost many fortunes," agreed Doc. "But some of the greatest treasures he uncovered my father chose not to exploit."

Doc Savage's eyes grew reflective.

Getting up from his chair, the bronze giant went to a huge safe in one corner. It would have done credit to a bank. Giving the dial a preliminary spin, he worked the combination and threw the great steel door wide.

From a cubby hole, Doc removed a teak box. He set this on the great inlaid table. It was unlocked. He lifted the ornate lid.

From within he pulled a yellowed square of parchment, very aged, and showing signs of having been waterlogged.

"This is the only proof my father brought back from the island," Doc said.

"What island?" wondered Monk.

Without answering, the bronze man set silver paperweights on each corner of the parchment.

"What is it?" asked Ham, dark eyes sharpening.

"Looks like a map," grunted Monk.

"A kind of a map," said Doc. "But it came into my father's possession in a damaged state. See the blurry area? Squid-ink writing. Obliterated. The only part that was unaffected was a landmark drawn in a different ink, a vegetable preparation that resisted salt water."

Monk and Ham crowded closer.

On the parchment, drawn in a reddish-brown ink that suggested dried blood, was a rough outline of a brooding death's head set atop a promontory.

"A skull, for sure," said Monk.

"A mountain peak in the shape of a skull," said Doc Savage. "That was all my father had to go on. He called it 'Death's Head.' But that was not its true name."

"What was?" inquired Ham.

JUST then, a huge man charged through the door. He was a big hulk of a fellow, and from the ends of his beam-like wrists hung blocky fists the size of husked coconuts.

His pomade-smeared hair almost scraped the top of the door jamb.

"Renny," said Monk, grinning.

"Holy cow!" exploded Renny, striding in. "I got here as fast as I could!"

"You are already aware of the nature of the problem?" suggested Doc.

"Man alive, yes. I already looked the big booger over. I'd suggest we haul him off the way you move a house. Place logs under him and set them to rolling."

"How do you propose to get the creature's body onto the logs?" challenged the bronze man.

"Crane. Riggers. Heavy tackle."

"Can you think of one suitable for the task at hand? This is not a concrete block, but a formerly living body. Probably every major bone is broken, if not pulverized, by its fall. Moving it will be like hauling a very large sack of bone meal."

Renny frowned. That meant he was happy, for he was most pleased when facing an engineering problem that forced him to use his brains in new ways. Colonel John "Renny" Renwick was one of the great civil engineers alive.

"We can build something!" he exclaimed.

"We can try," Doc said. "But time is of the essence. The authorities have requested that we complete the job as soon as humanly possible."

Rolling up his flannel sleeves, Renny boomed, "I'm game to start right away! We can roll him down to the Hudson River and load him on a barge. Drop him in the Atlantic."

Doc shook his head. "I have just made arrangements to buy a pier warehouse on the river, where we can store the body temporarily."

Renny demanded, "Why not just float him out into the ocean and give him a sea burial?"

"Perhaps. But while I was up north in my Fortress of Solitude, I realized that if we are to continue our work following in my father's footsteps, we will need a more handy place to store our airplanes. Driving all the way out to the airport in Queens every time we need to reach a distant destination will cost us valuable time."

Monk beamed. "I get it. A kind of boathouse-seaplane hangar combination."

"Precisely," said Doc. "There is one that is not in use. I purchased it at a good price. We will relocate the remains to that space. There I can study the creature until we arrive at a solution for appropriate disposal of the remains."

"I say we cremate it!" Monk exclaimed.

Separating his cane into two sections—the hollow barrel and the hidden sword blade of Damascus steel—Ham added, "Perhaps rendering the brute would present the best solution. Cut him up into sections, like a horse in a glue factory."

Doc Savage silenced them with a golden glance. There was frost in the big bronze man's eyes and a smoldering something that might have been repressed anger.

"Ham, locate the person who brought the creature to the city. I assume he is known."

Ham laughed. "Is he? The police are hunting him right now. He's a showman and film director named Carl Denham!"

"Find Denham."

"Righto, Doc." Clicking his cane back together, Ham exited the room.

Doc Savage addressed Monk.

"Organize control of the crowds."

"Got it," said Monk.

Lastly, the bronze man turned to Renny Renwick.

"Hauling logs into the city on short notice would be impractical," said Doc. "Telephone poles should work just as well."

Reaching for a desk telephone Renny rumbled, "Let me make some calls."

BY noon a line of tractors had been assembled on Fifth Avenue. The police were pressing the Sunday crowd back with raised nightsticks. No blows had to be struck, however. Monk went among the crowd and made his most ferocious faces, frightening away a good portion of onlookers and rubberneckers. Many who had heard of the monster ape mistakenly jumped to the conclusion that the dead creature had come back to life.

Overhead, three Navy dirigibles were hovering silently.

Monk Mayfair craned his bullet head upward.

"Where'd the gasbags come from?"

"I requested them," supplied Doc Savage.

The dirigibles began to valve gas, dropping down between Manhattan towers. It was a risky maneuver, so they performed it one at a time. Soon, they were floating serenely overhead, their steady shadows filling the street.

Mooring lines were dropped and Doc's men—all handy around airships—rushed to gather them up.

"Tie them to the creature's wrists," directed Doc Savage.

"I'm already beginning to see the light," marveled Ham.

This was done. Great chromium steel shackles had been

affixed to the brute's wrists and ankles—a sad remnant of its captivity. Only one had survived his midtown rampage in sound shape. The other three were scavenged and welded into place. There were eyelets built into these bonds for the restraining ropes and slave chains.

Once every line was tight, the airships dropped water ballast, causing them to lift anew.

A grisly spectacle took place on Fifth Avenue as they watched.

One by one, the creature's hands and feet began to rise, as if the great dumb brute were coming back to macabre life. But this was not the case. The eyes remained closed in the battered face.

Rising, the monstrous limbs looked puffy and bloated, like hairy boneless balloons, giving the unreal situation an added dose of unreality.

Arms and legs lifted sufficiently for Renny to order the first telephone poles to be rolled into place. These had been trucked in from a telephone company storage yard in Brooklyn. One was set under the primate's lifted skull, the other under his hairy haunches. Then the inert limbs were lowered.

Doc Savage called from his car radio, "Release all lines."

The lines dropped, landing with dull, whip-like thuds. Men rushed to collect them. They dragged these ropes toward the tractors, fixed them to reinforced tackle hitches.

The tractor engines started up next. Renny directed these machines.

Grunting and spilling malodorous exhaust fumes, the tractors inched forward. They sounded like a team of mechanical horses struggling with a load too great to be pulled. It was tough going. Teamster drivers began to curse and groan inarticulately.

But slowly, relentlessly, the hairy corpse began to move. The hands swung up over his shoulders, arms following.

The leading telephone pole positioned under the bloody skull began to roll. Another one stood ahead of it. With agonizing slowness, the head of the creature rolled onto the fresh log.

Now the head and shoulders bumped up onto the first pole that had been laid.

"It's working," Renny boomed. His face was one long horse-frown. That meant he was delighted. Renny was funny that way. The happier he was, the longer his face became.

It took all afternoon and the first part of the evening, but between the tugging tractors and with a construction crane brought in to lift the stubborn portions, they got the titanic loose-limbed creature onto a set of rolling logs.

Pulling the black-haired corpse toward the Hudson River after that was a mere matter of removing the rollers after the feet fell off them, and relocating them by crane to the head. Homes are moved in this fashion. But houses are built on wood-beam sills, designed to support walls. There was nothing supporting this massive burden.

The work continued to midnight. The body undulated along on its rollers, broken bones making grisly grinding noises as it progressed.

A brilliant crescent moon was up and made the scene unreal. By this time they had the great ape positioned so that its tapered skull was pointed toward the gaping doors to the great warehouse erected on a long pier facing New Jersey on the other side of the Hudson.

"We can park a lot of planes in this barn," Monk said, giving the interior a once-over. "But how are we going to keep it a secret?"

"I have invented an imaginary import-export concern for that purpose," said Doc Savage. "When this operation is complete, I will have a sign put up, suitably aged and faded, as if an existing company had relocated to this spot."

"Yeah? What are you gonna call it?"

"The Hidalgo Trading Company."

Monk grinned broadly. "Nifty name."

Turning the body had been the most difficult part. Now they had to do it again. Here the dirigibles again came into play.

This time they settled very close to the street.

Again the lines were transferred from tractors to the dirigibles and when they engaged their engines, the airships were practically dragging the corpse at a jog designed to execute a rude turn.

Once the body was in position, the tractors took over once more. Pulling the body into the gloomy warehouse interior was just a matter of Diesel fuel and man sweat.

A hastily constructed wheeled platform had been set there to receive the body. Renny had organized a work gang for that task. They had assembled the thing from ordinary building materials and truck tires, then departed, taking their carpentry tools with them. Only scatterings of sawdust remained.

When the massive doors closed on the great brute, it marked the last time ordinary eyes rested upon the creature that had once been called "King" Kong.

Chapter II

ELECTRIC LIGHTS BURNED long into the night on the eighty-sixth floor headquarters of Doc Savage. Outside, a cloudbank extending for many miles concealed the moon and stars from the sight of man. Rain was a promise that hung in the night air. The cool smell of it was leaking through the bullet cracks in the row of high windows running along the western wall. Temporary patches had sealed most of these, if imperfectly, until the bulletproof panes could be replaced. They had not been designed to stand up to military machine-guns.

The Man of Bronze was busy assembling cases of test equipment from the vast laboratory that occupied most of the floor. To these, Doc added books on zoology taken from the massive bookshelves of the adjoining library.

Monk Mayfair ambled in from the reception room, where he had been making telephone calls to the newspapers.

"Doc, I dug up the name of the girl who was carried up here by that overgrown gorilla. Called herself Ann Darrow. At least, that was the name she gave when they hauled her off the ledge outside. But no one's seen her since."

"She may no longer be important," commented Doc.

"Funny thing is, they say that Kong carried her all the way up here and after he was shot by those Navy warbirds, he set her down, gentle as can be. Sounds kinda human, huh?"

"Very human," admitted Doc, returning to his work.

Deep into the late evening hours, Ham Brooks came charging into the reception room. He was dragging a round-faced man along by the scruff of his rumpled coat collar. The new arrival was unshaven and unbalanced of eye. A battered hat sat comically askew on his head.

"Doc, permit me to introduce Carl Denham. He appears to be a little under the weather."

Monk squinted skeptically. "Looks drunk as a boiled owl to me."

"Drunken owls," said Carl Denham, exhaling fumes of alcohol, "are shining saints next to me."

Doc Savage appraised the man in silence.

"Your story would be appreciated."

"It's in all the papers. Read it for yourself." One bright brown eye squeezed shut. "You know, you look kinda like that Doc Savage fella."

"That is my name."

"Can't be. Doc Savage is almost ten feet tall. A regular Paul Bunyan. He's got eyes that shoot thunderbolts and everything he touches turns to pure eighteen-karat gold." A flicker of pain touched his weathered features. "Unlike yours truly."

"Exaggeration," said Doc.

"Damned Ninth Wonder of the World. Right behind ol' Kong."

"How did you find him in the first place?" asked Doc.

"Map. Curse it. A map got me there. Got it off a Norwegian ship's captain—damn the day I ever met him."

"I see," said Doc. "Now you find yourself in a lot of legal hot water."

Ham interposed, "I agreed to represent him in court, Doc."

"There might be a better approach to this tangle," suggested Doc. "Sit down, Denham."

Denham sat. He neglected to look behind him to see if a chair was handy, so he landed on the seat of his pants, on the carpet. He seemed not to notice.

Looking up at Doc Savage, he barked, "For the luvva Mike, but you are tall. Almost as tall as...."

Monk suddenly asked, "What happened to the blonde girl, Ann Darrow?"

"She and my first mate Jack Driscoll eloped, or something." He pulled his trouser pockets inside out. Nothing came out. Denham frowned. "I gave them my last dollar to do it with, too."

Denham's bleary bloodshot eyes seemed to go farther out of focus.

"Where is it?" he asked thickly.

"The body, you mean?"

Denham hitched up his trousers belligerently. "Damn right I do!"

"Housed in a safe place," related Doc. "How did you get Kong to the city, Denham?"

"Tramp freighter."

"The skipper's name?"

Denham tried to say the name, but his alcoholic tongue got tangled in his mouth. The name came out sounding something like "Oglethorpe."

"Englehorn," supplied Ham Brooks. "The freighter *Wanderer* is still docked on the Hudson. Hasn't left yet."

Doc directed, "Contact the harbor master. Have it detained."

"Oglethorpe's innocent, I tell you," roared Denham. "It was all my doing!"

"We are not interested in pressing charges against the freighter captain," advised Doc.

Denham said nothing to that. He seemed to become lost in his thoughts.

"He's supposed to take her back," he mumbled finally.

Interest flickered in Doc Savage's metallic mask of a face. "Her?"

"Penjaga. A native wise woman. You wouldn't understand."

Urgency crept into the bronze man's well-modulated tones. "Where is she?"

"Put her on the *Wanderer*. After the big monkey... fell."

Doc said sharply, "Denham, you will remain here. Ham, watch this man. Monk, come with me."

Doc Savage left, Monk Mayfair ambling in his wake.

THE *Wanderer* lay at anchor, a dark hulk that showed seaworthy lines. Doc Savage judged her to be capable of doing fourteen knots at her best clip.

A watchman stood at the bottom on the galvanized iron stairway, looking uneasy.

"Permission to come on board," requested Doc.

"Who's asking?"

"Doc Savage."

"Heard of you." He stepped aside. "All right, go ahead."

"Thank you."

Doc mounted the gangway. With the unerring instincts of a man who had sailed on many kinds of ships over the seven seas, he made his way below, finding the captain's rough quarters.

He knocked once, then threw open the door.

A middle-aged man with a graying mustache sat behind a desk, fiddling with an open pouch of tobacco. He looked up with sharp eyes black as buttons.

Doc asked, "Captain Englehorn?"

The skipper shot to his feet, slamming his palms on his desktop. "Who are you to come barging in?"

"Denham directed us to you," explained Doc.

Englehorn grunted. "Denham. They arrested him, have they?"

"No, but he is in protective custody for the moment."

Englehorn rolled a plug of chew in one cheek, began masticating it with the placid deliberation of a narrow-skulled cow.

Doc said, "The old woman who is named Penjaga, but called

Keeper. Where is she?"

"In her cabin. I don't think she feels like talking, though. I had to break the bad news to her. She took it hard. Not that she's shed any tears that I saw. But you could see the grief on her face."

"Tell her Clark Savage, Junior, wants to speak with her."

"Eh? She know you?"

Doc nodded. "We have met."

Captain Englehorn eyed Doc Savage skeptically.

"I never laid eyes on you before. And that woman ain't ever been off Skull Island, but that I took her away. That can only mean—"

"You are correct. I have visited Skull Island. Long ago."

"And here we thought we were the first white men to enjoy that debatable privilege," sighed Englehorn.

"Convey my request, if you will," pressed Doc.

The captain left the cabin, returning a few minutes later with a woman who seemed to shrink into herself. She had wise eyes that reminded one of an elderly tortoise. She might have been a hundred years old, or older.

"You have changed little," said Doc with sympathy.

"I have lost all. Kong...."

Doc nodded, "I know. I was far away when it happened. I had no idea."

"Your father. He is well?"

Doc shook his head sadly. "Died only months before. Murdered. The perpetrators have been dealt justice."

The old woman winced. For a time, no words seemed to encompass the moment.

Doc broke the silence.

"The body of Kong has been removed to a safe place, not far from here."

"No wild animal will devour it?"

"There are none here capable of that," assured Doc.

"Lord Kong must be returned to Skull Island," she said firmly.

"And he will be," promised Doc.

With that, the old woman lowered her seamed face and wept....

DOC SAVAGE conferred with Captain Englehorn and money changed hands.

"I started this little adventure," Englehorn muttered. "Only fair that I bring it to a fit conclusion."

"I will let you know when to move the *Wanderer* into position," Doc related.

Doc joined Monk Mayfair topside. The rusting and flame-scorched deck was all but deserted. Lines rattled skeletally in the river breeze.

"I don't savvy any of this," the hairy chemist admitted. "What's this all about, Doc?"

"It is a very long story," Doc offered. "One that should be told in full. But first we must prepare the body for transport."

"I figured out that part already," muttered Monk.

THEY drove to the long covered pier jutting out over the Hudson River. Parking at the side, they entered through a small door.

Renny met them there.

"I scrounged up everything in the way of tarpaulins I could," he informed them. "Decided that sailcloth would work best. Took some doing, but I think I have enough for the job."

Doc saw the stacks of sailcloth piled on wooden pallets and nodded. He turned his attention to the large form in the center of the cracked concrete flooring.

As if in state, the cold corpse of Kong lay on a massive rubber-tired platform that was a reinforced parade float.

"Ham will be ridin' me about this for years to come," mused Monk.

Doc looked at him curiously.

Apish shoulders shrugged. "He's tryin' to say that me and Kong here fell out of the same banana tree."

"Kong may have been closer to human than anyone imagined," said Doc, turning on additional lights until the gloom was dispelled from the warehouse interior.

"You could fit a fleet of planes in this joint," grunted Monk. Staring up at the high rafters, he added, "Maybe a dirigible, too."

But Doc Savage had already carried his equipment over to the head of the dead creature. Unpacking several cases, he began selecting tools.

"Monk, in a few hours the undertaking establishments will open for the day. Embalming fluid will be needed. And dry ice for packing. Several tons of it. Renny, you see to the latter."

"Got it," said Renny.

Monk grunted, "There ain't enough of either stuff in town to take care of this big palooka."

"We must do the best we can," advised the bronze man.

"Gotcha. On my way, Doc."

Monk and Renny left Doc Savage to his thankless task of preparing the body of King Kong for a final return to the land of his birth....

Chapter III

IT WAS NOW the late afternoon of the Monday after the spectacular fall of King Kong. A drizzle had descended over lower Manhattan. It made the cold sidewalks sizzle faintly, and automobile tires on the streets hissed as they raced about. Pedestrians hustled from corner to corner, huddled under umbrellas or holding sodden hats to their heads.

Sunset was not far off. Already the low-hanging unbroken cloudbank was flushing in the dying light. Normalcy had returned to New York City.

Trying to keep front pages dry, newsboys hawked their papers on every corner.

"*Wuxtra!* King Kong corpse missing! Monster gorilla vanishes from view! Mayor's office mum! Governor won't talk! Read all about it! *Wuxtra!*"

Papers were snapped up. But for all the ballyhoo that was promised by news butchers, there were precious few additional facts to be gleaned, other than what the cries of the street urchins carried.

As night fell, a rusty old tramp steamer warped up to the end of an unnamed warehouse on a wharf jutting out into the Hudson. The name on her stern was picked out by dismal dock lights:

WANDERER

Riverward doors rolled open. In the years to come, those

doors would open countless times to release and later receive all manner of aircraft and seagoing vessels operating under the fictitious name of the Hidalgo Trading Company. But on this sullen afternoon, the freighter was there to receive cargo.

Within, a great form lay sheeted beneath yards and yards of sailcloth, hastily sewn together. Workmen from the garment district had been recruited for this task. They were sworn to secrecy, paid off, and released back to their ordinary lives, never to speak of the strangest work ever to come their way.

As a shroud, their handiwork had a makeshift quilted look to it. But not a hair of the body beneath showed anywhere. The suffocating stench of formaldehyde hung in the cavernous confines.

On the deck of the *Wanderer*, the main cargo hatch had been pried open, revealing a huge hold lined in stainless steel. The boom of a great deck crane swung out. A rusty hook dangled from a woven-steel cable. It came to a rocking stop just before the open doors.

In the yawning interior, lights had been doused, so that only a few illuminated the gloomy vastness. This precaution, as well as the blocking freighter, would obscure the transfer operation from prying eyes.

Doc Savage stepped forward to signal the hook to drop lower. Deck hands complied with this silent order.

Renny Renwick was perched atop the great sailcloth tent that protected the immense body of the largest land creature ever to walk the Earth. He was checking a tangled arrangement leading to a steel turnbuckle ring that gathered together strands of heavy wire crisscrossing the form, holding the body and its dry-ice packing together.

Renny lifted a thumb so large it might have been a tent peg. "O.K.," he rumbled.

At the landward side of the interior, Doc Savage, Monk Mayfair and Ham Brooks put their backs into pushing the wheeled platform forward, toward the open door and the anchored freighter.

Amazingly, the platform began inching ahead. The combined strength of Doc and Monk accomplished that. Ham did his level best, but unlike the others, he was no Hercules.

As the platform moved, Renny used a boat hook to capture the dangling turnbuckle, drew it in toward him. Catching it in his monster hands, the big engineer muscled the iron contraption into the ring of steel holding the wiring together, and made it fast.

Turning, he bellowed, "Let 'er rip!"

Doc and Monk put every straining muscle into the task.

The platform began rolling faster. Ponderously, it picked up speed. Rubber tires ground grit and dust into the concrete floor.

The leading tires came to the edge of the warehouse floor, went off the lip and the platform banged to a stop, hanging precariously.

This was sufficient clearance to allow the crane to begin lifting.

"Careful!" boomed Renny. "Take 'er slow."

The crane reeled in cable, the hook jerked erect. Suddenly the platform was suspended a few feet in space. Below, the constant drizzle made the dirty Hudson River water speckle and dance.

Renny made haste to jump off the patchwork sailcloth covering.

Landing on the floor, he joined Doc and the others, who were keeping a respectful distance.

The platform heeled, rebalanced itself, and was deliberately swung out of the warehouse confines. With great care and caution, the hook brought it over the scorched deck, then began depositing it into the waiting cargo hold.

As the body was lowered from their sight, they watched in respectful silence.

Came a muffled *thump*, and a rocking of the freighter at her anchor chain told that the platform had been landed safety.

After a few minutes, the cable withdrew, showing the empty hook, dripping rain.

The main hatch was hastily closed. Doors landed with the thudding finality of a coffin lid slamming shut.

"That's that," announced Renny.

Ham Brooks looked to Doc Savage.

"Are you going back with it?"

The bronze man shook his head sadly.

"No. Once was enough."

On the bridge, three figures appeared. Captain Englehorn was recognizable. As was Carl Denham, looking clear-eyed and determined now. His old self. Restored and rejuvenated.

Penjaga the Keeper stood at his side. She waved a sad hand in silence.

Doc Savage lifted an answering hand, and bid farewell without a word. There was something in his golden eyes that was not like any emotion his aides had ever before seen there. Not even on the day Doc had learned that his father had died.

With a noisy rattle, the *Wanderer* weighed anchor and the throbbing engines began to make themselves heard and felt.

The freighter warped away, showing its rusty old stern.

No one stood on the broad fantail deck to wave a final farewell. Pelting rain had driven most of the passengers and crew below.

Dusk had turned to night during the transferal. Now the myriad lights of Manhattan were coming on.

The lights of the *Wanderer* were few. Soon enough, they were lost in the monotonous gray rain.

Peering out into the mists, Ham Brooks observed, "It took a lot of pulling of strings to let Denham go along, but the city fathers finally agreed."

Monk grunted, "After cutting corners and all that red tape to let him bring that monster into the city, they could hardly clap him in the Tombs without a stink bein' raised."

Renny boomed, "Well, the city has calmed down, anyway. People will start forgetting it ever happened."

"Not me," said Monk. "I saw that big monkey climb our skyscraper. I ain't ever gonna forget that! I was observin' from an autogyro when he took that header to the pavement."

Doc Savage did not contribute to this exchange. He was moving about the warehouse interior, closing the electrically controlled doors and shutting off the lights, one by one.

Ham walked over to join him.

"You have so far declined to explain your history in this horrid matter," he ventured.

"It is a very long story. But one worth telling. Let us repair to our headquarters for the evening."

LESS than twenty minutes later, Doc Savage took his customary chair behind the exotic reception room table that served as a receiving desk. His golden eyes held a faraway light. The brisk animation that normally imbued the irises, like the snowflakes in one of those glass globes that contain miniature snowstorms, were eerily quiescent.

Once more, Doc had on the desk the parchment map which was obliterated—all but the rude drawing of the mountain peak that resembled a human skull.

"This story begins with a man all of you have heard about, but none of you had the pleasure of meeting. My grandfather, Stormalong Savage."

Ham said, "Jove! They called him 'Old Stormy.' He captained a clipper ship during the days of the tea trade. Considered to be one of the best blue water men who ever lived."

"Yes," said Doc. "As you are aware, the Savage family is perhaps the first of the prominent New World families. There was a Savage in Jamestown. It is among the earliest recorded surnames in North America. Savages made their mark from Maine to California since that time. But Stormalong Savage was the first of our line to be classed as a legend in his own lifetime."

Doc Savage's men took comfortable chairs. The bronze giant was normally a man of few words, but they sensed that the story to be told might take most of the evening, and they didn't want to miss a syllable of it.

Doc resumed speaking. "That model in the corner is a replica of Stormalong Savage's ship, the *Courser*. On it, he made the run from Baltimore to Siam and back, breaking records on a regular basis. That was back in the 1860s, at the height of the tea trade as it was in sailing days."

"Whatever happened to him?" grunted Renny.

"Lost at sea," said Ham. "Correct?"

"Partially correct," qualified Doc. "There is much more to it than what history records. When the era of the clipper ship had passed, Stormalong took his ship to the South Seas seeking a different kind of treasure."

Doc Savage's eyes were upon the model of the *Courser*. He seemed to be far back in time, no longer present in the room.

For a good minute the only sound was the ticking of their wristwatches.

"This story that needs telling began not long after the six of us went our separate ways following the Armistice, over a decade ago."

Monk said, "That's how we first met. In the trenches."

"I cut my eyeteeth on barbed-wire entanglement," allowed Renny.

Ham said, "We didn't see or hear of you for over a year after that."

"My father saw to that," said Doc. "He had plans for me. The war interrupted those plans. He was determined to get me back on the path he had ordained for me since before my birth. 'To right wrongs and punish evildoers,' he used to say. To this day, I still do not know what motivated him."

"Heck," snorted Monk. "That's simple. He devoted his whole

life to the same creed. He just wanted his only son to follow in his footsteps—that's all there was to it."

Doc Savage shook his head gravely. "No, there is more. Perhaps one day I will understand the thinking that compelled a man to entrust his first-born son to an endless parade of scientists and other experts from the age of fourteen months into adulthood, molding him along scientific lines. But he gave me only glimpses and gleanings of his thought processes. No clear answers were ever forthcoming."

"There was a vogue back before the turn of the century to school up children to be virtual supermen," offered Ham Brooks. "No doubt he first conceived the idea from those experiments."

"We may never know for certain," admitted Doc.

"What about this Skull Island Monk mentioned?" prompted Renny. "That's what I want to hear about."

"As you all know, we only recently endured a hazardous adventure on a previously unknown spot near New Zealand called Thunder Island."

Monk grinned. "Yeah. Johnny Littlejohn is still studying his notes on that trip. He's talking about writing a book on the only known survival of prehistoric life into the Twentieth Century."

"Thunder Island is not the only such place of its kind," interjected Savage, "Skull Island—or Skull Mountain Island, to give it its complete name—is quite similar in some ways—although very different in others. It is of Skull Island that I must speak tonight."

Outside, the dismal drizzle was painting the high row of windows in running transparent watercolor tones. As they waited for Doc to go on, the rain picked up in intensity, became like drumming fingers, urgently encouraging the Man of Bronze to get on with his tale.

"It all began with a telegram from my father," began Doc....

Chapter IV

THE STRIPS OF letters pasted on the yellow telegram still looked freshly typed as Clark Savage, Junior, reread them on the steamer *Hurucan,* which was bringing him home from France.

CSJ RETURN TO STATES ALL SPEED STOP
AWAIT ME IN SAN FRANCISCO STOP
XAVAGE

That was his father. Brisk and to the point. And more than a little cryptic. When he wished to convey urgency, he always spelled his last name with an X. Why he did so was beyond fathoming. He had many such quirks.

Not for the first time did Doc Savage wonder what was so urgent as to summon him home on the very first day of his discharge. How had the old man known he was at liberty? Well, he had friends in very high places. Probably no mystery there. No doubt a great many officers in the U.S. and other allied armies had kept Clark Savage, Senior, apprised of his son's activities—where wartime censorship concerns permitted, of course.

Doc—he had picked up the nickname in the trenches—reflected on the strange turn his life had taken. In his first year of medical school, he had enlisted in the war against the Kaiser, where his skill patching broken bones, bullet wounds, and saving soldiers' lives had caused his comrades to name him that. He liked it. Liked it from the start. He had always been Clark,

29

Junior. Now he was Doc Savage. It had the flair of the Old West, along with a note of respect accorded to a medical man.

On the bed of his bunk lay a strew of metallic objects. These were the components of a Colt .45 automatic, along with a Thompson Annihilator submachine gun and a German MP18— the latter the first machine pistol ever devised. He had disassembled all three in order to bring them home with him. Their mechanisms fascinated him. He picked up the pieces and examined each, his active imagination working.

The automatic's design was barely ten years old, but already attempts were being made to improve upon it. The German machine pistol was more recent than that. The Thompson gun had been invented for trench clearing operations, but the war had ended before it could be fielded. Doc had come into possession of one of the prototype models, which had been given to him after the war concluded because the brass thought he was the right man to test it. Doc soon discovered that the Thompson had a tendency to jam, and the muzzle was difficult to hold level when in operation. Not that Doc ever had any trouble with that. He could fire a .50 caliber Lewis gun without the need of a tripod mount.

What if the ferocious firepower of an Annihilator gun could be harnessed on a frame nearer to that of a Colt automatic? Both employed the same .45 caliber round. What a weapon that would be!

Doc toyed with the pieces. He had no access to a machine shop. But at his first opportunity, he vowed that he would attack the problem.

That is, if his father allowed him to pursue this.

From the first dawn of self-awareness, Doc had been subject to his father's indomitable will. There was no brooking it. Quitting medical school to join the army was the first time he had stood up to him in a contest of iron wills. It had not been easy. It might not have been acceptable, but for the simple fact that Clark Savage, Senior, was every bit the patriot as his son.

The nation had called its young men. And Clark Savage, Senior, could not, in the end, thwart his son from enlisting. So it was done.

Now, it was time to pay the piper.

Reluctantly, Doc began stowing the loose pieces back into his kit bag. His metallic features were becoming set. San Francisco lay only hours away. It was difficult to guess what awaited him at landfall.

NIGHT was holding off when the liner pulled into the Embarcadero.

Clark Savage, Senior, was standing in the front of the receiving crowd, towering a full head taller than any of the others, his hair streaked with threads of premature frost.

His rugged face was a weathered mask of brass. His eyes looked eerily pale against the wind-burned skin that had known a thousand suns, and countless climes. Gold they were, but clear and almost transparent. Unlike his son's eyes, which seemed to be filled with minute golden flakes that were never still. The first time Doc had read Jack London's *Sea Wolf,* he was struck by how much like his father schooner master Wolf Larsen was, possessing the same rangy, symmetrical musculature—right down to the challenging golden eyes.

Shouldering his kit bag, Doc strode down the sagging gangplank.

"Father," he said simply. There was not much emotion in the greeting.

Clark Savage, Senior, returned the favor. He did not smile. A brush mustache sprinkled with silver made his mouth look grimly serious.

"Come. We must hurry."

"What is wrong?

"Explain on the way. Hard voyage?"

"I came by way of the Panama Canal. Reckoned it would be faster than landing in New York and coming west by rail."

"Sound thinking."

"Where are you staying? The Savoy?"

"You will see."

The waiting cab took them only a short distance to the sea wall by the coal pier at the foot of Mission Street. There rocked a familiar black two-masted schooner, rocking with the tide. Brass railed and copper-hulled, she was a sleek beauty. The name on the bows was ORION. Her tilting mast poles stood bare.

"Let me apologize for offering you such a meager berth after so long a crossing," Clark Savage, Senior, was saying.

"I was born on a ship, Father."

"Yes. As I recall, this very one."

They boarded the schooner. She was as Doc remembered her, ketch-rigged for easy handling, spic-and-span from her clipper-style bow to her taffrail. The white pine deck looked freshly holystoned.

From the crew's quarters scuttle, emerged two stolid-faced men with coarse black hair and coffee-colored features. They were short and squat, and while their muscles showed no definition, there was no questioning their raw strength.

"Indians?" asked Doc of his father.

"Mayans. They do not speak English. We have four in all."

"Strange crew."

"Mayans keep secrets."

Doc nodded. "During the latter months of the war, we used Choctaw speakers to pass messages by field telephone and wireless. The Germans mistakenly thought it was a code they could break; actually it was a language they could never translate."

"So I have heard." Turning to his crew, Savage barked out rapid orders in the Mayan tongue. They leapt to work.

"I just told them to cast off."

"Where are we bound?" wondered Doc.

"Where would you like to go?" countered Savage Senior, eyes snapping golden fire.

"Are you giving me a choice?"

"I thought after the ruinous wars of old Europe, fresh scenery would do you some good."

Doc Savage regarded his father intently.

"I understood that your summons was urgent."

"It is. But I remain interested in your answer."

"I have always wanted to see more of Asia. I enjoyed many happy hours in the South Seas."

"Fortunately, our itinerary takes us in that general direction. Therefore, you will get your wish. I will stow your things below."

Clark Savage, Senior, took his departure without another word.

Doc Savage watched the unspeaking crew cast off lines and prepare the *Orion* for departure. He wondered what it was all about.

Deciding time would tell, Doc pitched in to make the schooner ready to leave port.

The sails were raised. The anchor was brought on board mechanically. Powered by her auxiliary gasoline engine, the *Orion* warped out of the slip like a seagoing angel with canvas wings.

Slipping through Golden Gate in a light chop, Captain Savage at the helm, the graceful schooner cleared the Heads and passed into the North Channel in smart time.

Standing in the bow, Doc Savage felt very strange. He was born on this very boat, below deck. She had been anchored off Andros Island in the Bahamas group. He never knew why his parents were coved there. His father always avoided the question rather artfully. For a long time, Doc labored under the mistaken belief that he had been born on the Andros Island situated near the Aegean Sea. His father had told him only the island's name, which he had looked up in an Atlas, never dreaming that there were two islands by that identical name.

Now the *Orion* was taking him across the Pacific. And the reasons would probably be a long time in coming....

SUPPER was simple fare. Simple, but substantial: Mashed potatoes; fresh T-bone steaks in unacknowledged honor of his return from Europe; green beans; squash. Stick-to-the-ribs stuff.

They ate in silence at first.

A thousand questions passed through Doc Savage's mind. In many respects, he barely knew his father. He had been an intermittent presence from his earliest memory. Always off on one adventure after another. He seemed more like a distant uncle than a parent, and that peculiar feeling persisted.

It had been his father's money that paid for the procession of scientists who had reared Doc during his formative years. Intensive study. Hard work. Constant travel. Challenging years, they had been. But fulfilling, too. Approaching his twentieth year, Doc looked thirty.

Invariably, Clark Savage, Senior, stepped in to evaluate the progress of his son. His experiment. Then he would be gone.

Doc had a vivid recollection of a group of older boys piling on him for no discernible reason when he was thirteen. He beat them all—only to discover that his father had paid them to administer a beating. It was no act of aggression, but a way to toughen up Doc for the difficult life that lay before him. It had worked, of course, but at the time the ambush had the appearance of unnecessary cruelty.

Not until Doc had gone off to war did he understand that the stratagem of continually pushing him beyond normal limits had undoubtedly saved his life.

Questions, questions. Always questions. Rarely any answers.

Doc considered his first question, changed his mind and said, "I am thinking of not returning to medical school, father."

"Doesn't matter."

Doc looked at his parent. Finishing medical school had been

a supernal goal. But now the old man seemed disinterested.

"I expected an argument," said Doc.

"The war broke me financially, Clark. Long story. There are no funds available to continue your training."

The admission so shocked Doc Savage that he withheld comment. He had none. What was there to say?

"What will you do?" he asked at last.

"One thing I learned from your grandfather was that the world is full of treasure, just for the taking. One simply has to find it."

"Is this a treasure-hunting expedition, then?"

Seeming not to hear, Clark Savage, Senior, went on, "Your grandfather has been missing a very long time, you know."

"Is there word of him?"

"After a fashion."

"Go on."

"The *Courser* has been sighted, adrift in the Indian Ocean. Dismasted. No hands, no bodies on board. A derelict ship."

"After all this time..." said Doc quietly.

"My intention is to run her down and search the ship for clues."

"Count on me."

"I counted on no other answer from a Savage."

Doc went back to his meal. "If we make a swift crossing, we can reach the Indian Ocean by the first of the year. That will give us three months to operate before the monsoon rain cycle begins all over again."

No sooner had the last word left his mouth than Doc realized that had been his father's plan all along. Hence the urgency.

Savage Senior ate in silence for a time, then looked up. "What are your plans, son?"

"Plans?"

"Assuming that we survive this venture—and I intend that we do—what are your plans for the future now that you are a man and have no filial obligations to complete your training?"

"I have become very interested in mechanical studies," admitted Doc.

"Engineering?"

"Weapons. The revolver is a thing of the past. A new weapon of war has been devised. A portable machine gun that a soldier can carry efficiently. But it is bulky and the ammunition canister rattles when toted. I have been thinking that this Annihilator submachine gun can be improved to the point that a man can carry it in a holster at his side, as conveniently as a pistol."

Clark Savage frowned. "I had hoped for a loftier goal."

"A great war has just concluded. Despite the proclamations that this was the War to End All Wars, there will be another one, fought with even more fearsome weapons. We must stand ready to defend the nation. Better, more efficient weapons will be the key."

"Well put. But my comment stands. I had hoped for something loftier."

Clouds passed before Doc's metallic orbs. "This will occupy a few months at best. After that, we will see."

"Yes, we will."

THEY took their coffee on the forward deck in stoneware mugs. The father drank his black, while the son preferred it with cream and sugar.

"Don't count on cream for much longer," the father cautioned.

"I am thinking of giving up coffee altogether. Bad for the nerves."

"It was a habit you picked up in France, I imagine. Stimulants were previously denied you."

"Grandfather is certainly dead," ventured Doc after a silence.

"Many have assumed that for years now. But nothing is certain, not where Stormalong Savage is concerned."

"To hear that his ship still floats is remarkable. Most clippers lasted only a generation, at most."

"They were built for speed, not to endure," agreed the elder Savage. "The *Courser* first put to sea over fifty years ago. It is like a man living to be one hundred and thirty years in age. Not impossible, but highly improbable."

Doc stared off into the stars. "He was seeking a new fortune. I wonder if he ever found it?"

"If so, that fortune might still be there for the taking."

"My thought exactly."

They sipped in silence for a time. Conversation was difficult. Father and son, yet comparative strangers. The elder Savage was not profligate with his words. The son took after him in many ways—but in his own unique fashion.

"I have many questions for you, Father. Questions that I have pondered my entire life."

Finishing his coffee, Clark Savage, Senior, looked his son square in the eye and said, "I fear that I have few answers I care to share with you. Good night."

With that, he walked off.

Doc Savage followed him with his gaze, thinking, *Who is this man who is my father? Why is he always a stranger to me?*

Chapter V

A T HONOLULU, HAWAII, they took on supplies:
Fresh vegetables, dried fruit and meat, along with other
staples. And a new calendar. For they happened to make landfall on the first day of the New Year, 1920.

The *Orion* remained in port less than a half day. Doc Savage
wanted to go ashore and test his land legs. He got as far as the
dock area. Walking on dry land felt peculiar. His body wanted
to rock with the motion of the perpetually-unsteady deck he
no longer rode upon. The unsteadiness dissuaded him from
exploring further.

It was as if the heaving Pacific still had him in its grip. But
he knew from his studies that the balance mechanism of his
inner ear had adjusted itself so well to the pitch and roll of the
Orion's deck that the delicate structure remained in sympathy
with the phantom Pacific.

Returning to the *Orion* reluctantly, Doc conferred with his
father.

"How soon do we sail?"

"Immediately."

"The difficult part of this undertaking begins now."

"We have sufficient supplies," returned Savage Senior.

"That is not what I mean. I think you know that."

"Under sail we will make a straight run to the Philippines,
then turn south to Sumatra. That will be our next landfall."

"Under fair conditions, that will cost us six days."

38

"Double that. For I do not expect fair conditions. The monsoon season is not quite concluded. Once we reach the Indian Ocean, we will be propelled by the northeast trade winds every league of the way. Should be able to make up our time then."

Sail was unfurled and once again they were back on the tide.

Honolulu and its lush green mountains fell astern like a dream island. Soon, the *Orion* was bounding along the waves. With the greater expanse of the Pacific behind them, the character of the voyage changed.

Clark Savage, Senior, set the tone at last light.

"Starting tomorrow," he said, "you will address me as Captain, not Father. As befitting my first mate. Is that understood?"

Doc stiffened. "Yes. You make yourself very plain. But why?"

"Discipline must be maintained. For the good of all."

"Have it your way. Need I salute?"

"No. Superfluous ceremony is unnecessary. Economy is what is needed now. Economy, and discipline."

"If my mother were here, I wonder what she would say?"

Captain Savage replied nothing. He went about the business of bossing his taciturn crew.

DOC SAVAGE spent what free time he could scrounge during the first week of the crossing in his cabin, reassembling the Colt pistol and the Tommy gun. There was a small machine shop below, for repairs. Doc obtained permission to work with the tools therein.

He began fashioning a weapon from blocks of steel and other metal forms. It was slow going, but the work occupied his spare time.

Once his father looked in on the work in progress and grunted something noncommittal.

"You disapprove?" challenged Doc.

"After that last slaughter, the world could do with fewer weapons."

"The world needs better weapons to prevent future slaughters. And war is sometimes glorious. After all, we won."

"This war. What about future wars? Can any nation, no matter how powerful, win them all?"

Doc Savage offered no answer to that. It was a sobering thought.

He resumed his work. For his idea to pan out, he would need to simplify the firing mechanism of the Annihilator gun in order to miniaturize it. Doing so required adopting a caliber substantially smaller than a .45. Doc hoped that a .38 would do. But he was beginning to wonder if .22 caliber shells were his only practical recourse. Not much stopping power in a .22 slug. Yet a rain of them would do the job if the rate-of-fire could be stepped up....

THAT night, Doc took First and Middle watches.

Most of the crew slept below. One or two came out on deck and stood at the stern, as if dreaming of their homeland. They never smiled, never seemed happy. Their faces might have been hewn of some mineral that combined the softness of flesh with the strength of stone.

Doc wondered how his father had prevailed upon them to crew his ship.

Attempting to draw any of them into conversation proved futile. They appeared to know no English. Worse, they shunned it. It was all he could do to get them to say their names. Ikan. Kish. Ichik. Chicahua. They were easily remembered.

Doc turned in at dawn but slept only three hours. He had been given the cabin in which his mother had birthed him. The thought made him restless. As little as he knew about his father, his mother was an even greater mystery. Sometimes, if he relaxed, he could almost recall her face. But that might have been a trick of the mind. He had been so young when she died, it was as if he had never had any mother at all....

Skipping breakfast, Doc went topside and began the routine

of exercises that was the first item of discipline that his father had instilled in him when he had barely learned to walk. Long ago, this ceased to be a choice Doc made. He just naturally went about his routine.

Stripped to the waist, his bronze muscles gleaming, he attracted the attention of the Mayans, who always watched, but never spoke. It was evident even on their impassive faces that Doc's system of exercising his body was beyond their comprehension. In their primitive world, life was hard, work strenuous. The muscles were naturally exercised in the course of daily life.

Captain Savage came over and watched his son. A satisfied expression seemed to fall over his rugged face.

"Imagine you had a hard time keeping this up in the army," he observed.

"I made do," allowed Doc.

"Good. You always had excellent habits."

Captain Savage strolled off.

After a while, Doc completed the last part of his physical regimen and joined the crew in their shipboard work. They acknowledged him with glances and nods, then all but ignored him.

Observing one pointless attempt at conversation, Captain Savage drew his son aside and said, "I do not wish them to know English. It would ruin their value to me."

"Where did you find them?"

"In Central America. Hidalgo, to be exact. The Mayan empire vanished many generations ago, no one knows how or why. But pockets of descendants survive. I am cultivating these men. They know many secrets. Perhaps from them it will be possible to discover the mysteries of that vanished race of men and the empire that history barely records."

"As you wish, Father."

"As I command."

"Yes, Captain."

Chapter VI

THE RUN TO the Philippines was uneventful. The weather was splendid, prevailing winds favorable. Without fail, the sun shone every day. Contrary to expectations, it grew so predictable that Captain Savage began grumbling that he could stand a little rain as a change of pace.

Doc Savage went about the routine of the schooner and devoted himself to his private work whenever possible. He was making slow progress. The problem of caliber remained a stubborn one. He really preferred a .38 load. But more and more, the .22 made increasing sense. In addition to the obvious fact that one could fit more .22 shells in an ammunition clip than any higher caliber, a greatly reduced firing chamber called for a compact round. This appeared to be the inescapable logic of the problem.

To take his mind off the matter, he removed the heavy stock, replacing it with a lanyard for greater portability. A lesser man required the butt stock in order to steady the devastating weapon while in operation, but Doc Savage's massive arms could control it easily. This despite the muzzle's stubborn tendency to climb off target of its own accord.

One night, Doc worked through the entire evening. He had the forenoon watch that day. Unsatisfied with the ammunition capacity of the standard twenty-round clip, he began fashioning a drum magazine for the Annihilator. It was easily machined, and when he had it formed, Doc had doubled the sturdy submachine gun's ability to emit rounds without reloading. All that remained was to test-fire it.

When he was finished, the bronze giant climbed back on deck and went in search of his father. There was no sign of him.

Returning below, Doc knocked on the captain's cabin. There was no response. Placing an ear to the panel, Doc listened. His acute hearing could detect a man's respiration through any reasonable thickness of wood. But no such sounds came to his sensitive eardrums.

Throwing open the door, Doc found the bed unmade. That in itself was alarming. His father had instilled in him very regular habits; making his bed upon rising was one of them.

Going from nook to nook, Doc sought the missing man. He employed his keen sense of smell, but it ultimately proved useless. His father's personal cologne permeated the schooner interior.

He was nowhere to be found. Doc even checked the crew quarters up in the forecastle, but the tight arrangement of bunks wedged into the bow area held no cubicle fit for a man.

Returning to the main cabin, Doc retraced his search, with an eye to what may have been overlooked.

Behind a bulkhead stood the gasoline engine, seated on a platform. An access door permitted inspection, but Doc did not possess the key. So Doc picked the padlock with a small tool—another useful although disreputable skill he had picked up during his unusual schooling.

Opening the hatch, Doc was assailed by the stink of gasoline. A quick examination showed conclusively that the gloomy, malodorous hold harbored only mechanism, no person.

Shutting the hatch, Doc relocked the thing, metallic features grim.

In desperation, Doc picked the lock of a steamer trunk that he knew was too small to contain his father, even if he were a skilled contortionist.

Inside, he discovered several complicated devices. A set of

hydrophones, such as were used for submarine detection. A much more elaborate apparatus that Doc finally determined was a photophone—a device for transmitting sound via a beam of light—which had never come into general use. There were other, even more arcane devices, including, Doc was puzzled to discover, a wireless telegraph instrument in dire need of repair.

Mouth set, Doc relocked the trunk.

Climbing back on deck, Doc called out. "Captain! Captain! *Father!*"

No answer came. Only the rushing of water along the sleek hull.

Doc accosted the first man he came upon. Chicahua the boatswain, whose name meant "Strong."

"Captain. Savvy?"

The man shrugged, returned to coiling line.

Doc grabbed another.

"Have you seen the captain?"

The Mayan just stared, uncomprehending as a block of wood. Only his obsidian eyes betrayed awareness.

Doc flung him away, called out, "Father! Where are you?"

But no reply came.

A hasty search of the below-decks area brought the same result as before. It was maddening. The impulse to repeat the search came and went. Several times, Doc fought it. He knew that he had exhausted every possibility.

Back on deck, he brought a pair of field glasses to his eyes and began scanning the surrounding ocean.

Crinkling blue waves, shimmering with sunlight, were all he spotted.

A telescope was next employed. This gave better range and sharpness. But nowhere did he spy any sign of Captain Savage.

The dory sat upside down on its chocks. Doc stripped the canvas covering, exposed the dry hull. It had not been put off.

Having exhausted all possibilities, Doc Savage went to the bow and cast his mind back to the evening before. There was nothing in his father's manner to suggest any trouble. Not with the crew, nor the boat. No, he was certain his father had communicated nothing unusual.

Of course, the old man was so reticent that it was often difficult to plumb what was going through his brain. He was a man who had grown accustomed to keeping his own counsel. Especially after he had been widowed.

Mastering his quaking emotions, Doc observed the crew. They were going about their business as if nothing untoward had happened. That was suspicious. Surely, they understood that the captain was no longer on board.

Or was he…?

DOC considered and discarded many possibilities. Had his father gone overboard in the night? No, a splash or cries for help would surely have reached his ears.

Of course, if he had been waylaid, and tossed over the rail while unconscious, that would be a different matter.

The coffee countenances of the Mayan Indians remained unreadable. But nothing in their manner, or the way they went about their routine, suggested outward concern or guilt.

Slowly, a theory began forming in Doc's brain.

He decided to test it.

Pretending to be searching among the coils of manila rope and deck clutter for clues, Doc sidled up to a Mayan who was giving the deck a scrub.

Doc made a show of walking in circles, looking puzzled. On one turn around that part of the deck, he slipped, knocked the unprepared crewman against the rail.

The man sprawled awkwardly. Doc helped him topple overboard with a canvas-covered toe.

The splash that came was quite distinct, satisfying Doc that he would have heard any similar commotion even down in the machine-shop cubicle.

The Mayans began making a commotion. Their cries were impossible to translate, but Doc imagined that they were the Mayan equivalent of "Man Overboard."

Withdrawing to a spot behind the broad deckhouse, Doc Savage waited.

His patience was rewarded by the thud of booted feet coming up the companionway.

The silvery head of his father popped into view, cold golden eyes looking startled. Harsh words rippled from his lips as he yanked on his black captain's cap.

The Mayan crew began shouting and gesturing to the stern, where one of their own was bobbing like a black-haired cork in the turbid wake of the *Orion*.

Orders were rapped out. The lifeboat was stripped of its canvas weather sheeting and swung out on davits. Captain Savage took command of it.

Climbing aboard, Doc Savage said calmly, "It was all that I could think to do to flush you out."

"You shoved a man overboard?" Captain Savage roared.

"I had a clumsy moment."

Crew lowered the lifeboat and the dory smashed into the Pacific, which was living up to its name that day.

Unshipping the oars, they rowed toward the splashing man. He could swim well enough, for he began doing a breaststroke in their direction.

When they met, boat and man, Doc Savage assisted him into the boat. It was Chicahua.

"Please convey my apologies," said Doc, indicating the wet Mayan.

Captain Savage did so. Or appeared to do so. Doc couldn't make out the lingo, even after hearing it for more than a week.

Captain Savage directed his full attention to his son.

"I have a mind to—"

Doc interrupted him more calmly than he felt.

"Where were you hiding, Captain?"

"Who said I was hiding?" the other returned.

"I searched every nook and crevice. From the lazaret to the fo'c'sle. You were nowhere to be found."

"We are sailing into unsettled waters. I wanted to test your mettle."

"And?"

"You have very unorthodox methods," Captain Savage said grudgingly. "I expected you to concentrate your search so that you uncovered my hiding place."

"Why go to all that trouble when flushing you out of hiding was so much more satisfactory?" countered Doc.

The old man fumed in silence as they rowed back to the *Orion,* which had struck sail and was lying dead in the water.

As the boat was hoisted back to the stern deck, Captain Savage observed, "You have cost us valuable time."

"Which we can make up, if the winds favor us," pointed out Doc. And there was a twinkle in one golden eye.

THE winds favored them. By afternoon, they were making a brisk ten knots.

Her canvas cracking in the wind, the *Orion* leaped and crested the placid waves. She seemed energized by the chance to race with the wind.

Doc Savage went about his work more content than he had been so far in the voyage. His father had tried to teach him a lesson, and Doc had returned the favor.

It was a good feeling. All his life, Doc had been his father's son. These last two years away at war, and now back feeling as if he could lick the world, made him feel more like his own man than the son of Clark Savage, Senior.

"They hung a nickname on me in France," Doc said over dinner, which had been chilled by a thick, frosty silence.

Savage Senior looked up from his fish stew.

"What's wrong with Clark?"

"Nothing is wrong with it! That's your name."

The old man grunted. "So what did they call you?"

"Doc."

"Gunmen and gamblers are called Doc. Ever hear of a rounder named Doc Holiday?"

"Maybe Doc Savage will replace him in the history books. Some day."

The captain's frost-rimed eyebrows shot up. "You mean to tell me that you're keeping that name?"

"Why shouldn't I? It suits me."

"Not so much now that you cannot return to medical school, eh?"

"I have not ruled out completing my studies some day, Father," Doc returned patiently.

Captain Savage spooned fish stew into his mouth for over a minute before he uttered, "I wonder what your mother would have thought, having a son grow up to be known as Doc."

Doc Savage became very quiet. He had often wondered that very same thing.

Chapter VII

CLEAR SAILING ENDED when they entered the Philippine Sea. A blow sprang up and began to worry the rippling sails. The Mayans got busy tending the unruly canvas.

Doc Savage stood at the wheel. More and more, that duty fell to him. He was good at it. He had practically started life at this station. One of his earliest adult responsibilities had been steering the *Orion* when he was only eight years old. He had to stand on a crate in order see over the deckhouse roof.

Captain Savage was conning the waters ahead with his old spyglass.

"I am thinking that we might steer south to Borneo and go around this soup," he remarked at last.

"We'll have to run down Makassar Strait to the Java Sea, and then on up to Karimata Strait," said Doc. "That will cost us several days."

"A bad blow would have us at her mercy. These are no waters to fool with."

"You are the captain."

"Steer a course south by southwest, Mister Savage. Lively."

"Aye, aye, Captain."

Doc spun the ship's wheel, watching the compass card respond to the sudden alteration of course. The schooner heeled sharply, carving a new wake to the south.

"These are bad waters we are sailing into," the elder Savage said after a time.

"Pirates?"

"Pirates, and far worse."

Doc Savage asked, "What can be worse than pirates?"

"Headhunters!"

Doc said sharply, "In this day and age? I understood that the British had suppressed that practice a generation ago."

"Nothing so deeply rooted stays suppressed forever."

Doc Savage said nothing. He searched his mind for what he knew of headhunting in this region of Asia. Borneo came to mind. There had been a long custom of headhunting in Borneo. It was an important part of the Dyak way of life. Christian missionaries had all but obliterated the grisly rite.

"From now on, we sail with pistols on our hips," Captain Savage told him.

"I will have to reassemble mine."

"Belay that Tommy gun. It's too wild-shooting a contraption to be cutting loose with on a ship. You could riddle the sails to rags or sieve holes in the hull, if you lost control of the weapon."

"Aye, sir." A quiver of disappointment touched Doc's sun-bronzed face. He had come to appreciate the destructive qualities of the Thompson Annihilator submachine gun at close quarters. But his father had an excellent point. The weapon disgorged bullets in punishing streams.

The passage along the southern coast of Borneo was on the starboard side. Choppy waters told that storms were brewing in these waters. But nothing sprang up that pushed them off course, or inhibited their headway.

Most shipping consisted of the striped-sailed Malay *proas* of the region. Most flew the yellow Sarawak flags with their red and black crosses. They skimmed along briskly, often passing the schooner.

"Pick up any Malay in your travels?" asked Captain Savage.

"Some," Doc said modestly. In truth, he was fluent.

"Good. Malay is the common tongue in these parts. Serve

you well to keep your command of it very sharp indeed."

"*Ya, Kapten.*"

The *Orion* ghosted along, dwarfed by the high-decked Chinese junks that choked these waters. Other boats—a continual flow of them—passed in either direction. These ranged from lateen–rigged sailing vessels to modern merchant craft, making their way from port to port in greater Indonesia.

A native outrigger canoe drew alongside them and its dark-visaged crew watched with interest, as they paddled along Indian-style.

"Malays?" asked Doc.

"Sea Dyaks."

"Pirates?"

"Or worse," said Captain Savage. "They send out scout boats to observe and report back on coastwise traffic."

"They seem very interested in us," Doc observed.

The Dyak crew stared and some pointed at the working crew on the *Orion's* deck.

Talk volleyed back and forth, barely distinguishable.

"They appear to be puzzled by your Mayans," Doc suggested.

"And intimidated, too, I should hope," shot back the elder Savage.

"Is that another reason you picked them?"

"Pirates and other seafaring brigands depend upon sizing up ships and their crews," said Captain Savage carefully, never taking his eyes off the Dyak oarsmen. "Through experience, they come to comprehend how a crew will respond to an attack, based upon their nationality. A Japanese crew will fight—or not—differently from a British one, or a crew consisting of Hindus."

Doc nodded. "They cannot place your Indians in their lexicon."

"Which will make them chary of the unknown risks involved."

"Now they are interested in us," Doc pointed out.

"No. In our eyes. I hear the Dyak word for 'gold' passing from lip to lip."

"Probably new to their experience, too," said Doc.

"Among the Dyaks, there dwells a type of shaman or pan-jandrum known as a *manang*. When a Dyak is trained to become a *manang*, the ritual includes a pretend splitting open of the skull with an axe, followed by the placing of gold over the eyes. These allow the brain to perceive the absolute, and their eyes to see spirits."

"They believe that we are white *manangs?*" suggested Doc.

"That, or they are so backward they may think our eyes are made of true gold."

Doc went to the rail, and fixed his penetrating flake-gold orbs on the Dyak who seemed to command the outrigger.

The Dyak captain met his gaze with a steady frank stare of his own. But the longer Doc stared, the more the other fidgeted.

Finally, the Dyaks all averted their eyes.

After a time, the outrigger fell back, unable to keep pace with the swift schooner.

"Well done, Mister Savage," said the captain. "Carry on."

MUCH to their surprise, the expected gale failed to material-ize. To the contrary, the winds died and the schooner began to lose headway.

Before an hour was out, they were all but becalmed. The sails slackened, drooping like forlorn ghosts.

Doc spun the ship's wheel to no good effect. The compass swam and wavered lazily.

"Looks like we'll have to wait for a fresh breeze," he said.

"Won't be long, I'll wager."

The crew fell to standing guard at every corner of the deck. Machete handles thrust up from their belts. Revolvers hung from Western-style cartridge belts.

As they watched, other craft swept by, propelled by oars and husky dark men whose broad backs bent rhythmically to propel them.

Some hailed them. Others just stared. Dusk approached and the sun began its inevitable descent into the sea.

As night fell, they wallowed in the Java Sea, utterly becalmed now. Rigging hung and swayed idly with the rocking of the boat.

Seeing an opportunity, Doc Savage stripped to his underwear and threw a line overboard. Hand over hand, he shinnied down this off the port rail and into the chop. He entered the water like a human knife, making practically no noise.

Under cover of darkness, Doc swam about, enjoying the warm feel of the water on his bare skin. He had learned to swim at an age before he could talk in complete sentences. Years later, his father had sent him to the South Seas where he lived among the pearl divers of Paumoto. There, he had learned to live in the water almost as naturally as a porpoise. The ability to hold his breath for long periods while swimming beneath the waves was taught to him. It was one of the more enjoyable periods of his young life. Not many of those youthful sojourns had been wholly pleasant. Doc could recall many a time when his father or one of his tutors tested him, by placing him in difficult or dangerous situations.

If necessary, Doc could dive and remain under water for nearly twenty minutes. If he properly charged his lungs with oxygen beforehand, that is. There was a trick to it: Filling the lungs with so much oxygen that they became saturated with it. One only had to be careful not to dive so deep that one's charge of air ran out before the surface could be reached.

After a time, shouts could be heard. They were coming from the deck of the *Orion*.

"Clark! Clark!"

Doc Savage declined to answer to his old name.

"Where are you?"

Doc lay on his back, floating calmly, watching the moon

slowly rise. It was a very spectacular moon. It gave him a cool feeling after the heat of the day. He felt no urgency to respond to his father's frantic calls.

Gobbling talk went back and forth. The Mayan language, no doubt. It sounded like the guttural tongue the crew spoke. When they deigned to talk, which was seldom.

Captain Savage's voice called out again. "Clark! Clark! *Son!*"

Underwater, Doc Savage smiled. Pleased bubbles dribbled out from between his teeth.

After a suitable interval, Doc Savage began to strike back to the *Orion.* He found the line he left trailing from the stern and climbed it with the smooth agility of a long-armed baboon.

Topping the deck, he made his appearance. His bare chest looked metallic in the moonlight, like bronze dusted with silver.

"Did you call?" Doc asked pleasantly.

Captain Savage's golden eyes stared coldly. "Where did you get to, Mister Savage?"

"I went for a swim."

"In these villainous waters?"

"They felt refreshing."

"I expect my First Mate to remain on board until I give him permission to leave."

The worry on his father's face more than made up for the shaking anger in his voice, Doc thought. It gave him a satisfied feeling.

Doc asked, "Did you look for me in your secret hiding place?"

"Of course. It was the first place I looked. Did you figure out where it was?"

"Not yet."

The captain squinted one eye until it became a mere glint of gold. "I gather that you imagine that we are square now," he said evenly.

"Furthest thing from my mind, Captain," said Doc, poker-faced.

"Well, we are. So leave it at that. I'm giving you the next watch. Fetch your weapon."

Doc went below and got his automatic. Checking the action after inserting a magazine, he stuffed it into the waist of his pongee pants, at the small of his back where it would not inhibit movement.

NIGHT stole along like a black blanket being dragged about. The moon came and went. Cloud scud swallowed it, disgorged it again, and fresh scud came to gobble the lunar crescent once more. Light therefore was a haphazard thing.

Doc Savage had learned to see exceptionally well in the dark. Some thought he had freak eyes, like a lion or a tiger. Their gold color gave rise to that belief. In actuality, it was only that nature had given him excellent visual acuity and he had learned all the tricks of perceiving by night.

So it was that during one of the periods of no moonlight Doc spied a dugout canoe come stealing in the direction of the *Orion's* stern.

Six men huddled in the low craft. Paddles made stealthy sounds as it was pushed along.

Hardwood tubes longer than a tall man were lifted as the craft approached. Blowpipes. Fierce weapons in the night. Silent and very deadly.

Moving to the stern, Doc brought a Very flare pistol.

As the low craft drew near, Doc lifted the Very pistol. Before pulling the trigger, he aimed carefully, then shut his eyes to protect them from the incipient glare.

The muzzle vomited a rocket that burst into a star shell overhead. Night was splashed with chemical day.

From the craft erupted loud sounds of surprise and outright consternation. Dark heads ducked as if from grenade shrapnel.

Opening his eyes, Doc sent a .45 slug in their direction. He picked his shot well. It snapped a thick blowpipe from the fist of a startled warrior.

That was enough to change their minds. Digging hard with their paddles, they turned the dugout about, fleeing toward shore like a skimming ghost.

Captain Savage appeared on deck, a revolver clutched in his raw red hand.

"Trouble?" he demanded.

"Nothing a star shell and a well-placed lead slug couldn't deflect," said Doc.

Captain Savage watched the dugout disappearing into the murk of night.

"One may mean others. Keep a sharp watch, Mister Savage."

"You get some sleep."

"I will. If a wind should spring up, I want you to raise the crew. Catch that wind and get us out of this foul spot."

"I rather like it," said Doc.

"Trouble is nothing to borrow in the Java Sea."

Doc almost smiled. "I don't want to borrow it, but rather send it back where it came from. With interest."

Sparks stirred in the old man's golden eyes. "War has got into your blood, I see."

"Adventure has gotten into my blood. Turn in and I will see you in the morning."

Captain Savage went below. Doc moved to the bow, searching the Java Sea with the eyes of an eagle and a swelling heart. The trip was becoming interesting.

Chapter VIII

OVER BREAKFAST, DOC SAVAGE described the occupants of the dugout which had attempted to steal up on the *Orion*'s stern.

"They were tattooed, and their skins were shades of brown, with a tinge of yellow," finished Doc. "Their faces were blank of expression, and hairless. It appeared that they shave their eyebrows, as well as their faces. They wore red headbands, from which long feathers stuck up."

Captain Savage took this in, remained silent. After pondering a while, he spoke.

"Sea Dyaks. Bad customers, if they are on the war path."

"Tell me about them."

"Fierce warriors. More burly of build than the average Malay. Sometimes Sea Dyaks will join Malay pirate crews, as oarsmen. But they prefer to stick to their own kind. Their weapons are the *duku* chopping blade, curved *mandau* long sword, an iron-tipped spear they call a *lonjo,* and the *sumpitan.* That latter is a blowpipe, which has no equal in all the world. In the bad old days, they took heads."

"They might still," remarked Doc.

"That they might. Whether pirates or headhunters, the sooner we are out of these waters, the better I will feel. If a *balla* fell upon us, we would very shortly be in a bad way."

"*Balla?*"

"A war fleet of *bangkongs*—long shallow craft, stealthy and

57

fleeter than the Malay *proa*. Eighty feet long with a ten-foot beam. Ninety men at oars. Muzzle-loading brass guns positioned in the bow and at the sides. They run covered with a roof of *nipa* palm leaves, which extends the length of the craft. When they attack, the raiders climb onto the roof and attack from that position, leaping onto the decks of the victim ship, yelling like Comanches, which incidentally they resemble when they are in dark war paint and feathers."

"My Annihilator gun would make short work of them," said Doc firmly.

"One boat, yes. Perhaps two. But twenty? With each one crammed to the gunwales with blowpipes spitting sudden death at you?"

Doc said nothing. It was a sobering mental image.

His thoughts suddenly leapt to another subject, one that had been bothering him since he first set foot upon the *Orion*.

"It is perhaps acceptable to speak of this now, since my training is now behind me. Do you think my mother would have approved of your plan?"

"I *know* she would have approved," Savage Senior said shortly.

"How can you say this with such certainty? She passed on just as it began."

"It was her idea as much as it was mine," snapped the elder Savage.

Doc was shocked speechless for a moment. The thought had never occurred to him, never crossed his imagination as a possibility. He had always assumed—presumed—that the decision to place him in scientific hands had been his father's—a result of or reaction to her unexpected death.

After a moment, a strange ululation began issuing from Doc's parted lips. It began as an undertone, a faint whisper of sound. Soon it built, note upon note, into a musical cadence that filled the room with a haunting half-melodic refrain.

Captain Savage looked about perplexedly. "What is that peculiar noise?" he muttered.

Doc abruptly compressed his lips. The sound ceased.

His father eyed him dubiously. "Did you make that… that whistle?"

"I confess that I did," said Doc, coloring slightly.

"Explain it, please."

"You will recall, Father, that when I was young I went to India."

"It was part of the master plan for you. Yes, I recall it."

"There, an old Hindu yogi taught me many skills. The power to control the mind. How to repress the emotions. To be master of one's own body and brain."

"It was a subject thought fit to study—although I recall some dissent among the more rigidly scientific advisors," allowed the captain.

"The yogi was very skilled in the suppression of his own emotions," continued Doc. "But he had a habit. He trilled like a songbird when he was excited by something."

"What does that have to do with you?"

"I picked up the habit from him," explained Doc.

"Well, get rid of it!"

"I have tried. But much of the time I don't know that I am doing it. When I notice, I can shut it off. But not before."

Savage snapped, "It is a ridiculous and unbecoming sound for a grown man to make, Clark."

"I do not disagree," replied Doc. "But I'm afraid that it has become a part of my mental makeup."

The elder Savage stared at his son a long time with his striking golden eyes, as if seeing him clearly for the first time in a very long while.

"Perhaps it is a good thing that your training was interrupted," he muttered at last.

"How so?"

"You are at risk of becoming a freak. It is not too late to school some of this infernal freakishness out of you."

Doc said nothing. He did not think that his trilling habit was that unfortunate—merely a strange side effect of a fantastic upbringing. He had long ago let go of the notion that he was a normal man. Savages were not normal. He was something more. Supernormal, possibly.

After a while, Doc remarked without emotion, "I am what I am. I am the alloy that your single-minded will made of me."

"Room for improvement always exists," said Savage Senior, pushing his plate back and rushing from his chair. "Let us be about our day, Mister Savage."

"Aye, Captain."

EMERGING onto the deck, they found the crew going about their business like the mute automatons that they were.

Captain Savage took the wheel. He drew in a great breath, held it, and released it slowly, like a man exhaling the smoke of a particular flavorful and aromatic cigar.

"First Mate, mark this air well."

Doc glanced over. "Sir?"

"Draw it into your lungs. Hold it there."

Doc did so. He held it a long time before releasing it.

"What do you smell, Mister Savage?"

"Copra. Fish. Salt. Human sweat."

"Yes, yes. But the mixture. Commit the mixture of these smells to your memory. Your grandfather taught me to do this. You could place him on any deck in any sea on God's green footstool and he could tell what part of the Arctic Ocean or the Banda Sea he was transiting by its unique conglomeration of local odors."

Doc inhaled a second time. This time, he let the aromas of the Java Sea pass more slowly along his olfactory receptors.

"Give the mass a name," Captain Savage suggested. "One that will fix the combination in your mind for future reference."

"I will call it 'Java.'"

The captain shook his head. "No. Too broad. This is but a part of the Java Sea. There are other parts. You must learn them all."

"To what end, Captain? I do not foresee a life on the sea."

"Your future is a blank slate—a *tabula rasa*. This knowledge will do you no harm and it may do you a great deal of good."

"Very well. 'Middle Java' it is."

"Carry on, Mister Savage."

Doc went in search of something to do. The Mayans ran the ship so tightly it was difficult to keep his hands busy during a normal passage.

THEY passed northwest through the Greater Sunda Islands and into the Karimata Strait, into the lower reaches of the South China Sea. Doc tasted the air at every stage, committing it to memory, wondering what had been the life of his Grandfather Stormalong.

He recalled hearing of a mythical Alfred Bulltop Stormalong, a New England sailor, of whom tall tales had been told. Captain Stormalong was a giant, a nautical Titan standing some thirty feet tall, who captained a clipper ship so large that its masts were hinged so they didn't catch on the moon. It was named the *Courser.* Doc had assumed—again wrongly—that his father's father was named after the imaginary seaman. But further investigation showed that the myth had been inspired by the living man. It had made a tremendous impression on young Clark when he first learned that. It was like discovering that your grandfather had birthed the legend of Paul Bunyan, or Robin Hood.

Past Singapore on the starboard side and Sumatra to port, they went up the Strait of Malacca where pirates were rumored to lurk in hidden coves amid mangrove swamps.

"Here is where we may be tested," Captain Savage cautioned him.

"Pirates don't frighten me."

"Overconfidence does not become a Savage."

Doc swallowed a mild rejoinder that came to mind. He had just emerged from a great war, an undertaking so vast that mere freebooters seemed no more dangerous than flies. But it never paid to imagine one's unfought battles as victories before they were had. So he followed his father's advice—even if it rankled him.

"The Great War was a far cry from the wars in which you fought, Father," Doc said calmly. "Those wars were fought on land and at sea. Now we fight in the air and under the sea as well."

"We are not at war now. We are on a sacred mission."

"Where are we bound?"

"Up the Strait of Malacca to the Nicobar Islands."

Doc nodded. He had only a vague idea of the Nicobar Islands. But he liked the sound of them.

The lush island of Sumatra drew his attention often. Here, the smell of rubber plants overpowered other wind-borne odors. The Dutch controlled the area. Their rubber plantations dotted the landscape. But these were not visible. Only the great green mountains running along a north-south line.

Captain Savage drew near and started a conversation. "That river yonder leads to Belawan, one of the principal ports in these waters. Your grandfather knew it well. Up in those mountains far inland lies a plateau ringed by smoking volcanoes. On this plateau live a strange people. The Karo-Bataks. Ever hear of them?"

"No," admitted Doc.

"The Karo-Bataks were a seafaring people once," related the elder Savage. "An inland sea once existed where forests now flourish. This unnamed and now-lost body of water was the center of their lives. One day, long ago, an earthen dam or wall broke, sending the sea of the Karo-Bataks spilling into the ocean. The exposed seabed gave rise to vegetation, but failed to collect sufficient rain water to replenish the sea, so the Karo-

Bataks were forced to become rice farmers and hunters."

"Nothing wrong with that," said Doc.

"The Karo-Bataks," continued Savage, "possessed a written language resembling ancient Phoenician and were as skillful at chess as the most sophisticated European. In the generations since they lost their inland sea, they built villages which they called 'islands' in their languages. In these villages, they erected homes built along the lines of ships, with thatched roofs that curve fore and aft like ships. In fact, they call them 'ships,' even though they are built on stilts. It has been many generations since their sea ran away from them, and they know nothing of real ships or islands, but these concepts survive in how they have organized their communal lives."

Doc Savage waited for the point of the story. There was always a point, he knew.

"Sounds picturesque," prompted Doc. "Even idyllic."

"When your grandfather discovered these people," Savage offered, "they had fallen into the foul pit of demon-worship. The men lived idle lives, while the women did all the work. Their greatest challenge was to travel from village to village, to visit their many wives, who gave them money to waste on gambling."

"Far from ideal," conceded Doc. "But I fail to see your point."

"I will pass on to you the advice your grandfather gave me when I was about your age. 'Build yourself a boat, and once you have found it, never lose your sea.'"

Doc Savage considered this for some time, his thoughtful eyes on the green peaks which concealed the plateau of the lost seafarers.

"I have been thinking that I would rather like to have my own airplane," said Doc.

"You cannot live on an aeroplane," reminded the elder Savage.

"Or perhaps a submarine."

Captain Savage walked off without comment.

THE STRAIT OF MALACCA had a rank smell. Doc tasted it at intervals. It smelled of treachery and bloodshed, as fit its reputation. This was a haven for Malay pirates. The night watch was doubled.

Days came and went and the sailing was fine. It was common for native boats to sidle up alongside and look over the *Orion* and its unusual crew.

Once, a dugout canoe scooted by and a gruff voice called over.

"Ari ni penatai nuan?" Where are you from?

Doc looked to his father.

"He is speaking the language of the Dyaks," Captain Savage returned. "He wants to know whence we hail." The captain replied in the man's own language. "The schooner *Orion*. Out of San Francisco, U.S.A."

"Kini ka nuan?" Where are you bound?

"Andaman Sea."

"No port?"

"We make landfall where we will," said Savage Senior. "And you?"

The man smiled broadly, displaying teeth that were nearly black. *"Belelang."* Wandering about.

"You have very fine heads, Men-with-Eyes-of-Gold." And the Dyak canoe captain laughed as he urged his rowers onward.

"Headhunters?" asked Doc, after his father had translated the exchange.

"Or humorists. It is difficult to tell."

Whichever they were, they did not return. That day.

Chapter IX

THEY MADE LANDFALL at Port Blair, the capital of the Andaman and Nicobar Islands Union, which sprawled south of India and west of Burma. It had been an infamous penal colony going back generations, and remained so to this day. There was no sign of that storied institution, however.

As they approached its palm-frond-tossed shore, they had sighted the so-called Nicobar pigeon, whose metallic green plumage suggested anything but a common pigeon.

Watching a flock of the gray-headed, white-tailed birds fly by, Doc remarked, "They are believed to be unique among birds, although perhaps related to some extinct species, such as the dodo."

"What is that, Mister Savage?" asked his father, who was conning the port ahead.

"*Caloenas nicobarica.* The Nicobar pigeon."

Captain Savage grunted wordlessly.

"What does Nicobar mean, I wonder?" said Doc, shifting his gaze to the port in the splendidly blue Andaman Sea.

"It is based upon a Tamil word, I understand. It means 'Naked Man.'"

"Strange name for an archipelago," said Doc.

"These are strange waters," admitted Savage Senior. "It is thought that the name Andaman derives from the Sanskrit, and is a corruption of Hanuman, the Hindu monkey god. Why this would be so eludes me. Britain holds sway here. Before that, the Danes controlled this sector."

"We should see about purchasing a wireless telegraph while we are resupplying," suggested Doc.

The elder Savage frowned. "Useless for our purposes. The *Courser* carried no such instrument," he said finally.

"But other ships do, and if we are to locate her in the vast Indian Ocean, the power to communicate with other vessels may prove invaluable."

Captain Savage gave the matter further thought.

"We will see what we can learn about her last position before splurging on dubious mechanisms," he allowed.

By which Doc understood that he had succeeded in moving his father's mental machinery in a more positive direction. A large victory in principle, but possibly a major one in practice.

The Mayans were tying the springlines to the dock bollards when a representative from the British government came up the dock. He wore tropical whites and a pith helmet, which he doffed upon approach.

"Good day, gentlemen. Permit me to introduce myself. I am Talbot Friday, His Majesty's Port Officer for this jurisdiction. We were not expecting you. I regret to inform you that the Governor is not available to receive you. He is upriver, on a pressing matter."

"Captain Clark Savage, Senior. Good to make your acquaintance. We are in search of the dismasted clipper reported floating in the vicinity."

Doc thought: *That is my father—getting down to brass tacks.*

Doc put out his hand. "Clark Savage, Junior, late of France and No Man's Land."

For the occasion, Doc had changed into the only fresh clothes he possessed—his military uniform.

"Good to have you. Come, we'll have tea and I will tell you all you need to know."

OVER English afternoon tea, they exchanged news of the

world.

Doc took the lead. Younger and more personable than his father, his participation in the Great War had impressed the official, who soon dropped his British stiffness.

"The *Courser* was a marvel in her day," Friday said with reserved respect, and a trace of admiration. "Weatherly, yet constructed for speed."

"The finest kind," said Captain Savage approvingly.

"What was her last position?" asked Doc.

"Southwest of here. In beastly empty waters. It was a wonder that we've had any sightings of her at all. These are trackless seas, if you know what I mean. Trackless and treacherous."

"How can that be?" asked the elder Savage.

"Pirates, you know."

"Malays?"

"Malays and Dyaks. Mainly Dyaks. They seem to like to take an occasional run down into those lower reaches."

"What could they possibly want there?" wondered Captain Savage.

Friday shrugged elaborately. "No one seems to know. But those waters are haunted—troubled and taboo. No one goes there. Positively no one. Or if they do, they scarcely ever return."

Doc interjected, "From the last reported positions of the *Courser*, where might she have been?"

"Drifting north by northwest. That would plot her deep down into the Indian Ocean, where dry land is scarce indeed."

"Surely there are islands?" asked Captain Savage.

"Isles perhaps, and curious fogs."

"Fogs?"

"Perpetual pea soups, I am told. Not that I have ever been down in those vasty parts. We have enough of a job of work watching over these scattered islands."

Friday took out a map and two stickpins, pressing the latter into the blue grid.

Captain Savage leaned forward and his eyes sharpened.

"If I know my trade winds, that would suggest she is being blown from this area." He placed a sun-bronzed hand on the expanse of the Indian Ocean west of Sumatra.

"Hardly narrows it down, you know," offered Friday.

"Sir, up until these reports, I have had no inkling if the *Courser* lay marooned at the northern pole or sunk in the deeps of the South China Sea."

"I understand it had been a good ten years since there was word of her," the official said sympathetically.

"Longer."

Friday took a sip of steaming tea. "Surprised she floats, unmanned after all this time," he remarked.

"The reports say the masts were sheared off," offered Doc.

"Right. Rather remarkable. Suggests a frightful blow."

Captain Savage retorted, "I would question if any blow could dismast a stoutly-constructed ship such as the *Courser*."

"No ship is invincible, or storm-proof," Friday said pleasantly. "We all recognize that, I trust."

"Aye. But I practically grew up under her foresail. Her masts are stout. A blow sufficient to snap them as cleanly as reported should have sent her below."

Friday smiled crookedly. "I shall not weigh in against your superior knowledge, but facts are facts. She was seen here and again there by two different ships' crews. Both reported that the clipper floated along, entirely seaworthy as to her hull integrity, but utterly shorn of her masts, spars and rigging."

"Perhaps a pirate crew looted her, and stole away with her timber," suggested Doc Savage.

"Doubtful," said Captain Savage, shaking his silver-streaked head.

"I am inclined to agree with your father," disclosed Friday. "Such freebooters as prowl the Indian Ocean have no use for masts of clipper magnitude. Nor would the wood be of much value. Else, the ship would have been picked over, reduced to a skeleton, and no longer be afloat."

"Was there any report of her condition?" asked Captain Savage.

"I have the wireless communiqués here," said Talbot Friday.

He produced two Manila envelopes and emptied them. The reports went around the table.

Reading them, Captain Savage's seamed features gathered and smoothed, seeming to alter his appearance of age and maturity. It was as if he were gaining and losing entire decades with each facial alteration.

Doc Savage read with an impassive countenance.

AFTER a moment, his trilling issued forth. A sharp elbow in his ribs brought this social faux pas to his attention. He got control of it.

"This report speaks of a large splash of blood at the taffrail," said Doc.

Friday nodded. "Yes. Unpleasant point."

Captain Savage took the report and read silently.

"Could mean anything," he said curtly.

"It could," allowed Friday. "But where Dyak pirates have boarded shipping, they often take the crew to a central point and remove their, ah, heads. A taffrail is rather like a chopping block to them."

Doc commented, "This report suggests that the bloodstains, while not fresh, were not old either."

"What makes you say that?"

"Dried blood quickly turns brown," replied Doc, drawing upon his medical knowledge. "But even dry, monsoon rains would wash any such stain away over a period of months, if not weeks."

"Sound point. So you are suggesting that the crew were beheaded comparatively recently?"

Captain Savage interrupted. "Let us not go too finely into theories, gentlemen. It is only a supposition."

"Blood is blood," said Friday. "And there was quite a lot of it."

"Confound it, I do not wish to be jumping at conclusions when there are facts yet to be ascertained!"

And the coarse grain of Captain Savage's voice was such that the room fell silent.

Pouring himself another dollop of tea to freshen his cup, the official went on in a quiet and respectful tone of voice.

"I imagine that you will want to sail with the dawn."

"Sooner," snapped the captain of the *Orion*.

"Really? After all this journeying, surely a sound bed in a solid hotel room would be more to your liking."

"It would," said Captain Savage. "But every hour may count."

"Perfectly understandable, if not commendable. Yet I fear, if you hope to effect a rescue, that is sheer fantasy. Surely you grasp the facts of life as they present themselves."

"Sir," Captain Savage returned, his voice cold and shaking, "the *Courser* may have been reduced to salvage and her decks awash with blood, but my father, Stormalong Savage, will not be declared dead until I have seen his cold clay cadaver with my very own eyes."

"Jolly good!" Talbot Friday lifted his cup. "Let's all drink to a swift family reunion and a happy conclusion."

But the official was the only one to raise his china cup.

Doc Savage and his father read the maritime reports over and over, sifting for clues and gleanings, golden eyes fixed. They were of one mind and one will now.

Chapter X

BEFORE THE SCHOONER *Orion* departed Port Blair, Doc Savage spent his last thirty dollars buying crates of .45 caliber ammunition from a native general store.

As he lugged them up the gangplank balanced on one shoulder, Captain Savage asked, "Expecting another world war?"

Doc shook his head. "A Thompson Annihilator gun fires 1,500 rounds per minute. These will not last long."

"You have unbounded confidence in that contraption. In my time sailing the Seven Seas, I have found that one well-placed shot usually settles a matter."

"It was either more ammunition, or a radio."

"If the latter item," the captain said gruffly, "you would have wasted your money. For I have in storage a wireless telegraph set in need of repair—although I doubt it will be of much practical use. I seem to recall you have some mechanical knowledge. You might put it to use, if you have a mind to."

Doc suppressed a grin. He had been hoping for exactly that answer.

After laying the last heavy crate in the storage, Doc returned topside.

"Spectacular day," he remarked. "Shame to see it go."

"Other days lie ahead," returned the captain. "We must be off."

The Mayan crew began making preparations to depart.

They went out with the evening tide to conserve the gasoline supply. The trade winds were easy to catch and they were soon heading south at a fair clip: Six knots. The winds were brisk and lively.

As the Nicobar Islands fell behind them, and they pushed southeast through the Bay of Bengal in the direction of the Indian Ocean, Doc, at the wheel, asked a question he had been holding in reserve until they were at sea.

"Captain, a thought troubles me."

"Out with it, Mister Savage."

"A dozen years gone is a long time to expect a man to remain among the living."

"It is. I will admit to that."

"Yet you hold out hope for Old Stormy."

Captain Savage drew in a studied breath. "Stormalong Savage ranged the entire world in his day. He has been shipwrecked once, marooned on twice that number of occasions, and left for dead three times that I can attest. I have seen him sail into the teeth of Nor'easters, tropical cyclones and typhoons, driving his ship and crew along with him like a general possessed and dead certain of his destiny. A man of that stature does not perish easily."

"Surely you understand that Grandfather is mortal."

"Hercules was said to be mortal," Savage said stiffly. "Yet imperishable in his own way."

"A man must die when his time comes."

"I will speak openly to you, since no ears can eavesdrop on my words. When I was young and crewing on the *Courser*, I thought my dear father was made of metal more than flesh and blood. I believed with all of my might that Old Stormy could not be killed by man or machine. I came to think of him as a modern Titan."

"A young boy can be excused for thinking such thoughts," said Doc, reflecting that he wished he had enjoyed the luxury of such a strong connection with his own father.

"True. But now that I am older than he was then, I still feel the identical way about him. Envisioning him as deceased—at present that lies beyond my imaginative powers."

Doc considered his response. A door seemed to have opened in the conversation, a door that had never gaped open between them. A thousand questions rose in his mind. There was no end to them.

Instead, he said only, "I fervently hope that your judgment proves sound."

"I wish you had met him," said Captain Savage.

"Your faith in your father is showing signs of cracking, sir."

Captain Savage turned, metallic eyes challenging. "What do you mean by that remark, Mister Savage?"

"You said 'had.' As if you have foreclosed on the possibility."

"So I did, so I did."

"A slip of the tongue, Captain?"

"My faith in my father remains unshakable."

There was an awkward pause, as if the father expected the son to offer something in the same vein.

But Doc Savage knew not what to say. So he remained silent.

"We will know soon enough," Captain Savage said gravely. "Carry on."

"Aye."

Doc set his eyes on the course ahead. The setting of the tropical sun made a flamboyant splash in the Bay of Bengal, setting it ablaze with a hot liquid light that glared and spread and soon enough died.

When his watch ended, instead of going to his berth, Doc took the faulty wireless telegraph instrument into the machine cubicle and began tinkering with it. He soon had it in good working order.

DAWN broke over the schooner *Orion* as she passed into the northeast reaches of the vast Indian Ocean. The waters of this quarter of ocean were a cool blue to the eye and the scent of it cleaner and fresher than any encountered since the long Pacific crossing. No doubt the seasonal trade winds had something to do with that.

Doc inhaled the sultry air at intervals, marking the scent combinations and committing them to memory, with the exact hue of the sea as a visual reference. Neither were absolutes, he knew. Weather and other meteorological factors could influence changes. But as the *Orion* cut across the face of the ocean, Doc became increasingly confident that he could chart a reverse course blindfolded and make port safely.

He wondered what had become of his father in the intervening years. In his own youth, he had seemed a forward thinker. Open to new ideas. Now, he appeared to be stuck in the Nineteenth Century, if not clinging to it.

Doc wondered, not for the first time, if the whole idea of training him for his life's work had not been his mother's after all. Had she been the visionary, and his father only the economic engine for that vision?

Doc reflected upon his father's life. Trained as a civil engineer, he also studied law, medicine and other disciplines, as if attempting to fit three lifetimes into the delimited span of one ordinary existence.

Clark Savage, Senior, had known war. Many of them. He had attempted to enlist in the U.S. Cavalry when only eleven, but Old Stormy had put a stop to that. Later, the son got his way. He had fought Indians in the Southwest, then returned to civilian life. Called back into service during the Spanish-American War, he had distinguished himself as a Rough Rider, hoisting the first United States flag to fly over captured Havana.

A man of many parts, boasting multiple careers packed into a comparatively short life. Bridges, lighthouses and railways bearing his stamp still stood from the Red Sea to Patagonia. It was difficult to accept that one man could have done so much. But the records did not lie.

It was never spoken aloud, but the elder Savage was said to

have performed diplomatic services for President Roosevelt. It was always assumed that he did espionage work. This was never discussed openly.

There was also the undeniable fact that the father had relinquished his parental duties to a host of surrogates, leaving the son to learn a difficult emotional self-sufficiency while mastering manly skills ranging from hunting and trapping to going without sleep for days at a time.

It was, Doc reflected, an amazing youth and early manhood. An Apache taught him how to survive in a desert. A Zulu warrior how to track through jungle. He wintered with Eskimos and ate whale blubber and seal, as they did. A summer working roundup on a Wyoming cattle ranch was not enough for the cowboy in him, but the skills developed for the man would last a lifetime.

Was it all worth it?

Time would tell. The future, as his father had said, was a blank slate. All that mattered now was finding the *Courser,* and picking up whatever strange sea trail it might provide.

One important thing had changed. Where before, Doc Savage had held out no hope that Stormalong Savage still survived, now he felt an inner thrill, almost a supernatural presentiment that Old Stormy had managed to cheat the Grim Reaper one more time.

If so, what stories would he tell…?

Chapter XI

SOUTHWEST OF SUMATRA, the Indian Ocean stretches for leagues without landmark or interruption. There are no islands to be found on any marine chart, no rocks or reefs, and no possessions. Only the vast blue equatorial waters and the vaster azure sky above.

The January sun beat down on the heads of the *Orion* crew. Tropical trade winds cut the heat to a balmy seventy-five degrees, but when they paused, the temperature shot up to nearly ninety.

The trades blow from the northeast between January and March. Once they caught a good one, the schooner had blowing wind to her back all the way from Great Nicobar Island. She made good time. Trailing fishing lines from the stern brought them plentiful supply of edible fish, mainly yellowfin and skipjack tuna, as well as the odd grouper and dorado.

Once, they caught a squirming cuttlefish, but only Doc Savage seemed to enjoy chewing its rubbery tentacles. They salted what they could not consume, and laid it in the larder for later.

Such boats as they encountered were deep-sea fishing vessels, and the odd copra sloop. A group of Japanese tuna boats were the only ones traveling together. Few would be expected to speak English.

As they passed these, Doc got on the wireless telegraph instrument and hailed each vessel, asking if the *Courser* had been sighted along this course.

Two days along, and the answers had all been in the negative.

"We should be on the correct course to overtake her," said Doc, poring over a large marine chart in the captain's cabin below deck.

"I have no doubt but that we are," said Captain Savage firmly. "Do not forget that a clipper ship bobbing along without masts will not be visible any great distance. For it is a proud suit of sails that make her prominent against the deep."

"True."

Captain Savage leaned in to scrutinize the chart more closely. He seemed to be reading it with something more than his eyes and brain, as if the chart were some arcane tool of the divinatory arts.

Tracing a brassy finger southward, he murmured, "The counterclockwise gyre dominating this area might carry her to approximately this spot."

The finger came to rest on a blank blue spot southwest of Sumatra.

"Set course for this position, Mister Savage."

Doc read the longitude and latitude, committing them to memory.

Climbing back to deck, Doc unlocked the wheel. He steered by instinct as much as by his compass heading. He was coming to know these waters in a way he could not express.

They were sailing close to the wind, sails set for that purpose.

The seas were by now running high, and the black schooner knifed through the swells and rollers, her rails coming close to going under a time or two, but never dunking. Her weatherly properties showed plainly.

Captain Savage stood in the plunging bow with a sextant and stopwatch, checking their position. He seemed satisfied with their course. Spyglass in hand, he worked his way forward to the bowsprit.

Savage Senior conned the way ahead, giving port and starboard their fair share of attention. His manner was growing intense, in the quietly contained and self-possessed way that had been his for so long as Doc had known him.

Half a day farther south, with the sun baking the deck planking and the Mayans going about their business as if they were impervious to heat and humidity, Captain Savage showed his first sign of excitement.

"Hard to port!" he cried.

Doc spun the wheel smartly. The *Orion* responded, her prow digging into the heaving waves. Curving and heeling, sails fluttering like wings, she made a smooth course alteration.

Captain Savage had his spyglass up again, leaning into it as if barely restraining himself from leaping in the direction of his forward vision.

"Dead ahead!" he called back

"What have you sighted, sir?"

"Something that suggests a profusion of feathers. Sea Dyaks wear headdresses decorated with rhinoceros hornbill tail-feathers, which symbolize their war deity, Singalang Burong. Mark my words. A *bangkong* lurks ahead."

In the lurching seas, it was difficult to discern very much. Wave crests concealed the ever-shifting troughs.

Doc held the wheel steady. The sun was beginning to sink toward the water, as if it had become too heavy.

"We are going to lose the light," warned Doc.

Captain Savage turned his gaze to the west, as if noticing the sun's position for the first time. He began speaking in K'iche, issuing curt orders.

Doc still had gleaned nothing much of the Mayan tongue, but from the snappy actions of the crew, he knew the command must be: Put on more sail!

Fresh canvas was hauled up. The sails filled. Briskly, the *Orion* lunged ahead.

They foamed along, running close hauled, canvas cracking and tugging at her stays.

Doc held the wheel like Atlas holding up the world. The

rudder might have been fixed in place by bolts, so straight a course did he steer. The compass card did not deviate one point.

Suddenly, Captain Savage cried, "Sheer off! Sheer off!"

Doc turned the spokes with easy grace. The helm spun like a great wagon wheel.

"What is it?" he called ahead.

"A damned *balla*."

Doc said, "Dyaks?"

The elder Savage came rushing back. "A dozen *bangkongs*. Take in all sails before they spy our canvas. Lively now!"

Locking the wheel, Doc leaped to the downhaul lines. Responding to similar unintelligible orders, the Mayans likewise fell to.

Snapping canvas came down smartly. The *Orion* slowed, began wallowing in the swells.

At the stern now, Captain Savage trained his spyglass across the waves.

Doc stood alongside him. He had his binoculars in hand.

"See them?" asked Doc quietly.

Captain Savage shook his head. "No longer."

"That is a good sign."

"They run lower than we do. Easy for them to sneak up upon us under cover of darkness, undetected until it is too late."

Doc trained his binoculars on the upheaving swells. All he perceived was leaping blue water, which flung off white spume.

By now, the solar disk had touched the Indian Ocean's horizon line and fiery blood seemed to spill in lurid gouts. They made discernment difficult.

A half hour came and went. Then an hour. Captain Savage paced like a two-legged tiger.

"So far, so good," said Doc. He was back at the wheel, feet planted like tree trunks.

When nearly two hours had passed, Captain Savage folded up his spyglass and called for all sails to be raised.

"Resume course, Mister Savage."

"Aye, sir."

The *Orion* was soon under weigh. Night had fallen. They ran without running lights. The chances of encountering—never mind colliding with—another vessel were beyond remote.

Above, the moon was a slender crescent, its ghostly light wan and weak.

"Unlikely we will spy the *Courser* in this infernal blight," complained Captain Savage.

"I would like the watch tonight."

"Very well, Mister Savage. It is yours to have."

"Thank you, sir."

DOC SAVAGE took the evening watch after his supper. He rushed through the meal because he was eating alone. His father had the wheel, appearing reluctant to leave the deck for any reason.

Doc brought him a cold meat plate, which was silently accepted.

The atmosphere on deck was electric. Even the taciturn Mayans seemed more alert than usual.

Doc commented, "We seem to have avoided those Dyaks."

"Or not. They could be sweeping around us even now, with the fell intention of surrounding the schooner."

Doc sniffed the air.

"What do Dyaks smell like?" he asked suddenly.

"What does that have to do with our present situation?" asked the captain.

"People of Asia have remarked that Europeans smell of meat. The Mayans smell of corn. I am thinking, in this darkness, I might detect a boat filled with some eighty Dyaks by their distinctive personal odors."

"You would have to possess the nose of a bloodhound to scent them more than a few yards."

"You are forgetting my training, father," Doc said gently.

"So I am," returned the elder Savage. "Sea Dyaks consume fish at sea, pig and yams and chicken when on land."

Doc inhaled slowly, then released the captured breath.

At length, he reported, "I smell no unfamiliar people."

"Very good, First Mate Savage. Keep your eyes peeled sharp and your canny nostrils flared all the length of your watch. Our lives may depend upon it."

The captain sat down on a coil of line distributed on the quarterdeck and ate methodically. He had locked the helm, there being no need to alter course, even slightly, from their present heading. By night, with the trades steadily blowing, the *Orion* practically ran herself.

Doc Savage patrolled the length and breadth of the schooner as the night marched on. His eyes, amazingly acute, were nevertheless limited by the smothering darkness. The air had cooled, but only to about seventy degrees.

At each turn about the boat, Doc tasted the air and listened intently.

The sound of Dyak paddles was something with which he had already acquainted himself. They didn't creak like Western oars in metal oarlocks would, but they had their own distinctive rustle and gurgle.

No such sound reached his ears. Still, Doc refused to relax.

Midnight came and went without incident. The Mayans withdrew to their communal bunks in the forecastle below. All became quiet on deck.

A playful wind made the mainsail ripple and pop. Other than that and the running of the waves, a delightful quiet had descended.

Doc enjoyed the peacefulness of it all. During his upbringing, he had been handed off from one expert or scientist to another. Money had changed hands. His safety had been paramount. He was rarely left alone. Sometimes he ached for solitude. The war had been worse in that respect. So these quiet moments were like wine to him.

A flick resembling an insect shooting by his ear made Doc drop suddenly to the deck.

He waited, head cocked. No other sound came. His eyes searched, saw nothing. His ears captured a faint buzz.

An insect, to be sure. But the flicking sound past his ears was identical to that of a blowpipe dart whisking by. Doc had expected any attack on the *Orion* would have begun with the soft whisper of Dyak darts.

Doc climbed to his feet and resumed his stance at the wheel.

The way ahead was darker than the inside of an octopus, blacker than its ink. But the open ocean felt as safe as a green meadow. It was so large and spacious that no danger of collision was likely.

Doc soon relaxed. His thoughts drifted back to his storied father. Had the loss of his young wife, only weeks after Doc had been born, congealed his emotions? Clark Savage, Senior, had never remarried. It was all a poignant and unfathomable mystery....

BY the radium dial of his wristwatch, Doc noted the time to be four-fourteen in the morning. Not that there was any morning to be seen. The crescent moon was very high up and seemed very far away.

Overhead, the stars were splendid, a necklace of diamonds stretched across the night sky. The cool illumination trickling down from them was not brilliant. More on the order of a leakage from some other realm. A half light that tricked and fooled the eye into thinking there was more apparent light than existed.

So it was that Doc Savage was very surprised when he came upon the hulk looming in his path.

There was moonglade, of course. Sparkles, glimmerings and diamond points of dancing moonlight all around. This display aided in the discovery.

The hulk reared up ahead, slightly to starboard, looking like the Flying Dutchman ship of legendry. Her hull was black, the streak running its entire length, white.

Doc spun the wheel hard to port and locked it. Then he found a hurricane lantern, lit it, and set the wick low.

Taking it to the bow, he lifted the glowing lantern.

The mellow shine was fair. Good enough to reveal portions of the ship. She floated high in the swells, rocking like a drunken sailor.

His heart pounding high in his throat, Doc raised the wick, producing more light. But the throw of illumination proved insufficient to make out details.

Doc scrounged up a battery flashlight. It was a risky thing to do, but he used it.

The concentrated light played along a handsome hull. He lifted the beam, discovered no sails, no masts—although the latter might be missed in the murk.

Finding the rail once more, Doc raced the beam along until he came to the stern.

There, in distinct ivory letters, was the name of the vessel:

COURSER

Chapter XII

STRIKING THE SHIP'S bell was out of the question, so Doc slipped below and knocked sharply on the captain's cabin door.

A querulous voice responded. "What is it?"

"Ship sighted, sir."

"Name of vessel, if any?"

"It is the *Courser*, Captain."

The old man shot out of bed so fast that Doc was taken aback by the speed with which the door opened to reveal snapping golden eyes.

Captain Savage looked at him as if half incredulous.

"You are certain of this, Mister Savage?"

"The name is plain on her stern, sir."

Captain Savage seemed to stagger a moment. Doc almost reached out to steady him, but refrained out of respect for the old man's nautical dignity.

"Await me at the wheel, Mister Savage. I will join you directly."

"Aye, sir."

A short time later, Captain Savage was striding toward the bow, fully dressed and as awake and alert as if he had been on duty all of the evening. His pewter hair was combed smooth against his fine skull, attesting to the fact that he had neglected to don his captain's cap.

Doc passed the flashlight into his hand, saying, "You can make out her name with this."

"Chancy, with a Dyak war party in the vicinity."

Doc lifted the hurricane lantern. Its more diffuse light painted the surrounding sea, brought out the other ship with a stark clarity.

The majestic old clipper could be discerned far to port now, leaping and crashing in the rollers, rocking aimlessly from side to side. A moon-silvered derelict of the sea.

Carefully, Captain Savage clicked the flash beam on and chased it over the long sweeping lines of the other vessel. The expression crossing his sun-seamed features depicted the pain of a sailorman recognizing a crippled ship.

The light lingered on her figurehead—a plunging war horse, armored and wild, forelegs lifted in defiance.

After only a few seconds, he doused the light and said hoarsely, "I do not need to see her name, Mister Savage. I know that fine old ship as I know the back of my own hand. She is the *Courser*. Prepare to bring us alongside her."

"Aye, aye, Captain."

The crew was summoned from their sleep, and Captain Savage took the wheel, executing a sharp turn calculated to backtrack toward the *Courser*.

They warped in close and drew alongside the heaving opposite deck. Cork fenders were set upon the starboard rails. The Mayans employed boat hooks to keep the hulls apart until the *Orion* settled down.

Using the K'iche tongue, Captain Savage ordered, "Strike sails."

Sails were brought down.

"Grapples to hand."

Grappling hooks and lines of Italian marlin were brought from storage lockers, made ready, and the crew began throwing them with practiced skill.

Soon, the two vessels were lashed together rather perilously. The mighty clipper ship dwarfed the tossing schooner.

The *Courser* rode over a dozen feet higher than the *Orion*. It was impossible to see the deck from their inferior vantage point. But from a distance, it had appeared deserted.

"Who will go first?" asked Doc.

Captain Savage hesitated. For the first time, Doc detected a trace of fear, as if his father didn't wish to discover the worst the foundering old clipper had to offer.

Finally, he asked heavily, "Are you requesting the privilege, Mister Savage?"

"I am, sir."

"Then be about it."

Doc clambered up the ratlines, going up like a spider monkey climbing a tangle of vine. From the crow's nest, he flung a grappling hook and snagged the mahogany rail. Fastening the loose end snug around the mast, he went across, hand over hand, making it look easy.

Reaching the rail, the bronze giant dropped quietly onto the deck, his canvas shoes muffling his landing.

It was moist and the aged teakwood under his feet felt spongy in spots, like balsa wood that had been left out in a tropical rain.

Doc moved along the deck, using his flashlight carefully, not letting the beam rove too much. There was still the danger of Dyak boats hereabouts.

Doc found the main mast and examined where it stood splintered. His trilling issued slowly from his parted lips. Astonishment was the flavor of the sound. Only a great force could have accomplished such destruction, he realized.

The other masts were likewise sundered. Curiously, the direction of these other breaks was haphazard. The splintering ran in different directions, as if beset by opposing forces.

Going to the rail, Doc called down to the *Orion*.

"All masts sheared close to the deck. No gale did this."

His father shouted up, "Cannon shell?"

"No. Not to my eyes."

"Then what, Mister Savage?"

Doc hesitated. "I cannot venture a guess."

"Resume your duty, sir."

Doc returned to his investigation. He went below and moved among the cabins crowded together near the main stateroom. They were deserted.

No one had slept here in a very long time, he saw.

There were splashes of blood. A dying half-starved rat. Cobwebs. Vermin. Cockroaches and copra-bugs.

Returning to deck, Doc went to the taffrail in the clipper's stern and found a mass of jellied blood at its base. It was concentrated in one spot. The area looked like a rude chopping block and the thoughts his imagination painted of the fate of the crew were not pleasant, although they were exceedingly vivid.

Doc returned to the *Orion* to report.

"Not a soul on board, Captain," he said after shinnying down the main mast.

"You are certain of this?"

"Absolutely."

Captain Savage hesitated. "At first light, I will see for myself."

"We are twice as conspicuous by dawn light," Doc cautioned.

"What I wish to see, I wish to see under honest sunlight," said the captain carefully.

THEY boarded with the dawn, tossing grappling hooks upward to snag the weather-beaten rail, and climbing trailing lines until they could drop over onto the great deck.

The Mayan crew remained with the *Orion*, on guard, their revolvers and machetes handy.

Captain Savage examined the sprung masts first and the pain

evident on his sun- and wind-burned features was acute.

"You are correct, Mister Savage. No gale did this horrific damage. Nor shell, either. It would be impossible to aim artillery so accurately that only the masts were taken away, and the rails to survive undamaged as they have."

"It is difficult to guess what might have contained the force to snap all three masts in identical ways," offered Doc.

"I agree. But your eyes tell you the same tale that my eyes do. So there you have it."

Doc scrutinized a clump of spidery, rotting ratline that lay athwart the port rail. It had come loose during the uprooting of the masts, obviously.

"There must be an explanation," he said firmly.

Captain Savage directed his piercing gaze on his son. "As I recall, you were a great reader of Sherlock Holmes in your youth. Have you any theories of a deductive nature?"

"As I recall, you disapproved of my taste in authors."

"I have always been partial to Shakespeare, as you are well aware."

"Shakespeare wrote about human affairs," countered Doc. "Conan Doyle taught me to look at the world through scientific perceptions."

"Well, here is your opportunity to vindicate that wasted portion of your youth," returned Captain Savage sternly.

Responding to the challenge, Doc moved about the deck, examining each splintery stub in turn.

"Had any wind or man-made power done this," offered Doc, "the masts would have necessarily toppled in such a way as to ruin deck and rails—if not the superstructure."

"I observe the same thing that you do. Pray, continue."

"If the masts did not fall down, they must have gone up."

"Preposterous!"

"See for yourself, Captain. The way the splinters are grouped on each mast heel, unmistakably twisted."

The elder Savage fingered one splintery stub, removing a tendril of wood for closer examination.

"Sails caught in a gale would not create this," he murmured. "The canvas would be sundered before the masts began turning in their collars."

"We have already established that," said Doc. "Each mast was individually torn loose and carried away."

Challenge burned in the old man's eyes. "By what? I await your explanatory theory."

Doc considered this for a long period.

"Occam's Razor suggests one possibility," he mused. "Something wrenched the masts loose and flung them in such a way so as not to damage the rest of the *Courser.*"

"Yes, yes, I comprehend your drift," said the elder Savage impatiently. "But by what miraculous agency?"

Doc pondered this question. "Were we living in the days of Ulysses, I would have suggested a Cyclops. But it would appear that only a giant approximately the size of Alfred Bulltop Stormalong could have accomplished this easily. He was said to stand thirty feet tall."

"Myth and legend are not acceptable to the scientific mind," snapped Captain Savage. "You are jumping at conclusions, sir."

"Sir, my conclusions appear sound. I see no other alternative."

Captain Savage stared at his son with reserved incredulity.

"Next, you will be leaping from tree to tree like Tarzan of the Apes," he grumbled.

"Or mast to mast," said Doc, suppressing a smile. He was pleasantly surprised to learn that his father had read that book.

Realizing that his son had already demonstrated that feat, the old man made an impatient gesture that could only be interpreted as, let's get on with it.

Doc led his father to the taffrail, beneath which a bloody blob sat in the sun, looking like a dead jellyfish engorged with plasma.

"Heads were taken here," intoned Captain Savage after a difficult silence.

"I would judge within the last two months, perhaps less," offered Doc, after toeing the encrimsoned matter carefully.

Savage Senior favored him with a sharp glance. "And you judge this how?"

"My medical training, sir."

"Such as it stands," said Savage glumly. "But I do not doubt you in this particular matter. The way of the Sea Dyak is to remove the heads as trophies and dispose of the bodies at sea. If we wish to know who perished at this ugly spot, we must locate the trophies of war. For they always carry them away."

"Does that mean we are now in the business of hunting Dyaks?"

Captain Savage nodded solemnly. "Beginning with the *balla* operating in these reaches." His voice was very firm, the tone akin to a vengeance vow.

They went below, Captain Savage leading. He lit his hurricane lantern to light the way, and its mellow glow made the varnish of the golden oak paneling below gleam brightly.

CAPTAIN SAVAGE went directly to the master's cabin, which was in disarray, the bed stripped of all linen. Chests stood open and empty. He ignored these things and stood before a mirror. It was dusty, but amid the dust were pale streaks.

"My father had a habit of using his mirror to mark messages in soap," Captain Savage told Doc. "It had the advantage being impermanent, and could therefore be erased with water."

A word appeared to be scrawled in the glass, barely readable now.

" 'King,' " said the captain, frowning. "Without proper context, I fail to fathom the meaning."

"I believe that second letter to be an 'O,' not an 'I,' " suggested Doc. "Perhaps this is an attempt to write *bangkong*."

"Either way, it is insufficiently informative," snapped Savage

Senior.

They exited. The other cabins were not only deserted, but appeared to have been emptied of any meaningful possessions.

"Looted, no doubt," decided Doc.

"Looted, or carried off by the crew at landfall," countered the captain.

"Possibly," admitted Doc, looking about.

Having made a cursory investigation and finding nothing of interest, Captain Savage went to a spot where the mainmast was anchored below the decking. He carried with him a brass key.

"Where did you get that?" asked Doc, curiously.

"From my pocket. Your grandfather gave me this long ago."

Doc watched with impassive interest as the elder Savage inserted the brass key into what appeared to be a knothole in the surviving butt of the missing main mast.

A click resulted and, when the captain withdrew the key, a block of wood came with it. The block proved to be hollow, one side of which was a hinged lid.

Setting this on a chart table, Captain Savage opened the terminal lid. It was cunningly wrought, obviously of Oriental construction, but the box opened to his manipulations.

Out came a curl of parchment. Captain Savage unrolled this item and laid it out on the scarred table.

"A map," said Doc.

"Yes," Savage Senior growled. "But practically useless now. See for yourself."

If it were a map, the important section had been obliterated. The lower portion of the chart was a dark smear of ink. Salt water had destroyed its writing so that now it was unreadable.

But the top half of the map had been drawn in a differently-colored ink, one which had withstood the ravages of salt water.

This took the form of a drawing. It appeared to show a knoll or hill whose top had been eroded into the semblance of a human skull. Above this bald knob floated what appeared to be two seagulls soaring on outstretched wings.

"A landmark," said Doc.

"Aye. A landmark such as I have never heard tell of in all my years at sea. Looks like a headland, judging from the circling seagulls."

Doc looked closely. "Those don't look like gulls."

"Of course those are seagulls. Look at their relationship in size to the fearsome hill."

Doc remained unconvinced. The drawing was crude, but the details were interesting. The bird's beaks were unusually long and pointed, like those of storks.

"The top is very rugged, more akin to a mountain peak," Doc suggested.

"If this is a mountain," the elder Savage insisted, "then those are the largest seagulls known to man. They would put an albatross to shame."

Doc ran a sensitive fingertip over the drawing, like a blind man reading Braille dots. "I wonder if those birds are vultures. Look at their heads—bald with predatory beaks."

"Buzzards are not common in this part of the world."

"Can we assume this map relates to the Indian Ocean?" asked Doc.

"We must, until proof otherwise presents itself."

Doc was forced to agree. But still… those birds resembled carrion birds of prey.

"This map may be a clue to the last landfall of the *Courser,*" Captain Savage insisted. "We must proceed on that assumption."

"No argument there," agreed Doc. "But where might it lie?"

"Sumatra, perhaps. Or Java. These are the largest land masses hereabouts."

"If so, wouldn't we know of such a natural formation? It would be famous the world over."

"Perhaps you are correct. We can safely rule out India to the north and Australia to the southwest."

"Could be an island," suggested Doc.

"There are no islands known to possess such a landmark. No. More than likely this is a rock formation of a wild, unknown country. 'Death's Head.' We will call it that for now."

Carefully rolling up the map, Captain Savage mounted the companion to the bright morning sun, Doc following.

After the close darkness of the hold, the climbing tropical sun dazzled their eyes.

They blinked the piercing rays out of their sun-sensitive retinas.

Doc's alert eyes went to the rail. He failed to see the grappling hooks by which they had first boarded the old clipper ship.

Rushing to the spot, he looked down to where the *Orion* should be.

His musical trilling piped up, wild and excited, tinged with fury.

"Sir, the ship!"

Captain Savage arrived at the rail, puzzled of countenance.

"What is it?" Then he saw the awful truth.

Bright blue water squirmed and danced where the schooner should be.

The *Orion* had vanished!

"My ship!" croaked the captain, his tone disbelieving. "Gone!"

Chapter XIII

ON CLOSER INSPECTION, a series of scarlet bulls-eye rings wavered on the spot where the schooner *Orion* should have bobbed in the swells. Sunlight on the water made the tableau difficult to make out, but when they spotted them, their meaning was unmistakable.

"Bodies dropped overboard, one by one," Captain Savage judged, stern features darkening.

"I count only three rings," said Doc.

"One of my Mayans may live yet," snapped Savage, his harsh gaze raking the surrounding ocean.

Of the *Orion*, there was no sign. Only trackless rollers, laced with sea foam.

Doc moved to the opposite rail.

"'Ware darts!" his father called after him.

It was an unnecessary warning, but it may have saved Doc Savage's life nonetheless. He reached the rail, leaned over, and spied a *bangkong* lurking directly below!

Under the rattan awning, a sinister array of blowpipes were trained upward in anticipation of his arrival. Puffing sounds came, expelling fletched missiles.

Doc retreated ahead of the soft whispers of death flicking by. One hand, moving with amazing reflexive skill, snapped out and grasped a passing dart by its feathered tail.

Doc had his automatic in hand. Cocking it, he called out, "Dyaks below!"

They met in the center of the deck, put their silver and bronze heads together.

"We dare not approach the port rail lest they pepper us with impunity via their poisoned darts," said Doc Savage, lifting the one he had captured. It was a very long splinter of bamboo, shaved tip heavy with a pasty substance.

Captain Savage frowned. "We cannot remain here. The devils are certain to attempt a boarding."

Doc looked about. Far away, he could see the tops of two masts, and a glimpse of canvas. The *Orion*. She was being carried away by the trade winds, making remarkable time.

"I can overhaul her," assured Doc.

"Impossible!"

"Have you forgotten that I sailed on the *Titanic*, and survived in the water without benefit of a lifeboat?"

"I have not, sir! And I will not lose you to a similar disaster."

"What are our chances marooned on this hulk if I don't try?" countered Doc.

The old man looked uncertain. The pressure of the moment paralyzed him. Without his ship, he seemed helpless.

Doc took command. "Create a diversion."

"Who is master here?" Savage roared in frustration.

"This is Stormalong's ship, not ours," Doc advised.

Captain Savage accepted Doc's .45 automatic and looked at his fists filled with steel.

"Distract them," instructed Doc. "Let me do the rest."

He leaped to the starboard rail and went over, clambering down using his metal-hard fingers to go from hull plank to hull plank, using the loose seams for handholds.

Reaching the surface, Doc charged his lungs with air and slipped beneath the waves.

The sound of repeating gunshots reached his ears before the warmish waters of the Indian Ocean swallowed him.

The quickest and safest way to the outrigger was under the

Courser's keel. Doc propelled himself in that direction, releasing air bubbles one at a time.

He reached the other side and came up on the starboard gunwale of the warrior-packed *bangkong.*

All Dyak eyes were aimed upward at the deck of the *Courser.* Doc looked up, too.

Two sun-burned fists popped in and out, firing downward. The muzzles flared tiny barking tongues.

A Dyak took a direct hit and screamed. Another lost his ironwood pipe. A third hefted a long spear, but lost his balance while throwing it over tattooed shoulder in preparation for launching. He landed in the brine, losing his weapon.

Doc Savage came up on their blind side, still holding the single Dyak dart he had captured in mid-air.

Reaching up, he began sticking the nearest warriors with the vicious needle of death.

They jumped up, howled wordlessly, immediately succumbing to their own native poison. During the commotion, Doc Savage yanked hard on their gunwale.

The result was consternation and confusion redoubled.

The longboat spilled warriors, their feathered headdresses toppling. Doc used his fist to crack a few heads, wreck jaws and render a portion of his foes insensate. Those who did not fall into the drink created tangles of limbs in the crowded dugout.

A few warriors wielded monstrously-long blowpipes, capped with detachable iron spear points. They scrambled to get these into stabbing position. Blowpipes at close quarters are not efficient weapons. Nor can they be brought to bear on an unstable platform with reliable accuracy.

Doc kept rocking the outrigger. Feet kicked at him. Doc seized ankles, yanked warriors into the water, smashing their skulls with knuckles of iron.

Long and short swords came out. Oblong rattan shields were raised. Doc emerged from the water and picked up a sturdy blowpipe as long as he was tall.

He employed this to fend off the first knife man. The tube was swiftly hacked to fragments, but this maneuver bought the bronze man sufficient time to pick up a fallen *mandau* and begin hacking.

The longer sword made short work of the *duku* wielders. Using his superior strength, Doc lopped off hands at the wrists, literally disarming his swarming foes.

More blades came up. Hands grasped for bare bronze arms.

Doc shook them off, removed a head with a sidewise swipe. It splashed into the water, rolling wildly like a buoyant ball.

By now he had a curved *mandau* in one hand and a thorn-like *duku* in the other. He used the latter as a throwing knife. It was not made for that purpose, but his superior size and strength allowed him to pierce an ink-decorated chest with his first throw.

Picking up another, Doc clove a skull at its crown, exposing living brain.

In the close quarters of the benched-seated boat, fighting was not easily accomplished. So it was that the Dyaks began retreating from this bronze-skinned giant who dwarfed them all.

Above, Captain Savage leaned over and began raining hot lead upon the combatants. They began falling with surprised grunts and outcries of mortal pain.

Soon, the waters around the outrigger were floating with the dead and wounded.

Doc ended the battle by inserting a *mandau's* sharp tip into the face of the apparent captain of the outrigger, transfixing him. The Dyak sat down hard, keeling over with his dark eyes rolled up into his blank-faced skull until only the whites showed.

A silence ensued. The groaning of the wounded punctuated it at intervals.

Doc looked up.

Captain Savage stood at the rail, weathered brassy face a frown, a smoking pistol in each fist.

"Hold your position," Doc called up. "I will be back directly."

"Son. This is madness. There is no catching her! The *Orion* has the wind at her back."

"No other choice," called back Doc.

Inserting a *duku* knife into his belt, he returned to the water and struck out in the wake of the fleeing schooner. The grisly gray blades of cruising shark fins came and went, vanishing below to feed on hapless dead flesh.

IT was not so mad as it seemed, this plan of Doc Savage's.

The bronze-skinned Hercules knew he could not overhaul the *Orion* in a race. But this was not a simple contest, as he saw it.

The *Orion* had sailed off in order to isolate them aboard the *Courser.* When the Dyak outrigger failed to follow, Doc judged, whoever now commanded the schooner would surely turn back to seek the fate of his fellow warriors.

It was a fair guess. And it proved accurate.

After an hour, the schooner tacked about clumsily. The sails had not been raised correctly. Whoever had control of the wheel was attempting to turn the boat by brute force alone.

This meant that headway would be lost.

Sure enough, the luffing canvas lost their wind, collapsed. The *Orion* began to wallow.

At that point, Doc began swimming in earnest. He kept an eye out for sharks, but encountered none. They would follow the blood, and the bronze giant, entirely unscathed, was swimming away from the gory patch of death and dismemberment.

Nearing the schooner, he paused, treading water.

There were no signs of a crew of any size. Three dark heads moved about the deck, one at the wheel. There had been three empty seats on the *bangkong,* so Doc was reasonably certain that he faced only a trio of foes.

Moving on an intercept course with the approaching *Orion,* Doc charged his lungs and submerged.

He floated beneath the waves until the dark prow came knifing in his direction.

Doc allowed the copper-sheathed hull to pass over him, then kicked for the surface, head emerging at the stern, where the Dyaks would be unlikely to be watching.

A line trailed in the water. It was not regulation marine line, but a hand-woven fiber cord. No doubt it was an artifact of the process by which the *Orion* had initially been boarded.

Doc seized this cord, testing it, and determined that it might hold his weight.

Hand over hand, he ascended. The crude line strained. Fibers popped and parted. It began to look as if he would not make it.

With a snapping snarl, the line finally gave under his 200 pounds of rock-hard muscle.

By then, Doc had neared the stern rail and quickly transferred his grasp to its smooth brass. It was slick with some sticky fluid, and Doc had to scramble to keep his grasp.

Coming over the rail, Doc knelt, allowed the last brine to silently string off him. His metallic hair was already become dry, a weird property it possessed. He saw that his hands were ensanguined with fresh blood.

When he was ready, Doc moved forward, gleaming *duku* in hand.

He passed a welter of blood by the starboard stern. That told a grisly tale and redoubled his resolve to retake the *Orion,* and so to avenge his father's slain crew.

The Dyak at the wheel stood closest. He was jerking it back and forth, as if testing its response. He seemed to be enjoying himself, for he bounced on the balls of his bare feet, like a boy playing with a new toy.

But he died like a man.

Doc stole up behind him and smothered his mouth with terrible digits of bronze. The other brought up the sharp *duku* knife and slit his tattooed throat lengthwise.

Doc lowered the squirming body, stood on it to keep spasmodic death throes from hammering the deck and alerting the others. He swiped the blade clean of gore, lest dripping blood drops give away his position.

Doc moved for the next man, keeping close to the deckhouse walls.

That stealthy approach did not go so well.

Doc made no sound, but the Dyak was pacing the foredeck restlessly, looking ahead with jet eyes that combined a penetrating fierceness with an incongruous blankness due to their lack of eyebrows, vainly in search of the war canoe that had been left behind to finish off the last of the *Orion* crew.

Taking a turn about the forecastle, the warrior suddenly spotted the bronze giant approaching in the shadow of the deckhouse. Perhaps the sudden scent of fresh-spilt blood alerted him.

Doc rushed forward to meet him, a terrible, towering figure. The Dyak squealed, shrank back. That alerted his brother pirate.

Suddenly, both were plunging in Doc's direction, *mandaus* out and flashing menacingly.

A knife against two long swords does not favor the man armed only with the shorter blade. But Doc Savage was no ordinary man.

He lifted both arms, making himself look even larger than he was. He vented a war cry he had learned in Arabia—one that started deep in the pit of his stomach and seemed to scrape the eardrums with its piercing howl.

This had a decided effect on the others.

They abruptly recalculated the odds. One backed up. The other attempted to dodge to one side on bare feet.

As it happened, the latter veered in the direction of the port rail and Doc Savage swept a hand up and sent the *duku* blade sizzling after him.

The blade struck in the shoulder with a meaty bite, and the man pitched over the rail, trailing a satisfying scream.

The surviving Dyak, seeing that the bronze colossus was no longer armed, discovered his mistake. He came in again, *mandau* waving menacingly.

Doc dived for a coil of heavy line, brought it up in both hands, then flung it with strength that was prodigious.

The swordsman caught the heavy mass full in his unprotected chest and had the wind knocked out of him. He also lost his sword. It went skittering and spinning along the deck.

Struggling to extract himself from the hempen tangle, the Dyak scrambled in search of the fallen blade.

He discovered it when the blade tip suddenly appeared under his sagging chin. Doc raised the man's head, gave him the full power of his golden gaze.

Seeing those terrible aureate orbs, the Dyak screamed.

Doc addressed him in Malay.

"Adakah terdapat lebih anda di atas kapal?" Are others of your breed aboard?

The man hesitated.

Doc employed the head-taking *mandau* sword to raze the eight hornbill feathers sticking up from the Dyak's sweat-stained headband. This produced a sudden change in attitude.

"No, no!"

"Terima kasih." Thank you. Doc removed his head with a swift, sidewise swipe.

The man never knew what happened. His rolling face remained as blank after death as it had been before.

Doc picked up the bisected body and disposed of it over the side. It wasn't long before shark fins were slicing toward the spot, which soon began boiling with the fury of their feeding.

By that time, the *Orion* was tacking back toward the derelict clipper ship. Soon, she was coming up alongside the *Courser.* Doc Savage had cleaned the decks of blood and bodies. His face was very resolute.

Chapter XIV

CAPTAIN CLARK SAVAGE, SENIOR, took command of the schooner *Orion* with a stern visage and a mouth that was like the cold edge of a sword blade.

He seemed at a loss for words. Finally, his snapping eyes met those of his son.

"Your training has repaid all the wealth I have poured into it," he said stiffly.

Doc Savage said nothing.

"Put another way," he added, his voice thick with clogged emotion, "you have exceeded my expectations, Mister Savage. Congratulations on a job masterfully accomplished."

"Thank you, sir," returned Doc, inwardly gratified even if his outward mask registered nothing of the sort.

"There will be heads on board," Captain Savage said, upon surveying the deck.

"What makes you say that, Captain?"

"My eyes. There were none in the war canoe. I see none on this deck. Therefore, they must be below. Dyaks do not waste trophy heads, which they consider to possess supernatural power."

"I will investigate," said Doc.

"I am the captain. This is my solemn duty." He surged for the deckhouse companion.

Doc followed him below.

They expected to find utter ruination, but there had been no time for that.

On the dining table reposed three fresh heads and a fourth that was dry and shrunken, its eyes and mouth sewn shut. It rested upon a pewter platter.

Grimly, Captain Savage examined the fresh specimens first. He recognized them as Ikan, Kish, and Ichik.

"Where is Chicahua?" wondered Doc.

"That remains to be discovered," Savage Senior said gravely. "But we will accord these sad remains the proper burial at sea that they deserve for their loyal service and sacrifice."

"Aye, Captain."

They turned their attention to the fourth head. It was not freshly-taken. Withered and black with age, it brooded, eyes closed, mouth sewn shut. Yellowish teeth showed dimly behind coarse black thread.

In the gloom they thought it might be a human head that had become bloated and deformed in its death corruptions.

"Looks to me to be a man of Africa," pronounced Captain Savage. "Possibly a Zulu."

"No," said Doc. "Not a man. An ape."

Captain Savage examined it with undisguised distaste. "I stand corrected. A Kongo gorilla, from the size of the beast."

"No gorilla ever grew so large," countered Doc Savage.

Captain Savage cocked a quizzical eyebrow. "What is it then?"

Employing a knife, Doc picked at the head, testing it for flexibility. It had been taken long ago, he decided.

Doc paid special attention to the top of the skull. He found a lack of bone there, but upon further probing, decided that the bone plates were floating free.

Doc's peculiar trilling wandered the scales for a period of time.

"What is it, son?"

"This gorilla is a juvenile. The skull plates have not yet fused."

"Nonsense! Observe its prodigious size. Larger than the head of a full-grown man."

Doc employed his blade tip to lift a flap of scalp. The brains had been removed and the brain pan stuffed with dried grass, but the bony crown had not been disturbed. The top of the skull was composed of separate plates.

"A youth," decided Doc at last. "Not more than three years old."

Captain Savage snorted. "What manner of ape would this be?"

Doc did some fast mental calculations. "One that, when fully grown, might stand a dozen or more feet tall."

"Absurd! Science has catalogued no such creature. The prehistoric record is silent on this score."

"Only a juvenile would have such an arrangement of skull plates," insisted Doc. "They fuse after several years. This is a young specimen of an anthropoid unknown to the Twentieth Century."

Silence held them for over a minute.

After due consideration, Captain Savage intoned, "We will dispose of it with the others."

Doc said swiftly, "Captain, please reconsider. This head may be of great value to anthropologists."

"Such a foul thing does not belong on a clean ship like the *Orion*, Mister Savage."

"I will keep it in my cabin," promised Doc.

"Very well. If you must. But we have a crew member to find. See to the sails, while I undertake the task."

DOC returned to the deck and examined the canvas while his father rummaged below. They were intact, although they drooped from lack of maintenance. The rigging was a limp mess.

After a period, Captain Savage came clumping up. Doc turned, startled—for he heard two sets of footfalls.

A prolonged trilling signaled his surprise. For Captain Savage emerged with the last member of the crew, Chicahua, who served as boatswain to the late crew.

"Where did you find him?" asked Doc.

"In my secret hiding hole. He discovered it."

Doc looked blank, which for him served as a mask of surprise.

"I was unable to locate it," he admitted.

"Chicahua may be the better man," Captain Savage returned. "At hide and seek, at any rate. He has told me his story. Blow-pipe darts accounted for the others, who were taken unawares by Dyaks crawling up from the port stern rail."

Doc nodded. "I found one of their climbing vines."

"The Dyaks had dragged the dead and wounded to the taffrail and were chopping their heads off when Chicahua heard the commotion. Seeing that he was outnumbered, he attempted battle, regardless of the peril to his life."

Hearing his name, the Mayan hung his head.

"Chicahua was forced below," continued the captain, "but made a pretense of going overboard by throwing a bundle of rope into the water, which duly sank. He forthwith concealed himself in the secret spot, trusting to obtain his vengeance at his first opportunity."

"He looks ashamed of himself," said Doc.

"He is contrite. One of the seamen who perished was his brother. We must spare him the sight of their heads."

They got under weigh, waiting until nightfall to dispose of the heads with due ceremony after Chicahua had returned to his lonely bunk forward.

The matter of the *Courser* was settled after a brief discussion. Doc returned to the foundering clipper and scuttled it by opening every aperture that would admit seawater.

When this proved too slow, he blasted holes in her planking to speed up the process. It felt like shooting a lame horse.

Clark Savage, Senior, refused to witness the sinking. He went to his cabin, leaving word to be called topside when the deed was done.

Doc Savage alone watched the ocean swallow the damaged clipper. She slipped low with great speed, began listing to port. The ancient deck was soon awash. Brine sloshed the boards one last time, then the old clipper began vanishing from view.

Doc had the strange sense of the great masts also slipping from view. But there were no masts to go down in the traditional manner. Her holds filling with heavy ocean, the clipper heeled and rocked. Her stern went down first, which threw the *Courser's* bow high into the air.

The last portion of her to go below was the proud plunging warhorse that had given the *Courser* her famous name.

AFTER being called back to deck, Captain Savage ignored the swirl of water that marked the demise of the *Courser.* Stone-faced and stern-eyed, he took his customary position at the helm. From time to time, he took fresh sightings with his sextant.

They sailed west, in the direction of the Maldives.

"I must find Death's Head," said Captain Savage after an hour of silent contemplation.

"We could sail the Indian Ocean for years in search of it—if it exists."

"It exists," Savage Senior said firmly.

"As it stands," reminded Doc, "it is only a sketch on a map of unknown origin and purpose."

Captain Savage stood firmly silent.

"If it were I who was lost—or you—Stormalong Savage would scour the seven seas for us," he observed.

"I am prepared to scour the universe, if necessary," said Doc. "But I would feel more confident if my objective were a certain one."

"We will communicate with maritime traffic, inquiring if the landmark is known to sailors of this sea."

"I will see to it," said Doc.

DOC SAVAGE worked the radio set when he could, reaching out via the International Morse Code. His message was the same each time:

SEEKING PROMONTORY IN THE SHAPE OF A SKULL. RESPOND WITH EXACT LONGITUDE AND LATITUDE OF LANDMARK. REPLY SCHOO-NER ORION IN INDIAN OCEAN.

Return dots and dashes offered no concrete information. One reply came from a British warship:

SCHOONER ORION. YOUR LANDMARK BE-LIEVED SIGHTED FAR WEST OF SUMATRA BY THE FRIGATE BUCKINGHAM. NO EXACT COOR-DINATE. GOOD LUCK.

Doc took out a marine chart.

West of Sumatra lay island groups, such as Nias Island and the Batu and Hinako Islands and Telos, and their associated barrier reefs and rocks. Although obscure, they were charted. Any bald knob resembling a human skull would be well known to coastwise mariners, he knew. That meant an unknown land mass.

Going topside, Doc explained his findings.

"We are either looking west or south," he said after revealing the message.

Captain Savage considered this for several minutes, his brassy brow furrowing and unfurrowing, adding and subtracting from his apparent age as he did so.

"Mister Friday spoke of fogs southwest of the Nicobars. I should think that any obscure island might be fog-bound, and thus evade detection and charting."

"It is a line of attack," agreed Doc, "if a thin one."

A silvery eyebrow cocked upward. "You have a more concrete course to offer, Mister Savage?"

"I do not."

"Then let us plot a concrete course and make the best of it."

"Aye, Captain."

Together, they pored over their charts, noting the position of the *Courser,* and drawing a line from it on through the earlier reported positions.

Captain Savage again regarded the chart like a seer looking into a crystal ball. One finger moved over the map, as if feeling for something.

"I would sail westerly along this heading," he said at last.

Doc could not make out his reasoning. He decided that reason may not have anything to do with it.

"It's as good a course as any," allowed Doc.

They were soon breaking waves along the new tack, sails having been restored to apple-pie order. The sun finished climbing to the noon hour, then began its slow, sizzling descent. The winds were fair, the air hot but breezy.

More shipboard responsibility had fallen onto Doc's shoulders since the loss of the crew and he no longer had the spare time to work on his new weapon.

Reluctantly, he decided to abandon it. The bronze man reassembled the Annihilator submachine gun and stowed it away for safekeeping. Upon reconsideration, he loaded the drum and then put it away. He wished he could test it, but that was out of the question on shipboard.

The *Orion* might or might not be beating away from the rest of that Dyak *balla.* There was no telling. It remained a puzzle exactly what a Dyak war party was doing so far from their home shores. These were not safe waters for pirating. Too many vessels were of the international variety, and many armed. No sheltering harbors or coves to flee into, either. Leagues of open water were not the friend of sea rovers.

It was a mystery. As much a mystery as the giant gorilla skull that was unquestionably that of a juvenile....

Chapter XV

SAILING WESTWARD BROUGHT the *Orion* to a patch of fog just as the day began to die. The setting sun showed as a hazy scarlet ball that sank heavily into a horizon line that could not be seen in any compass point.

They slipped into the fogbank, the schooner's clipper bowsprit vanishing into a soupy haze.

An eerie silence overtook the ship. The warm white murk smothered the sails, streamed along the deck, and muffled what little sound the schooner made in her passing.

The waters here were calm, more like an inland sea than a great turbulent ocean.

They were sailing with the wind, making fair time: Twelve knots.

Captain Savage had the helm. Doc paced the length of the 125-foot deck, attempting to pierce the cottony fogbank with his ever-restless golden eyes. But the misty stuff defeated even his superb visual acuity. All that was discernible was the yellowish glow of the *Orion's* running lights painting streamers of fog as they rode along.

"This must be one of the pea soups of which Friday spoke," Captain Savage remarked gruffly.

Doc nodded, concentrating on his hearing.

He heard something. Swiveling his head around, he tried to catch the sound.

A gray-headed albatross swept by, appearing so suddenly

that Doc almost missed it. The sea bird flew low—low enough that it could be glimpsed momentarily as it passed through a thinner patch of fog, before vanishing again into the thick soup. No sound attended its flight. It might have been a winged phantom of the sea. Had Doc been looking the other way, he surely would have missed it.

Rushing back to the wheel, Doc reported, "Albatross. Headed due west."

Captain Savage nodded. "Land nearby. What do the charts say?"

From memory, Doc recited, "No known islands for hundreds of nautical miles in any direction."

"In that case, the question becomes, is that bird fleeing land—or heading toward it?"

"The albatross can fly for hundreds of miles, resting at intervals by alighting on the waves," offered Doc. "We can assume there is something in either direction of its flight track, but we cannot judge which direction that might be."

"Did you get a good look at the bird?"

"Good enough, but brief," admitted Doc.

"Flying low?"

"Rather low. It barely cleared the mast heads."

"Fatigue might cause that condition," Savage reckoned.

"Or it is preparing to alight."

Captain Savage frowned, making his silver-dusted mustache droop. "We will have to choose a direction, and then trust in luck."

"Dame Fortune is a fickle mistress," responded Doc, returning to the bow.

Captain Savage held the wheel for a time, not deviating from his course. The bill of his peaked cap threw his sharp eyes into shadow, dulling their gold.

At length, he spun the wheel just enough to correct course to west by southwest.

Doc made no comment or criticism. The direction the albatross was flying was as good a guess as its reverse heading. Time alone would reveal the wisdom of the decision.

THE endless fog required that both captain and first mate stand watch all night long. Too many days of this would take a severe toll but, for now, they were up to the challenge. They spoke little, remaining attentive to their tasks. Their clothes became moist and clammy, which, while unpleasant, would help keep them awake and alert.

Far, far into the night, Doc Savage's ears picked up other sounds over the crinkling waves.

He listened intently. The sound was subtle, ineffable, combining a rhythmic hiss with movements that were so muffled that they could not be made out.

Worse yet, the sounds seemed to be coming from no special direction.

Doc swept from port to starboard, then worked his way amidships, dousing all running lights as he did so.

"What do you hear?" hissed Captain Savage.

Doc motioned for silence.

Moving to the stern, Doc found that the noises appeared stronger there, yet still difficult to make out.

Doc waited. The conglomerate noises appeared to be approaching.

Unexpectedly—given their sharp-eared surveillance—the commotion drew very close and echoed all around them.

Doc raced forward to the headsails and took hold of a line, attempting to arrest its noisy knocking.

All around them in the weird murk, the unmistakable sound of Dyak men at their oars swept by. They were making unbelievable time, thanks to their shallow draft and two tiers of oarsmen, paddling like tireless automatons.

Doc and his father dropped to the deck, alert for the whisking noise of flying darts.

But no such sound materialized.

Instead, the *balla*—for that was what it must be—ghosted past, apparently oblivious to their presence. The fogbank was that thick.

Doc Savage lay flat to the polished pine deck, head down, his automatic clutched in one bronze first. He did not cock it, lest the telltale clicking of its action carry.

After a time, Doc stood up. Holstering his pistol, he helped his father to his feet.

"These Sea Dyaks are astoundingly far from their home preserves," said Captain Savage in a low, concerned tone.

"They have a definite objective," agreed Doc.

"Aye. And they are going in the same direction as we."

"Good enough reason to stay our course," decided Doc.

"Like the albatross, they will have to cease their rowing and rest, trusting to the tides to carry them on," the elder Savage pointed out.

Doc nodded. "No doubt. We are certain to overhaul them. The morning sun is likely to burn off this fog, exposing us to their crews."

"We will take that chance," decided the captain. "For now, they are racing along, at their top clip, seeking a break in the fog."

"You do not think they will come about and make an ambush?"

Captain Savage shook his head gravely. "I do not. Clearing this horridly clammy atmosphere means their lives, exposed as they are. I do not think they perceived us."

"Nor do I," added Doc

"Best you turn in, Mister Savage. Be fresh for the morning watch. Rest assured, I will call you if need be."

"Very well, Captain."

Doc retired for the night and fell asleep so rapidly it was as if he hadn't a concern in the world. He had learned the mental trick of sleeping on command from a Ubangi witch doctor. The trait had served him well in the noisy mud of the trenches of France.

The same soothing sounds of water against the schooner hull that had greeted him upon his arrival into the world some twenty years before lulled him to sleep....

Chapter XVI

MORNING WAS ACCOMPANIED by a brisk wind, which filled the straining sails, impelling the *Orion* along at a steady ten knots.

The sun burned away some of the cloying fog, but failed to dissipate it. Visibility became more amenable to distances, but the fog often closed in, as the wind moved its streamers and tendrils around.

Doc Savage worked the sheets, along with the Mayan crewman, Chicahua. All sails were wet, which made handling strenuous. The canvas fluttered in the wind like frightened ghosts towering over them.

When every sail was properly set, the bronze man took the helm from his father.

"I have matters well in hand," he told the captain.

Relinquishing the wheel, Captain Savage said, "Hesitate not to summon me from my bunk, First Mate."

"Count on it," replied Doc.

Overnight, Captain Savage had piloted the schooner on a more westerly tack in hopes of sailing around the *balla*, should it lie ahead.

As the *Orion* broke along wave caps, lunging like a frisky colt, that possibility became more and more certain. Even if the Dyaks could maintain their brisk pace—an impossibility in terms of human endurance, Doc knew—the schooner was sure to come upon them at this pace.

Every sail strained with the sheer joy of the exuberant wind. Canvas snapped smartly as the air bit into it. Such sounds carried, Doc knew. Even over the wind.

Holding the wheel to a steady course, Doc ranged the surrounding sea with his penetrating eyes. He had flown in Spads, Jennys, even a few captured German Fokker airplanes, stood watch in an observation balloon, but nothing equaled a good sailing ship in a running sea.

Noon came and went. All was peaceful upon the vast continual heave of the Indian Ocean. Far to the south, storm clouds hung along the horizon, as if a careless artist had daubed them there with blue-gray water colors.

Doc continually sniffed the air for strange scents, but the wind blew so strongly that it was likely to keep any odors from reaching him, if they were away from windward.

The crosswind began abating as the afternoon marched on. The *Orion* began to slow to a more decorous pace. It was still good sailing.

ALONG about three bells, Doc spotted something ahead to starboard. A bit of white bobbing on the foam. It had a cottony look.

Steering toward it, he kept his eyes upon the object. It seemed to be moving.

Gradually, the white thing came into sharper focus.

"Fetch the Captain," Doc ordered Chicahua.

Although the Mayan appeared to understand no English, he went clomping down the companionway, presently returning with Captain Savage, who was donning his black captain's cap.

"Albatross resting upon the waves, Captain," Doc reported.

Opening up his spyglass, Captain Savage went to the bow and trained the instrument upon the resting bird.

The albatross jerked his head about, as if watchful of its surroundings. Otherwise, the sea bird sat there placidly, the swells raising and lowering it in long undulations.

"If we can startle it," suggested Doc, reaching for his sidearm, "it would fly off toward land."

Captain Savage shook his gray head.

"Gunshot sound might carry too far. And an exhausted bird should be left to take off when it has the strength to reach its destination. No, we will circle it, until it decides to leave the water. Stand by to tack."

"Very well, Captain," said Doc, as Chicahua rushed to slack up the sheets.

"Ready about! Hard alee."

Doc spun the wheel, steering the *Orion* about in a long sweeping arc. As she came around, the after boom was hauled aweather. Doc pointed the clipper-style bowsprit at the floating flyer.

From their first view of it, the albatross had looked almost contented to rest upon the waves. But as they began their circuit, its agitated head turned this way and that, growing more pronounced in its evident distress.

Doc remarked, "He seems afraid of us."

Captain Savage stroked his mustache thoughtfully, "He is afraid of something. Albatrosses have little fear of boats. No sailor would shoot one down for the sport of it. Bad luck would surely follow. Recall Coleridge's 'Rime of the Ancient Mariner?' No, they are our friends, and we, theirs."

Coming around, they saw that the sea bird's outward semblance of calmness belied a terrible truth.

For the entire right side of the sea creature proved to be a gory smear.

"Wounded!" said Doc.

The spyglass came up and Captain Savage muttered, "Wing is off entirely."

"Shot?"

"No. Clipped. As with a knife, or perhaps by a jaw. Crocodiles have been known to take a snap at the odd roosting albatross."

"Hungry Dyaks might have attempted to make a meal of this one," ventured Doc.

"Best we investigate. Up for a swim, First Mate?"

"Aye, Captain."

DOC stripped down to his undershorts and went down a dangling line. He found the water warmer than expected, and swam for the resting sea bird.

It attempted to swim farther away, but its legs lacked the paddling power of an adult swimmer. Doc soon caught up with it and took it in hand. It vainly flapped its surviving wing, but could hardly fly away.

Tucking the wriggling bird under one arm, Doc returned to the *Orion*.

Going up the line one-handed was not practical. Doc managed the climb by taking the bird's good wing in his mouth, freeing both hands to clasp the rope. The albatross was too fatigued to complain much. It squawked only once.

Topping the rail, the bronze man set the unhappy bird on the poop deck.

Prying up the stump of a wing with his rigging knife, Doc examined the wound.

"Bitten off," he pronounced.

"Crocodile," said Captain Savage. "There's our explanation."

But Doc Savage was not yet done with his study.

"Crocodile teeth did not do this," he said, finally.

"No?"

"I have examined crocodiles, and this is not the work of their teeth."

"Have you a theory, Mister Savage?"

"The teeth that did this were reptilian, if I am not mistaken," Doc said at last. "But what species of reptile, I cannot state with certainty."

"Well, small matter. It stands to reason that this unfortunate bird escaped being consumed close to some nearby shore. It could not have floated very far in its present deplorable condition."

Doc nodded. "Less than a half day's sail. We might light upon land before nightfall if we are lucky."

"Keep a sharp watch, Mister Savage. I will catch up on my sleep and join you for supper."

"Aye."

Doc Savage took his stance before the *Orion's* wheel. He was paging through his remarkably retentive memory for reptiles whose dentition would fit the creature that had crippled the albatross.

He could think of none. It bothered him greatly, but this fact did not register on his brazen countenance, which shone under the dying afternoon sun.

Chapter XVII

NO LAND WAS encountered that day.

Night fell with the startling splendor of the tropics. The fog gathered, thickened and before long a waxing crescent moon was illuminating it with an eerie, almost spectral light.

"Better night than last," remarked Captain Savage, after coming up from his nightly sleep.

"The wind appears to be dying," cautioned Doc.

It did die. Before the evening was very far along, the sails began to flap and droop. No amount of adjusting made any difference in their headway. They had drifted out of the ever-blowing trades.

Once again, they were becalmed.

"We have been saving our fuel for just such an occasion," reminded Doc.

Captain Savage nodded silently, then made a tour of the deck. Doc left the useless wheel, following him.

"I agree with you, First Mate, but I have in mind that *balla*."

"No sight or sound of it for nearly a day," Doc pointed out.

The Captain of the *Orion* turned to face him. "If this were your ship, what would your decision be?" he demanded.

Doc hesitated.

"Before you answer," his father interrupted, "I will remind you of what our late President, Mr. Roosevelt, so famously said: 'In any moment of decision, the best thing you can do is the right thing, the next best is the wrong thing, and the worst thing you can do is nothing.'"

Doc considered. "With all due respect to Mr. Roosevelt, I would await developments. The motor can be brought to bear at any time, should it be necessary."

"A sound point. For we have no present emergency. A true emergency may lie ahead of us. In which case, we will be thankful for all the fuel we have on board."

"I am glad we agree," replied Doc.

"However," added Captain Savage, "my decision stems from my observation that the tides are carrying us along ever so slightly. As long as we are making headway, and the ship is secure, what matter if our sails are filled or empty? The difference between one knot and ten is a matter of time, and nothing else. We have time."

"Aye, Captain."

Before long, they went below, leaving Chicahua to stand watch while they dined on pemmican and sea biscuit, enlivened by steaming black coffee.

"Time will tell if we are on a profitable course, or not," mused Captain Savage.

Doc nodded wordlessly. He didn't feel like conversation. His eyes were thoughtful and far away, the gold flakes that comprised the irises oddly quiescent.

Uncharacteristically, the old man felt like talking.

"I am wondering how you can be certain that no crocodile ever molested that poor albatross?" Captain Savage asked after a lengthy silence.

Doc paused. "I have wrestled alligators in Florida and hunted crocodiles along the Nile. The teeth of the crocodile are pointed like daggers, and spaced apart in a distinctive way. The saw-tooth bite I examined was neither crocodile nor alligator, but resembled both. My guess would be a monitor lizard."

"Monitor lizards—in the landless heart of the Indian Ocean? *Impossible, sir!*"

"Exactly. But I cannot place the toothmarks. They suggest instead serrated blade-like teeth. However, they match nothing in my experience."

"You have lived less than a score of years," grumbled the captain. "No doubt there are many things not yet in your personal lexicon."

Doc did not dispute that, but he was bothered still.

Dessert was dried apricots. They ate sparingly since dried fruit doubled as emergency rations.

The meal was not quite concluded when they heard a peculiar thrashing and slapping above their heads. A squawk as of a frightened bird followed. Then the pelican-like rattle and paddle of something treading the deck that did not go about on human feet.

They grabbed for their pistols and pounded up onto the deck, weapons jutting before them.

IN the moonlit fog, they discovered Chicahua standing at the stern, his machete out, and waving both bare arms in a kind of frenzied frustration.

Captain Savage called out in K'iche.

The Mayan turned, eyes stark. His face was gray—terrible. His brown arms trembled.

He spoke one word over and over again.

"*Camazotz! Camazotz!*"

"What is he saying?" asked Doc.

"He says that a bat carried off the wounded albatross."

"A bat?"

"If I understand him correctly. The word he keeps repeating is that of a Mayan god, *Camazotz*. The name means 'Death Bat.'"

Captain Savage began questioning the man.

Words gobbled out of Chicahua's pulsing throat. He gestured broadly, as if trying to convey hugeness.

"He said a bat as large as the mainsail. A bat whose wings were like twin jibs."

Doc's face was touched by a frown. "No such bat exists, as you know."

Captain Savage turned, drew up on his heels. "Are you questioning my crewman's veracity, Mister Savage?"

"No," returned Doc in a reasonable voice. "Only pointing out that bats are not carnivorous, except where it comes to insects. Nor would one be large enough to carry off an albatross, even if they had a taste for meat."

Captain Savage's jaw snapped shut. He offered no retort. It was undeniable truth.

Doc began searching the deck for signs.

He found that scratches and scrapes had scored the portion of the poop deck where the albatross had been left to die. The wood appeared to have been raked, as if by wild talons. Kneeling, the bronze man examined these.

"No bat made such markings. They are too big for an eagle."

Captain Savage shone a lantern on the scattered markings. While this produced more light, it did not admit more clarity into the situation. The marks stood out in sharp relief.

"If I did not know better," he said slowly, "I would ascribe these talon-marks to a quadruped animal. There are signs of lesser and greater feet."

"Ask Chicahua to describe the bat in more detail," requested Doc.

Captain Savage fell into low converse with his agitated Mayan.

At length, he reported, "Chicahua describes a creature with a bald bony skull like a buzzard, wings like membranous sails and a whip-like tail belonging to the Satan of the Bible."

"He is not describing a bat," Doc said flatly. "Or a buzzard, for that matter."

"I know what you are thinking."

Doc looked at his father. Golden eyes locked.

"You are thinking that he is describing a prehistoric flying reptile," said the elder Savage.

Doc nodded soberly. "Chicahua's 'bat' *does* fit the description of a Pteranodon, or other pterosaur."

"I am not unfamiliar with these things, Mister Savage. But they no longer exist in our time. Science has spoken with finality on the subject."

"I wonder..." said Doc slowly.

"What do you wonder, Mister Savage?"

"Flying reptiles are believed to have been fish eaters. I wonder if a Pteranodon might not find in a fish-eating albatross a tasty meal?"

Captain Savage declined to address that supposition.

They went back to the task of manning the *Orion*. But the silence that followed the carrying off of the hapless albatross left them with an uneasy feeling.

The feeling persisted, then worsened twenty minutes later when they spied a white wing floating upon the waves off to port, visible through the yellowish miasma.

Doc spotted it first.

It stood on the tossing tide, a forlorn fragment of a once-graceful sea bird. There was no blood. It looked perfect, as if clipped off by very sharp shears.

Doc called the wing to his captain's attention. Savage joined him at the port rail as the *Orion* swept past the sad remnant.

"Clearly a left wing," he pronounced.

"Yes," agreed Doc. "The creature must have consumed the albatross on the fly, discarding the wing as inedible."

"It is a good sign. It means whatever carried off the bird traveled this way. We are on course for landfall."

Doc said nothing.

"Something troubles you, Mister Savage?"

Doc Savage stared past the sails grouped ahead of him. "It

is a bad sign that we are sailing toward the rookery of an unknown bird that cannot be found in the taxonomy."

Captain Savage did not disagree with that. His mouth became grim. The sun-weathered lines of his face began showing his age.

As they sailed on through what increasingly struck them as a primordial mist such as was said to exist before the dawn of time, their attention continually went to the shrouded sky as much as the befogged sea. Unseen things with wings could be heard from time to time. Pulsings and thrashings stirred the swirling atmosphere high above.

Or was it a trick of their imaginations?

Chapter XVIII

THE SWIRLING FOG grew more yellow as the evening wore on.

Time passed. One bell. Two bells. Three bells. Nothing changed but the color of their shrouded surroundings.

Deep in the night, with the quarter moon ghosting in and out of view—a hazy lunar lantern never quite showing itself—Doc Savage began detecting a change in the oppressively heavy surrounding atmosphere.

First, a smell touched his sensitive nostrils. It smacked of something strange.

Doc inhaled deeply, allowing the odor to be fully absorbed.

After several draughts, he realized that he did not smell a single unusual scent, but a conglomeration of them. Foliage mixed with fetid animal smells. He attempted to distinguish them, but it was no use. It was as if the *Orion* was sailing into a ball of odors that belonged to some awful other realm.

Doc went below, roused his father.

"Captain, I smell land."

Captain Savage climbed back to the deck. He strode to the bow, sniffed several times and nodded his head in silent agreement.

"I will have Chicahua take soundings," he decided.

Chicahua fell to with a plumb line. Positioning himself at the bow, he dropped the lead weight time and again; after a while, he called out a burst of words.

"Bottom," translated Captain Savage. "Twenty fathoms. Land ho for certain. Steady as she goes, Mister Savage."

Doc nodded. The smells grew more alive, or alarming. He had never encountered such a packed knot of indescribable odors. His mind struggled to separate and categorize them. But the task proved too daunting. There was no making sense of it.

Chicahua continued his strenuous work with the heavy rope and lead plumb.

A few nautical miles along, he gave out a howl.

Captain Savage hurried to his side. He began feeling of the line.

Locking the helm, Doc rushed forward.

"What is it?" he demanded.

"Take this in hand, Mister Savage and discover for yourself."

Doc grasped the line, tried hauling it up. It could not be raised.

"Snagged," he decided.

Captain Savage shook his pewter-haired head. "Feel the vibration."

Doc steadied his bronze hands. After a moment, he realized that he could feel a dull thumping moving up the stubborn line that could not be budged.

Doc looked his question.

"Octopus walking up the line," explained the captain.

Doc looked doubtful.

"There are devilfish in deep waters larger than Science has yet catalogued," said Captain Savage. "I suspect we have encountered a curious specimen. If he gets a tentacle around our rail and is able to anchor his suckers to the bottom for traction, he may be able to capsize us at will."

"An octopus that size would have to weigh in excess of three hundred pounds—"

Captain Savage had his knife out and began sawing the line, saying, "If we act fast, we may be able to salvage the situation."

The keen blade dug, bit hard. Strands began parting.

All the while the rope jounced as the unseen climber made its ponderous way up the heavy cable.

A tentacle broke the surface—slickly black, as thin as a whip at the tip. It began groping blindly, seeking the rail.

Doc did not wait for more of it to surface. Unshipping his automatic, he took aim, and snapped the top off with one sure shot.

An explosion of frustrated bubbles broke the surface as the maimed tendril whipped around, then sank from sight.

The cable no longer vibrated.

"Heave to," cried the captain.

They began hauling up the line. It came up easily now, and they soon had the lead blob on deck.

The cable appeared undamaged.

"We had luck," breathed Captain Savage. "Best you return to your station."

Doc rushed back to the wheel as Chicahua resumed taking soundings. The Mayan looked uneasy in the extreme.

ANOTHER hour passed without eventuality. Doc was mentally calculating the probable size and weight of the discouraged octopus and decided that it might rival the Kraken said to slumber at the bottom of the ocean, patiently awaiting the end of the world, upon which it would awaken.

Out here in the vast Indian Ocean, nothing seemed fanciful, or far-fetched. It was a strange feeling.

The smells grew worse. The metallic stink of blood was mixed in with them. Doc had thought he might have caught a whiff of blood before, but now he was certain of it.

Night still reigned when, through the yellow-white pall, something sprang to life beyond the heaving jib spreader.

High in the air ahead of them, it appeared to be a bonfire, dimly perceived through the spectral swirl.

After a minute, a second bonfire started up, to one side of the first.

The blazing apparitions stood off to port, burning holes in the mist.

Captain Savage was attempting to make them out with his spyglass when he called back. "Steer toward this phantasm, Mister Savage."

"Aye, sir."

Doc spun the wheel. He pointed the bow directly at the fiery phenomenon.

Moonlight was not much help. It had been all but smothered by the ghostly white murk.

They crawled toward the apparition, Chicahua taking soundings every few minutes. Doc stood ready to throw the wheel hard over to avoid land or reefs.

Through the fog something reared up the closer they got to it. Something vast and eerily titanic. Twin fires burning on a huge promontory. That was all they could make out through the hazy atmosphere.

Then, the vision began to resolve itself.

Two fires, yes. Two blazing eyes, they had seemed. But now the truth became clearer.

Two fiery holes, they were. Twin burning eye sockets on a great weathered skull floating in the fog.

"Death's Head!" sang out Captain Savage. "We have found it. Hard alee!"

Eyes fixed on the uncanny headland, Doc Savage responded smartly. He was thinking of the rough drawing below deck, and the size of the unidentified birds that had circled it. Now he was dead certain that they were not ordinary seagulls....

Book Two:

SKULL MOUNTAIN ISLAND

Chapter XIX

I T WAS A fearful, disturbing thing as they beheld it now.
The map discovered on the *Courser* had been crude, but
the resemblance to a great, weathered human skull in real life
was remarkable. Cloud shadows cast by the moon paraded
across its cold countenance, animating it in an uncanny way, as
if dark thoughts were being projected onto its troubled brow.

"Death's Head," repeated Captain Savage in a voice border-
ing on awe.

"You mean Death's Peak," corrected Doc. "A mountaintop,
after all."

"Aye, if a small one."

"I am reminded of the hill on which Christ was crucified,"
mused Doc. "Golgotha."

" 'The Place of the Skull,' " commented his father. "It, too,
was reputed to resemble a great skull. It fills me with dread just
to gaze upon its grim countenance."

Captain Savage had taken the wheel. They were near land.
No question about it.

Doc could make out a soft chuckling of lapping water against
stone, not very far away. Surf sounds came and went.

"Mister Savage, go forward with a light. Look for shoals.
Snags. Breakers. Anything that might rip out our bottom."

Doc found a flashlight and surged toward the stem.

He speared his light ahead. The beam made a swirling cone
in the thickening yellow miasma.

"Sheer to starboard," Doc called back.

Somewhere on the island, something screamed in response to the carry of the bronze man's voice. It climbed like a wild thing, and was nothing human.

Captain Savage manipulated the wheel. The rudder responded. The *Orion* heeled smartly.

"Another!" warned Doc. "Hard aport!"

Soon, it became clear the waters all around were jagged with reefs. Doc pulled cartridges from the loops in his gun belt. He began tossing them ahead, listening for splashes or metallic clinks. He heard more clinks than splashes.

Doc's ears, sharpened by intensive training—much of it while blindfolded—enabled him to place the dangerous spots by hearing alone.

Between the light and Doc's ingenious soundings, they found a break in the shoals and passed through safely, into what appeared to be unobstructed waters. A lagoon. A wavering slice of moon was mirrored in it.

They cleared the last snags, began to make a circuit of the island—which is what it must be. An unknown isle in the vast Indian Ocean.

Little could be seen of it. Only the skull peak with his baleful burning orbs. Even these subsided to a vague yellow-red glow as they put the face of the skull behind them.

More rock fangs showed, jutting black as basalt in the darkling waters. The sloppy chuckling sounds made by the tide sounded ghoulish to their ears.

"I am reminded of the submerged reef that bedevils the Caribbean, called by mariners the Devil's Backbone," muttered Captain Savage.

Doc nodded. "I recall it. Many ships lost their keels to its rocks."

Captain Savage studied the disturbing patterns in the water, his mustache bristling with worry.

"Drop anchor!" he ordered sharply. "Strike sails!"

Doc fell to the task, releasing the chain from its windlass drum so that the anchor entered the water with minimal commotion. He joined Chicahua in bringing down the sails.

Soon the *Orion* lay placidly at anchor, her sails furled.

"We will wait for morning," said the captain. "The mists should burn off by then."

Doc was sniffing the air carefully.

"What do you smell, Mister Savage?"

"I do not quite know."

"Sea Dyaks?"

Doc shook his head slowly. "If they are here, I do not detect them amid the overpowering odors coming from land."

Something cut in front of the irregular knob in the shape of a skull. Something sharp-winged and bat-like. There was the suggestion of a whipping devil's tail. It made a fleeting pass, vanished from view.

Spying this, Chicahua muttered, *"Camazotz."*

Although they kept their eyes sharp, the winged thing did not return.

THEY waited for the dawn. It came soon enough. The mist began burning off.

When the outlines of the island became clear, they could discern its approximate shape. It was a great jungled plateau, the high point feathered with palm crowns.

Before the steep main portion, jutted a long finger of land. The sere countenance of Death's Peak brooded over this finger like the face of judgment.

Between the highland part and the peninsula stood a tall barrier that had not been visible by night.

"A wall," breathed Doc. "Of incredible size."

There was no gainsaying it. A great structure had been erected the entire breadth of the peninsula's inner neck, covered with decorative carvings that could not be made out clearly. It stretched from one side of the island to the other. In the center was a double gate and running atop the entire length a walkway of some type. In the center of which, directly over the gate, a great brass gong reflected the rising sun.

Captain Savage unlocked his spyglass and trained it upon the structure. He appraised this with the practiced eye of a civil engineer.

"No native islanders built that," he decided after a careful study. "Have a look for yourself."

Doc accepted the glass and used it. He studied the workmanship of the wall, with an eye for age as well as construction.

"Over forty feet high," he pronounced. "Perhaps two thousand feet across."

"How old would you judge it to be, Mister Savage?"

"Ancient. But kept up to this very day. There are no signs of neglect or decay."

Savage Senior nodded. "I would tend to concur. We have passed through uncharted waters to an utterly unknown location."

Doc surrendered the spyglass. "This place bears investigation, I agree. Do you think grandfather could be marooned here?"

But Captain Savage failed to reply. He had the spyglass up again and was seeking some other sign.

"Raise anchor," he said at last. "We will circumnavigate this place."

Chicahua, apparently understanding simple nautical commands couched in English, went forward and worked the pump brake of the Armstrong mechanism that hauled up the anchor chain in stages. It came rattling up the hawsehole.

Once it was on deck, Doc got the anchor squared away. He did this bare-handed, a remarkable feat that caused Chicahua's eyes to widen.

All sails were raised and the *Orion* began its slow circumnavigation of the incredible island. They chose not to engage the auxiliary engine for fear of attracting unwanted attention from the isle's unknown inhabitants—if any. This called for deft sailing, but the greater risks called for such a precaution.

Captain Savage continued raking the shoreline with his ever-present spyglass. Beyond the jutting lowland digit, the bulk of the island reared high, its sides tall and scored, rather like the White Cliffs of Dover, but darker and more rugged and difficult to scale.

"Plutonic rock, I should say," he appraised.

"If so," returned Doc, "that would mean this island may be the tip of a larger land mass now swallowed by oceanic waters."

"Stranger things are possible," admitted the captain.

They could see that the great wall bisected the entire island on its easternmost edge, not counting the low-lying peninsula. It ran right to the sheer edge, which afforded no opportunity for access by sea.

Captain Savage mused, "This is a formidable feat of engineering, as great as the Great Wall of China. Greater! For that barrier was made of stone, which resists the elements. This wall is faced with what appears to be mortar, which must be continually maintained against the ravages of time and kept up where necessary."

"There are no records of any people capable of such work in this part of the world," agreed Doc.

Here and there, amid the wilderness of fanged reefs surrounding the island, could be discerned places where the ground sloped down to the sea. But they were rare, and invariably too treacherous to permit a sailing vessel the size of the *Orion* to put in safely.

They moved all the way around the bleak shoreline, at times steering around stony pinnacles resembling dark stalagmites jutting up from the lapping water, finally coming back to the approximate spot where they had first spied the skull-faced mountaintop. It took most of the day to do so. The island was that large.

They realized that the great peak was further inland than it had first seemed. Its brooding mass dominated the plateau on which it stood.

There, the fires still burned. Someone was feeding the flames.

"Inhabited for certain, Mister Savage."

"But no sign of Dyaks, at least," returned Doc.

Captain Savage's voice became stern. "Do not jump to unsupportable conclusions, First Mate," he warned. "The *bangkongs* of the Sea Dyak are constructed so that they can be taken apart and carried overland. The *balla* was headed in this direction, as I reckon. They might have beaten us here, and secured their canoes in the jungle, out of view."

Doc frowned. He was studying the great grim prominence that they were calling Skull Peak, now baking in the morning sun.

Captain Savage noticed this. "You have an observation to share, have you?"

"The size of that peak is impressive," Doc said slowly.

"I would class it with the Rock of Gibraltar. What of it?"

"The winged creature we all saw pass before it, by comparison, would have to possess a wingspan of fifty feet."

"Preposterous!"

"If a deep-sea octopus can reach the size of the one we encountered last night, I would respectfully suggest that, in this strange spot, very little can be so classified."

"Point taken, Mister Savage. But I will have to see your pterosaur with my own eyes to credit it."

AS the morning mist continued to burn off, birds began to rise off from the jungle.

At first, these feathered creatures appeared unremarkable, although they could not be identified at this distance. They climbed, swooped about, then returned to their perches, to all appearances acting like ordinary birds the world over.

Doc kept one golden eye on the plateau of the isle, expectantly.

He was rewarded when something as black as a bat lifted into view on spasmodic wings, climbed high, then settled into a soaring series of circles, gliding closer and closer to the open water.

"Sir, high to port."

Captain Savage almost dropped his spyglass when he spotted it. He trained the tube on the gliding black thing.

After he fixed it in his glass, and followed it for a time, he announced, "Mister Savage, it appears that I owe you an apology."

Doc had his binoculars up and studied it. His trilling came to life, low and amazed.

"Rhamphorhynchus," he said.

"I am familiar with the name," allowed the captain. "But I understood that they never reached a size any greater than a common crow."

"In Jurassic times, this was true—according to the fossil record," replied Doc.

"In that case, we have stumbled across an island that the Deity forgot."

As they watched, a second, then a third pterosaur lifted into the sky. All behaved much as albatrosses do, soaring and gliding, occasionally diving into the sea and bringing up a tuna or some other fish in their long, needlelike jaws. These they gobbled whole, fishy tails wriggling as they disappeared down the creatures' gullets.

After one had gorged its fill, it began circling aimlessly. Doc watched its bald black head, noting the tiny eyes, and thinking how much like a combination bat and buzzard the ugly thing was.

Craning its head around, a blood-red eye on one side of the creature's skull fell upon the white sails of the *Orion*. Abruptly, it convulsed its membranous wings and angled toward them, spiked tail snapping about.

"Coming this way!" Doc warned.

"Strike sails! Strike sails!" Captain Savage hollered.

They fell upon the lines. Canvas began rattling down on their hoops.

They got the mainsail down all right, but before they could go to work on the other sheets, a great shadow fell over the deck. A sharp hiss breathed down upon them.

Doc had his automatic out, cocked it, and began blazing away.

A smoking round went through one wing. But it was like poking a hole in a sail. There was no other result than the hole. Black wings gathering, it descended. Convulsing, its four claws gathered to clutch and snatch.

Doc shifted his aim. Squeezing the trigger, he broke one of the bony spars that framed the translucent membrane of the right wing.

This brought results. Throwing back its head, the *Rhamphorhynchus* gave forth a piercing scream. Flapping its surviving wing wildly, it attempted to regain altitude. But it was too late for that.

The creature stumbled, collapsing on the forward deck. There it fluttered in distress, extended claws scratching the planking with desperate jerks.

Doc moved toward it, fascinated, his trilling mixing with the distressed sounds of the wounded monster.

Somehow, it scrambled painfully to its feet and stood there, head switching this way and that, resentful red eyes glaring at them, like a distorted stork.

From the helm, Captain Savage yelled, "What are you waiting for, Mister Savage? Dispatch that monster!"

Doc Savage hesitated. Here was a specimen of prehistoric life rarer than the rarest jewel. To destroy it went against his scientific training, against logic.

Wheeling, Captain Savage barked out words in the Mayan tongue.

Chicahua came striding up, a thin cane tube in one brown

fist. He inserted something long and thin into one end, applied that end to his lips and puffed out his wide cheeks.

A feathered dart blew out the other end and embedded itself into the creature's round black body. The thing jumped, began stamping about in circles, ruby-red eyes glaring furiously, and emitting weird gasping noises.

It did not take long for the poison to do its work.

The *Rhamphorhynchus* flapped madly, its head swayed and the ruby eyes began closing. Its mouth snapped open and closed, exposing crocodile teeth.

When it collapsed onto the deck, a glaze of death had already touched the closing orbs.

"Curare poison?" asked Doc.

"Mayans also have their blowguns," Captain Savage retorted stiffly. "And you are expected to snap to when ordered, Mister Savage."

Chapter XX

THEY USED BOATHOOKS to jockey the dead *Rhamphorhynchus* to the starboard rail and pitch it over the side. It made an ungainly pile going overboard. One wing—the broken one—caught on the brass railing, or rather its hook-like talon did. Doc unhooked it with his rigging knife.

The splash it made was sloppy, but the thing failed to sink. Crimson pooled in the water. The head floated the way a dead fish would, one eye staring sightlessly. Angular wing portions poked up from the brine, and the tracery of its wing veins showed as a grisly webwork.

Doc Savage watched it for a time, lost in thought. His golden eyes whirled with a busy briskness.

At length, Doc left the rail and faced his glowering captain.

"I will not reprimand you, Mister Savage," his father began. "I detected no cowardice in your demeanor. No doubt you regretted the dire necessity of the responsibility before you."

"Thank you, sir."

"But I will not brook a repetition of such hesitancy. We have a mission to accomplish. Is that perfectly understood?"

"I understand, Captain."

"Let us see to our shared duty, then."

"What are your orders?"

"We will reconnoiter the island posthaste. Sunset is not far off."

"I will make ready the dory."

Doc got the sturdy little boat squared away to go over the side.

When he was done, the bronze man addressed his father.

"A landing party of two persons would leave the *Orion* virtually undefended against attack, and the remaining crewman unable to sail off by himself."

"I know that!" snapped the elder Savage. "Your point, First Mate?"

"Allow me to go ashore alone."

Captain Savage gave that suggestion considerable thought. He seemed of two minds. Finally, he said, "I give you three hours. No more. If you do not return within that span of time, I will be forced to go after you, jeopardizing the ship."

"Thank you, sir. I will not need the dory."

"Carry on, then."

Doc Savage unbuckled his gun belt and stripped to his duck trousers. He donned a Bowie knife in its belt scabbard.

Throwing a line over the bow, the bronze giant began to climb over.

He was startled to see a trio of black tentacles reach up and pull down the dead *Rhamphorhynchus*. It went under with a great noisy gulp.

Doc decided to take the dory, after all. He retrieved his gun belt, donned it grimly.

He lowered the dory off the other side of the schooner, away from the disturbed water.

Taking the oars in hand, he pushed off and began rowing shoreward.

BEACHING the craft on a sandbar, Doc immediately smelled the smoke of a cooking fire. He upended the dory on the sand and began his reconnoiter.

Moving inland, he at first noticed that the lush foliage consisted of swaying palm trees of various varieties, and spidery ferns. Intermixed were leafy trees with great branches. This was no ordinary jungle. Some of the growth he could not easily classify.

The phenomenon of still standing on a pitching deck, a legacy of having been aboard ship for so many weeks, plagued him. The bronze giant put it out of his mind, and soon he failed to notice it. It was an example of the mind-over-matter mental discipline he had learned in the Orient, long ago.

There was a village. He gave it wide berth, found a coconut palm, and climbed it by the simple expedient of looping his belt around the glass-smooth bole and "walking" up the trunk by shifting the leather loop upward every few steps. It was a very efficient manner of ascent.

Reaching the thick crown, Doc grabbed a cluster of supporting fronds and peered downward.

A cluster of huts lay in the shadow of the great wall. The people who inhabited were ebony of skin, and went about in clothing not far removed from the primitive.

Studying them, the bronze man failed to categorize them. They were not Malays, nor Indians. Some of their barbaric dress suggested faraway Africa. Yet their faces and limbs displayed the scarring and tattooing that smacked of the Maori and other South Seas island people.

Several minutes of observation caused Doc to turn his attention to the fabulous wall of impressive construction. It was carved. The decorations did not register on his consciousness as anything he had ever seen or studied.

Doc decided to make for the wall.

Unfortunately, as he started down, the feathery palm fronds rustled. Or perhaps it was the wind. Either way, the sound attracted attention.

Doc squeezed the slick bole with his muscular thighs, arresting his descent. He hung exposed, one hand free, the other wrapped around the trunk.

More quickly than he could react, Doc was surrounded by

dark warriors bearing stout and very lethal spears. The points appeared to be chipped stone. Flint, perhaps.

A warrior attempted to hurl his projectile at Doc.

The bronze man set himself and one metallic hand snapped out, catching the spear by its hardwood shaft.

A rumble of surprise came from the assembled warriors below. Plainly, this display of physical prowess made a tremendous impression upon the warrior band.

Reversing it, Doc sent the spear back at its hurler. The point chucked the dirt precisely between two toes of his naked feet.

The warrior jumped backward, shocked at the speed with which his weapon came whistling back at him.

The other warriors were equally impressed. They hopped back, then began laughing uproariously.

Doc decided to join in their laughter. It did not have the friendly effect the bronze man had hoped for.

Another spearman drew back and let fly.

Doc ducked that one. The point struck the trunk in the spot where his head had a moment before been silhouetted. The stout shaft quivered strongly.

Doc extracted the spear, examined its tip. Flint.

This one Doc used to make a different point.

He sent it flying toward another palm trunk, transfixing it. This way it would not come back to harass him.

A third native gave it a shot. He set himself exactly in the style of an Olympic javelin hurler, then launched.

Doc caught that one easily and, reversing the weapon, sent it after the previous spear. It landed directly before the other.

More spears came hissing at the bronze man.

He caught them all, sent them flying in the direction of the other palm.

He missed only one. That spear—the one he had artfully placed between the toes of his first attacker—landed in a jungle pool, and sank from sight.

The warriors stood mute with empty hands. Their striated faces were unreadable. They might have been impressed, angry—or simply without emotion.

Satisfied that they were disarmed, Doc slid down the trunk.

The men of the village approached warily.

Doc ducked behind a monstrous tree of another type. It reminded him of a sprawling baobab tree, which were native to Africa.

When the warriors had mustered up sufficient courage to creep around the fat trunk in search of the bronze man of great prowess, he was no longer there.

In fact, Doc had climbed the far side of the tree, reached the topmost branches and by walking along them barefooted, reached an adjoining tree, silent and unseen as a slithering serpent.

From this, he leaped to another. Then another, feeling very much like the storybook character, Tarzan.

Finally landing in a bushy tree isolated from the others, Doc looked about for a way to the wall that would not put him at risk of ambush.

There was little danger of that, the natives having failed to figure out where the bronze giant had gotten to. But Doc had begun enjoying this method of traversing the thick forest.

Locating a strong vine, he cut it with his knife, until it was of a usable length. Fastening a loop, he employed it to lasso a high branch farther along, thus vindicating his summer spent on a Wyoming cow ranch when a mere stripling.

Snagging a bough, Doc launched himself into space.

He swung a fair distance, and cushioned his landing against the target tree with his great steel-thewed legs.

After that, he climbed the vine to the anchoring branch, where the bronze giant undid the lasso.

A few more maneuvers like that, and Doc Savage came within easy reach of the massive wall.

UP close, the structure was even more imposing than it had been, seen from afar. The wall was plain and pale, apparently faced with some form of mortar that withstood the ages. Simple railless staircases built into either side of the frame led up to the wide top of the structure.

The ponderous double doors were of wood, constructed from great vertical planks fitted together, and framed in iron. A colossal bar, also of hardwood, was fitted into huge decorative brackets, as if to bar the portal from something on the other side gaining entry.

Examining its details gave Doc Savage a disquieting sensation. It seemed impossible that human beings could have constructed such a Cyclopean arrangement.

Doc moved closer to better study the only decorative element, the ornate iron brackets. And as he absorbed the details, his trilling piped out briefly.

For the designs were uncannily similar to a pair of stylized dinosaur skulls! Triceratops, Doc decided from its huge horny brow projections.

From the other side, Doc heard disturbing sounds. Thrashings as of disturbed branches. Snapping noises. A roar. Other commotion. It was quite a contrast to the relative peace of the native village sitting on a long spit of jungle and tranquil beach.

Doc considered the twin staircases built into the face of the wall, on either side of the massive portal. They represented the handiest way up. Unfortunately, they were too exposed. To mount either one would risk disclosing his presence to the inhabitants of the village.

Gathering up his lariat, Doc moved further along until he reached an area so thick with trees, it concealed that stretch of wall. Giving the lasso a spin, he tossed it expertly, snaring a projectile on the wall itself. Swinging toward it was impractical, if not unnecessarily dangerous.

So Doc solved the problem by tying the loose end to the tree trunk. The vine was stout. Doc used it to go hand over hand, as a circus performer might. The expression on his features was untroubled by worry. He might have been unconcerned about the perilous fall to the jungle floor below, or he might have been enjoying himself immensely. It was impossible to tell.

Finally, Doc reached the wall at a point beneath the ornate ebony frame that upheld the great beaten-brass gong.

Climbing up to the top, he stood and looked over to the other side.

Death's Peak brooded over all. In its hollow eye-sockets, twin fires blazed and crackled. He could imagine their roar. Black smoke curled from some natural aperture, like a chimney, above the smooth dome.

Doc's trilling came, low and melodious. A kind of awe threaded it.

For the bronze man knew at a glance that this was no natural configuration. Human hands had shaped the rocky summit into the semblance of a human death's head, and had done so such a very long time ago that the ages had eroded and smoothed out its stark lines, giving it the appearance of a freak natural formation.

Sealing his lips, Doc suppressed his sound of surprise.

Something was shaking a cluster of palms due east of the peak—something moving through the jungle growth. Something large enough to cause towering trees to react to its passing!

Chapter XXI

IMMEDIATELY, DOC SAVAGE began wishing that he had brought along his Annihilator submachine gun. This intuition struck him even before he could obtain a glimpse of the thing moving through the jungle.

A blunt black head poked up, craned about. Its skull was a glossy black, and had the pebbled and plated look of snakeskin. The black hide was shot with short threads of orange, like that of a salamander. Beginning at the top of its forehead, a crest of irregular horns paraded down its spine.

On either side of the dark head, small green eyes peered about. They had the look of lizard orbs, slit-irised and cold as gems dug out of a cave. Surrounding these orbs was a pattern of smooth skin, forming an effect of interlocking curved blades alternating black, red and white. This pinwheel-like ornamentation had the hypnotic effect of drawing attention to the tiny staring eye, as well as magnifying it to terrifying proportions.

Doc Savage watched closely. He knew that no dinosaur hide had ever survived to be studied by modern scientists. So only theory existed. Most assumed that reptiles of this magnitude displayed brown, gray or green skins, as befitting their lowland environments.

But this monster was a smooth reptilian black. Its coloration was fabulous in its unusualness. So striking were the markings that it took the best part of a minute before Doc Savage realized he had no clear idea what he was looking at.

A few seconds more and there was no question about it.

Here was a creature that might have descended from a full-grown *Tyrannosaurus rex!* A monster out of primeval times. A thing that once ruled the Earth, but lived no longer. It seemed preposterous, utterly impossible.

Yet there it was. Stalking about on its massive hind legs, muscular forelegs grasping and releasing tree branches as it pushed aside those which impeded its progress.

Doc's trilling filtered out, held, and careened up and down the musical scale. It seemed a fitting sound for the occasion. It might have been the ululation of a prehistoric creature—whether bird, lizard or other—of this lost island. In civilization, Doc had come to feel self-conscious about it, and quickly throttled it. Here in the wilderness, the bronze man gave it free rein.

Finally, Doc allowed the sound to trail away, and he began thinking.

Whoever had built that formidable wall with its double doors had unquestionably done so to keep something terrible at bay. There was no doubt that the creature crashing through the close-packed trees was a likely candidate.

And if there was one loose, no doubt there were others. No dinosaur could survive into the Twentieth Century without having parents and forebears—if not siblings.

Doc considered his options. He reflected on his mission: To seek any sign of Stormalong Savage. It was by no means certain that Old Stormy had been shipwrecked on this spot. But Doc could not assume otherwise. Not if there was any chance that his grandfather still lived.

Doc decided to walk the length and breadth of the wall before executing his next move.

Farther along, to the south, he discovered a hut-like dwelling place built atop the broad runway. It was uninhabited, but clearly this was not normally the case. Remains of a meal lay about, along with other signs of recent habitation.

There were items of a sophistication that seemed unconnected to the simple villagers who were certainly now in search of him. One was a mirror. It might have been taken off any shipwreck or vessel that passed by. But it was the product of a manufacturer, not an artisan.

Doc left everything as he found it and continued his traverse of the imposing wall.

The promenade was scrupulously maintained, and showed signs of having been swept of wind-blown dirt and debris regularly. It appeared to function as a long watchtower, for the purpose of monitoring the jungled plateau beyond.

DISCOVERING nothing else of interest, Doc decided that there remained only the quest. To push on into the high plateau, or retreat to the *Orion* for further instructions or reinforcements.

It did not help his decision-making that one hour of the allotted three had already been exhausted. The sun was slowly setting.

The decision was taken out of his hands when a pair of enamel-red wings lifted off from somewhere in the misty distance below. Doc recognized that a pterosaur was on the hunt.

After swinging about aimlessly, it began beating toward the wall. As it neared, Doc could see its eyes resolving. Their color was a chilly bone-white.

Watching it, Doc sensed that those glittering orbs were focusing on him. Flashing to reach shelter, the bronze giant got behind the great brass gong.

Running may have been a tactical mistake, for the metallic blur of his sprint attracted the searching thing's attention. It arrowed in, showing itself to be covered in a kind of feathery down that brought to mind a cardinal on the wing.

Doc hunkered down as the thing fluttered and flapped about the gleaming disk, perhaps seeking its last meal of the day before returning to its rookery.

The creature was stubborn, if not persistent. Whenever Doc

switched sides to thwart it, the thing moved around to the other side. It made no outcry. Only the muscular creaking of its wing ligatures sounded, reminding Doc of squeaking bats on the wing.

Doc yanked his Colt from its worn holster and decided to risk a shot. Risky, because he did not want to attract any further human attention.

Before he could line up on the flapping harridan, it faltered in its flight, one claw-tipped wing inadvertently striking the brass gong.

The metal resounded, brought forth an answering roar somewhere in the jungle.

It also sent the scarlet pterosaur screaming into the sky, frightened by the unexpected noise.

Doc had conserved a bullet—but at what price?

The answer was soon in coming.

The echoing reverberation had naturally carried to the lumbering Tyrannosaurian carnivore. Its horned black head turned, and one mesmerizing eye fell upon Doc Savage retreating from the noisy gong. Dying sunlight glinting off wobbling brass also drew its attention.

The dinosaur started in the direction of the commotion.

The noise of its approach—a wild snapping of broken branches and trampled bushes—alerted Doc. The bronze man saw what was coming.

Retreating down the inner side of the wall made the most sense. There were handholds and purchases that allowed this. But just as Doc started down, a wild roar caused him to freeze in mid-action.

Jumping to the runway promenade, Doc took in a sight often depicted in the paintings of naturalists and others. It was a primitive struggle out of the dawn of time.

In its rapid progress—the speed of the thing was startling—the meat-eater stumbled across another monster of his original era.

It was a long-necked sauropod with a tail twice as thick and elongated as its other end, resembling a Brontosaur! It had not caught Doc's eye because it was a dull brown in hue, dappled and mottled by patches of variegated green.

They were vegetarians, Doc knew. In fact, the head of the sauropod was inserted into the crown of a deciduous tree that resembled a magnolia. It had been munching on some tasty bulbs. Now it peered about with semi-sleepy orbs the color of walnuts.

As it happened, the mud-hued plant-eater was dining placidly in the path of the lunging Tyrannosaur. Now it swung its sleepy-eyed head in the direction of the approaching commotion, revealing a startling thing.

The sauropod possessed a long prehensile trunk, resembling that of a Mastodon, with which it had been feeding!

From his high vantage point, Doc Savage could see that a collision was inevitable.

Given that the black-and-orange Tyrannosaur—or whatever it really was—was a predator of unsurpassed power, Doc knew what was coming next.

In that, he was in for a surprise.

The upright dinosaur gave a roar that exposed yellowed teeth like gleaming stalactites in its cavernous mouth. The inner mouth was a pale pink, mottled with gray.

The piebald sauropod veered its small head on its long muddy neck, seeming slow to react. Its doom appeared almost upon it.

With a casual grace, the big brown brute swept its slab of a tail about, first in one direction, then in the reverse. The whip-like tip of its tail snaked upward. Like a cow flicking at a pesky fly, it laid it against the side of the meat-eater's head. The sound of this impact carried as if a locomotive had landed atop an elephant.

There came an audible crack. The black Tyrannosaur gave a sideways lurch, vented a queer grunt that possessed no menace, then took two halting steps, after which it keeled over on one

side and began beating its long spiked-ridged tail in its death
throes.

The sauropod went back to its meal. The other did not rise
again. Its skull had been caved in.

The most ferocious of dinosaurs, a relative of the fabled tyrant
lizard—felled by a casual swipe of a sleepy saurian!

THAT decided Doc. He was going to investigate this lost land.
He started climbing downward, this time on the inner side of
the incredible wall. There was a portion veined with tough, thick
creepers, and these tendrils were as handy as a ship's ratlines
for climbing purposes.

What Doc discovered moving downward caused him to fight
the urgent impulse to trill in utter disbelief. He stifled the sound
after the merest warble of melody.

The wall on this side was much more impressive. The other
side of the portal was framed in great stone blocks, improved
by durable mortar. On this side, Doc discovered as he scrambled
down to the ground, stood pillar-like pediments, at the top of
which crouched two matching statues, carved to resemble great,
crouching gorillas.

Below, decorative bas-reliefs depicted another pair of dinosaur skulls, and what appeared to be a pair of cuttlefish, or
perhaps they were nautiluses.

Most amazing of all, when the bronze giant reached the
ground, he found himself standing in the shadow of a life-sized
carving of a species of horned Tyrannosaur—an artistic ac-
complishment that staggered the imagination. It was similar
to the one Doc had observed, but had other attributes that
suggested an evolutionary offshoot of *Tyrannosaurus rex*.

Looking up, Doc saw a parade of unusual dinosaur skulls
spaced at intervals along the top of the wall itself. He could not
immediately place them.

Had this wall been built so long ago that men possessed the
knowledge of prehistoric creatures? Man and dinosaur were

supposed to have lived in different eras.

Yet here stood concrete proof this had not been the case on this remote island for centuries up to this very day.

Fascinated, Doc tore his attention away from the seemingly-impossible structure, and studied the land it faced. He saw a mountainous primordial wilderness, thick with gnarled trees that seemed out of place in this weird island in the Indian Ocean, and slashed by ravines and broken upheavals of land.

Nearby, a short distance and in line from the imposing portal, stood a man-made platform which aroused alarm. It was surmounted by twin stone pillars, intricately carved, with an iron ring set in either one.

Death's Peak brooded over it all like a curse, or a symbolic warning made concrete by an awesome hand. Low on its east-facing flank, from the jagged mouth, poured out a cascade of tumbling water. Here and there, visible through the undulations of the varied terrain, shimmered a winding river. Doc wondered if its source might not be the mountain that wore the fixed face of Death.

But the most unnerving element of the evil-looking formation was the twin fires blazing in its eye cavities. They imbued the stony countenance with a malignant vitality, suggestive of an ancient intelligence glaring at him in warning.

Do Not Approach Me, those hellish orbs seemed to say....

Chapter XXII

DOC SAVAGE REALIZED that his best course of action would be to climb to the top of Death's Peak and investigate the fires burning there. They could only mean a camp, possibly a habitation for a cave-dwelling group of people.

But to reach the strange landmark, he would have to cross over many miles of primeval wilderness. An impossibility to do before darkness came. Not to mention the perils of traversing a seemingly prehistoric terrain.

Again, Doc Savage took to the trees. High in one, he located a vine which would serve as a makeshift lariat. With his Bowie blade, he cut this to a working length and began his journey from treetop to treetop.

Sometimes, he swung. Other times, Doc leaped from branch to branch where they interlaced. The growth was so thick that he could almost walk part of the way through the jungle lanes, so green they dazzled the eyes with their varied hues of emerald, jade and chlorophyll.

This brought the bronze man over ravines and rifts in the rugged plateau.

The trees were not empty of inhabitants. There were dragonflies whose wingspans rivaled the seagull. Undulating millipedes that looked unnatural flowed around trees, seeking the latter for food.

Once, Doc passed over a deep and jagged cleft in the riven rock. Dark things seemed to be scuttling down in its depths.

He paused to scrutinize it from on high, found he could only discern furtive movements, decided further examination could wait, and passed on to the next arboreal perch. His skin crawled until he put it behind him.

This took him to within easy reach of a lesser summit. If he could reach the top, that vantage point should give him a better view of Death's Peak.

The sides were sheer, but scalable. Dropping out of one tree, he landed on a rocky cliff. From this spot, he began to climb, using hands and feet. The going got rougher.

Doc slipped off his shoes and left them on a convenient crevice. This allowed him to use his amazing prehensile toes for leverage.

There was an odor clinging to the eminence. It seemed half familiar but Doc could not immediately place it. The island air was choked with competing scents.

Higher and higher, he climbed, pausing only to make certain that no predators were about.

A slithering nearby told of a serpent gliding through dirt and rocks. But Doc avoided it by moving around the mountain, finding a different way up. This proved a tougher climb, but he was equal to it.

Once, he hit an outthrust ledge that looked unassailable.

Taking a resting position, Doc used his vine lasso and cast it blindly upward. Three tries and the vine flopped back, discouragingly. Doc hauled it back, organized for another attempt.

On the fourth try, he snagged something. Pulling the lasso tight on its slip knot, Doc resumed his careful climb.

He reached the lip of the rocky ledge, and lifted his head carefully over it, to see what might lurk there.

THE vine had caught a treelet whose roots were dug into the stony façade, clinging to a precarious existence. It appeared solidly anchored, so there was no danger of it ripping free under his weight.

A movement came. Doc's eyes flicked in that direction.

A figure crouched on the flat escarpment. Dressed in skins that might have been peeled off the belly of a dinosaur, hair white as milkweed, a woman regarded him with dark eyes much brighter than the surrounding skin of her face.

An old woman, Doc saw. She possessed a seamed face that suggested incalculable age. A human turtle's visage. The eyes sharpened and she gave vent to a venomous hiss.

At a momentary loss for words, Doc raised a quelling hand.

"Friend! Savvy?" he asked.

"You speak English?" she croaked.

"Yes!"

"You are called Savvy. Is that your name?"

"Savage," said Doc, bewildered in spite of himself.

The old woman crept toward him, turtle head canting curiously. Gnarled fingers rose, making arcane gestures.

"You have the eyes, I see."

"I do not understand."

"You have the golden eyes of the—"

Suddenly, she turned, rushed to one end of the ledge—the southerly one.

Doc Savage took that opportunity to clamber up onto the ledge. He observed the crone in studied silence.

The old woman was listening to a crashing of brush.

"What is that noise?" asked Doc.

Her hissing admonishment made Doc think of a feral cat.

Something was moving through the underbrush, something whose progress could be traced by the quaking and twitching of brush below.

Doc attempted to peer through the thicket. There were thorny bushes he could see. Whatever moved through those was either well protected by hides—or armored like a dinosaur.

After a time, the thing moved out of sight and hearing.

"What was it?" asked Doc quietly.

"Slasher. Perhaps a deathrunner."

"What are they?"

"Creatures of death. Horrible things. Smart as men. Smarter than some men."

"How do you come to speak English?" asked Doc.

The old woman turned to face him. She looked him up and down and then up again.

"You have the eyes of a kong. Strong. Fearless."

"Kong?"

"Do you not know of Kong?"

"No," admitted Doc.

"Pah!" spat the crone.

Doc paged through his memory. *Kong*, he recalled, was Cantonese, or perhaps Mandarin. It meant "fear" or "dread." But they were a long way from China. A very long way. The word probably did not mean the same thing here.

Doc asked, "What is your name, old woman?"

"My name, you would not be able to pronounce without long practice. But you may call me Penjaga, which in the Malay tongue means Keeper. I am the storehouse of the stories of my people, what you would call a wise woman. Now, why have you come to Skull Mountain Island?"

"Is that what this place is called?" countered Doc.

"In English, yes. In Malay, it is *Tengkorak Gunung Pulau*. In other languages, the words sound different, but mean the same thing."

"Who taught you English?" demanded Doc.

"Pirates. Long ago. Few come to Skull Island. Fewer leave alive. Why do you come here, Gold Eyes?"

"I seek a man also named Savage."

Penjaga squinted. "Your father?"

"No. Grandfather."

The old woman scrutinized his strong, bronzed features.

"You are young, I see. But not so young that you could not

raise a beard. Why no beard?"

"Men of my generation do not grow them. They are out of fashion."

"You do not look very much like him," she decided.

"Who? Kong?"

"No, not Kong," Penjaga said impatiently.

"What are you doing on this ledge?"

"I am watching for the hunters of heads," replied the crone.

"Dyaks?" asked Doc.

"I do not know what they are called. But many landed two suns ago. They prowl and creep through the jungle, seeking heads."

"I will not let them harm you, Keeper," said Doc reassuringly.

The old woman expectorated upon the ledge.

"Pah! I do not fear them. It is not my head they seek. It is Kong's."

"Who is Kong?"

The old woman did not reply. She fell to studying his youthful face once more.

"No, you do not look like him at all," she clucked.

Growing impatient, Doc said, "I wish you would answer my questions."

"I must be certain of you. Yes, you have the eyes. Kong has them. So does Old Stormy, curse his crabby old bones."

"You know of Stormalong Savage?" Doc said, excitement grading his mellow voice.

"Did I not speak his name?"

"Is he—dead?" asked Doc.

"How would I know? I have not laid eyes upon him since the headhunters arrived. He is probably out chasing them, the long-legged fool. One man against many. They spit death from their mouth staffs. Perhaps by now they have brought him low."

Doc Savage had been so stunned he had not uttered his

trilling. It came now, rising in cadence, ventriloquial in its effect. It caused the old woman to duck and jerk around, as if fearing some unfamiliar avian attacker.

It took her nearly a minute before she realized that the bronze giant was making that sound.

When the truth dawned on her, she straightened and began getting her barbaric finery together.

"You are very short."

Taken aback, Doc blurted, "Short? I stand considerably over six feet tall."

"Short for a Savage," snapped Penjaga the Keeper.

Doc said nothing. He wondered how she had meant the word. Did she consider white men to be barbarians?

A shadow fell over them. There was a rattle overhead and pebbles began drooling down, bouncing away noisily.

Doc Savage looked up sharply.

A NARROW face unlike anything he had ever imagined stared down at him. Dragon-like, yet also bird-like, it was riotously feathered in hues of emerald and silver. Its bare midriff and bony arms were covered in gray-green scales rather than plumage, ending in fierce raptor-like talons that clutched spasmodically.

"Slasher!" hissed Penjaga, ducking for the shelter of the straggling rock-rooted tree.

The eyes of the thing shone with a piercing lizard-orange gleam, but a spark of something more glittered deep within. Its mouth opened, disclosing thin blade-like teeth, and suddenly Doc understood why the old woman called the thing a slasher.

Moving like lightning, Doc whipped for the tree and got his lariat loose. Why he did so when he had a pistol at his side, he did not know.

In his youth, he had learned many cowboy rope tricks. One was the Houlihan, a cast that was designed to snare unwary horses or calves.

With only the briefest of backthrows, Doc let fly.

The avian thing was scrambling downward, jaws agape, displaying vicious triangular teeth.

The loop dropped over the narrow tufted head, and snared the thick-plumed neck beneath. Hissing, the thing gathered itself for a leap.

Holding the other end, Doc raced to the opposite end of the ledge, away from the crouching old woman, and leaped off the edge into dizzy space.

Chapter XXIII

THE LEAP INTO space was no maneuver borne of panic. The bronze man had calculated the situation and knew exactly what he was doing.

Vine clutched in both hands, Doc dropped down to land on a rocky tumble of stone he knew to lie below. He had memorized such landmarks on the way up.

The vine stretched, went tight, and with a snapping sound, yanked the ungainly slasher from its crouching perch.

Emitting a wild scream, it came careening down, a flailing bundle of shimmering plumage and scales. Raptor claws splaying wildly, it slashed and ripped at empty air.

One foot-talon swiped in Doc's direction, but the space was too great for contact.

Doc caught a glimpse of a sickle-like central claw vicious enough to rip a man open.

Landing on the rocks, Doc watched the powerful creature go tumbling past.

He released the vine.

Scrambling for purchase that did not exist in empty air, the avian monstrosity finally crashed into the stony base of the mountain. It made an ugly sound as it dashed its life out against the obdurate masses.

There followed a distinct crack that Doc knew was its neck bones snapping, or possibly a shattered section of spine.

Doc watched to be certain of its death.

The body jittered, spike-feathered tail twisting and whipping in its death throes. The lean head flopped and lay still, hot orange eyes staring sightlessly.

Only then did the bronze man get a clear look at it.

It was small for a dinosaur, and feathered like some fantastic chicken, except where it showed plates resembling the armored underside of a crocodile. The body was supported by plumed legs ending in two-toed bird claws. Despite its abundance of feathers, the ostrich-like thing possessed no wings, as such. It was nothing like any creature the bronze man had ever seen, or discovered in the paleontological books. Like many young boys, dinosaurs had fascinated him. Doc had spent hours in New York's American Museum of Natural History studying its murals and fossil display.

This was no known dinosaur. It might have been related to some now-extinct prehistoric bird, such as the wingless moa. Some of those creatures were so large and powerful, they could kill a man with a single kick of their clawed feet.

A bizarre Latin construction suddenly popped into Doc's mind: Dinoavisaur—terrible bird-lizard!

CLIMBING back to the ledge, Doc rejoined the old woman, Penjaga the Keeper.

She was reluctant to come out from the spindly shelter of the tree, but finally did agree to do so.

"Tell me of Stormalong," requested Doc.

Instead, she pulled at him, saying, "We must go. Where there is one slasher, there are many slashers. And a scarlet-streaked deathrunner to lead them."

"I do not understand."

"Do you understand sudden death? Come!"

She picked up a gnarled length of hardwood, which she used for a walking stick, but which Doc suspected was really for self-defense.

The woman led Doc up, across the face of the mountain and

to the summit, where they stood facing westward. There, Doc looked in the direction of Skull Mountain—its true name, he now knew. The empty eye sockets boiled with grayish-black smoke, as if the rock formation was some bizarre type of volcano. Through the wormy columns, fitful fires blazed.

"Whose camp fires?"

"Not camps. The headhunters have profaned the lair of Kong. They hope to deny him his rightful refuge, the better to set their snare."

"Why?" asked Doc, putting aside for the moment the identity of Kong.

"They seek in their foolishness what they believe to be a great treasure."

"Which is?"

"The head of the last kong."

Doc nodded. "Kong is a man, then?"

"Do you know nothing?" Penjaga flared.

Doc flinched. "I have just arrived on Skull Mountain Island. I know nothing of Kong."

"The headhunters know of him. They have been here before. Long ago. They took the head of a young kong."

Suddenly, Doc thought he understood.

"Kong is an ape?"

Penjaga shook her white head impatiently. "Kong is the god of Skull Mountain Island."

"I do not understand," said Doc, showing more patience than he felt.

"You keep saying that! Did you never hear of the legends?"

Penjaga was guiding him down the face of the mountain. Rough steps were cut into it. From a distance, they would not be discernible. But here, one could pick the way down if one were careful. Penjaga was exceedingly careful.

They reached the base of the mountain and she led him back in the direction of the great wall of Skull Mountain Island.

On the way, they came to the flat plain where the elevated altar was erected. Two stone pillars stood upon it with their iron rings, which made the bronze man think of the days when slaves were shackled.

"What is the purpose of that?" asked Doc.

"The Atu chain their maidens there. They sacrifice them to Kong."

"You mean the people who dwell on the other side of the wall?"

"Who else could I mean?" Penjaga retorted.

Passing the grim relic, they came to the towering wall. The light was dwindling.

"Where do I need to go to find Stormalong Savage?"

"Who can say? Not even Kong. Never mind that old fool. We must get to safety. It is more dangerous after moonset."

She led Doc to the base of the massive carven wall, halted in its shadow.

"The gate cannot be opened from this side," Doc pointed out. "The bar is on the other side."

Penjaga glared at him. "I do not live on the other side of the wall, short Savage."

Doc looked his question.

She raised her gnarled walking stick. "I live atop the wall."

"There are no stairs on this side," Doc pointed out.

"I can climb the vines," Penjaga said, turning and taking fistfuls of creepers into her strong, claw-like hands.

And she did. Like a spider monkey up the gnarled creepers. Doc was astounded, although it did not register on his metallic face.

Following, Doc soon overhauled her and paced his climb so he could catch her if she faltered. There was no danger of that. Penjaga had the agility of a girl many years younger.

Reaching the top of the wall, Doc Savage stood up and said, "How old are you, Penjaga?"

"By your reckoning, more than one hundred years."

Doc smiled politely at the obvious exaggeration. That was improbable, of course.

Still, the old woman sounded serious.

Doc looked the old crone over in the dying light of day.

She appeared to be of a higher type than the jungle natives who lived below the wall on their isolated spit of jungle. It was very puzzling.

"Where are your people, Keeper?"

"Gone. All dead. You ask too many questions that are not of your business."

"My apologies," Doc said politely. "I have only come to this island because my grandfather's ship is thought to have been shipwrecked here."

"Yes, yes. Moons and moons and moons ago. It is gone now. Swept out to sea, never to be seen again. It is gone."

"I must find Stormalong Savage," said Doc earnestly.

"Then you must wait for sunrise, Gold Eyes. There is no point in throwing your young life away in the night seeking one who may already be dead."

"You suggested that my grandfather was searching for the headhunters. Why?"

"He knows that they seek the head of Kong. He may think he can save Kong from the headhunters. He is a fool. The headhunters will need saving from Kong."

"Describe this Kong for me, please," requested Doc.

"Ferocious as the most fearsome lizard. Terrible in his wrath. Thunder and lightning are themselves afraid of him. That is Kong."

"And you say he lives on Skull Mountain?"

"Yes. They have torched his lair now. But Kong will punish them."

Suddenly, Doc recalled the statues that resembled gorillas carved into the fabulous wall of antiquity.

"Do you know what a gorilla is?" he asked.

"No."

"But you know the word ape?"

"Yes."

"Is Kong an ape?"

"No. Kong is mightier than any ape. Mightier than any mountain. He is the ape that walks like a mountain."

Doc Savage could see that he was getting nowhere with the old woman.

At length, he said, "I must return to my ship."

"Am I stopping you from doing so?" she flung back.

"No, of course not. I only—Would you like to come with me? You might be safer there."

"I have lived here for many, many moons, growing wiser every passing year. I am safer here than you are on your ship, Gold Eyes. Especially once Kong learns of you. Kong does not like ships, or the men they bring to his domain."

"I see."

"Kong was the one who broke the ship of Stormalong Savage and pushed it out to sea so that it could bring no more outlander men to Skull Mountain Island."

Doc considered the querulous crone's words. His thoughts flashed back to the mirror message written in soap back on the *Courser*. Not King—*Kong!* Evidently, it had been a warning.

"You saw this happen?" asked Doc.

The old woman shook her white head slowly. "No, I heard it happen. I know the sound of Kong when he snaps great trees in his hairy hands. This was the same sound. Thunder is no louder. *Less!*"

"Tell me more," invited Doc.

"When I looked out over the lagoon, the masts and sails of the ship were floating in the water and Kong was pushing it out to sea," Penjaga said firmly.

Doc studied the old woman for signs of mental instability.

"It would take a creature taller than four men to accomplish that feat of strength," he pointed out. "Perhaps taller than five men."

"Kong," the old woman said seriously, "is taller than *ten* men!"

That, of course, was ridiculous. Kong would have to stand fifty feet high.

Night was falling now. "I must be going," Doc Savage said at last.

"Take the staircase," said the old woman. "You will not be seen from the village."

"Thank you," said Doc, who moved in the direction of the stairs.

The old woman blinked. She had attempted to follow the big bronze man with her sharp yet wise turtle eyes, but long before the metallic giant should have melted into the gloom of night, his path could not be traced.

Shaking her head slowly, Penjaga retreated to her wall-top hut.

Chapter XXIV

DOC SAVAGE FILTERED through the jungle until he reached the shoreline. This he traced down to the spot where he had beached his dory.

It was still there. He uncovered it and placed it in the surf, gave it a running shove and, holding onto the stern, levered himself into the cockpit.

Doc let momentum carry him out into the still lagoon before unshipping the oars and sculling around the fanged rocks.

In his heart was a high strangeness. Stormalong was alive! At least, he had been not very many days before. But the Dyaks were also at large. That complicated matters.

Doc glanced back at the spit of jungled land that lay in the shadow of the massive gated wall. The light of campfires could be discerned through the dark clumps of foliage and towering palms. The natives obviously preferred to remain in the relative safety of their huts after nightfall.

And above it all, thrown into smoldering shadow by the sun setting behind it, stared Skull Mountain, its countenance as dark and menacing as the gorilla skull discovered on the *Courser*. Leaping fires deep in the hollows of its empty eyes made the featureless face appear demonic.

Doc turned his back on it and concentrated on working through the breakers.

Clark Savage, Senior, was pacing the deck of the *Orion* when Doc spotted him. He made no sound to draw his attention.

But soon, the captain noticed him coming in the deepening twilight.

A line was dropped into the dory cockpit, and then another. Doc made them fast and climbed up the pilot ladder that hung over the port rail and lay against the hull planking. Doc climbed this rapidly.

Once on deck, Captain Savage barked, "You are past due, Mister Savage."

Doc got straight to the point. "Stormalong is on this island. Alive, as of two days ago."

Captain Savage stood as a man thunderstruck. His snapping eyes began to moisten. He checked them, stifled all outer emotion.

Squaring his shoulders, he said in a low, thick voice, "Let us hoist the dory, and then we will talk."

This was done.

BELOW deck, they ate a cold meal. Cooking was too risky. Food smells would carry inland if the wind blew that way.

Doc told the story of his adventure, leaving out only superfluous details.

"I do not believe the account of this fifty-foot Kong," snapped Savage Senior when Doc was finished.

"Nor do I," said Doc. "Yet the story the old woman related to me explains the condition of the *Courser* as we discovered her. And that was the name scrawled in soap on Old Stormy's mirror."

"I rule nothing out."

"Nor will I," concurred Doc.

"The immediate problem before us is this: Dare we await the dawn to embark upon a rescue?"

"The dangers of the island are great by day, much greater by night," countered Doc. "And if the Dyaks are here—and I do not doubt that part of the story—we are taking a terrible risk leaving the ship undermanned."

Savage Senior flared, "I know that!"

"I am prepared to go back," asserted Doc. "Now. To conduct a search."

Captain Savage leapt out of his chair. He began pacing, his face twisting, weathered seams coming and going.

"Hang it all, man! We are undermanned. Outnumbered! By the stars, the Dyaks have more boats than we do. We could be surrounded by their *balla*, and what then?"

Doc counseled, "The situation may appear hopeless. But it is not."

Captain Savage eyed him coolly. "Have you a strategy in mind, Mister Savage?"

"I have my Annihilator submachine gun. With it, I would rule the jungle even by night."

"Have you unlimited ammunition?" Savage flung back. "Have you the ability to carry it all through miles of trackless jungle?"

Doc admitted that he did not—on either count.

"Then your plan would work only if all other factors fell in your favor. Would you chance that they would? Would you risk your life on such a reckless gamble?"

"I am not afraid of that island, or what dwells upon it," Doc said firmly. It was not bravado. Ordinary fear had been schooled out of the bronze giant. The war had not changed that part of him—only tempered it in the fires of experience.

"We have no choice but to await the coming of dawn," said Captain Savage finally. "No choice under the North Star…"

Doc nodded. "I will not disagree with you, then."

"I want to find Old Stormy as much as you. More so, sir! But we must apply common sense to the situation, not youthful impetuosity. Courage is a strong motivator, but we must win out in the end. We cannot have any Savages perish in this foreboding spot. So many of our forebears have died in the far corners of the Earth that our numbers have dwindled to a select few."

Doc reflected that, out of the relatives of whom he was aware, he knew only of his father's brother, Alex Savage, whom he had never met. There were no other known blood relatives.

"I see the wisdom of your thinking," said Doc quietly.

"Oil your machine gun. We will have need of it. Now leave me and let me think. Thank you, sir!"

Doc Savage took his departure.

Everything in him ached to leap into the water to return to Skull Mountain Island. But he wouldn't disobey his captain, or his father.

In his cabin, Doc began breaking down the submachine gun, readying it for the coming battle.

After he was done, he reached down under his bunk and extracted the dried ape head from his sea bag, and fell to studying it anew.

There was no question that it was a juvenile specimen. Age was impossible to judge, except approximately.

Full grown and whole, it might stand nearly fifteen feet tall. That struck Doc as preposterous, even with the evidence sitting on his bunk, even after witnessing a prehistoric sauropod topple a rampaging Tyrannosaur with one mighty sweep of its tail....

THEY slept most of the night. It was not easy. But the gentle waves of the lagoon lulled them to sleep. So they slumbered, with Chicahua standing silent watch on deck. He stood like a statue carved out of mahogany in the stern, which faced the island.

Obsidian eyes conned the surroundings.

There was a moon, a waxing quarter moon that was often covered by racing cloud scud. The ocean winds were brisk. The *Orion* heeled and rocked pleasantly. They had muffled the ship's bell, lest it ring disconsolately with the stronger breezes. The sails had been struck, of course. Otherwise they would have drawn curious natives from their village to investigate. It was assumed that the villagers had canoes, but none had ventured out into the lagoon since their arrival.

Chicahua was thinking of his brother, missing him deeply, when the first *bangkongs* came ghosting around the headland. They approached silently, propelled by oarsmen skilled in the art of stealth. The moon was behind a cloudbank resembling a rag thrown athwart the stars, so they arrived cloaked by darkness.

The hunched rowers made good progress. When moonlight returned, they dipped their oars in a smooth breaking action, and the ships—there were only three of them—came to a slow, definite halt. The warriors ducked under the thatched awning of their split-bamboo deckhouse, feathered headdresses quivering as if in anticipation.

For a time, they were indistinguishable from the breakers that studded the dark lagoon.

Ten minutes passed. Twenty. Then the moon was consumed by another racing cloudbank. With an eerie silence, the Dyaks began sculling toward the anchored schooner.

They were like ghosts crewing ferries over the River Styx. Approaching the *Orion*, a Dyak positioned in the bow stood up and balanced a long spear atop one bare shoulder. He let fly.

The projectile shot true, plunking into the water on the windward side of the vessel.

Hearing it, Chicahua rushed to the rail, peered into the darkling waters.

He saw nothing. The night was too dark, the surrounding waters were more easily heard than perceived.

And while the Mayan was studying the impenetrable darkness, the three noiseless *bangkongs* separated and began to silently surround the helpless schooner.

Chicahua finally gave up on determining the cause of the strange sound in the water. It might have been a fish leaping upward for a tasty minnow. Turning, he cast his dark gaze over the surrounding lagoon.

As it happened, a shaft of lunar light shot down from a rift in the moon-smothering cloud, disclosing one boat laying not twenty yards from the lee side of the *Orion.*

Before the Mayan could react, a second spear shot through the night.

It landed beside him, *thunking* into the deck planking with deadly intent.

From every Dyak throat, wild yells of challenge issued. War cries!

Chapter XXV

CHICAHUA FACED TWO necessities.

The first was to preserve his life against imminent peril. The second was to ring the ship's bell and thereby alert his captain.

Dropping to the deck, the Mayan found the shelter of the gunwale. He began crawling along the polished pine deck, on his belly like an anaconda. He uprooted the still-quivering spear, dragging it along with him.

He expected more spears to drive their sharp points into the deck, but none came. His ears, alert to the deadly whisper of arriving poisoned darts, heard only the lapping of waves against the schooner's hull.

Reaching the mainmast where the bell hung on its gimbals, Chicahua rolled over onto his back, employed the tip of the spear to poke at the cotton batting that had been stuffed into the brass bell to prevent it from ringing as the boat rocked, dislodging it.

Next, Chicahua removed his blowpipe from his belt, inserted into the cane tube a clay pellet normally used to stun small game, and placed one end to his grim lips. His cheeks puffed in, then out.

The pellet struck the bell, causing it to *dong* once, disconsolately. Inserting another, he made the bell ring again, louder this time.

Commotion sounded below. The whisking of bare feet in

motion.

"What is wrong?" came the stern voice of Captain Savage from the half-open deckhouse door.

Chicahua rattled back rapid words in K'iche.

Crawling to the deckhouse, Chicahua pried open the door. He scrambled down the companion steps, lost his footing, landing hard at the bottom.

Captain Savage helped him to his feet.

They exchanged quick words in the Mayan tongue.

Doc Savage hovered nearby. He asked of his father, "What is happening?"

"Sea Dyaks. Three *bangkongs* stole up on us. That means nearly two hundred Dyak warriors. We are surrounded."

"Not as long as I have this," said Doc, patting the receiver of his Annihilator submachine gun confidently.

"You place a great deal of store in that clumsy weapon," returned Captain Savage. "If you stole up on deck, they would cut you down in a hail of spears and poison darts before you could unleash very much lead effectively."

"I can try," whispered Doc stubbornly.

"We must find another way. They have not boarded us as yet. Perhaps they want to parley."

He noticed the Dyak spear that had fallen from Chicahua's hand. Picking it up, he scrutinized the pennant of red hair hanging from the haft.

"No doubt this is hair torn from the scalp of a war trophy," murmured Captain Savage.

Doc fingered it, shook his head firmly. "Orangutan hair. They are common in Borneo."

Captain Savage said, "Unless I am very much mistaken, this is the sign of a desired truce."

Climbing to the door, Captain Savage pushed it ajar and cupped his hands over his mouth. He began calling out to the raiders in their own tongue.

"Bercakap fikiran anda." Speak your piece.

A volley of words came from beyond the railing. Captain Savage listened, then translated for Doc's benefit.

"He is saying that his name is Monyet, son of Ramba, a mighty chief among the Sea Dyaks of Sakkaran, which they call Skrang," Captain Savage told Doc. "Monyet means 'Monkey' in their language. No self-respecting Dyak *penghulu* would name his son Monkey, but we will humor him for the moment."

Switching to the Dyak tongue, the senior Savage demanded, *"Apa yang anda mahu?"* What do you want?

The return reply was not understandable. In frustration, the Dyak switched to speaking Malay. *"Gencatan senjata."* Truce.

Captain Savage nodded. "As I suspected, he wishes to parley under a flag of truce. I will give him permission to come on board."

More words went back and forth, and one of the *bangkongs* approached under sculling oars. Soon, it was scraping the starboard side of the *Orion*.

Captain Savage and his tiny crew stepped out into the open, ready to repel boarders if treachery was in the offing. Doc left the Annihilator in the deckhouse, but had placed it just inside the open door, where he could flash to it if need be.

By this time, the Dyak prince had climbed onto the thatched awning of his vessel. Chicahua obediently draped the pilot ladder over the port side, and Monyet climbed up nimbly. He wore only a loincloth and a red headband crowned by upright hornbill feathers. On his hairless brown chest shone a protective necklace of beaten-gold breastplates.

The Mayan's dark eyes drilled into the Dyak's own. Flinty sparks seemed to pass between them, but Chicahua only made hard fists with his fingers. He had stepped out on deck unarmed, as commanded.

Monyet stood alone on the deck, resplendent in his barbaric finery, his posture that of a man unafraid. The Dyak warriors crammed in the waiting *bangkongs* bristled with spears and short blades and long blowpipes. These were the source of his bravado.

Doc Savage saw that this was the same man who had hailed them from a dugout canoe back in the Java Sea—the taunting one who said that they had very fine heads. They had thought him to be a scout for marauding pirates then. In reality, he was the leader of a war party.

The Dyak looked them over with insolent eyes. Words rippled from his lips. He made a very long speech. At the end of it, he spoke two words over and over, gesturing to help convey the meaning.

"Antu pata," he repeated, frustration tingeing his tone.

Captain Savage frowned. *"Antu pata. Antu pata.* I believe that means 'head trophies.'"

Switching to Malay, he called out, *"Trofi kepala?"*

"Ya!"

"They want that ape's head back," whispered Doc. "But why?"

"I will ask him." More words volleyed back and forth, growing hot and accusatory.

"Monyet says that the head we have was harvested by his father, Ramba, who is now dead. He has brought it back as an object of power, so that the spirit of his father will protect him as he hunts the mighty Kong."

Doc undertoned, "Father, if we can't fend them off, it makes sense to surrender the head. We can always recover it later."

The elder Savage shook his head. "It is not that simple. He says that he demands satisfaction for the killings of his men aboard the *Orion* when they had mastery of it."

"Point out that they slew most of our crew," said Doc dryly.

"I have done exactly that. This is why he suggests a contest instead of battle."

"What kind of contest?"

"Dyaks have a unique way of settling differences, Mister Savage. The two antagonists, with their seconds, retire to the beach and they immerse their heads in water until one of them can stand it no longer. The man who takes the first breath loses."

"That does not sound like much of a contest."

"The purpose of the second," said Savage Senior, "is to hold his man's head down so that he does *not* lose."

"That makes it sound more interesting," said Doc. "Tell him I accept the challenge."

"I will do so."

The Dyak listened to the sharp words coming from the lips of Captain Savage and something like a smile splashed his dark face, showing teeth that had been filed down.

Captain Savage turned to Doc. "It is done. We will meet on the beach at dawn."

"What about the natives?"

"The Dyaks say that the natives are afraid of his men. They will leave us alone. Now if you please, Mister Savage, fetch up the gruesome head and show it to this man as proof that we have retained it."

Doc pitched below, returning with the head in a swatch of burlap.

Fixing Monyet with his own flake-gold eyes, Doc Savage approached, the severed and dried ape head cupped in both muscular hands.

When it was presented to the man, Monyet's eyes lit up. For the first time, the Dyak prince truly smiled, and it could be seen that his filed-down teeth were nearly black from chewing betel nut. His grin was a dark caricature of a smile, evil in its hideous reverse hue. From his expression, he might have been offered the greatest emerald ever mined.

"This trophy," said Doc, "evidently means much to the man."

"Trophy heads are to the Dyak warrior what 'counting coup' is to the Sioux," explained Clark Savage, Senior. "We are to bring it to the beach. The winner of the contest may claim this grisly trophy as his property."

Doc nodded. "Ask him about Kong."

Captain Savage rattled off some quick words.

The answer came flying back.

"He said Kong is the monarch of this island."

"Ask him to describe Kong."

The Dyak employed a lot of gestures, most of them vertical.

Captain Savage translated. "He is saying that Kong is an ape greater than any found in Borneo or Siam. The earth shakes when he walks. The great demon-lizards flee from his path. His roar causes the full moon to fall from the sky. He is saying that Kong dwells on Skull Mountain, but they have denied Kong his refuge with their bonfires. Now they hunt Kong. Hunt him for his head."

"Whose head is it that they have now?"

"A younger ape. Captured years ago. It was a great prize taken by this man's father almost a generation ago. Now that his father has died, he seeks one of his own, the greatest head trophy imagined—the head of Kong, the *binatang tuhan*. That means beast-god."

Doc considered this answer.

"Tell him we will meet him on the beach at daybreak."

This was conveyed, and the Dyak suddenly leaped for the starboard rail. He favored them with his evil grin one last time. Then he hooked one tattooed leg and then the other over the rail, scrambling down the pilot ladder, managing to make his way to the rocking dugout canoe.

Oars were employed to kedge off from the schooner *Orion*. The rowers took their places under the thatched awning, and with near-military efficiency, the three *bangkongs* joined up in the lagoon and paddled away, making only gurgling sounds that were almost indistinguishable from the action of tides upon the black breakers.

Captain Savage turned to his son, his metallic eyes grave.

"We have only an hour to prepare you for the contest of your life."

Chapter XXVI

CAPTAIN SAVAGE WAS saying, "The rules of the contest are very simple. The man who keeps his head below the waterline longest wins, therefore the man who is forced to come up for air first is declared the loser."

"What happens to the loser after that?" asked Doc.

"According to Dyak custom, he has been shamed. And if the matter is legal, held responsible for restitution. In this contest, your opponent is seeking to save face for his war losses, and reclaim his trophy head. He may also secretly hope that you drown, which is a very real possibility for either party, given the solemn responsibilities of the second."

"I won't need a second."

"You cannot violate the rules, Mister Savage. This is their game. Chicahua will be your second."

Captain Savage turned to the silent Mayan. Chicahua's face remained one of fixed stone, but his obsidian eyes smoldered. He began explaining the contest and its rules. Chicahua listened attentively, then asked a question in his native tongue.

"He wants to know if he can be the Dyak's second, not yours," Captain Savage reported.

"Why?"

"He wants to hold the man's head underwater until his lungs burst. He has not forgotten his brother, and what was done to him."

Doc said, "Assure Chicahua that I will win this contest."

"I am certain Chicahua has every confidence in you, as have I. But he wants blood atonement."

"Perhaps we should leave him on board, to guard the ship," suggested Doc.

"No. Chicahua must be your second. Leave it to me to watch him. We will take no weapons. Is that clear?"

"Risky."

"These are the rules of engagement in this contest. No weapons. A truce has been declared for this purpose. We must abide by it."

"Very well," said Doc. "Is there anything else I will need to know?"

A thundercloud of a frown settled over the captain's brassy features.

"There is something I wish I knew," he said slowly.

"And that is?"

"Three *bangkongs* came. But are there more? Were these the only survivors of the crossing to Skull Mountain Island, or are others lurking in the bush?"

"If there are, they could stumble upon Stormalong at any time."

Captain Savage shook his head gravely. "I daren't ask the Dyak headman about him. Too risky. Once the contest is settled, we return to the war path—all of us. If he does not know about Stormalong, so much the better."

DAWN crept up not twenty minutes later, rising in the east, spreading a warm rosy light upon the bony dome of Skull Mountain. It made the landmark look as if it were rising out of the fires of perdition.

Doc watched the sun climb, noted the play of light crawling over the hollow-eyed face of the mountain peak. Men made that once. But what manner of men? Surely not the barbaric natives.

When the sun's hot lower edge lifted free of the horizon,

three *bangkongs* came around the headland.

"They must have found a way to scale the sheer cliffside," ruminated Captain Savage.

"If they did, so can we."

"We will leave that for later. Come."

They dropped the dory off the side. All three went down the pilot ladder unarmed. Chicahua handed the severed ape's-head trophy to Doc, who stored it under a bench seat.

Rowing, they reached the sand of the shoreline ahead of the Dyaks, beached the craft and stood waiting.

Calmly, Doc Savage removed his shirt. The play of muscles in action was something that would make Hercules incarnate shiver in envy. Although not overmuscled, the bronze man showed thews that were like bundles of piano wire. The cables and ligaments flexing on the backs of his hands and neck had an alarmingly solid look, resembling metal bars rather than mortal cartilage.

As the Dyaks approached, their gaze fell upon the patiently waiting giant of bronze. A ripple of fear crossed their blank, hairless faces. Weirdly, their deep-set eyes stared out of their skulls with an unnerving sharpness.

Soon, the *bangkongs* were grounded and drawn up onto the sand.

The Dyak band stepped barefoot onto the beach. They wore only their bark loincloths and feathered headbands. Many had elaborate tattoos on their necks, which Captain Savage had explained were talismans believed to keep their heads on their shoulders during battle.

Captain Savage and the Dyak chief approached one another and fell into low converse. Terms were being settled. The elder Savage produced the head held by Chicahua. That seemed to settle matters.

Satisfied, the two captains returned to their crews to make preparations.

Two rattan mats were brought from one boat and laid on a

flat finger of coral reef, near the water's edge where it was shallow, yet deep enough to immerse a man's head if he could not surface.

"We must build a bonfire as a station to which to repair at the contest's end, or to drag the incapacitated," said the captain.

Doc and Chicahua gathered dry driftwood, palm fronds, and other materials. They made a pile, which the captain set alight with a flint striker. Soon, it was blazing nicely.

Captain Savage made a minor ceremony of placing the severed ape head trophy before his champion's fire.

About a dozen yards to the south, the Dyaks had their own fire burning merrily, its flames whipped by fitful sea breezes.

The Dyak leader went first. He strode down to the water's edge and took a position upon one of the rattan mats laid on the flat finger of coral reef, which served as a platform. His second followed him, stood thigh-deep in the water beside the reef. The latter man held two ironwood staffs two feet longer than he. They appeared to be blowpipes. Curls of dried human hair were attached to them.

With great ceremony, Monyet removed his gold breastplates and handed them to his second. He was attired only in his simple loincloth now.

DOC SAVAGE did not follow immediately. He had been charging his lungs. He continued to do so, bringing deep draughts deep into himself.

The Dyak chief, seeing this, decided to follow suit. He quickly began inhaling deeply and ferociously, expelling long breaths and taking in fresh ones.

Doc observed him carefully. Monyet clearly knew something of the proper way to charge the lung tissues with life-giving oxygen, but his technique was different from those of the pearl divers under which Doc had learned the dangerous art.

Time alone would tell whose technique was superior.

Finally, Doc entered the surf, walked with calm deliberation to the coral reef, and stepped on his mat. There he locked eyes with his opponent.

The Dyak glowered back, no trace of fear in his blank, deep-set eyes.

A Dyak second handed his leader a long blowpipe. This was shoved into the ground, and served as an anchor and support staff for the combat.

Chicahua came up and did the same, accepting the other blowpipe from the opposing second. It was stout enough to serve the purpose.

Doc grasped the thing with one cabled hand.

A Dyak dignitary, wearing a more elaborate costume than the others, strode up and began a speech. It went on for quite a while.

At the end of it, Doc asked, "What was he saying?"

"Ceremonial ritual," replied Captain Savage quietly. "He was invoking the spirits and asking that justice be done. It is time."

Doc gave his lungs a final charge. Monyet did the same.

They grasped their anchor poles. Both men knelt and placed their heads under water.

At first, a hush accompanied this action. The ordeal had only begun.

Men crowded closer to watch, eyes greedy for the spectacle of combat.

A single bubble of air dribbled up from the Dyak's nose. None from Doc's. A second air bubble popped the surface, then a third.

Yet no air bubbles were released by the big bronze man.

A minute crawled by, then two. More air bubbles came—a little flurry of them. The sense of tension grew, and overtook the crowd. They began chanting.

"*Labon! Labon!*" they cried over and over again. Fight! Fight!

Finally, a big bubble came from the spot where Doc Savage's head was submerged.

The Dyaks went wild. "*Labon! Labon!*" they roared.

The three-minute mark was reached. The Dyak's shoulders began to struggle. His second bent down and laid both hands upon him—one on his hair, the other on the muscular back of his neck. He forced Monyet's head to stay submerged.

Now it was a struggle for life.

Doc released another big glut of bubbles. But his bronze shoulders remained resolute. The bronze skullcap that was his hair might have been an inert thing in the water.

"*Labon! Labon!*" howled the Dyaks wildly.

Chicahua stood poised to step in, but his eyes, flicking between the broad back of Doc Savage and the Dyak's jittering muscles, decided him. He remained on his feet.

His obsidian-dark orbs went to the cheering Dyaks. Flint struck no more fierce sparks. The look on his face, while outwardly impassive, was one that bespoke confidence.

"*Labon! Labon!*" went up the frenzied cry.

Now the Dyak leader was fighting for his life. Air came streaming upward, breaking in furious bubbles. Mewing sounds came from beneath the water. He clutched his staff with a frenzied fury. He was a man at war with himself. He fought to win, but also struggled to live. Both impulses were in direct conflict with one another.

Doc Savage remained resolute. Air drooled up, this time in an orderly trickle of tiny bubbles. It was as if the bronze giant was releasing his pent breath the way a smoker blows smoke rings. Sometimes, he made as if he were expelling a struggling breath. Other times, it was as if he was playing with the release of the contents of his lungs.

At no point did Doc seem to be in distress. And the agonizing minutes were rushing by. Four. Five. Six—

Finally, the Dyak leader went into convulsions. He seemed to lash out at his second, desperate to bring his head back to the reviving realm of air. But his second, determined that his leader not lose the contest, redoubled his strenuous efforts. He pushed down hard, as if prepared to drown his leader rather than see him lose face.

The Dyak gave a final squirming twist, then collapsed.

The chanting of the crowd turned into a low groan, then subsided into a long snaky hiss.

Monyet's head was quickly pulled up. His jaw hung slack, his face utterly bloodless. The eyes were rolled up in his skull, as if dead.

A groan rose up from a dozen Dyak throats. It was over.

THEY dragged him back to the fire dedicated to him, where wet mud was thrown into his face. This brought him around in time.

All eyes were on the Dyak leader. Hands were slapping his slack face. He began to cough and hack out water from his tortured lungs. He seemed dazed, unable to focus.

Few eyes were on Doc Savage, calmly releasing air bubbles from his nostrils. Chicahua stood sentinel, his eyes feasting upon the features of the Dyak murderers of his brother. The Mayan's triumphant smile was tempered by a darker emotion. It could be seen in his unblinking gaze.

Captain Savage tore his gaze from the ministrations designed to bring the Monyet back to his senses.

"Clark, you may stop now," he said firmly.

Doc Savage allowed another minute to pass before he lifted his head. He took in a single relaxed sip of air and seemed unaffected by his long immersion.

"Evidently," he said calmly, "the Dyak technique for swimming underwater is not as advanced as the pearlers of Paumoto."

Captain Savage nodded. "No doubt the natural lung capacity of your opponent played a role, as well."

Doc looked to Chicahua. Something in the dark depths of his eyes was not good to see.

Doc warned, "Chicahua is not satisfied."

"He will obey. He is a good sailor."

They went toward their own campfire, to await the fate of the Dyak leader.

The man was coughing unbearably. Hands continued to slap Monyet's face, yank on his hair, and pull his fingers, until he looked so bedraggled all semblance of royalty had departed from him.

Seawater poured from his nostrils. Doc stepped in to turn the man over. There was some resistance, which the bronze giant shrugged off with his powerful shoulders.

Doc laid the man on his belly on the sand and applied pressure to his back. Seawater poured out. The awful hacking resumed, then subsided.

Standing up, Doc withdrew.

"Tell them he will live," Doc told his father.

Captain Savage repeated the words in the language of the Dyaks.

Before very long, the leader rolled over and sat up. He had to be held to remain erect. His eyes held a beaten, confused light.

"What comes next?" Doc asked his father.

They were destined never to know.

Two things transpired in close order.

From the surrounding jungle fierce war cries resounded, followed by a storm of flint-tipped javelins raining down.

Two unwary Dyak warriors were immediately transfixed through the chest. They sagged to the sand, fatally impaled. Others scattered in all directions.

In the melee, Chicahua raced to reclaim his borrowed blowpipe. He also grabbed up the blowpipe that the Dyak leader had used for support.

Blowing the former clear of brine, he inserted something into it and, taking the tube to his mouth, expelled a powerful breath.

A dart flew out. It would have struck the Dyak leader, but

for one of the frantic warriors scrambling to get out of the way of the rain of spears. That unfortunate man took the dart in his face and gave out a shriek of fear.

This attracted the attention of others, who ran to claim some of the spears that had not found human targets.

Spears were shouldered, leveled in Chicahua's direction.

Doc Savage plunged in then. Metallic fists began raining blows. Knuckles broke noses, jaws, knocked heads askew on their necks. The audible crunching of spinal bones and other mortal injuries could be heard.

"To the dory!" shouted Captain Savage. "To the dory! The truce is broken."

Chapter XXVII

FOR THIS ONCE, Doc Savage dared disobey his father. Rushing to the beached *bangkongs*, he began smashing them where he could, using great rocks he scooped up from the surf.

Spears continued to rain down, but none came near him. They were all aimed for the clot of Dyaks milling about the beach.

Only then did Doc rush to join the others at the dory.

They got it off, jumped in and began paddling furiously. This made them a clear target.

Spears began chucking into the water. But only a few. All missed. Doc rowed with Herculean energy, propelling the dory away.

On the beach, natives and Dyaks became embroiled in a great combat.

"With any luck, they will destroy one another," said Captain Savage.

"Unlikely," said Doc. "The natives have the numerical advantage."

While this was true, the Dyak warriors were not without prowess. Spears having been expended, the battle turned to one of hand-to-hand combat.

Here, it was a boiling mass of human flesh and bone. Knives were brought out and used. Sharp iron grated on bone. Blood flowed.

Unarmed, the Dyaks were getting the worst of it. A retreat was called.

Surviving Dyaks took to the surf, battled to get their boats into the water. They managed to get only one *bangkong* afloat. It began leaking badly, but they bailed with gourd drinking cups and somehow managed to keep it afloat.

The other Dyaks fought for a time, then melted into the jungle, pursued by native warriors bent on finishing them off. One of them had the presence of mind to snatch up the blackened ape's head trophy. He tucked it under an arm and vanished.

THEY reached the *Orion* and boarded it. From the rail, Doc and the others watched the last spasms of the battle on the beach. Few Dyaks were now visible.

The shore area was soon cleared of fighting forms. The dead and wounded lay on the sand and rocks, chests heaving. Moans of the dying could be heard distinctly.

Doc's flake-gold eyes went to the foundering *bangkong*.

"The Dyak leader seems to have survived," he remarked.

Captain Savage had found his spyglass and was studying the crew of the vanishing vessel as it found its way around a headland.

"Yes, he lives. And he will be in a foul mood until he avenges this insult done to him."

Captain Savage turned to Chicahua.

"You disobeyed me, bosun," he said starkly. Then, realizing that he was speaking English in his anger, the captain switched to K'iche.

Chicahua hung his expressionless head and said nothing.

"He has avenged his brother in his own eyes," said Doc sympathetically.

"He has done nothing of the sort! The killer still lives."

"We have shown them that we are more powerful than they. They will be afraid to cross us in the future."

"Is that why you showed off as you did?" returned the elder Savage.

"I wished to make a point."

"There is a difference between winning a contest of strength and rubbing salt into the wounds of the vanquished, Mister Savage," the captain said bitterly.

"I had the psychological, as well as physical, advantage, and I pressed it home," explained Doc quietly.

"The days to come alone will speak to the wisdom of your actions. Now how are we to search for Stormalong, with conditions such as they are?"

"By searching for him," returned Doc. "Nothing has changed. The Dyak prince is temporarily incapacitated. His warriors have been scattered. The war party is demoralized."

"The ones we encountered, yes. But what if twice that number are holed up on Skull Mountain? What if they descend upon us, howling for blood?"

"In that sense, nothing has changed since yesterday."

Captain Savage made motions as if to contradict his son, but realized that Doc Savage spoke the truth. Nothing had changed, in that wise. The Dyak enemy would or would not attack, by their own lights.

Squaring his shoulders, the elder Savage swallowed whatever he was about to say.

"Come," he barked finally. "We must lay plans for the rescue of Stormalong Savage."

THEY assembled their weapons in grim silence. Doc looked for a fresh shirt, then realized that his Army uniform might serve him best, since it generally resembled the coloration of parts of the jungle of Skull Island.

Captain Savage came up from below, lugging a locked trunk. Doc eyed this. "What is that?"

"We may have use of its contents. Time enough for explanations, if we do," he said shortly.

Doc did not press the matter.

They raised all sails, took up the anchor, and cast off.

The black schooner ghosted around the island, keeping clear of the reefs, in the opposite direction from where the Dyak *bangkong* had disappeared. It seemed to be the most prudent thing to do.

They sailed past the spot where the north edge of the wall stopped, and their eyes drank in its vast height, its gargantuan size.

"Nature did not build that," mused Captain Savage. "The pharaohs would have been challenged to construct such a thing."

"I suspect that this island has a deep history," remarked Doc.

The Captain steered carefully, while Doc and Chicahua employed boat hooks to fend off the rocks. The going was slow. Fortunately, the *Orion* was a shoal craft, built for operating along the stony eastern U.S. coast and in shallow, reef-bedeviled Caribbean waters. The schooner possessed no fixed keel, only a removable centerboard ideal for lagoons such as this one.

As they progressed, Captain Savage studied the sheer cliff-side walls. They looked as if beasts had scored them with gigantic talons.

For an hour, they moved through the morning light, threading the fangs of stone jutting up from the chuckling waters.

"Heave to," commanded Captain Savage suddenly. "This looks like a likely spot."

Doc glanced up. Here the cliff side was broken in several places, possibly from some past earthquake or volcanic eruption.

They lay under the cliff side, which was virtually unscalable.

Captain Savage unlatched the trunk and removed some unusual objects. An old muzzle-loading rifle was produced. The captain proceeded to charge this with black gunpowder. From the trunk he took a small three-pronged grappling hook and some light fishing line.

Affixing the line to the grapnel, he inserted its iron shaft into the muzzle-loader. Only then did Doc notice that the barrel was specially constructed to receive it.

"Remarkable device," Doc commented.

"I devised it myself for just such eventualities."

Aiming high, the captain set the walnut stock to his shoulder and squeezed the trigger.

A prodigious quantity of fire and black-powder smoke erupted from the muzzle.

The iron grappling hook disappeared into the sky, trailing rope.

Doc watched it climb. The unwinding coil at his father's feet rapidly diminished.

The grapnel faltered, fell back. On the way down, it snagged a cleft with a dull clang, seemed to hold. Doc doubted that he could do as well in one sure shot.

"You may do the honors, Mister Savage."

Reaching over, Doc gave the dangling line a firm yank. It held. He tugged again.

"Anchored solidly, sir."

"Since you are the heaviest of us, it stands to reason that you should be the first to test it."

"Begging your pardon, Captain, but if the line won't stand my weight, we may have difficulty retrieving the grapnel and line. May I suggest that you go first, followed by Chicahua? That way at least two of us will succeed if the line should prove insufficient to bear the load."

"Well reasoned, sir. Stand aside."

Captain Savage took hold of the cord and began his ascent.

Doc watched his father climb. He did so in a natural manner that showed that he valued stealth, not speed.

Captain Savage got half way up and discovered that there were handholds. He switched to them, releasing the line.

Doc motioned for Chicahua to go next.

The Mayan was also methodical in his climbing, probably in emulation of his captain.

They made it to the lip of the cliff before Doc followed. He went up with great speed and agility, and after the first few yards, ceased to be concerned about the line's ability to support his weight. His Annihilator submachine gun hung from a lanyard attached to a leather strap crossing his chest, along with an extra magazine of ammunition. The rounds in the loaded drum rattled and shook noisily as he went up.

REACHING the top, Doc began coiling up the line. He hid the grapnel and coil in a thicket of thorns where no one, human or otherwise, would be likely to root around and accidentally discover it.

Captain Savage began drinking in his surroundings.

Before them stood a stretch of clearing, tumbled with boulders and lesser rocks, beyond which a veritable wall of dense tropical jungle loomed. The explosion of green growth was overwhelming.

Over this profusion, pterosaurs wheeled, resembling fantastically constructed vultures, their downy bodies displaying striking hues, their membranous wings catching the morning rays like living sky sails.

"Astounding!" the captain said, with a trace of awe in his rough-hewn voice.

"We have stepped back into time," agreed Doc.

"That we have, Mister Savage. That we have."

Unholstering his revolver, Captain Savage struck out inland.

Doc and Chicahua followed, heads swiveling back and forth, eyes alert for any movement. Doc had his weapon cradled in his great arms, making it look small, like an overgrown pistol.

They progressed inward for some time, marveling at the profuse vegetation that grew wild and unchecked. There were giant conifers, towering hardwoods, woody cycads resembling monster pineapples. Bamboo grew in isolated stands, in great profusion. Ferns abounded, waving sultry green hands. All over, thorny rattan vines infiltrated the lush emerald phantasmagoria. Filtering sunlight infused everything with a luminous chlorophyll blaze.

"I feel as if I am in the Cretaceous Era," remarked Clark Savage, Senior.

"I see evidence of the Jurassic," suggested Doc.

"It is clear that this island stands alone and unique in its natural evolution. What do you make of it, Mister Savage?"

"From what I have seen thus far," said Doc thoughtfully, "we had best be prepared for anything."

Insofar as fauna was concerned, they saw only insects of remarkable sizes and properties. Once a serpent slithered by, and it seemed unremarkable until it corkscrewed spirally up a tree at their approach, and suddenly sprouted gossamer green wings.

Launching itself into space, it swiftly glided to a nearby tree and, once striking a branch, wrapped itself around that limb like a whip snapping around its target.

The wings folded up in some ingenious manner and the reptile slipped into the crown of the tree, undulating out of sight.

Seeing this, Chicahua sank to his knees and breathed, "Kukulcan!"

Doc observed, "I seem to recall that Kukulcan was the name of a Mayan deity."

"Yes. The so-called Plumed Serpent. Identical to Quetzalcoatl of the Aztecs. It would appear that the myth has some reality—although far from the land where it still flourishes."

"Very far," agreed Doc.

Captain Savage motioned for Chicahua to rise and continue along.

The awed Mayan did so, but his obsidian-black eyes remained on the tree until it fell behind them.

There were no paths as such, just spaces between clumps of vegetation. But as they moved inland, the ground sloped down, and a great plain opened up before them. It was dotted with weird trees whose tortured limbs were sinuously outflung in the manner of snakes engaged in combat, but they were not so close packed as before.

The smell of smoke hung in the air, biting at their eyes and nostrils. Their eyes went to the craggy crown of Skull Mountain, enwrapped in a gray haze that made it seem to be smoking, like a volcano rousing to sulphurous life.

There had been a rain during the night, and Doc wondered if it had quenched the fires burning in the hollow orbs of the monster mountain. From this direction, it was impossible to ascertain. Skull Mountain stood in profile, but it seemed as if the smoky haze was issuing from its eye sockets and cliff-like jaw, like a threatening exhalation from subterranean regions beyond human ken.

"I do not like the look of that mountain," Captain Savage commented.

"It does not look real," agreed Doc.

"We will avoid it, if at all practicable."

A sky-reflecting pool of blue drew them and they made their way to it.

Chicahua pointed and said one word, *"Cenote."* Doc recognized it as a Spanish term for a sacrificial well of the kind scattered throughout pre-Columbian Yucatan.

"Remarkable," said Captain Savage, kneeling before the placid body of water.

"It appears to be an ordinary pool," said Doc.

"Have you forgotten your childhood? Do you not recall when you first learned to swim?"

A flicker of something strange crossed the bronze man's sun-kilned visage.

"On Andros Island. I was not yet two. You tried to teach me to swim."

"And you were reluctant to enter the water."

"I hesitated," amended Doc. "So you threw me in bodily."

"Yes, into a 'blue hole' very much like this one. Andros was dotted with them. It is amazing to see a similar body here. No doubt this connects to an underwater cave, if not a network of them. That is the arrangement on Andros."

"As I recall," continued Doc, "I became disoriented and almost drowned."

"A boy who lives on a boat, if he is to survive, must learn to swim," countered Captain Savage gruffly. "I would have rescued you, but you found your way back to the surface without assistance. And you appear no worse for it."

"No worse, but looking at this particular blue hole, I feel a vague disquiet."

"Nerves, nothing more. We shall press on."

They moved forward, making little noise except for the rattle of Doc's ammunition drum. He decided to exchange the heavy drum for the smaller magazine clip, but this precaution produced no appreciable lessening of noise. So Doc switched back.

Another quarter mile of walking and they came upon something that caused the two Savages to draw to a halt and become very quiet.

It was a coconut palm. It lay across the way, toppled and twisted in a most extraordinary fashion.

Doc Savage was the first to speak.

"If I am not mistaken," he ventured, "this palm has been subject to the identical destructive forces that toppled the masts of the *Courser.*"

Chapter XXVIII

CAPTAIN CLARK SAVAGE, SENIOR, walked around the fallen palm, frowning darkly. It was a very thick specimen, fully three feet around.

He gave his full attention to the splintered mass that was the stump. It remained attached to the fallen bole by long twisted strands of tough wood. It was evident that something powerful had brought it down.

"Kong?" wondered Doc.

"Nonsense!" retorted his father. "A hurricane could have done this. I have seen tropical cyclones that have uprooted entire groves of stout trees and twisted railroad tracks into fantastic shapes, by the relentless action of their concentrated wrath."

Doc looked around. "There are other trees," he pointed out. "They stand untouched."

"A freak of nature," Savage hurled back. "Tornados have been known to pluck children from their mother's arms and deposit them safely in treetops or upon barn roofs."

"I do not question this. But this break is fresh and there are no signs of tropical disturbance in the vicinity."

"There is nothing more deceptive than an obvious fact," snapped the captain.

Doc regarded his father steadily. "That is a quote. It sounds familiar to me."

"Conan Doyle, if you must know."

"If I am not mistaken," said Doc, "Sherlock Holmes spoke

those words in 'The Boscombe Valley Mystery.'"

"Holmes is a fictional character, sir. I am quoting an author, not a figment of said author's imagination."

Doc repressed a smile. "Then allow me to offer a counter quote from the same source. 'When you have eliminated the impossible, whatever remains, no matter how improbable, must be the truth.'"

"I believe the actual statement to be, 'Eliminate all other factors, and the one which remains must be the truth.'"

"Both are factual," stated Doc. "And you are changing the subject."

"No giant ape did this, I tell you," insisted the captain. "Again, from Doyle: 'It is a capital mistake to theorize before one has data. Insensibly one begins to twist facts to suit theories, instead of theories to suit facts.'"

" 'There is nothing like first-hand evidence,'" countered Doc, stubbornly.

" 'You see, but you do not observe. The distinction is clear.'"

"We are getting nowhere," said Doc, secretly amused by his father's knowledge of one of his favorite authors. "I suggest we look for spoor."

They dispersed in three directions after Captain Savage gave Chicahua clear instructions not to stray far.

Doc had learned to read sign like a Red Indian. He began looking for subtle but telltale indications of tracks. He quickly found them.

Grass had been crushed and trampled in spots. The spots were very large. But studying them formed no clear impression in his mind. Mentally, he attempted to fit the footprint of a gigantic ape into these flat depressions. His calculations suggested an ape of incredible proportions, possibly twenty feet tall.

Doc dismissed these calculations out of hand. An ape of a dozen feet height was fantastic enough, but he had been half-willing to entertain it. But nearly twenty—? It was ridiculous on the face of it.

Still, facts were facts and spoor, spoor.

The tracks vanished into the tropical forest. Laying his Annihilator on the ground, Doc went up a woody, creeper-festooned cycad, found its topmost point, and peered in all directions.

He saw nothing that stood over twenty feet tall, other than Skull Mountain. From this vantage point, the haze-enwrapped formation's profile with its drawn, hollow cheeks still could not be seen clearly. Through the early morning mists, its stark, forbidding countenance brooded over all. This filled Doc Savage with a cold grimness—as if he walked in a land ruled by unconquerable death.

Of the rumored giant gorilla, there was no sign. But Skull Island was an amazing conglomeration of terrain. There were ravines deep enough to conceal such a monstrosity—if one existed. Stretched out amid the jungles and forests, Kong might evade detection. For a time.

Dropping down to the ground, the bronze giant recovered his weapon and went in search of his father. He made his way carefully, drum cartridges rattling with every step.

Doc came upon his father watching a purplish crab as large as a Collie dog cracking open a fallen coconut.

"I am here," he said quietly.

"I know. I could hear the rattle of your approach. I will remind you not to fire that thing without my express permission."

The robber crab sat industriously cracking the coconut shell with one large lobster-like foreclaw. It was easily three feet in circumference. Around it stood a great deal of jungle debris— broken husks, splintered bamboo shoots, even an unusually large tortoise shell that had been dragged to this spot.

"Are you familiar with the common palm thief, Mister Savage?"

"Yes. Also known as the coconut, or robber crab. Scientific name *Birgus latro.*"

"Good. Observe that one closely."

"It is doing what is natural for it," said Doc.

"Obviously. But that is not what I am referring to. I watched this creature climb that palm and snip off a coconut, which fell to the ground, unbroken. It had hoped the fall would begin the job it is now attempting to complete."

"The robber crab is a land animal, as I recall."

"Quite so. It is the largest arthropod in the world, hence its impressive size. It subsists upon coconuts and other such food. Under pressure, it will eat garbage and even meat. But that is not what I am trying to get you to see."

Doc approached the thing. It was a mottled purplish-blue, strikingly different from the red or green of a water-dwelling crustacean. Its jointed legs and horny shell were very robust. Its monstrous foreclaws and waving antennae made it resemble a deformed lobster.

"I fail to detect anything unusual about this one," he admitted.

"You have perhaps encountered fewer of these than have I. But then I have lived longer than you, and consequently ranged much farther."

Doc nodded, holding his tongue. He wanted to say something assertive, but decided to let his father have his point.

"Evidently, I am missing what it is you wish me to perceive," Doc said reluctantly.

The elder Savage intoned firmly, "I again invoke Doyle: 'You know my method. It is founded upon the observation of trifles.'"

Doc studied the crab from all angles, but the only result was that something akin to perplexity crawled over his metallic mask of a face.

" 'The world is full of obvious things that nobody by any chance observes,'" prompted Captain Savage, again drawing from Conan Doyle.

"I give up," admitted Doc.

"That crab, Mister Savage, is but a child."

Doc circled the busy creature, but his knowledge of crustaceans was not up to seeing what his father had perceived.

"If true, and I do not doubt it," Doc said finally, "that would mean that a full grown one would be the size of a man."

"Conceivably larger. We are in a land where evolution has run wild—or where the guiding hand of the Almighty has been conspicuously negligent."

"Whichever it is," said Doc, "it would be better to avoid this one's parents."

"Agreed. Let us be off. Mind your weapon."

They collected Chicahua, who eyed the robber crab with vaguely stunned eyes. He had never seen a crab of such size and coloring before. That fact was plain on his stolid coffee-colored face.

They came upon another crustacean attempting to climb a shaggy palm. Its dexterity was remarkable. It scooted up the slick bole like a grotesque bruise-colored spider.

Chicahua took a hardened clay pellet from his dart pouch, and inserted it into the blowgun. Aiming carefully, he sent a pellet bouncing off the carapace of the thing. It halted, seemed puzzled, for it waved its mandibles oddly, then continued its climb.

"Why did he do that?" asked Doc of his father.

"Perhaps he was testing the crab."

"For what?"

"A Sherlockian clue. Did you not hear the noise of the clay pellet striking?"

"Yes. It sounded very soft." Suddenly, Doc understood.

"That is another infant crab," he pointed out. "It must be the season for them."

"Exercise due caution," warned the captain. "I would not ignore the possibility that larger specimens can be found hereabouts."

"If the crabs and insects grow to such prodigious size," remarked Doc as they moved along, "could a human have also reached a comparable stature?"

"If you are asking if Skull Island harbors giants such as the Bible speaks, I would not venture to speculate," Captain Savage said impatiently.

"This island very much reminds me of the one described in the renowned novel by Jules Verne," suggested Doc. *"The Mysterious Island."*

"If you ever reach the point in your life when you come into possession of a submersible of your own, Mister Savage, perhaps you will choose this place as your home anchorage. You might become the Captain Nemo of the Twentieth Century."

"That has never been my ambition," Doc said quietly, wondering if his father was mocking him.

"A man with a submarine should have a use for it," Captain Savage pointed out reasonably. "And you will need a crew."

"I made friends in the war. Good friends. I imagine we will reunite at some point in the future."

"Then there is your crew, sir."

Doc shook his head. "Not these men. They have ambitions of their own. One is an engineer like yourself. Another a chemist. He taught me a few things. These are not subordinates. These are leaders of the future."

"Even the leaders of the future need to be led," Captain Savage pointed out. "Perhaps you will take the role of a super-leader."

"I fail to follow," admitted Doc.

"Never mind. I had for a moment forgotten that your training has come to an unsatisfactory conclusion. Let us focus on the business of finding my father, your grandfather. Be watchful."

"I see that you brought along a Very pistol," Doc noted.

"Only as a last resort. Were I to unleash a star shell, it would no doubt trigger the curiosity of your grandfather—but also invite investigation by hostiles."

Doc gave the receiver of his Annihilator a hard spank. "We are more than equal to them."

"Let us hope that our reconnoiter does not result in unnecessary wholesale slaughter. Once we have discovered Old Stormy, we will have reached our objective and may depart at will."

Doc looked about him. "There may be other things of interest on this island."

Captain Savage nodded sagaciously. "At another time, I would enjoy mapping this place for posterity. But my sole objective is rescue."

They marched on. Doc was in the lead. He seemed to be tireless. His submachine gun clutched in his formidable hands appeared as light as balsa wood.

They came to a river, its banks dotted with waving bulrushes.

"We do not have axes with which to construct a makeshift crossing," Captain Savage reminded. "We will have to follow its course until we find a way across, or encounter what we will."

Doc nodded. "Swimming across would be foolhardy, given our unfamiliarity with the things that may dwell in these inland waters."

"I am glad to see that you are exercising due restraint. It is an excellent trait in commerce, or combat."

THEY moved along the riverbank, single-file. The course of the stream twisted like a dark dragon that carried them to the edge of an area of rain forest. The banks were choked with tall, waving cattails and other reedy growth.

From time to time, Doc plucked a thistle plant from the ground, examining the fuzzy spikelets. He pocketed a few, but neglected to explain why he did so.

They entered, feeling the cool canopy of interlacing overhead branches touching their faces and arms. It was a great difference in contrast to the savannah they had been traversing. Here, the soil was rocky and moist. Their feet sank a half inch with most steps, two in some spots.

"'Ware quicksands," warned Captain Savage.

"I smell a trap."

"It is much the same thing. Mind your footing at all times." Savage Senior turned to give Chicahua the same counsel in his own language.

But Chicahua, who had been trailing behind to protect the rear, was not in sight.

"Halt! We have lost sight of Chicahua."

They waited for him to catch up.

Listening, Doc said, "I do not hear him moving through the brush."

"Chicahua can be very stealthy when he wishes to be."

"No one is that stealthy," insisted Doc. "We should backtrack."

Silently, they reversed course.

Captain Savage walked with his sharp eyes scanning the greenery ahead. But Doc kept his gaze upon the ground, seeking sign.

Abruptly, he touched his father's shoulder. Captain Savage turned. Doc motioned for silence, and pointed to the ground.

"Tracks cease here," Doc undertoned.

They looked up. Overhead hung a spidery lacing of boughs, ferns, lianas, vines and creepers. Something rustled up there. A section of dense greenery shook and crackled.

"Robber crab?" suggested Savage Senior.

Doc shook his head. "Its coloration would stand out," he countered.

Doc raised his cumbersome weapon, sweeping the area of disturbance.

Something launched itself into space. It was impossible to see what, owing to the verdant gloom.

Captain Savage whispered, "What was it?"

"Pterosaur, possibly," said Doc.

"Could one have carried Chicahua away?"

"The specimens I encountered attempted to do the same to me." Handing over his weapon, Doc added, "I am going to investigate."

Captain Savage accepted the submachine gun and said, "Take no unnecessary chances. Chicahua is a valued crewman, but you are my only son. Remember that."

"Yes, Captain."

Doc went up the tree, carrying only his sheathed Bowie knife, in the event he would need it.

He reached the top without making much noise, or rustling the foliage.

Poking his metallic head up from the canopy, the bronze giant scanned the surrounding sky.

The blazing sun made his eyes hurt. He shaded them and normal sight soon returned.

High to the east, a great feathered thing was gliding along. It looked like a fantastic prehistoric chicken, although it possessed other, less familiar, attributes.

Its feathers were purplish, not unlike that of the robber crabs, but its underside and portions of its arms were the hue of muted emeralds.

Doc recognized the creature as similar to the thing he had encountered on the mountain, that the old woman Penjaga had called a slasher. His mind flashed back to the original naturalists who had unearthed the first dinosaur fossils. They believed them to belong to gigantic birds. The first generation of paleontologists had subsequently reclassified them as reptiles. The truth, is seemed, lay in the middle. Not dinosaurs. Dinoavisaurs!

As Doc observed it, the avian monstrosity searched the foliage below, its hot orange eyes questing about menacingly.

Doc could see its plumed legs hanging vulture-like, talons distended. There was nothing in those hooked claws. No man, or other prey.

That was a relief. Reinserting his head into the canopy, Doc went in search of the missing Mayan.

"Chicahua!" he called out.

No answer came, no reply of any kind. Neither sounds nor motion.

Doc moved about carefully, golden eyes roving, missing nothing, but finding nothing either.

At last, he returned to the original tree he had climbed, and began working his way back to the forest floor.

When he was halfway down, Doc called out, "No sign of him."

Captain Savage failed to respond, and Doc took that to mean he was not encouraging conversation that might carry to hostiles.

But once he came within sight of the ground, Doc saw that his father was no longer standing on the spot where he had left him.

The bronze giant dropped to the ground, his powerful leg muscles cushioning his fall.

Coming erect, Doc made a circuit of the tree.

"Captain!" he called in a stage whisper. No reply echoed back. Not even his own voice.

Doc was forced to raise his voice. "Captain! Captain! *Father?*"

This time his voice echoed back, hollow and unanswered.

Chapter XXIX

DOC SAVAGE WRENCHED to a halt. There was no sense in running around in aimless circles. Concentrated thought, not wild action, was what mattered.

Deliberately, he made his trilling sound. It became one with the jungle, coursing through its cool confines, like a creature composed of pure melody searching for its soul mate—a call more supernatural than animal.

After a minute, Doc suppressed the sound. He listened for a replying whistle.

It came. It sounded human-like. But there was an uncanny quality to it that evoked the unknowable.

Doc made his trilling again, stopped after twenty seconds or so.

Seemingly in response, the uncanny whistle came again. Its duration exactly matched Doc's own. Only then did the bronze man realize that this had been true of the first interval of whistling.

Doc essayed a third tune, this one limited to seven seconds.

After a pause, seven seconds of a whistled bar came and went.

This allowed Doc's supremely acute hearing to zero in on the sound's source. It came from northeast. Doc struck off in that direction. This time he kept his lips compressed and his boots made no sounds on the rocky soil.

As Doc moved, something struck him at the side of his head.

He had not sensed the attacker, but immediately dropped to

the ground, eyes questing about.

Something clattered to the ground. Doc spotted it out of the corner of one eye, reached for the thing.

Bringing it up to his face, he saw that it was a clay pellet, identical to the ones that Chicahua used.

Doc looked about, saw no movement around him.

Carefully, he stood up.

Again, a pellet struck him—tapping him on the chest. This time Doc had been listening for the preliminary intake of breath, followed by a powerful puff of air that preceded the expulsion of the tiny missile.

Doc veered off in that direction.

He found Chicahua crouching under a great cluster of fan-like ferns that might have originated in the Devonian Period.

"Where is my father?" asked Doc, joining him in the lacy green shelter.

Chicahua attempted to pantomime a reply, but Doc had difficulty following, much less interpreting the man's gestures.

Suddenly remembering the Mayan's use of the non-native term *cenote*, Doc switched to Spanish.

"*Habla Español?*"

"*Si. Un poco.*"

It stood to reason that the man might have picked up some Spanish, and Doc wondered why this had not occurred to him before.

As it turned out, Chicahua's Spanish was rudimentary at best. But it allowed the conversational trend to become somewhat more efficient.

According to what the man seemed to be conveying, Chicahua had been distracted by something moving through the bush and paused to get a clearer view of it. The need for silence had prevented him from warning Captain Savage.

"*Qué?*" asked Doc.

"*Hombre.*"

"Qué aspecto tenía?" What did he look like?

"Gigante."

Doc asked Chicahua how tall was this giant.

Chicahua wasn't certain, or perhaps his grasp of the Spanish terms for feet wasn't certain. But he showed eight fingers.

"Eight feet tall?" asked Doc in Spanish.

Chicahua nodded. With a finger, he tried to draw the giant, but a finger in the dirt is no fine instrument for artistry. He depicted something that might have been a man, or a simian monster. The head was a mass of hair.

"Negro?"

Chicahua shook his head. *"Blanco."*

Doc could not tell whether Chicahua meant that the man was white-skinned or his hair was white. It was frustrating.

Doc decided that he had gotten all he could out of Chicahua and that it was high time for action.

He signaled the Mayan to follow.

THEY MOVED in the direction where Chicahua had spied the man, who evidently had melted into the dank forest almost immediately upon being seen.

The search brought a sign of Captain Savage's boot heels. They were very distinct for a time, then seemed to peter out. This was the way of it. The forest floor could run for yards sufficiently soft to take prints, then change to a rocky material that left little trace.

Doc tried every trick he knew. Looking for mica specks that might have been disturbed was an old cowboy tracking trick. Sunlight would glint more brightly on the freshly exposed side, but there was insufficient sunlight present in the canopy for that, never mind the fact that mica was unlikely to be found in such a lush locale.

Grass or reeds depressed by a boot would take their time rising, and Doc looked for these, but found none.

Captain Savage, if made prisoner, would know to break branches or make some similar disturbance to show the direction in which he was being conveyed.

Nothing such as that revealed itself.

At length, Doc came to a halt.

"If we stray too far in the wrong direction, we are only making matters worse," he said.

Chicahua seemed to understand.

They paused, standing back to back protectively, covering one another's blind spots, searching their surroundings with their penetrating eyes.

At a loss for anything more productive, Doc gave forth with his trilling sound.

To his astonishment, the whistle he had heard before came filtering through the forest. And it was not coming from Chicahua!

Fixing its location with his ears, Doc signaled for the Mayan to follow him carefully.

Doc kept on, one hand on the butt of his automatic. He had not unshipped it before now due to the risk of firing at shadows that might be friendly.

The whistle came again, and this time Doc made the answering call.

His keen ears attempted to unravel the flavor of the thing. It sounded as if a human throat had produced it, but why had the caller not spoken up?

"Captain?"

No reply came.

"Is anyone here?"

No response.

Doc switched to Malay.

"Jawaban!" Answer me!

Still no response. He offered his trilling sound and this brought a clear comeback.

A lilting whistle, pleasant but eerie, traced the air, leaving a haunting echo after it died away.

Picking up his pace, Doc Savage marched in its certain direction. Chicahua followed, wordless and alert, machete swinging in one fist.

Soon, they broke into a clearing, a space of some thirty yards in circumference where the jungle seemed to hold back.

In the center of the clearing stood an upright thing of fabulous construction. Generally, it resembled a man-sized ostrich—but one assembled out of an avian nightmare in which an ostrich body, eagle talons and chicken legs had been scavenged. The long, narrow face brought to mind a cross between a lizard and a monkey, but was neither.

Ebony of plumage, crisscrossed by haphazard scarlet slashes, it stood on two scaly bird-form feet. Deep violet eyes regarded him with a wise intelligence.

Doc studied the strangely-still thing. He realized that it was some species of feathered dinosaur that science had yet to describe, or categorize. In its unwinking sapphire eyes lay a cold, calculating intelligence. Doc began to suspect that this might be one of the slasher pack leaders Penjaga had called a deathrunner.

This creature greatly resembled a slasher, but looked more powerful, and differed in other anatomical details. Its lower jaw was more pronounced and sported a tuft resembling a rough beard. But the eyes were the thing that was most different. Unlike the slasher's orbs, which were placed further apart in the manner of a bird or a reptile, these were set well forward, staring with a cold sapphire malignancy.

It made no move, offered no threat, so Doc began to circle it warily.

Closer and closer, they got to it. Still it stood rooted, as if in fear.

One three-clawed hand slowly lifted, displaying a sharp set of talons. The claw scissored open, but otherwise the creature stood rooted in place.

Then, the thing's powerful jaw parted, displaying vicious yellow-ivory teeth and a thin black tongue.

Out of that aperture came the whistling that had seemed so human.

A rustling of feathers erupted all about—and suddenly the sky was filled with more of the scaly plumed things!

The slashers descended in a mass, landing on the outer perimeter of the clearing.

Doc Savage had the eerie feeling that he had fallen into a clever trap within a trap, conceived and executed by a creature of near-human intellect.

His trilling was yanked out of him, unbidden.

And from the scarlet throat of the creature, came an answering whistling, beautifully half-human, but also menacing in its cool superiority.

As one, the nightmare flock advanced on him.

Chapter XXX

DOC SAVAGE COCKED his Colt .45 automatic and whirled on the nearest slasher, a stork-like monstrosity plumed like a tropical macaw.

The weapon convulsed in his steady hand, spouting saffron tongues of flame. Three smoking cartridges spat from the jerking receiver.

The slasher was knocked off its spindly bird-like legs and gave a screech of half-human horror.

The others charged in, screaming rage, hot orange eyes ablaze.

Doc swung around and knocked another off its legs, finishing it off with a single blunt bullet to the skull.

Chicahua was busy with his sturdy blowgun. Unfortunately, it proved ineffective. The poisoned darts had no immediate effect on his thick-hided assailant.

Doc had to deal with that one, too. He fired once, clipping a talon off an outstretched limb, then his gun ran empty.

Stepping in, machete in hand, Chicahua began hacking furiously, removing one arm and then parrying the other talon with the flat of his blade. Twisting and advancing, he maneuvered until he was in a position to strike a decisive blow.

A ferocious downward slice removed the upper and lower jaws of the thing, maiming its face horribly. Emitting weird strangled cries, it fled.

Others of the nightmarish pack hesitated, colorful eyes glaring. Then, they began creeping ahead on their raptor-like bird feet, stepping as turkeys do.

From somewhere close, a voice called.

"You! Kendra's boy!"

Doc searched his surroundings.

Up in a tree limb, half concealed, stood a man so tall he seemed unreal.

White was the color of his long hair and bushy beard. Sunlight filtering through the overarching canopy made his skin gleam as copper as a Red Indian. One cat-yellow eye winked at him mischievously.

"I mean you. Take to the trees! You can't fight them all."

Reversing course, Doc seized Chicahua by one arm, and flung them both in the direction of the sheltering forest.

The slashers pursued them. Some spread scaly arms and lifted off the ground, gliding short distances. The sapphire-eyed deathrunner remained behind, like a general calmly observing its troops, confident in the outcome of battle.

Doc proved faster than the nearest attackers. He found the base of the tree from which the call had come and pushed Chicahua ahead of him.

Chicahua grabbed the bole and began shinnying up it, eyes wide, broad face twisted in horror.

Doc followed him up, pausing only once to break off a stout branch and fling it at the head of the first slasher who reached the spot.

The thing grabbed the branch in its strong jaws, shook it violently and snapped it in two, like an angry chicken.

A cluster of them stood stamping at the tree roots, stretching angry arms, but otherwise acting helpless in a frustrated way.

Doc realized that they could not fly in the manner of birds, but only glide if they found a perch of sufficient height from which to launch themselves. Nor could they climb, it seemed.

Reaching a high vantage point, Doc looked for the copper-skinned wild man who had called him "Kendra's boy."

There was no sign of the hirsute apparition. Only then did it register on Doc's quieting mind that his mother had been named Kendra.

"Father!" he called. "Father? *Grandfather!*"

The buzz and drone of jungle insects was his only answer....

DOC SAVAGE motioned for Chicahua to follow him. They began working along the branches, farther inland where the weird slashers could not easily follow.

The burly Mayan was good at tree-work as he was in his forest craft. He almost kept up with the agile bronze man.

Doc had no clear objective in mind; only to reach safety, a place from which to take stock of the situation.

Reflecting upon the slasher ambush, he realized that his father had not fallen prey to any of those insane creatures. There had been no blood on the ground, or smeared on their claws or snouts. That much was a comfort. Cold comfort, perhaps. But it gave hope that his father yet lived.

Farther along, Doc spotted a glint of metal in the tree. It was dull, but metal nevertheless.

Going in that direction, moving from springy branch to springy branch, he discovered the object.

It was his Annihilator! Someone had left it there, wedged in the crook of a forked branch, its lanyard still clinging to it.

Slinging it over his shoulder, Doc waited for Chicahua to catch up, then pointed due west.

They made good time—or would have if they knew where they were going.

A fresh slash in a tree suggested a knife cut. Another farther along, caused Doc to alter direction.

Following the slashes—some of which dripped sap—Doc worked his way deeper into the jungle. He felt that he was getting somewhere. But in the back of his mind was the fear that the slashes had been made by the feathered enemies, and that he was being led into a treetop trap.

So when he came within sight of the tree house, the bronze giant was vastly more relieved than he was surprised.

The thing had been built by men. It sprawled across the adjoining tree, and boasted three stories. Many months had been spent in creating it. Ratlines and other bracing cords made it look vaguely like a ship.

Doc approached to within hailing distance and cupped huge hands before his mouth.

"Ahoy the tree house!"

"Ahoy back," called an unfamiliar voice.

"Who are you?"

"Have you not figured that out?" returned the age-cracked voice.

Suddenly, the welcome tones of Captain Clark Savage issued forth.

"Never mind all that now. Permission to come aboard is hereby granted. We are about to enjoy lunch."

"Father!" breathed Doc in a tone so low even Chicahua did not detect it.

They picked their way along the fat supporting branches to the vast mansion in the trees.

THERE were no doors, of course. Everything was open to the air, although there was flooring, and roofing after a fashion. Most of it had been constructed of split bamboo—decking, uprights and, where it was practical, walls. Dried palm fronds constituted the thatching.

In a central chamber—if it could have been styled that— Captain Savage stood over a rough-hewn table set low like a Japanese taboret, around which several cushions were arrayed.

Captain Savage reposed on one and called over, "Come! You are just in time."

Doc approached, Chicahua hanging cautiously behind.

"Permit me to introduce to you your illustrious paternal grandfather, my immediate forebear, Captain Stormalong Savage," the elder Savage said grandly.

The coppery old man of the trees, his face a profusion of white whiskers, eyed Doc Savage with orbs that were a startling yellow hue.

"I see you found your Gatling gun," he remarked.

"Yes, thank you."

Doc did not know what to say to the old man. He was not eight foot tall, as Chicahua had described. But he was easily seven. Doc had never met a man so vertical in his construction. He was garbed in a nautical uniform of an earlier day, patched in places with exotic hides. Incongruously, he was barefoot.

"I can see how the legend of Captain Stormalong got started," said Doc.

"See if you can surround some of this food," grunted Doc's father.

Doc took a seat, as did Chicahua, who remained mute throughout. The food consisted of fruit and vegetables, many unfamiliar to Doc, who thought that he had sampled every exotic viand from armadillo meat to turtle stew.

There were portions of white meat in the center of each plate. They steamed aromatically.

Doc took some into his mouth, and chewed it experimentally. He liked what he found.

"What is this?"

"What does it taste like?" returned Stormalong.

"It reminds me of coconut, except that it is plainly meat."

Captain Savage said dryly, "And what do you deduce from that datum, Mister Holmes?"

Doc considered briefly. "Coconut crab."

Old Stormy grinned in his beard. "They taste like their diets, do they not?"

"They do," agreed Doc, taking more.

They consumed their food in silence for a while, as the very hungry often do.

Finally, Doc made conversation. "This place would impress Tarzan of the Apes."

A feline yellow eye regarded him quizzically. "Eh?"

Captain Savage explained, "A literary allusion that I fear is lost upon you, father, having been marooned here these many long years."

"Oh. I myself am partial to Shakespeare."

Doc started. Did his father not say those very words to him? Well, the apple did not fall far from the tree, usually.

Captain Savage spoke up. "My son, your grandson, has a taste for cheap popular fiction."

"I seem to recall your addiction to dime novels far back," Old Stormy remarked.

"A youthful one, which I have long since put behind me."

Stormalong Savage bent a bright eye on Doc. "Did you ever hear of Nick Carter, young man?"

"Yes."

"That was your father's idol when he was not much younger than you are today."

"I would prefer to speak of the present, if all are agreeable," inserted Captain Savage with a thin trace of stiffness.

"Very well. You may begin by informing me how you discovered my hiding place," invited Stormalong.

"It is very simple, Father," returned Captain Savage. "I found the map you had secreted in the lower mast of the *Courser*."

"That map," said Old Stormy, "was all but useless."

"I will not quibble with that assessment, for most of it was obliterated. But it showed a prominence I dubbed Death's Head. We searched for that."

"And found it, I see," muttered Stormalong Savage. "I rue that day I set eyes upon its deathly countenance."

They finished their meal, which they washed down with

coconut milk, served in their half shells.

"How did you come here, Grandfather?" asked Doc, getting straight to the point.

"How I came and why I stay, may be two entirely different things."

"I would like to hear both."

"As would I," added Captain Savage.

"It was when I was among the Malays that I heard talk of an uncharted island they called *Tengkorak Pulao.*"

"Skull Island," translated Doc.

"Mount Skull Island, as the Atu natives term it. My days carrying cargo from San Francisco to Siam were behind me. The day of the clipper ship was over, but I still had the *Courser,* and the will to profit from it. You see, unlike your father, who liked to gallivant around the world, doing good deeds and not profiting by them, I was a merchant man by temperament. I sought treasure."

Doc nodded, fascinated.

"What I heard of Skull Island intrigued me. A place where animals dwelled who no longer lived. Imagine the price some specimens would fetch. But when I made landfall, I discovered greater treasure than those uncatchable beasts."

"Such as?"

"Have you not seen them for yourself?"

"If we have," interjected Captain Savage, "we have not recognized them."

"The jungle, man. The trees! Trees such as modern man has never felled. Teaks. Hardwoods. *Et cetera.* Man alive! Magnificent timber that, if carried off as cargo, a canny soul might name his own price."

"I see," said Doc, slightly disappointed. He had expected an explanation more romantic than valuable hardwoods.

"I suspect that you do not have all of my blood," clucked Old Stormy.

Clark Savage, Senior, offered, "He has a glint of your eyes, Father. And the Savage wanderlust, without a doubt."

"He reminds me more of his mother than he does you."

"Did you know my mother?" Doc asked quietly.

"Let us stick to the point," suggested Captain Savage.

Old Stormy said, "I met your mother only once, then I saw her no more. Alas."

A moment of awkward silence ensued.

Captain Savage picked up the dropped threads of the conversation.

"How did you come to be marooned here?"

"In the beginning of my great misadventure, I was not. My crew and I decided to study this island, the better to decide what to take from it. The days stretched to weeks, then to months. Do you know that there are the ruins of a high civilization not far from here?"

"We saw the wall," said Doc.

"That is but one manifestation. I refer to a ruined city, now crumbling to blocks. A mighty nation formerly resided here once, so long ago that one can scarcely credit the antiquity of it."

Doc perked up. "What happened to them?"

"What happened to Egypt? To Rome? They fell into decline, entered into internal disagreements, and began warring amongst themselves. The baser remnants—the Atu— dwell on the other side of the great wall. For generations, the high-minded survivors of the Tagu eked out an existence on this side, called the Plateau of the Skull."

"They made that mountain?"

"Their ancestors took what had been a suggestion of a skull and made it sharp and definite, carving where they could and employing the same durable mortar that faces the great wall on both sides. Passing time has eroded it."

"Why did they build the fantastic wall?" asked Captain

Savage.

Stormalong Savage was a long time answering that question. For a while it seemed that he wouldn't.

"Kong, I imagine."

"I have heard of Kong," said Doc. "I met an old woman who called herself Penjaga the Keeper."

"I know her. She lives atop the gate. Penjaga is the last of the Tagu, custodian of her race's knowledge and history. She knows all the stories, but most of all she knows the story of Kong."

"I have difficulty imagining a gorilla as large as a small mountain," Captain Savage said frankly.

Stormalong again fell into silence.

"Kong is the reason I am still here on Skull Island ," he finally offered.

"Go on," prompted Doc.

"I have told you that I sought treasure, but I never carried any out. Not a splinter of wood, or pinch of minerals. All because of Kong."

They waited for him to continue.

"We had been on Skull Island more than a year before it happened. I will not tell you the full story now. It would take too long. But Kong had run afoul of a raiding party of head-hunters."

"Dyaks?"

Stormalong nodded, fingering his beard. "Sea Dyaks. Nasty fellows. They were out headhunting. I do not know how they came all this way from Borneo. Blown off course, or responding to some ancestral call, I suppose. But they arrived one day. War broke out between the Dyaks and myself."

Lowering his cracked voice, Stormalong fixed them with his amber orbs.

"In the middle of that war came Kong. The Dyaks had taken for a trophy the head of a young female of Kong's line. The only other survivor of his mighty line, to the best of my knowledge. This enraged the beast-god, who then went on a rampage, when he discovered the pitiful, desecrated remains."

Doc advised, "Dyaks have returned to Skull Island. They have brought back that ape skull. Now they want the head of Kong."

"Fools. Sheer folly. But to my story. In his understandable rage, Kong came upon the *Courser* lying at anchor. He knew ships. Others had been to the island before us. Pirates, I imagine. Kong knew that ships such as the *Courser* carried white men to Skull Island and white men usually brought death and destruction to his domain. The Atu opened the gates of the great wall to permit him to reach Skull Lagoon. So Kong waded out to the *Courser* one day when my crew and I were reconnoitering the plateau. We saw him from an escarpment. He strode out into the water and snapped the masts off the *Courser* as easily as you and I break tree branches. The sails were naturally furled. He tossed the masts into the lagoon and gave the dear old lady a shove that sent her out to sea, alas—and away from my sight forever."

Captain Savage said solemnly, "We found her adrift last month. I regret to inform you that we thought it best to scuttle the *Courser*."

A gloomy silence fell over the table. No one spoke.

"After that," resumed Stormalong Savage, "we were forced to dwell here, awaiting the day of rescue when a ship blundered along, by accident or design."

Captain Savage laid a gentle hand upon his father's amazingly long arm. "Well, we have found you and we will carry you back to civilization as soon as you are ready to depart."

Stormalong looked into the eyes of his son. A curiously sad light leapt into them.

"I do not know about that, for I doubt that I will ever leave Skull Mountain Island."

Chapter XXXI

CAPTAIN SAVAGE SPOKE gently to his father.
"I have my schooner anchored not far off. Of course you may come along with us."

"I know that I can," countered Stormalong Savage. "But I do not think that I will. For I have lost my ship. I am a captain with neither vessel, nor crew. At my age, where will I find another, and what would I do with it?"

No one had a good answer for that.

"Excuse me," inserted Doc, "but you have been marooned here for some twelve years. Where is your crew?"

"Dead. All dead. Their ready luck ran out."

Doc pressed the point. "When we discovered the *Courser* drifting on the high seas, there were signs that heads had been taken from crewmen not long before."

"When Kong consigned the *Courser* to the mercy of the Indian Ocean, I had men posted on board, on guard." Stormalong sighed deeply. "What became of them, I do not know."

"Twelve years is a long time," said Doc.

"Kong separated the *Courser* from her captain less than four years ago," Stormalong corrected.

Captain Savage muttered, "It is possible for a crew of men to survive on the open seas for that length of time adrift and without the means to make for land, surviving on rain water and such fish as they could catch."

"Only to fall victim to marauding Sea Dyaks," added Doc.

224

"The Indian Ocean is so vast that one could drift for years before encountering another vessel, except by chance."

Captain Savage nodded. "Far-fetched, but we are in a far-fetched predicament." Turning to his father, he said, "Why did you not leave Skull Island before the loss of the *Courser*? I count eight years."

"I did not leave Skull Island," said Stormalong, "for a very sound and simple reason. I could not. For I was a prisoner of Kong, high in his lair on Mount Skull."

"Prisoner! For what purpose, father?"

"As near as I could make out, I was his plaything. Kong's sole friend and companion. This was after the loss of the female ape that had been his only solace in life."

"The brute treated you well?"

"He fed me. Kept me. Protected me. But it was a very long time before I could escape his lair. Most of my men perished attempting to succor me. Alas."

This sacrifice was accorded the silence it deserved.

"And that is the sad story of the last of the *Courser*," said Stormalong, fingering his profuse beard.

"You have not told how you escaped," reminded Doc.

"Oh, that. It seems that the natives on the other side of the island like to sacrifice maidens to Kong every so often. It was during the ceremony that Kong took me up in his hairy hand and bore me to the altar on the plain where the poor unfortunate girl had been shackled."

"I saw that altar," offered Doc. "And deduced its purpose in part."

"In picking up the maiden," continued Stormalong, "Kong set me in a tree, and from this I escaped. I imagine the old brute thought after so long in his company I had no impulse for freedom. But escape I did. He has been searching for me ever since. But he has never found me. I constructed this tree mansion over the years. It has served me well. Kong cannot enter this portion of the forest. It is too thickly treed and defeats him every time he tries. But I suspect that he knows I dwell here. I do not think he has forgotten me."

"I see," said Captain Savage.

"Tell us about the slashers, Grandfather."

"Vicious beasts. The very devil on bird-of-prey legs. I am reminded of the mythical wyvern and cockatrice, which combined the scaly bodies of dragons with the attributes of the bird family. Slashers run in packs, like hyena or wolves. Everything that walks is their prey. Man. Beasts. I have seen them lay open many a larger creature with their hooked talons."

"They seemed intelligent. They whistled in response to my call."

Stormalong pursed his lips and gave a credible slasher whistle. "Like this?"

"Exactly like that," said Doc, slightly startled.

"They learned to whistle from me. That is my sound signal. They merely mimic it."

"So who was whistling in response to my call?" asked Doc.

"At first, it was I. It was a little game, you see. I came upon your Indian and distracted him, so I could approach your father, and surprise him."

Captain Savage exploded. "And I *was* surprised. No, astonished! I make no bones about it, gentlemen."

Stormalong vented a hearty laugh that shook his long, bony frame.

"I used to surprise your father when he was young in just such a way. Well, I came upon him and he was so shocked he was speechless. When he told me that you were up that tree, I suggested a prank. He went along with it willingly."

Doc Savage eyed his father. The senior Savage—senior no longer—averted his gaze.

"So when you landed and gave forth your musical call, I returned with one of my own. But the slashers were about. One heard me—a Jabberwock!"

"Jabberwock?" asked Doc.

Stormalong laughed. "So I named them, with due apologies to Lewis Carroll. Penjaga told me that the Tagu called them deathrunners. That was the one you discovered standing by his lonesome. The sapphire-eyed devil that whistled. He was luring you into a snare, you see. You can always tell a deathrunner from a mere slasher by the deep violet hue of their eyes. Also, by the bloody streaks amid their dark plumage."

"I suspected as much," said Doc. "But you make them sound intelligent."

"The pack leaders are. The slashers simply follow the death-runners. When I realized your peril, I called out to you. It was too dangerous to jump into the fray, as I had no weapon other than your strange gun, which I did not know how to operate."

Doc Savage drank it all in.

"I thank you for the timely rescue," he said simply.

"It was the least I could do for my own flesh and blood. I am only sorry that our harmless prank turned into such a travesty."

"It was not your fault," said Doc graciously.

"Kind of you to say so, Clark. May I call you Clark?"

"I go by Doc these days."

"Doc. Splendid name! I never fancied the name Clark. Too bookish. My late wife forced it upon me, in naming your father. I wanted to call him—now what was it? Oh, yes. Nicholas."

"I would have enjoyed being known as Nicholas," admitted Clark Savage, Senior.

"I never told you that. But when I caught you reading Nick Carter, I could not bear to hold it against you."

"Well and good," said Captain Savage, seeming uncomfortable with the past.

Stormalong looked around the table. "Well, now that we have eaten our fill, what is there to do but discuss old times?"

Doc Savage interrupted, "I would like to see Kong with my

own eyes."

"That would not be wise," warned Stormalong. "He would no doubt endeavor to make a captive of you, as he did me."

"Why do you say that?" asked Captain Savage sharply.

"If and when you see Kong with your own eyes," snapped Old Stormy, "you will instantly know the why of it."

And that was all Stormalong Savage would say on the subject.

Chapter XXXII

THEIR REPAST CONCLUDED, they were given a
tour of the tree house of Stormalong Savage. They climbed
the spidery ratlines to reach its various platforms.

It began reminding Doc of a magnificent ship of the trees,
with clear analogues to decks and holds and other, similar
structures. There was a hammock for sleeping strung between
fat boughs, just as ocean-going sailors once slept in similar
arrangements in their crew quarters. For shade and privacy,
enormous ribbed sails such as decorated the Dimetrodon dinosaur back in the Jurassic were erected in strategic spots.

Even the thick leaves in the branches suggested natural sails
and rigging. It was like some jungle fantasy out of Kipling or
Haggard.

"Built by hand, every bit of it," the grizzled old sea captain
said proudly. "Of course, it was engineered for a crew of men.
Sadly, it houses but one."

"It is very much like a jungle home fit for a king," agreed
Captain Savage, showing pride in his father's handiwork.

Stormalong grinned widely. "It is a refuge from wild creatures.
For as you have already discovered, Skull Island is a relic of
antiquity. I have come to call it the Island that Almighty God
Forgot."

"There is no doubt of that," assayed Captain Savage. "I, too,
pronounced it thus—in nearly identical terms."

There were few conveniences, of course. Vines weighted with

blocks of wood served as simple devices with which to reach the ground. One had only to toss one off a platform constructed for that purpose and slip down to the ground. Clambering back up, one withdrew the line for storage and to confound any climbing creature, human or not.

Studying it all, Doc was reminded of the story of the Karo-Batak tribe, who, having lost their sea, kept their seafaring traditions alive in their architecture. But he thought better than to bring up the comparison.

Clark Savage, Senior, turned to his father. "Captain, I suggest that we repair to my ship, if for no other reason than to give you the opportunity to stand on a sound deck once more."

The grizzled old man looked sad of eye. He was a long time answering.

"Swear to me on your family honor that once I have done so, you will not sail off with me as unwilling supercargo."

"I so swear," Captain Savage said forlornly.

They shook hands and it was done.

Dropping lines over the edge, they slid down, all four of them. Chicahua insisted upon going first to face any danger, his broad machete lifted.

Striking out for the western shore of Skull Island, they began the long march to the sea. Chicahua led the way, swinging his machete as if he ached to encounter marauding Dyaks.

Doc Savage again took the lead, his Annihilator submachine gun cradled easily in his great arms. He seemed not to tire.

"I do not recognize that uniform, sir," Stormalong Savage said after a while, eyeing Doc.

"United States Army, lately separated. We have just fought a world war—the first in history."

"I trust our side emerged victorious."

"It did, sir."

"Bully!"

Stormalong Savage had a coil of plaited rope tied to his waist, from which hung three black balls.

"What is that, may I ask, Father?" began Captain Savage.

"I spent some time in the Argentine, as you might recollect. I there began practicing with the bolas. I find it among the most useful devices imaginable for whatever one encounters in these horrid woods."

As they walked along, Captain Savage paused once in a while to whistle.

"What is the purpose of that?" asked Clark Savage, Senior.

"If there are slashers about, it flushes them out of conceal-ment, the better to dispense with them."

"If there were slashers about," interposed Doc, "I would have detected them."

Old Stormy cocked a curious eyebrow. "By what means?"

"My son has possession of the most extraordinary olfactory receptors," supplied Captain Savage. "He means that he would smell them."

"He has taken after his grandfather, I see," said Stormalong, adding for Doc's benefit, "Slashers smell of carrion."

"I know," said Doc. "I committed their repulsive odor to memory on my first encounter with them."

"My son has the benefit of an unusual and extended educa-tion," said Captain Savage proudly.

"I can see that he has reached his majority a splendid spec-imen of manhood," agreed the most senior Savage.

"Actually, he is short by many months of that milestone. Over a year, in actual fact."

"Indeed! He looks to be a man of maturity."

"He is."

Doc kept silent. He was unaccustomed to being spoken of in such a way. He remained intent along the way ahead, absorb-ing everything he could. The presence of Stormalong was a distraction, however. He was very curious about his legendary grandfather. What conversation passed between the storied clipper captain and his own father was proving to be very revealing.

THEY passed through the jungle without encountering anything more noteworthy than the insects which seemed to belong to another time. Cockroaches as large as a thumb. Undulating millipedes longer than many snakes. Whenever anything with wings whisked by, they started, freezing in their tracks, thinking of Dyak darts.

The heat of the day was mounting and it made the going arduous in its way. They kept close to the riverbank, beside which cattails and tall thistles waved lazily.

"Is this channel dignified by a name?" asked Captain Savage.

"We call it the River of No Return," Stormalong replied.

Captain Savage grunted, "A fitting, but unfortunate name."

"It flows down from Mount Skull. I have often thought of it as a modern River Styx, just as I have sometimes imagined Kong to be a primitive Zeus holding sway over his fearful domain like the Monarch of the Gods looking down from lofty Mount Olympus."

Hearing this fanciful account, Doc and his father exchanged concerned glances.

They began wondering if Kong was real, after all....

Coming to the savannah-like plain, they turned toward the water. In the distance, a line of giant turtles was making its ponderous way. Doc and his father were struck by the enormous parrot-like beaks that made their jaws resemble powerful ploughs.

"You say that the war party of Sea Dyaks is in search of Kong?" asked Stormalong Savage of his son.

"Indeed. They seem fixated upon him."

"Then they are mad. Kong is too mighty for any man to best. He is a veritable Titan of old. Elemental as Thor, the thunderer."

"I would like to take the measure of this gorilla with my own eyes," Captain Savage said with a trace of skepticism.

Stormalong grinned in his bushy beard. "Oh, Kong is no gorilla. He is much too intelligent. Nor is he built along the lines of an African gorilla, especially. For one thing, his legs are too long. For another, he walks upright much of the time."

Captain Savage grunted. "Then I am doubly interested in this beast. I have been taught that man alone walks upright."

"Kong is unlike anything man—civilized man—has ever encountered. I believe him to be the last of his race. He has no mate, nor any prospects of one. His passing would be a tragedy of the highest order."

Doc interposed, "You speak of Kong as if he were human."

Old Stormy smiled thinly. "Kong and I spent many long years in each other's company. A bond was formed. We have looked into one another's souls. Such things do not fade. If I did not believe in his supreme might, I would be leading the charge to his rescue. But Kong does not need our puny assistance. He can handle the Sea Dyaks himself. I would stake my life upon it."

"You make him sound like a virtual demi-god..." Captain Savage asserted.

"He is. Kong is the absolute monarch of all that you see about you."

Passing safely through the grassland, they came to the ring of bamboo and palm forest that edged this side of Skull Island. It was impossibly green, sunlight picking out innumerable shades of verdigris.

"What is that smoke?" asked Captain Savage, his sharp golden eyes going to Skull Mountain's stern summit.

Doc spoke up. "The Dyaks have torched the lair of Kong, in the hope of denying him refuge."

Old Stormy shook his white head. "In that they are truly mad. For they will only enrage him. The braincase—if you will—of Mount Skull is a hollow chamber in which Kong keeps those things dear to him. His keepsakes."

"Such as?"

"The bodies of the maidens that have been sacrificed to him."

"Really?"

"Yes. He does not kill or eat them, although they perish in time."

"Yet he spared you?" said Doc.

"And the reason for that, as I have told you, is a thing you will realize should the fateful encounter ever come," pronounced Old Stormy loftily.

"Perhaps he was intrigued by your long white beard," suggested Captain Savage.

"Perhaps Kong was. You will have to ask him, if you ever obtain the opportunity." And Captain Savage authored a secretive laugh that made Doc Savage and his father exchange fresh glances of worry. Their meeting eyes seemed to ask, *Is he mad?*

In the jungle, they encountered nothing more remarkable than something that resembled a nest of ostrich eggs.

"I see that you could not have lacked for variety in your diet, Grandfather," noted Doc.

"Game is plentiful, if unusual. Smaller dinosaurs taste rather like game fowl. I have yet to encounter an ox or beef suitable for a steak. But I have made do."

As they passed the nest, Doc noticed one of the eggs was broken. An oversized rat had inserted its long snout into the cracks and was taking nourishment.

"That is the first mammal I have seen on this island," remarked Doc.

"They came with the ships," explained Stormalong. "They like the eggs the dinosaurs lay. If they keep up their raiding, before long the dinosaurs will be no more."

"Ironic," commented Captain Savage. "A mighty population of monsters, felled by low vermin."

"It is the way of the world," clucked Old Stormy.

They continued their trek, watchful for danger. But even four pairs of eyes could not look in all directions continually.

Something high in a tree shook the top of a palm, taking them by surprise. They froze in their tracks, forming a back-to-back circle.

The shaggy palm shook again, like an angry fist of green.

Carefully, Doc approached, Annihilator muzzle raised high.

"'Ware, son," warned Captain Savage.

Doc eased up to the palm, which was shivering madly now.

Another one also began quivering. Then on the opposite side, still another. It was as if the groves of coconut palms were being shaken by a mighty wind. But here was no wind. Only a sultry sea breeze.

Suddenly, purple-blue shapes began scrambling down from the shivering crowns.

At first, their striking size and coloration made Doc think slashers were dropping from the sky. But these were not feathered, but armored monsters.

For the palms were raining gigantic coconut crabs!

They scuttled down with the single-minded determination of mad things, using their pointed middle legs to clasp the boles. Each one was the size of a full-grown man.

Doc elevated his submachine gun, then realized it would be wasteful in this encounter. Too many bullets would be expended too rapidly, so he dropped it.

Doc had reloaded his Colt and this came up in his fist. Captain Savage had his revolver out and was already picking a target.

They began firing at the descending monsters.

The bullets, aimed true, split carapaces and shot off waving claws. But the coconut crowns continued to shake with fury. Soon there were more of the crab monsters than they could count.

Emptying his Colt, Doc reholstered his weapon and brought up the Annihilator. He drew back on the charging handle.

Pointing the muzzle at one crab midway down a bole, he squeezed the firing lever. The weapon shook and stuttered. Only the merest touch of the trigger, and the crab creature flew to meaty pieces, the palm trunk sheared along its width. It toppled with a splintering groan.

Turning, Doc aimed at a crab now on the ground and charging forward with remarkable speed, despite its massive foreclaws and its clumsy construction.

This, too, flew apart before a storm of .45 caliber lead.

Doc swept about the clearing, seeking another.

Two more were down on the jungle floor and slipping along the ground, looking like horny tarantulas constructed of purple shell.

Doc emptied the last of the big ammunition drum he had fashioned into them with the inevitable result. The substance of their inner matter splashed the surroundings.

The drum was now empty. Doc extracted it, hastily inserting the magazine clip, worrying that he had already wasted too much precious ammunition.

Once he had it firmly in place, Doc yanked the charging handle. Aiming for the handiest target, he pulled the trigger. Nothing happened! The weapon had jammed!

Hastily, Doc switched back to his automatic, reloading with a spare clip, resumed blazing away. He wasted no more rounds. Each target took only one slug to stop dead.

Doc looked about him. Stormalong Savage was leaping about like a man possessed, bolas whirling madly, pummeling into ruin any lobster-like crustacean he could smash. His father had accounted for two of the horny blue brutes. But more of the many-legged monsters were coming.

There seemed to be an endless supply of them. They emerged from the jungle, wriggling eyestalks regarding them with sullen interest.

Flinging his battered bolas at a descending crab, Stormalong managed to wrap one flailing monster around a palm trunk.

Turning, the spindly giant barked, "Too many to bother with. But follow me. I know of a way to defeat the things."

Having no other reasonable course of action, they followed the nimble old man, whose long whiskers flapped in his hurry.

Stormalong Savage soon led them to an azure pool known as a blue hole.

He waved them along. "Into the water. Come."

Old Stormy leaped in first. Doc's father followed, then Chicahua the Mayan. Doc dropped such weapons on the dirt that could be recovered later, because once immersed in water, they would be useless.

Doc was the last to go. He turned to see a small horde of crabs ambling along like beetles out of prehistory. They seemed determined to attack.

Doc paused to charge his lungs with air as much as he dared. He hoped that the passage would not be a long one. He felt a stab of disquiet about entering the pool, but charged that off to childhood memories of his first forced swim.

PLUNGING into the pool, Doc found it cool, but not cold. This was a surprise. Almost immediately, the light became a dim cobalt, then it shaded to a darker hue like the night sky just after dusk.

He spotted the flashing limbs of others. Stormalong seemed to be leading them.

The bronze giant swam by kicking his feet and propelling himself with great sweeping motions of his hands.

They passed through a narrow dark tunnel of what felt like volcanic basalt, into a wider passage which became very dark before it shaded into a pale blue that grew brighter and brighter with each lively kick of his feet. A light source ahead!

Abruptly, a hazy glow showed over his head, and Doc realized he was alone in the water. He swam upward. His smooth head broke the surface, golden eyes searching.

Overhead, light was splintering down from a narrow crack

high in a rocky ceiling far above. This illuminated the place.

The others had already pulled themselves onto a subterranean rock ledge, just above.

"Underground grotto," explained Stormalong, grinning down at Doc.

The bronze man climbed up. Taking a seat beside the others, he saw that the chamber was a natural one, but also that there appeared to be no other exit than the one they had employed in their escape.

"I imagine a return by this route is out of the question," said Captain Savage.

Stormalong said, "Not if the creatures run true to form. For they are likely to follow us."

It was true. Before long, a purplish monster appeared in the water, scuttling along the floor of the underground river tunnel.

It reached the edge of the ledge, where the tunnel stopped, and seemed at a loss for what to do next.

Others promptly arrived. They, too, began to skitter about aimlessly.

"They appear dumbfounded by the barrier," commented Captain Savage.

Stormalong smiled mischievously. "The ledge forms a lip. They cannot climb it, even if they could see us. Which they cannot."

"So what do we do?" asked Doc.

"We wait patiently."

"For what do we wait?" asked Captain Savage with a trace of impatience.

"We wait for them to face their inevitable and unavoidable fate," said Stormalong Savage in an unconcerned tone of voice.

Chapter XXXIII

WHAT STORMALONG SAVAGE meant by waiting for the coconut crabs to face their fate was over an hour in revealing itself.

In the interim, an unceasing tide of the purplish-blue crustaceans arrived and began crawling atop one another. For a time, it seemed that they might by this ingenious method form an armored pyramid and, in this fashion, clamber atop one another until they reached the lip of the rocky ledge on which the Savages sat, with Chicahua the Mayan squinting stark-eyed beside them.

But that was not their intent. The truth was that the confused crabs were at a loss for a way out of their predicament. They began to panic. It showed in their flailing limbs, the manner of which their claws snipped blindly at nothing.

"The coconut crab is a distant relative of the hermit crab," Stormalong was saying to pass the time. "The hermit crab, as you may know, is perfectly at home in the water. These creatures are not. They are entirely terrestrial."

A gleam of understanding coming into his golden orbs, Captain Savage suddenly said, "I see it now! They cannot swim. They do not possess gills."

Stormalong fingered his beard. "Precisely. Even as we watch them flounder about, they are drowning."

"Remarkable," said Doc.

"Not really," returned Old Stormy dryly. "This is how I have caught many a meal. I merely lure one of these thieves into a pool and await his inevitable and lamentable demise." Stormalong chuckled deliciously. "Then he is mine."

"There are too many to eat," pointed out Doc.

"No matter," said Stormalong. "In another hour, it should be safe to exit the way we entered."

The hour came and went. By this time, the crabs had ceased their aimless panicky scuttling. Their feelers began to droop, the nervous snapping action of their foreclaws growing feeble.

Soon they were still, although some continued stirring longer than others.

During the wait, Doc Savage thought of a question to ask his father.

"Captain, I am still curious. How did you know that first robber crab we encountered was a juvenile? I studied it carefully, and failed to discern your reasoning."

Before Captain Savage could reply, Stormalong inserted a question.

"Why do you call your own flesh and blood by that honorific, Doc?"

Captain Savage interrupted this time. "It was at my insistence, Father. I thought it best to maintain shipboard discipline. Inasmuch as we are among family, I will temporarily suspend the requirement."

Old Stormy remarked, "I do not recall ever requiring that curious custom when you sojourned on the *Courser*, Clark."

There followed an uncomfortable silence.

Captain Savage cleared his throat and replied to Doc's question.

"The reason you failed to discover the truth was twofold. First, you observed carefully, but you did not investigate. Had you tested the carapace of the crustacean in question, you would have discovered its undeniable softness."

"*You* did not," Doc pointed out.

"Correct. I did not because I needed not. For I did not study the crab, but its surroundings. And do you know what I discovered?"

"No," Doc admitted.

"I discovered what you failed to perceive, that nearby lay a tortoise shell. If you knew the habits of your coconut crabs, you would know that juvenile specimens are compelled by the instinct of survival to carry about a protective coconut or snail shell they scavenge. This, to protect themselves from predators until such a time that their own natural shells harden in adulthood."

"As Holmes would say, 'Elementary,'" murmured Doc.

Captain Savage reminded, "'It is, of course, a trifle, but there is nothing so important as trifles.'"

"Are you quoting Doyle again, Father?"

"I am citing common sense," snapped Captain Savage. "Now, shall we endeavor to escape these dank confines?"

"Capital idea!" said Stormalong, who had been an interested listener throughout the exchange.

They returned to the water, swimming over the charnel house of dead crabs and feeling their way through the dark tunnel of rock until they saw the light streaming down from the opening that was the blue hole ahead. It was an easier passage on this second trip, the terror of the darkness and the unknown no longer before them.

Emerging onto dry land, they reclaimed their weapons and resumed their course.

DOC SAVAGE was concerned about the long treacherous climb back to the waiting *Orion*, but said nothing about it. They would confront that instance when they came to it. No sense in risking the possibility of objections beforehand.

As they moved from savannah to jungle, Doc observed his grandfather. He was still getting used to the man's freakish height. It was rare that the bronze giant had been put into the position where he had to look up into another man's eyes.

Otherwise, Stormalong seemed spry enough, and had adapted well to jungle living. He was more akin to Robinson Crusoe than Tarzan of the Apes, of course. It was remarkable how the old man had taken to the hardships and privations of his exile.

Or was it an exile?

"Grandfather," Doc asked, "how has the living been here?"

"I lack for nothing except human companionship. That, I get from Penjaga whenever our paths cross. They seldom do. She keeps to herself and I hold firmly to my own preserves."

"Are there others such as her?"

"No, she is the last of her people. A once proud and mighty race, as I understand it."

Captain Savage spoke up. "We should preserve a greater silence, lest we awaken predators."

They fell quiet, the wisdom of the Clark Savage, Senior's words being as pointed as his tone.

The path soon took them to the edge of Skull Island, and the sheer plutonic cliffs that looked down upon the anchored schooner.

AS they approached, an unease fell over them. Doc and his father were of one worry. Was the schooner still there?

Coming to the lip of the edge, they peered over.

Below, anchored amid the fangs of stony reef, sat the *Orion*, just as they had left her.

Stormalong Savage came up and peered downward, his wrinkled face breaking up into more lines and creases. His feline-yellow eyes blinked.

"I fear," he said, "as hardy as I may be, I am not up to such a descent."

"I will carry you, Grandfather," offered Doc, retrieving the grappling hook and line from the thorn bush where it had been secreted. He began readying the grapnel.

"You may call to mind the legendary Hercules," Old Stormy

observed, "but I weigh a steady two hundred pounds. And I would be a dead weight to you."

"I can manage it," said Doc. "First, I must climb down to that ledge below where I can set the grapple. The difficult part will be to negotiate the climb down these high rocks."

Captain Savage urged, "Go ahead, son."

Reversing himself, Doc began his descent.

The hours of marching and climbing had not impaired Doc's muscular strength. The bronze man went down the high rocks, finding hand- and foot-holds as if he possessed the many feet of a spider.

Reaching the ledge, Doc set the grapple's hooked flukes in place, then dropped the line. Giving both a series of testing tugs, he looked up.

Somewhere in the distance, a great roar came. It seemed to reverberate, a blast of sound that was repeated over and over.

Doc came scrambling up.

The other Savage men stood waiting, heads turning and eyes seeking the source of the roar.

"Could that be Kong?" asked Captain Savage.

Stormalong shook his white head, "No. Kong does not make such a distressful sound. That is a bellow of mingled fear and rage."

"I have never heard the like," returned the captain.

"How could you? If I am not mistaken, that is the cry of a bull Triceratops."

Doc became interested. "A Triceratops? I would like to see that."

"We have no time," snapped Captain Savage impatiently.

The sounds of bellowing distress came again and again.

"What could he be fighting?" wondered Doc. "I hear no other sounds."

Stormalong said firmly, "Men. He is fighting men."

"Dyaks then," snapped the captain. "And they are not far off.

Let us be about our own business."

Abruptly, Doc Savage seized his grandfather and shouldered him unceremoniously. The old man started to protest, but the indomitable power of the bronze man's massive muscles checked him.

Doc used his belt to tie Stormalong's wrists together, and with the man hanging off him like a long, loose-limbed ruck-sack, swung out into space.

Doc moved down the cliff side, ignoring his grandfather's protests that this was undignified.

Reaching the grappling hook, Doc took hold of the line, tested it again and seemed satisfied.

This time, he wrapped cloth around the line to protect his hands and went down the rope in a series of breathtaking spurts. The old man hung on, and was down on the deck of the schoo-ner before he realized that the trip was over.

The only difficulty they had was when Stormalong's dangling feet struck the deck before Doc did. They upset.

Doc quickly extricated himself, and untied the old man's wrists.

"That," the old clipper captain said, "was quite an adventure."

"Are you all right?"

A youthful grin split the bushy white beard. "Now that I stand on the deck of a good ship," said Stormalong happily, "I feel like Ahab."

They looked up.

Doc expected to see Captain Savage at the high point of the cliff face. But he was not there. Nor did his stern mustached face peer down from the high stony lip, as would be expected.

"Where has that youngster gone off to now?" Stormalong huffed.

Doc said, "He would not tarry. It is not like him."

"I fear that you do not know your father as well as I know my son, Doc. It is just like him to change his mind at the last minute."

Grasping the dangling cord, Doc said, "My concern is that Dyaks changed it for him."

Stormalong stopped him.

"Are you forgetting something?" he asked pointedly.

Doc looked momentarily blank, then comprehension dawned on his impassive features.

"Ammunition!"

Plunging below deck, the bronze man returned with every pocket bulging with .45 caliber cartridges for his Annihilator drum.

Doc began the difficult ascent anew, his face a bronze mask of muffled concern.

Chapter XXXIV

DOC SAVAGE WENT up the line in half the time of his first ascent.

He made his way to the grappling hook, and tore up the side of the upper cliff with such speed that he sent small stones tumbling down. There was no time to worry about that now. His grandfather could dodge them, if necessary.

Topping the cliff, Doc pulled himself the last few feet by grasping a tough bush and levering himself up on the high, rocky ramparts of Skull Island.

Of his father, there was no immediate sign. Doc took to tracking his spoor.

It was simple. Trampled grass was slowly straightening. His acute eyes picked up these minute movements, rather like the ticking of tiny green watch hands.

There were other tracks, too, Doc saw. Barefoot men. Some had missing toes. Dyaks. No question about it.

A few yards of tracking and the situation became clear. Hearing approaching men, Captain Savage and Chicahua made for the trees. Dyaks were hunting them. They were not yet prisoners.

No doubt this maneuver was calculated to lure the Dyak warriors away from the cliff edge, where they were certain to spot the *Orion* far below.

Doc followed them, Annihilator at the ready, its recharged magazine rattling with fresh cartridges.

246

After a time, the tracks ceased to be distinguishable.

Doc looked for other clues, such as tree bark snapped to point in a specific direction or knife hash-marks on the boles of trees. He found none, soon realized that his father dared not make any such signs, lest they alert the jungle-wise Dyaks to his moving presence.

Doc decided to take to the trees, hoping that their higher coigns of vantage would provide a better view of the situation.

Using his acute sense of smell, he attempted to locate the personal scents of his father and Chicahua.

Moving along tree branches carefully to keep from making sounds or disturbing roosting birds, Doc detected the metallic smell of blood. A lot of it. He moved in that direction, losing no stealth as he increased his speed.

But the only human odors he detected were those of the fish-eating Dyaks.

Doc maneuvered to avoid them, but not entirely. If they were tracking the others, he needed to keep them within easy reach.

Once, a tiny tick caused the bronze giant to freeze in place. His supernaturally acute hearing fixed the sudden sound as coming from behind him.

Flake-gold eyes questing about, Doc spotted the bright-feathered fletch of a Dyak dart. It had just struck a spot not far from him.

Using his ears, Doc could detect soft, stealthy footfalls. The Dyak hunter was creeping around the bases of nearby trees, looking upward, blowpipe carried in both hands. His long weapon and tall hornbill feathers gave away his position.

Carefully, Doc removed the splinter-like dart from a nearby branch and moved with infinite quiet until he had positioned himself above the searching man.

Sighting with one eye, Doc held the dart point downward over the Dyak's black-haired head. He let it drop.

The vicious thorn landed perfectly, seemed to become just another feather decoration in the man's head.

The unlucky Dyak gave out a yelp of surprise. The sound was swallowed by the creeper-laced trees.

The man reached up, and snapped the projection. When his eyes fell upon it, recognizing it as his own handiwork, he simply sat down on the dirt floor and waited to die. It took less than a minute. He made no other outcry. He simply fell over on his side and expelled a final gusty breath.

Doc moved on, taking even more care. He encountered no more searchers.

In an area clear of trees, Doc discovered the Triceratops that had bellowed so loudly not a half-hour before.

The great gray beast lay upon one side, looking from a distance like a rhinoceros, but many times larger than the greatest African specimen of rhino.

Doc descended and approached the immobile thing.

The creature was dead. Gore splattered the surrounding grass. There were other odors. As had been the case with other dinosaurs encountered on Skull Island, this monster displayed distinct differences from known specimens, suggesting an evolutionary path that diverged at some point in prehistory, producing dinosaur offshoots not recorded in the fossil record.

Slipping around to the head, Doc discovered that the three horns—one on the tip of its nose and the other matched pair over the eyes—had been cut away and carried off. As trophies, no doubt.

The bony crest or frill that marked the Triceratops had been left intact. No doubt it was too unwieldy to remove, never mind lug off as a war prize.

Doc examined the creature. Its skin was a thick, pebbled hide. Touching it, the bronze man found it bristly. Here and there, in the interstices between the alligator-like scales, protruded long Dyak darts. The thing had been brought down by a dozen poisoned darts.

Spears had been used to worry it as it laid dying, Doc saw. There were large holes in the softer parts. One eye had been gouged out. That cruel act perhaps had induced its demise.

Thinking of the potent Dyak darts, Doc Savage climbed the beast and, finding an opening, began to skin out a portion with his Bowie knife. It was no easy task. A man of lesser muscular strength could not have done it. But after several minutes of hard work, Doc had cut out a rectangular patch and peeled it off the red inner meat.

Carrying it to the ground, Doc worked it with his knife until he had a heavy poncho, which he draped over his body, using a hole he had cut in the center for his head.

No doubt he looked bizarre. But now he was armored against Dyak darts where no skin showed.

Flapping heavily, the bronze giant moved on.

DOC SAVAGE came to a mud hole, paused. Deciding that his bronze skin was too shiny with perspiration, he stopped and began to smear his face and hands with a brownish-gray slop that provided cover against the ever-changing jungle background.

Looking like some primeval colossus, Doc continued on his way. It was difficult to move with his usual stealth, the flapping Triceratops hide making silence all but impossible. But the advantage he hoped it would provide him against sudden ambush was too great to abandon.

Soon, Doc detected the odor of a Dyak man. He swept in a circle toward the scent, seeking to slip up on the man, while keeping out of his sight.

As Doc moved closer, he heard a familiar clacking and nattering sound—a coconut crab.

Doc came upon the dead Dyak lying sprawled under a palm tree, where he died. A crab had come upon him and was testing the body for reaction. No doubt the crab was considering whether to consume the cadaver.

Slipping up from the opposite side, Doc examined the body while the crab continued to worry the corpse, like a dog digging at something interesting.

Doc discovered a dart in the man's shoulder. It was no Dyak dart. It was shorter, and the fletching was different. The dart had come from Chicahua's blowgun.

Satisfied that he was searching in the correct direction, Doc moved on, leaving the crab to its carrion meal.

Cautiously, Doc Savage allowed his trilling to range free. The sound mingled with the jungle noises, blended with them, seemed to belong, yet added a distinct note that would carry.

Doc did this at intervals, trying to sound like some feathered songster passing from tree to tree, trilling when at rest. The bronze man had only the vaguest notion of what songbirds might populate Skull Island, but he imagined the Dyaks were no more knowledgeable than he in that regard.

After a time, there came an answering whistle.

Doc paused, rotated his head, trying to fix the return call.

Memory of the whistling deathrunner came rushing back to him. Its mimicry had been uncanny. He knew the whistling was not the work of Old Stormy this time. That was certain.

Would his father be making the sound? Or was this a cruel trick of the bird-like deathrunners?

Doc drew back the charging handle of the Annihilator, cocking it. He was ready either way.

WHEN it happened, the ambush managed to come from an unexpected direction.

Doc had been moving from tree to tree, using the thicker boles as added protection, when up ahead, several Dyaks popped out of concealment.

They had been crouched amid a profusion of ferns, and these shook not at all before they leaned out, protruding blowpipes making soft *puff-puff-puff* sounds.

Doc recoiled, but not before he could detect the distinct ticks of darts striking against his Triceratops-skin poncho.

Finding cover, Doc quickly checked his arms and legs. No

dart marks. None had embedded themselves into any part of his hide poncho, therefore they must have been repelled.

Doc decided that to unleash his submachine gun would be to draw more attention than he wanted.

So he laid the weapon down carefully, and showed himself.

A blowpipe puffed and Doc flashed back to cover.

The dart whisked by, missing completely. It knocked aside fluttering leaves, finally falling to earth somewhere.

Once more, Doc showed himself. But this time from the other side of the sheltering trees.

This brought two more blowpipes into play. Darts spurted.

One whisked by his arm. The other found lodgment in his chest—fortunately in the interstices of the poncho.

Picking up a rock, Doc lobbed it toward one clump of ferns.

The rock found a head. The resulting sound was very satisfying. A meaty thud, followed by a falling form.

Pitching toward another tree, Doc worked his way around, moving with the practiced stealth of a jungle stalker.

Now it was a deadly earnest case of hide-and-seek. Darts flew. None stuck. The bronze giant was flashing from tree to tree like dark lightning.

Then he seemed to vanish entirely.

A sudden disturbance far to the south made the two surviving Dyaks believe that the bronze man had gone that way. In actuality, Doc had thrown a second rock to trick them into switching their piercing eyes away from his own location, which was much closer.

Stealing up from their blind side, Doc Savage ambushed one by seizing his head in terrible metallic hands and giving the head a sidewise wrench. The grinding of neck bones ended in a distinct snap.

Doc released the dead Dyak and lunged for the other one.

Alerted, the crouching warrior began to flee. It is impossible to aim and employ a blowpipe longer than the one wielding it while fleeing an adversary, so no darts flew in Doc Savage's direction.

The bronze man was forced to track him, lest the fleeing Dyak catch up to his war party and give alarm.

Moving up into the trees, Doc began following. He had picked up a fallen blowpipe and a long leather pouch of darts from one of the dead men.

Reaching a spot where he had clear aim, Doc brought the weapon to his open mouth.

The fleeing man somehow sensed the approach of death, for he suddenly turned, wide eyes frantic. He endeavored to spot his following foe.

It was the yellowish blowpipe that gave Doc away. It stood out against his gray and brown camouflaged body.

The Dyak was quick. He levered his weapon up and applied it to his lips.

The range was not good, he realized—for either of them. He did not fire, preferring to save his dart until he could creep closer to his intended victim.

That was his mistake.

Doc Savage took in a deep breath, held it, and expelled it down the pipe.

The dart thus released traveled many yards before it found a spot in the exact center of the Dyak's tattooed throat.

His eyes rolled up almost immediately, and he fell backward. The jittering of his feet started at once, as the poison entered his bloodstream and did its dark work.

After the feet settled down, Doc dropped from the trees and recovered his submachine gun.

He would remember that his superior lungpower gave him an edge that Dyaks could not equal.

Chapter XXXV

THE UNEXPECTED COMES in many forms. It can steal up on a man on cat feet. It can slide out from the underbrush on the scaled belly of a snake. Or it might creep along on bare feet and whisper its arrival, as would a stealthy Dyak assassin.

Doc Savage, moving through the jungled growth of Skull Island, garbed as no warrior before him, unrecognizable as himself, encountered the unexpected in a manner that, as alert as his senses were, surprised even him.

There had been a jarring of the Earth. A tremor. Doc felt it as he crept along, halted, every sense keyed to its highest pitch.

There was no second sound, nor movement of the ground.

Deciding that Skull Island had experienced a minor earth temblor, Doc continued the search for his father and the Mayan warrior, Chicahua.

Once more, the bronze giant experimented by issuing his special sound. As Doc attempted to warn of dangers unseen, the trillation blended with the chirring of insects.

Back came, after an interval, an enticing whistle.

Doc slowed his muscular gait, crouched down. Flake-gold eyes raked the surrounding ferns, skated up into the trees, missing nothing, it seemed.

Switching his attention to the first smells, Doc once more felt overwhelmed by what the jungle had to offer. Ripe odors. Heavy musky scents. It was almost too much to sort out.

There were patches of clearing here and there, and the bronze giant approached each one cautiously, not wishing to be exposed to skulking Dyaks, or predatory dinosaurs, which seemed scarce in this quadrant of Skull Island.

In one muddy patch, he came upon a footprint.

The outline was simian, fringed with striations that suggested that the extremity that made the impression in the mud was extremely hairy, in a coarse way.

The footprint was not new. Rainwater had collected in it. Yet the size of the depression was immense, titanic.

Trilling this time from sheer surprise, Doc Savage approached the thing, walking around it carefully. The crater measured over six feet long and half as wide. The big toe was larger than a grown man's head.

Mentally, Doc Savage calculated the height of the creature that had left that track and shook his head slowly as if in disbelief. All the while his trilling ranged the scale, all but unnoticed by him.

"It would have to be almost as tall as Alfred Bulltop Stormalong!" Doc whispered to himself.

Doubt tinged his vibrant tone. Kneeling, the bronze man touched the fringes of the track, examined the toe print for whorls or lines, such as would be found on any footprint this human-seeming. It was obvious that Doc doubted the validity of the impression—was searching for clues to suggest that it was man-made, a trick of the Dyaks or other natives.

But every indication showed that here was the footprint of an ape or gorilla that stood no less than twenty feet tall, and probably taller!

"Kong," breathed Doc, stifling his trilling.

Preoccupation is an amazing thing. When Doc had been pondering his discovery, he failed to notice—as he often did—his own trilling sound.

Now it came again, and once more it did not impinge upon his consciousness. The sound permeated the lush surroundings for a time, like the note of a woodland sprite transmuted into pure music.

When Doc finally noticed it, he clamped his lips shut.

Yet the sound continued uninterrupted!

Whirling, Doc took stock of his surroundings. He was not the author of his unique sound. That meant either his father had learned to imitate it and was signaling, or a deathrunner lurked in the vicinity.

Ears keyed up for the flutter of feathered bodies, Doc waited.

The trilling came from the southwest. Doc listened to it intently, confronting another example of the unnervingly incredible phenomena of Skull Island.

Annihilator submachine gun at the ready, Doc swung about, prepared for anything.

It came!

Out of the brush came a rushing. Screaming. The weird trilling stopped, or was swallowed.

Then Doc Savage stood face to face with a herd of bright-feathered slashers!

There was no escaping them. He opened up with the Annihilator. The weapon yammered and bawled, brass cartridge cases spewing out to splash in the water-filled track beside him.

Death screams and spouting gouts of blood showed the power of the handheld submachine gun. Doc had only to tap the trigger, and punishing lead hurled from the smoking muzzle. To keep the shaking barrel from climbing off target, he had to hold the weapon steady with its forward grip.

One—two—three slashers exploded in a gory paroxysm of plumage and entrails. The surroundings became splashed with red matter.

Shifting his aim, Doc depressed the trigger.

A stream of rounds cut the wild-eyed head off another slasher, sectioning it at the neck.

Howling and headlong, it strained at him, collapsed before

his feet, scaly arms flailing madly, claws clutching.

A rustle from another quarter caused Doc to whip about. He took aim at a patch of ferns where the green pattern was mixed with other, brighter hues.

Pulling back on the trigger, Doc made the weapon spurt fire. It quickly ran empty.

Out of ammunition! And the surroundings were alive with hot orange orbs and frantic, inhuman feet!

RECHARGING the drum magazine—a laborious procedure—with the remaining bullets from his pocket, was for the moment impractical. Doc still had the twenty-round clip. But it would not last three seconds. He threw the Annihilator over his back, where it hung from its carrying lanyard.

Pulling his automatic from its holster, the bronze giant began to retreat.

From somewhere came a crashing.

A harsh barking noise, metallic and vehement, also came from that direction.

Down went a slasher, its narrow, lean-jawed skull drilled clean through by lead.

Doc turned. Out of the brush came his father, smoking Colt revolver in one brassy, wind-burned hand.

Captain Savage waved a beckoning arm. "This way! This way!"

Doc started in that direction, made it only a few paces before something huge landed hard, blocking his path.

At first, Doc took it for another slasher. But this creature, while similar in its bird-like structure, was different in many other respects. It was larger, for one. Its eyes were placed further forward, and beneath them powerful jaws yawned, showing a glint of shark-like teeth. This, Doc realized, must be a deathrunner!

A pair of eerie violet orbs, inhumanly cold but innately intelligent, locked with his own. Its plumed throat puffed in and out, like a cobra flexing its hood. The hues of its plumage were an intense black streaked with luminous scarlet, as if permanently stained by the gore of its kills.

Like a serpent attempting to hypnotize a bird, the pack leader kept its cold gaze on Doc Savage. And from its fanged mouth emerged a sound that was equally hypnotic.

The trilling sound of Doc Savage—*issuing from utterly inhuman lips!*

Carefully, the bronze giant raised his automatic, took dead aim.

Squeezing the trigger, he fired once.

Amazingly, the horrible head jerked to one side, literally dodging the round with snaky speed. It understood pistols!

Doc fired again. Again, the feathered monster ducked successfully. He attempted to snap off a third shot, but too late. The weapon froze.

Up flashed one of the center claws of the deathrunner's bird-talon feet. Doc's eyes shifted to the sickle-like protuberance, recognized that it could eviscerate him in an instant with a ripping up-and-down slash.

There was no choice in the matter. Doc endeavored to retreat.

Plunging back into the jungle, he made for the shelter of the trees.

Behind him, the thing came like a mad ostrich blown up all out of proportion in size. It screeched. It trilled. It seemed to be mocking him as it came.

The spiteful crack of Captain Savage's revolver echoed several times. But still the mad thing came on.

Wrestling with his own Colt, Doc attempted to unjam it. But the mechanism appeared to be clogged with jungle grit. It couldn't be fixed on the fly. It was flee or perish.

Punching through a vegetation-choked jungle lane, Doc found himself suddenly in another cleared space—the last thing he wished for!

Doubling back into the trees was impossible. He turned, dropped his useless Colt and took up his Bowie knife, intending to make his stand.

A yellow-green slasher came out from nowhere and landed behind him. It must have been perched in the trees, waiting to pounce. Doc turned just as a three-fingered talon snatched wildly at him. He blocked it with his Bowie knife, then gave a wrench of his metallic muscles.

The weird thing upset, scaled arms flinging outward, swaying madly on one teetering talon.

Rushing in, Doc impaled its plumed throat with his blade, jerked it out ahead of a fountain of cascading blood. Its lizard-orange orbs began closing.

By this time, the deathrunner was out of the jungle and coming on hard, its gem-like eyes utterly without mercy.

Doc reversed the blade, set himself to throw it. He knew that this more intelligent specimen of a slasher dinoavisaur would not be slain as easily as its fellows.

Doc let fly. The blade—not designed for throwing, yet impelled by powerful muscles—turned end over end. The deathrunner ducked, weaving to one side.

The blade landed in the dirt with a distressing plunking sound.

Doc Savage stood unarmed.

Out of the surrounding greenery, more slashers came. Soon, Doc was all but surrounded.

Bending, he picked up a rock, held it ready to chuck. But there were too many slashers and insufficient available stones lying at his feet.

Far away, Doc could hear the frantic voice of his father. "Clark! Clark! *Doc!*"

Doc threw the stone. It smacked a slasher in the neck. Like an ungainly ostrich, it reeled backward. The others screamed.

Then kicking, striking as it came, the deathrunner pack leader began walking calmly and methodically toward Doc Savage, never taking its chilling sapphire gaze from his intended prey's own golden eyes.

Behind him, Doc heard another crashing of brush, more loud than any before, and understood for the first time that he was almost certainly doomed.

Book Three:
KONG!

Chapter XXXVI

FOR THE REMAINDER of his remarkable life, Doc Savage never forgot what happened next.

The deathrunner approached on splay-clawed feet, confident in his powers, certain of its victim's fate. It never took its eyes off Doc's metallic face, its scarlet-plumed throat expanding and contracting ominously.

Holding his lowered hands before him as if determined to sell his life dearly, Doc awaited its coming. He could not concern himself with the thrashing and crashing going on behind him. His attention was so fixated on his feathered foe that he ignored all sounds and smells emanating at his back.

The deathrunner danced forward. A shadow fell over it. A very large shadow, as if a great cloud had passed before the sun.

Seeing this, it glanced up. The open mouth opened even more. One might have said that its bony lower jaw dropped.

The look in the eyes of the creature changed abruptly. From a murderous intensity, it became one of fear—or awe.

For a black hand, hairy in the extreme, came out of nowhere and seized it like a human fist preparing to wring the neck of a chicken. But this was no simple chicken, nor was the hand an ordinary one.

It was the hand of an earth-striding colossus. And it seized the deathrunner by its throbbing throat, lifting it from sight.

Pivoting, Doc turned and watched the spectacle taking place over his head.

The hairy hand raised the deathrunner high. Another hand joined it. Together, they pulverized the suddenly screaming predator amid a noisy cracking of bones and dripping of gore.

Above this ferocious activity loomed a head. Towering. Gigantic. Unreal.

A bestial face peered down. Doc Savage found himself looking into simian eyes which possessed a quality that brought forth his amazed trilling in a confused tangle of musical notes.

For the eyes looking down at him—large as the husks of coconuts—were a startling amber-gold hue!

The creature regarded Doc for a moment, its ferocious expression shifting to one of monkey-like interest. Wide nostrils quivered. Then he reached down with one massive paw.

Normally, the bronze giant might have evaded it in time. But he did not. Astonishment held him rooted in place. The titanic creature, the uncanny way it had come up behind him unsuspected, caused Doc to doubt his senses.

Great fingers clamped about him, firmly but without the excessive pressure.

They carried him aloft.

Below, a brown-and-gold slasher had been sneaking up behind the bronze man. But taloned feet are not designed for perfect quiet. A fallen branch snapped like a dry bone underfoot.

Kong—for there was no doubt that this colossal monster was he—calmly lifted a foot and brought it down on the bizarre feathered thing with distressing finality.

The slasher became as flat as a flapjack against the ground. No outcry escaped its vomiting mouth.

The huge fingers bore Doc high into the air, dropping him into its opposite palm.

It felt like landing on a hot leather trampoline.

For a moment, Kong turned the bronze giant—that term seemed laughable now—in his great hairy paw, and made odd noises. His gigantic mouth hung open, revealing formidable teeth larger than shovels. The smell of Kong's breath was an overpowering mixture of fermented vegetable matter laced with the distinct stink of raw meat.

Then, noticing more slashers stamping and scattering like wild turkeys about his feet, Kong placed Doc in the crown of a tree and went to work obliterating them all.

The great gorilla—or whatever he was—casually reached down and took up flailing slashers in each hand. He did not bother to examine them as he had Doc. He simply flung them away, to smash their lives out against rocks or bushes or tree boughs.

Soon, the frenzied flailing and screaming had ceased. The jungle became still.

Brutish head swiveling around on its truncated neck, Kong decided that the task was finished.

He went to the nearest slasher body and picked it up. Examining the dangling legs, he noticed that they still quivered with nervous life. Opening his mouth, the colossal creature inserted one limb, then another, into his mouth, stripping the still-warm meat off the raw bones with his powerful incisors. Then he discarded the rest disdainfully, like a man finished with stripped chicken bones.

Reaching back for Doc Savage, Kong groped amid the tree branches, hairy visage distorted by various apish expressions.

But the bronze man was already clawing through the trees, hampered by his hide poncho and the loss of confidence occasioned by the failure of his weapons and the unexpected arrival of the towering simian, Kong.

Behind him, a bough cracked as a wrist as wide as a railroad tie forced it aside.

Precariously perched, Doc rolled and dropped to a lower branch. Thick black fingers grasped and groped.

Looking up, Doc spied the eyes of Kong questing about over impatiently flaring nostrils, his nearly-neckless head swiveling menacingly. Excited grunts spilled from his thick, mobile lips.

Again, it struck him with the force of a blow to the solar

plexus that the orbs of the great brute were uncannily like the eyes of the family from which he was descended. They lacked the golden flakes of his own, but their resemblance to those of his grandfather, Stormalong Savage, made Doc think he was hallucinating, or in some fevered nightmare.

But this was no dream. Kong now sought him. The ape reached out, began separating boughs, impatiently breaking off limbs as thick around as oak boles.

Doc scrambled deeper into the interlacing trees. He found vines, yanked one loose with a mighty surge and attempted to fashion a lariat from it.

But Kong would not be denied. He pushed his unstoppable bulk inward. His narrow hips collided with a palm. It splintered, toppled.

Another got in his way. Reaching down, the growling monster took it firmly in both hands and began twisting and wrenching, grunting with effort at every turn.

With a cracking sound, the palm was pulled up by its clumpy roots and Doc Savage clearly understood what had happened to the proud masts of the clipper ship, *Courser.*

Kong pushed in. His shoulders shrugged aside entire leafy crowns, which groaned loudly, then broke with a mad splintering.

Attempting to fling off his cumbersome Triceratops poncho, Doc was momentarily still. That was enough. Two blunt fingers pinched the poncho, tugged at it.

Doc discovered that he was being dragged inexorably in to the open. Metallic hands seized branches, attempted to hold on. The serpentine boughs broke under the tremendous pressure.

Twisting, the bronze man fought to extricate himself from the heavy garment. His great strength, intensified by two decades of remorseless exercise, proved sufficient. The thick hide tore with a groan. Doc pulled free. He lunged for the shelter of entwined branches.

An animal voice grunted as the poncho was revealed, empty!

Then the other great simian hand clamped around him, plucking Doc out of the trees. It was irresistible. He went up into the air as if riding an elevator, abruptly stopped.

Once more, Doc found himself face to face with the creature called Kong. Seen up close, it was an unlovely visage. The cicatrix of a long gray scar had twisted the right cheek out of shape. The parted mouth was a malodorous cave of yellowed canines, striated with age.

The eyes regarding him possessed a monkey-like curiosity. But behind them lay an open intelligence as well. More remarkable still, unlike simian eyes, the pupils showed white all the way around them. Their structure was astoundingly human-like.

This creature is no gorilla, thought Doc.

The expression in Kong's amber eyes was not menacing. It was vaguely warm, intrigued.

Below, a voice could be heard bellowing.

"Son! Son!"

Doc called down, "Father! Come no closer. It has me."

"Can you tear loose?"

Doc put his mighty muscles to the test. Placing both hands against a warm right finger, he applied pressure. Kong's digit gave slightly. The creature gave a surprised *cheep.* He pushed back. Doc could not budge the blunt finger after that.

"Keep your head down!" Captain Savage warned. "I am going to shoot the brute with my Very pistol. No doubt it fears fire!"

"No!" called Doc. "It has intelligence. And if he drops me from this height, I might not survive."

This heated exchange did not go unnoticed by Kong.

Head swiveling, his amber eyes fell upon Captain Savage, Chicahua crouched by his side. The Mayan lifted his blowgun.

With his massive foot, Kong scuffed dirt in their direction. It was a minor gesture from the viewpoint of the terrible simian, but a crushing storm of loam mixed with blood and dinosaur matter cascaded over the two.

They were forced to retreat from the dark rain.

Satisfied, Kong turned and began stalking in the general direction of Skull Mountain, Doc Savage carefully cupped in both hands.

Having no choice in the matter, Doc surrendered to the journey. Any attempt to escape would have to come later... when he was no longer vised in Kong's hot, unbreakable grip.

Chapter XXXVII

KONG STRODE OVER the plateau comprising Skull Island like the lord of all he surveyed.

Below, armored dinosaurs of many fearsome varieties swerved out of his path. Above, devil-tailed pterosaurs gave cry and took to the air. Nothing stood before him. Nothing dared stand before him. All fled. For he was Kong.

Striding purposefully, the tremendous creature that walked like a man made his unswerving way to his lofty lair, whose bald dome shone in the brilliant sun, appearing as white as true bone, its shadowed eye sockets contrastingly black as twin pits.

After a time, a strange and eerie calm settled over Doc Savage, cupped in his hairy hands. Perhaps it was the memory of his grandfather's story of being Kong's captive and held safely for many years. Possibly it was some instinct that told him that no harm would befall him.

Or perhaps it was simply the obvious and undeniable fact that Kong was carrying him the way one might convey a valued pet or property to his still-smoking retreat.

Soon, Kong came to the winding stream Stormalong Savage had dubbed the River of No Return. He followed its course until he reached a spot where it came cascading down from the highest point on the plateau. Skull Mountain.

Coming to the broad base of Skull Mountain, Kong began his ascent. For this, he transferred Doc to one leathery-palmed paw, holding him firmly but without undue pressure. He seemed to know or understand exactly how tightly he could squeeze a human without reducing their ribcage to kindling. Doc began to suspect that Kong had done this many times in the past.

The climb was perilous, arduous. Once, Kong stumbled when one foot came to rest on a loose ledge. Shale cracked. Kong stumbled and scrambled for better footing. But he succeeded.

Enclosed in his hot paw, Doc rested unharmed. Escape was impossible.

Approaching the granite summit, the air became heavy with smoke. Doc placed his hands over his mouth to keep out the lung-abrading fumes. They seemed more pungent than ordinary wood smoke, and Doc realized that something had been introduced into the fires calculated to produce a noxious pall intended to deny Kong his refuge.

Reaching the great cliff beneath the eye sockets of Skull Mountain, Kong was forced to use both hands. Here, he simply placed Doc on one shoulder, forcing the bronze man to cling to coarse hair with both hands.

The air here was a gray haze. The fires had evidently gone out, exhausted after days of burning. But the thickness of the lingering smoke was almost unbearable. This suggested hot spots still smoldering.

Giving vent to an angry roar, Kong deposited Doc on the ledge and began batting at the eye-socket entrance to his lair with impatient paws. The effort accomplished little.

Soon, Kong clambered in. Doc followed him with his eyes and saw that the interior was a cavernous chamber decorated with scattered calcium stalactites and stalagmites. In places, they met like closing fangs. Further in, there was a dark pool where water had collected.

Going to this, Kong began scooping up great sprays of water, dousing the smoldering remains of two bonfires—the same blazes that had made the hollow orbs of Skull Mountain burn so menacingly before.

This caused the last lingering smoky hot spots to be quenched.

Gradually, the air began to clear. A round hole in the top of the granite dome permitted some smoke to escape skyward. From this, natural illumination leaked, making it possible to see deep into the gloomy interior.

By this time, Doc Savage was endeavoring to work his way downward. Unfortunately, the rattle of the bullets in his pocketed magazine clip gave him away.

A massive black paw reached out and drew him back in, carefully depositing him on a high, inner ledge. The hand moved away.

Crouching there, Doc Savage studied the interior. It was like a spacious natural cathedral. The greater portion of the choky smoke had been drawn upward. Now the flue effect was acting to sweep out the last remnants. In a surprisingly short period of time, the air became breathable.

Kong sat down, facing Doc. Again their eyes met, and something resembling recognition came into the great quasi-gorilla's sensitive orbs.

But this was not a gorilla grown by some freak of nature to leviathan proportions, Doc saw at once. Kong's legs were too long. He tended to walk upright, which according to Science only man could do. The shape of his head was not the blunt bullet form of a gorilla's skull, yet he was nearly neckless.

Whereas Doc's wartime friend, Monk Mayfair, greatly resembled a terrestrial gorilla, Kong suggested both man and gorilla, while clearly being neither. His stomach was flatter than the gorilla's enormous paunch. His chest was a tangle of matted hair and multiple long-healed scars, in contrast to the bare hide gorillas showed in that area. And most amazing of all, the amber orbs were framed in white, imparting to them a nearly human aspect.

After several minutes of study, Doc Savage realized that he did not know into what category of animal to classify Kong. He belonged to no known genus or species. That he was an anthropoid ape was undeniable. But no ape stood twenty-five feet tall—which was Doc's final estimation of his height.

Mentally, Doc began filing facts in his head for a monograph he intended to write about this creature. Even as a captive, the bronze man retained unbounded confidence in his eventual escape. He noted that in places the bristling black hair that covered the apish form was turning gray, suggesting that Kong was very old, if not ancient.

After a period in which the great ape studied the bronze man from a respectful distance, Kong clambered to his feet and began a strangely human array of activities.

First, he picked up a dead palm tree that seemed to have been carried up to this aerie for the express purpose of serving as a cleaning tool. The dead cluster of dried fronds had largely fallen away from use, but Kong nevertheless wielded it as if it were a broom or rake. He used this to scrape all the simmering wet burnt wood into one corner of the chamber.

Once Kong had done this, he used his hands to heave out the detritus in large clumps. It went rattling down the side of Skull Mountain, coming to a clattering pile far below.

Satisfied with his toil, Kong looked at his paws. The gray-black ashes had smeared them, although outward inspection showed no color change.

Evidently, Kong was not pleased with the ashy deposit on his fingers and palms, for he ambled over to the dark pool and dunked his hands in. After splashing them around for a while, he dried them on the sides of his legs.

Grunting and cheeping, Kong looked about his domain.

There were shelves arrayed on the other end. Dimly, Doc could see that mummified bodies lay there in the clotted shadows, carefully arrayed in a neat row. His mind went back to what his grandfather had told him about the maidens who had been sacrificed to the so-called beast-god, whom Kong had kept as souvenirs—or whatever idea was harbored in the brute's dim brain.

Only Kong's brain did not appear to be so dim, after all. He showed a simian intelligence, but also something beyond that. His use of the dead palm bole smacked of the use of tools—a trait that Science insisted was limited to humankind.

As much as he desired escape, Doc Savage continued to study the chamber of Kong. There would be plenty of opportunity for escape later, after the beast retired for the night.

Especially intriguing was the apparent fact that Kong showed all outward signs of loneliness and the desire for companionship. Bereft of others of his kind, the titanic creature evidently considered Doc, and his grandfather before him, to be kindred beings, if only by virtue of the amber eyes and similar body shape.

NIGHT began creeping along, and the stupendous ape started showing signs of fatigue, or just the natural urge to go to sleep when the sun set.

After ambling over to see that Doc Savage was safely ensconced in the safety of his ledge—Doc could not help but feel like a toy on a shelf—Kong sat down and began scratching the rocky floor aimlessly.

It dawned on Doc Savage that the two bonfires had been constructed from dried palm fronds that Kong had arranged as a rude pallet on which to sleep—another sure sign of intelligence.

Various expressions played over the great ape's sometimes comical face. He grunted, seemed uncertain. Doc sensed that he was considering a climb down to harvest fresh fronds.

But having been denied the sanctuary of his lair by the fires, Kong was evidently too tired to execute the thought.

Slowly, laboriously, Kong laid his head down and began to drift off into slumber.

It was, until this point, the most incredible situation in which Doc Savage had ever found himself. Nothing that had transpired during the Great War equaled it. And that was a conflict that had shaken the world.

In time, the great creature turned over and cupped his head in his folded hands, very much like a child might. It was disconcerting.

Doc Savage allowed an hour to pass before making his move. He knew that sleep would be lightest in the early hours of the evening.

Examining his perch, the bronze man found that he stood easily a dozen feet over the floor of Kong's lair. It was not impossible to climb down if one were athletic. But the rocks were unstable. It was too easy to dislodge one. Doc had to employ great caution.

Removing the ammunition clip from his pocket, Doc removed each shell individually, left everything behind. He could hardly afford to abandon precious ammunition, but there was no choice in the matter.

It was time to start. The increasing darkness did not help. But after a time, moonlight began weaving spectral cobwebs here and there. Doc's eyes began adjusting to the wan lunar light and he felt confident in his plan of escape.

The bronze man did not climb down. He clambered up. There were cracks and crevices everywhere. He used them as handholds for his steely-string fingers—mentally thanking the human fly who taught him to scale brick buildings using only the indentations between the bricks—and soon reached a point where he could not be easily seen by the inquisitive ape.

His plan was simple. He was going to fling stones in the direction of the great opening in Skull Summit through which the beast-god came and went. His intention was to trick Kong into thinking that Doc had managed to escape, when in reality the bronze man remained concealed from those enormous amber orbs.

If the ape acted true to form, he would go off in search of his prize. Doc could escape Kong's fantastic aerie at his leisure.

But Fate has a way of foiling even the simplest and seemingly foolproof of plans.

Doc had collected several rocks of various sizes, filling his uniform pockets with them so he had a goodly supply of ammunition.

The bronze man never got to cast that first stone.

A new sound came to his ears—a scratching, stumbling kind of commotion.

Someone—or something—was climbing the side of Skull Mountain!

Chapter XXXVIII

MIGHTY KONG ROUSED. He shifted, snuffled noisily, and seemed on the verge of turning in his sleep, but subsided, like a mountain settling after an earthquake. Only in this case the mountain was the earthquake—a lumbering force of nature on stubby bowed legs, carrying in his upper body the power to destroy anything man had ever created, and much of what nature had wrought.

The skittering sound came again. Through Doc Savage's mind came a parade of thoughts, imagining what might be seeking the summit of Skull Island. A scuttling slasher? A serpent? Perhaps it was his own father, seeking Doc's fate.

After a time, a dark figure poked its head in, peering around.

In the dim light, Doc made out the movements, but failed to immediately discern what manner of creature possessed such a curious head.

After a minute, something entered on padding feet, sounding rather like a great cat.

Following it with his acute eyes, Doc soon realized that this was a lone Dyak scout. He wore only his hide loincloth and a brass-wire bracelet on one bicep. No tall feathers adorned his head.

Seeing Kong's bulk looming in the murk, the Dyak shifted to the rock walls and began working his way around, keeping to the stony crevices.

Doc watched him carefully from his shadowy coign of vantage.

The man carried no blowpipe. He clutched a charcoal-dulled knife in one hand, but made no move to use it. It would have been less than a thorn to Kong, anyway.

As Doc followed his progress, the Dyak made a circuit of the lair and, returning to the entrance, slipped out as silently as he had come. More silently, for so much as Doc Savage listened for it, no sound of the man's going reached his ears.

This forced Doc to wait even longer than he wished, but it had the added advantage of assuring him that Kong had lapsed into his deepest slumber. He never roused.

Time was now of the essence. Unless the bronze man was very much mistaken, the Dyak scout was rushing off to report that Kong had returned to his lair. Before long, a headhunting party would be arriving.

Doc Savage had no desire to face them alone, in this place of high peril.

Moving from crack to crevice in the riven rock, the bronze man reached the edge of the lair and climbed down until he stood on the solid ground of the great fanged cliff. Looking out, he ascertained that the sheer face of the mountain was clear of raiders. Then he slipped over the edge and began working his way to the rock-strewn base of Skull Mountain.

Doc no longer wore his Triceratops-hide poncho. But his bronze physique was still caked with dried mud. This served to keep off jungle insects and camouflage him where necessary.

The going was rough and, when he found the bottom, Doc slipped into the surrounding underbrush. There he merged with the waving ferns and dark brush of midnight, began making his careful and stealthy way to the coastal escarpment of the island.

REASONING that it would be better to locate the *Orion* than embark upon a far-ranging and possibly futile search for his father and Chicahua, Doc cut a straight line through wilderness to the northern cliff, then worked in the direction of the spot where the *Orion* lay coved.

He found it without incident. Peering over the edge, Doc spotted the grappling hook, still lodged in place. Naturally, his father would leave it there for him, even if he had returned.

Looking beyond it, Doc spied no lights on the *Orion*. Safety demanded that none be lit, so Doc took no special meaning from that bare fact.

Starting down, Doc went carefully. The day had been arduous and his muscles felt stiff. It was not cold, but it was much cooler, which had a strange effect upon him.

Doc reached the grapnel and transferred to the rope. He lacked the strength to slide down the rope, as much as he preferred to skid down it as fast as possible.

Instead, he dropped down in measured jerks, finally reaching the deck of the rocking schooner.

Before he reached it, Doc smelled blood.

Dropping to one knee, he touched the deck. There were blood spots everywhere.

Moving carefully, he found them wherever he went, even around the deckhouse, whose door was closed.

Rushing to the taffrail, Doc failed to find any clots of blood suggestive of a hasty beheading frenzy. He felt great relief, although it failed to register on his perpetually impassive countenance.

Moving back to the deckhouse, Doc attempted to ease open the door. It refused to budge. That meant someone had locked themselves in.

Doc evoked his musical trilling, let it run. It traveled up and trailed about the bare masts, seemed about to exhaust itself when a cracked voice called up from below.

"Is that you, grandson?"

"Yes," Doc called down. "Where are you?"

"Hiding in the cofferdam."

"The what?" asked Doc.

After a few minutes, feet tramped up the companion. After a rattling of a latch, the deckhouse door opened.

Stormalong Savage poked his grizzle-bearded head out. He peered about guardedly.

"Are they gone?"

"Who?"

"The Dyak boarding party."

"I see nothing but spots of blood," admitted Doc.

Old Stormy emerged on deck, looking a bit like an elderly giraffe. An old cutlass thorned one fist. "Watch out for tacks."

"Sir?"

"Carpet tacks. I smelled the Sea Dyaks coming, so I sprinkled the deck with tacks." He cackled. "Points uppermost, naturally. Then, I secreted myself in the cofferdam, and enjoyed their howls of consternation."

"Your scheme worked," Doc told him. "They must have stepped on the tacks and ran back to their dugouts. There are no Dyaks hereabouts, and hardly any tacks, for that matter."

"Dyaks, like Malays, always enter the water feet-first," explained Old Stormy. "Doubtless they swam back to the dugouts, there to remove the offending objects and lick their wounds. Back in the '80s, I used that trick to repel a felucca of buccaneers while sailing through the Milky Way breakers off Cape Horn. Won't work on boot-shod boarders, but most Asian pirates go barefoot like alley cats. Long ago, I instructed your father that a canny seaman always carried a ready supply—advice I am pleased to report he heeded."

"My father did not return?" asked Doc.

"No. And I would have climbed up that infernal rope to fetch you all, had I been free to undertake the task."

"Do not worry." After a pause, Doc said, "I encountered Kong. He carried me off to his lair, but I escaped."

"Then you are a better man than I, for it took me all of eight years."

"I understand now why Kong took you—and me, for that matter."

"Well, enlighten me."

"His eyes are virtually the same color as ours."

Old Stormy winked one yellow orb. "Nature plays queer tricks, doesn't she?"

"Yes. Where did you say you were hiding?"

"In the cofferdam. It's a void."

"Show me," directed Doc.

Stormalong led him below and to the rear of the hold, where the auxiliary gasoline engine stood in its enclosed compartment.

"A cofferdam," said Stormalong, "is a space between bulkheads. In these new-fangled ships, they are built around the engines so that spilt fuel doesn't mix with other substances, causing trouble."

"I have never before heard that term," admitted Doc.

"You sound surprised by your own ignorance," clucked Old Stormy. "I imagine that you considered yourself educated because you attended a university."

Doc said nothing. Penjaga had intimated the same disconcerting opinion.

The cofferdam lay under the steel plate supporting the engine housing. There was a bit of molding and when Old Stormy pressed it, a long and narrow panel fell forward. Doc stooped and saw that an agile man could hide within, if he managed to squeeze himself through the opening. It was no spot for the claustrophobic, thought Doc.

Shutting the panel, Doc stood up.

"I have to find the others," he announced.

"Bring me along."

"Someone has to guard the ship," Doc reminded.

"You left it unguarded when you found me, didn't you?"

Doc admitted that was the case.

"I know Skull Island better than anyone. You cannot deny

that."

Doc nodded. "The Dyaks seem bent on bearding Kong in his lair."

"They want his head," returned Stormalong. "Kong will pull theirs off their thieving necks and return each one to them, in his illimitable way."

"We can stop them, if we find the others."

"Agreed. Let us be about that undertaking, then."

Then, to Doc Savage's everlasting astonishment, Stormalong went to the dangling line and began to climb it hand over hand, showing that more corded strength and dexterity than he could ever imagine resided within the rawhide frame of his alarmingly-tall grandfather.

"I have always been better at going up the mast than clambering down it!" Old Stormy chuckled.

The old rascal! thought Doc.

The bronze giant was forced to wait on deck until the spindly giant reached the grappling hook and transferred to the rocks. After that, Doc commenced his climb, feeling considerably less spry and agile than his well-rested grandfather.

Chapter XXXIX

UPON REACHING THE cliff top, Doc Savage discovered his grandfather crouching down amid the tumbled rocks that fringed the high rim of the plateau.

"Is something wrong?"

"As I normally stand, I make a tempting target for snipers," replied Old Stormy in a reasonable voice.

Doc decided to follow suit. He, too, crouched as they surveyed the shaggy hump of island that stood before them.

Skull Mountain brooded some miles distant, no less foreboding because moonlight ensilvered its gloomy countenance.

"You see the hollow where he dwells?" asked the old sea captain, pointing a long finger at the landmark's right eye socket.

"Yes."

"In the other hollow are strange artifacts of a dead civilization. Treasure. Statuary. Other bric-a-brac. A great people shaped that prominence. They left behind their detritus, which would be worth millions to European museums."

"Who were they?"

"I do not know," confessed Stormalong. "But I have often wondered if, in times unrecorded by history, some of the people who still come to this island, the Malay and the Dyaks, might not be following some ancestral memory of a time when their distant cousins came and settled here."

"Difficult to imagine any civilized people colonizing an island filled with crawling death as this one," remarked Doc.

282

"Stranger things these eyes have seen in my sea-roving days," clucked Stormalong.

Moving into the jungle, the old man picked his way cautiously, as if hunting something.

He found a trailing vine and, after shinnying up a tree, cut the creeper down. Moving along, he began collecting stones. Three of them.

"When I was young, I spent some time down in the Argentine."

"So you said," reminded Doc.

"Eh? Yes, that's right, I did."

The long-limbed clipper captain sat down with his jungle salvage and got to work binding the stones until each was attached to a vine. Then, he tied the ends of the weighted cords to a central hub.

When he was finished, Stormalong Savage had made a rude bolas.

"A formidable weapon, if thrown properly," he said, upon standing up.

Doc nodded. He had experimented with them, too. They could be dangerous if not controlled properly. If wielded without care, a man might stave in his own skull.

They marched along, skirting the trees and walking along winding jungle lanes, sometimes crossing open areas.

"Venomous things drop out of the branches by night," Stormalong explained. "I do not refer to the redoubtable robber crab."

After a while, there were no paths and they were forced to make do by infiltrating through the jungle. The same trees Doc had traversed by day now felt weird and clutching by moonlight.

Overhead, he saw bats, then wondered if they might not be infant pterosaurs, disturbed from their roosts. They moved out of sight so rapidly, there was no being certain.

Once, they happened upon a gauzy web so large and thick

it was like a cloud squatting on the ground.

Stormalong pulled Doc back, hissing, "We will go around that snare."

Doc kept his eyes sharp for the weaving spider. He saw nothing, but a clicking as of hungry mandibles made the skin on the back of his neck prickle unpleasantly.

Old Stormy warned, "That web's tougher than rawhide, more sticky than saltwater taffy. Even a grown man would be hard-pressed to extricate himself."

Doc began recognizing landmarks. A certain tree. An outcropping of rock in the shape of a natural anvil. A stand of rattan-choked bamboo trampled by dinosaur feet.

Before long, they came to the spot where Kong had rescued him from the slasher pack. The damaged trees alone told the tale.

There, they halted.

Doc Savage spoke in a hush. "The last I saw of my father, he stood under this canopy," he whispered. "We might pick up his trail from this point."

But Stormalong was already sniffing his way ahead.

Moving quietly, Doc caught up with him.

"I see no sign," he admitted.

"Close your eyes and employ your nostrils," came the reply. "I am following scent."

Doc did so, and was immediately surprised at how much easier it was to discern individual odors without the distraction of paying attention to what his eyes told him.

"This is impractical," offered Doc, peeking often in order to avoid obstacles.

"But effective."

Doc's silence was his affirmative assent.

"The brain is so often filled with the world that we see," explained Old Stormy, "we do not fully comprehend the universe of its smells until we shut out the realm of sight."

Doc, who had spent some weeks in a school for the blind, learning the art of navigating the world while blindfolded to simulate loss of vision, suddenly realized that test had been one lesson where experience had not fully educated him.

Still, this jungle was no place to go about sightless. He opened his eyes and let his grandfather lead him, rather like a blood-hound—if bloodhounds could be imagined to stand nearly seven feet tall.

There was a renewed strength and vigor about his grandfather now. His energy seemed inexhaustible. Was it his old seaman's courage coming back, or did the quest for his lost son restore him? Doc couldn't tell. But it was a remarkable transformation. He could see how legends had sprung up around the man and his deeds. He was a giant in more than stature.

From a distance, a sound rolled across the treetops. It caused them to freeze in their tracks.

This was a roar. Bloodcurdling, bestial, and so great in volume it might have emerged from just over the rise. But it did not.

It was coming from the orb-like cavities of Skull Mountain, a massive moonlit sentinel in the distance.

"Kong," intoned Doc. "He is awake."

"Or he has been awakened," suggested Old Stormy.

"Which do you think it might be?" asked Doc.

"Kong has his ways. We will leave him to them. I smell humans. We will follow that olfactory track."

Before they had gone a few rods, Doc smelled them, too. Very faintly. His grandfather's sense of smell was astounding, exceeding his own, it seemed.

A shuffling of something alive and prowling sounded in the brush ahead.

They were upwind of it, so no scent carried to their distend-ing nostrils.

They listened.

"Not human," decided Old Stormy.

286 / A DOC SAVAGE ADVENTURE

"We will skirt it."

"And have it stalk us? No! In this jungle, you strike first—or end up in someone's belly. Follow me, grandson. I will teach you a thing or two about surviving on Skull Mountain Island."

Doc followed, not liking it one bit.

IT happened so fast that Doc had no time to react. Then it was all over.

Old Stormy had the lead. He was creeping up on the rustling sound. Abruptly, the unfamiliar noise turned to a mad dash.

Out of the thicket came a yellow-and-black slasher, mouth sealed, trying to be quiet. Picking his way forward, the ungainly two-legged thing displayed uncanny stealth. But little rain had fallen in recent days. The underbrush was dry. Detritus rustled beneath its stalking talons.

The slasher froze, emulating utter stillness. Its bright orange eyes sealed to slits in an effort to mask its presence.

It was all for nothing.

Old Stormy lifted his bolas and began spinning it, quickly shifting the deadly blurred disk over his head. When he let go, the whirling mass of balls wrapped themselves around the suddenly churning legs and brought the slasher stumbling down in a flash of feathers.

Coming in behind it, Stormalong Savage smashed its skull with a rock he picked up on the fly. The creature keeled over, began flailing, attempting to rise. But its cord-tangled feet were held fast. It screamed.

Stepping up, Old Stormy removed its head with a quick chop of his cutlass, which he pulled from his belt.

"That," he said, walking back to Doc, "is how things are done around here."

Doc stared. Speech was momentarily driven from him. He had just seen an elderly man conquer a vicious dinoavisaur with a blinding series of maneuvers.

Stormalong had not emerged from his battle entirely unscathed, however.

The force with which the gangling giant had wielded his cutlass had bent the blade severely. Noticing this, Old Stormy frowned unhappily, and tossed away the now-useless blade.

"Pity," he clucked. "I presented your father with it on the occasion of his taking possession of the *Orion*."

Doc gave the slasher a careful examination, paying particular attention to its prehensile three-fingered talons, then to the two-toed feet, which its retractable center claw capable of rending any living foe to ribbons.

"These claws are sharp as razors," he observed.

Stormalong said, "They make good weapons, if we had the means to wrest them loose."

Doc knelt, withdrew his Bowie knife and attempted to cut the middle sickle-like claw out. It was no easy task. The anchoring cartilage was tough.

But after a bit of red work, he had it free.

Standing up, Doc held the thing. He wrapped his belt around the base, to make a thong handle of sorts.

Then, he presented it to his grandfather. "For you. I have my Bowie blade."

"Gratefully accepted, sir," said Stormalong. "And well done, I might add."

After a time, they came upon Doc's Annihilator submachine gun, lying where it had fallen.

Doc looked at it, then picked up the weapon. He examined it carefully. It would need to be cleaned, he saw.

"I thought this was going to make me master of this island," Doc said thoughtfully.

"It failed you?"

"Not exactly. It discharges so many bullets that I ran out before I finished the job."

"That is the trouble with firearms," grunted Old Stormy. "No matter how sound the weapon, without ammunition it might as well be a lead ballast for all the good it will do you."

Doc considered the weapon. There were fresh .45 caliber rounds in his automatic. But only a few. Not enough to be worth the trouble to reload the drum. The submachine gun would spit them out in a quarter-second and leave him defenseless. The Colt was a better tool, owing to the fact that one could release each bullet individually.

"A gun is only as useful as its supply of bullets," Stormalong Savage observed. "A knife or cutlass will stay sharp longer than lead will fly. You would do well to remember this simple truth."

Doc left the Annihilator where he found it. It would only slow him down now.

They pushed on.

Another roar rolled out into the night, sounding like savage thunder. It hurt the ears, made them ring.

"Kong is angry," Stormalong said flatly.

"He may have discovered that I got away."

Stormalong squeezed his yellow eyes into slits. "That he might. And woe betide whoever gets in his way. For you and I have seen Kong at his best—curious, friendly, half-mortal. But there is another Kong—elemental, unreasonable, beyond bestial. He will slay anything in his path. He does not fear the Tyrannosaur, or the Triceratops. Men are like ants to him. Even the lightning avoids his fury."

Doc eyed his grandfather skeptically. "The lightning?"

Old Stormy grinned fiercely. "Possibly I exaggerate a bit. But Kong is—well, the Malay used to call him *Buhan* Kong. Lord Kong. Or perhaps the proper translation would be 'God Kong.' He is absolute lord and master of Skull Island."

As he spoke, the coppery giant fingered his long ivory beard. Discovering something within, he suddenly reached behind his neck and lifted off a thonged pouch that had been hidden beneath the profusion of whiskers.

"Penjaga gave me this long ago," he said, holding it by the hide-string loop that had supported it. "It contains herbs that

Kong finds unpleasant. She said it would ward him off. I do not know if they work, but Kong has yet to recapture me. I want you to wear it now."

Doc accepted the pouch, sniffed it, and decided it might be some sort of herbal irritant. He had to resist the sudden urge to sneeze.

Doc donned it to humor the old man.

"We will find the others and get off this island as soon as possible," he said.

Stormalong did not respond to that. Doc could tell that he had other plans—for himself.

As if fearing his imminent loss, Doc said suddenly, "Grandfather, I never knew my mother."

"That is too bad. She was a splendid woman. Kendra Robeson. That was a fitting name for her. Did you know that Kendra means 'wise woman?'"

"Yes. Also, 'champion.' I looked it up once. But what I am trying to convey is that, other than my father, you are the only relative I have ever met. I do not want to lose you."

"I have another son. Alex. You should seek him out. I named him after the celebrated Alexandre Dumas, whose *Count of Monte Cristo* I have read many times."

"Grandfather, I think you should return with us," Doc said gently.

Stormalong growled, "Let us worry about surviving this adventure before we concern ourselves with the disposition of the survivors. If any."

And that seemed to close the book on the subject, so far as Stormalong Savage was concerned.

They pressed on in a silence punctuated by Kong's terrible roars of rage. They put the grinding crack of thunder to shame. Doc began to wonder if the lightning might not be afraid of the beast-god, after all.

Chapter XL

MONYET, SON OF Ramba, prince of the Iban of Skrang, lay in a bamboo platform high in a sprawling tree. Here he had been placed by his warriors, where he would be safe from the dragon-lizards of Skull Island.

His lungs still ached. His brain throbbed. He had nearly drowned, there on the beach when the brazen devil with the golden eyes and the iron lungs had engaged in a contest of wills and lung prowess.

Monyet had lost. He had been shamed. He would avenge that shame, if it took him until the day of his death. This he vowed on the head of his father's greatest trophy.

One fortunate thing had come out of the terrible trial. In the confusion of the attack by the Atu natives, the trophy head of the young kong had been left behind by the white devils. A loyal man of Monyet's band had bravely captured it and brought it to the *bangkong* in which Monyet, sick and dazed, had been spirited away.

Now that sacred head sat at his side, where its fierce spirit would protect him until his scouts returned with news of their enemies.

The wait was long. Things scuttled through the sheltering tree branches. Once, a slender serpent slithered up the trunk beneath him, flicking its liver-colored tongue. The stealthy noises it made in its ascent were very odd.

Peering down, Monyet saw that it was creeping up the tree

trunk, climbing in some strange fashion. Some moonlight filtered down through the thick whispering leaves. But Monyet could not make out the way of the serpent. He could only see that it was the color of mud, streaked with yellow.

Fascinated by its creeping progress—for the Dyak had never seen anything like it, from Borneo to Sumatra—Monyet stared at the wedge-shaped head inching its roundabout way up the smooth trunk.

When it poked its lean snout above the platform, it stared at Monyet. The Dyak prince glared back, equally unafraid.

But when a pair of spindly hands reached up to steady the snake, Monyet saw how it had managed its peculiar ascent. The serpent possessed hands! Strangely human-like hands!

These it used to lever himself up over the edge. Now the Dyak leader could see that it possessed four limbs, like a salamander. But it was no salamander. It hissed, revealing a forked tongue. Bright fangs shone in the thin moonlight.

Biting his lip, Monyet reached out for his *duku* chopping blade and patiently waited until the serpent writhed within range, being propelled by its strange limbs.

A swift chopping blow, and the long body began twisting and wrapping its coiled length around itself.

Monyet kicked the coiling and uncoiling body off the platform to the dirt below.

He reached out and picked up the head, setting it beside the kong head. Now, he had two head trophies. Soon, he would make a pile of them, beginning with the golden-eyed enemies and concluding with the greatest of them all: *Buhan* Kong.

Far away in the night, a rumble came. It sounded like distant rolling thunder. Monyet ignored the sound, never suspecting that he was hearing the voice of his mortal enemy, the beast-god of Skull Island.

Chapter XLI

DOC SAVAGE DEBATED whether to trill, as a signal to his father and Chicahua, who remained among the missing.

They were making no measurable progress toward their goal. Night was far along now. The jungle seemed to sleep. Even the drowsy drone of insects was heard no more.

Stormalong Savage was talking.

"This portion of Skull Island reminds me very much of the Khorat Plateau in Siam," he offered. "That was back in the days when the tea trade was at its height. King Mongkut ruled Siam in that era. The tea leaves produced during his illustrious reign were unsurpassed in all the world. They fetched a pretty penny."

"Tell me about your life," invited Doc.

"The sea is my life," Stormalong said brightly. Then more sadly, "Or it was...."

"Men still sail ships," Doc pointed out.

"The Age of Steam has come. I am a sailing man. The ships of my day are all gone now, broken up for salvage or lying at the bottom. Even the *Courser.*" His voice cracked, and nothing Doc said could entice him to resume his account.

They moved along in silence, giving their full attention to the way ahead.

Here and there, Doc paused to examine stands of bamboo. Each time, he moved on, as if unsatisfied.

"What is it about the bamboo that interests you, Doc?" asked

Stormalong, seemingly back to his old self.

"I have an idea. I entertained it earlier, but had not time to act upon it."

"Yes? Go on. I am quite interested."

"I spent some time among the Cherokee," related Doc.

"A proud people. I fancy the Apache myself. Superb warriors. In my youth, before I went to sea, I harried them all over the Southwest as an Indian scout."

"The Cherokee taught me their skills," continued Doc, "one of which was to fashion blowguns and darts from nature."

"I see. You think to meet the Dyak enemy on their own terms?"

"Exactly. Their blowpipes are very long and accurate, but inefficient in other ways. They are difficult to carry and awkward to bring to bear in close combat."

A twinkle came into Old Stormy's eye. "I begin to comprehend your drift."

Doc came upon another stand, picked through it rapidly and swiftly began hacking at a long thin stalk with his Bowie knife. He whacked off one section at each joint.

After he had the section cut to size, Doc examined its interior. With his knife point, he dug out the membranes sealing the joint, exposing its hollow interior.

"This specimen is much shorter than the Dyak tubes," he explained. "But it has the advantage of greater portability and range, if the lungs impelling it are up to the job."

"I take it you think that yours are."

"I have been trained as no other man has ever been trained," said Doc quietly. It was not a boast. It might have been a statement of half-regret mixed with a trace of restrained pride.

Doc repeated the operation with other sections of the bamboo rod, then split a leftover length until he had created a brace. To this, he attached six short bamboo tubes, lashing them together with fiber cords he harvested by stripping rattan vines.

"I recognize the famed Pan-pipes known to the Greeks and Incas alike," said Old Stormy, "but I fail to imagine of what use that musical instrument will be to you here."

"Think of this as a repeating blowgun," said Doc.

A slow amazement crawled over Stormalong's coppery features. Fingering his beard, he watched the bronze man with growing interest.

From a small leather pouch in his pocket, Doc cautiously extracted a few of the Dyak darts he had earlier acquired. Sitting down, he removed the feather fletching, breaking off two inches of the long splinters, and discarding them. He handled the poisonous ends with great care and respect.

From another pocket, Doc pulled a handful of the milk-thistle spikelets he had picked along the banks of the turbulent river that flowed down from Skull Mountain.

Removing the feathers, Doc attached the fuzzy thistle tuft with what he took from another pocket. It was a long loop of ordinary thread.

Captain Savage watched with interest. "Thistledown?"

Doc nodded. "The Cherokee used it for fletching spines plucked from the black locust tree. Thistle has the advantage of filling the tube of a correctly-sized blowgun, forming a seal, thereby offering greater resistance to the breath of the blower."

A twinkle came into one narrowed yellow eye. "Which would translate into a higher velocity, with considerably greater penetrating power."

"That is my expectation," said Doc, finishing his work.

"Rather like employing a six-gun instead of a Winchester rifle."

"Exactly my thinking. At short range, they should be very accurate."

Pocketing his newly-made missiles, Doc stood up.

"What are the Dyak darts dosed with?" the bronze man asked.

"When at war, a paste made from the sap of the *upas* tree. Invariably fatal. But I have never noticed any *upas* trees on Skull Island."

"If I run out, as I am certain to do," said Doc, "I will need fresh poison. Perhaps if a venomous serpent can be milked safely. Have you any suggestions?"

"I do not. For I have managed to avoid all such encounters. But Penjaga knows the names of every plant and herb growing upon Skull Island, and their specific properties. She could advise you."

"If it comes to that," Doc said, "we will seek her out."

DOC started off, the multi-blowgun firmly in one hand, his pouch of darts handy in his pocket.

"You look more like a natural man, without that ugly weapon," observed Stormalong.

"I feel very much like Tarzan of the Apes," Doc admitted.

Frowning, Stormalong murmured, "I fail to follow your reference."

"Tarzan was a fictional man who was raised by apes until he achieved mastery of his jungle in Africa. It is a novel published just a few years ago."

Old Stormy scratched his bristly beard. "Sounds like the story of Romulus and Remus, but with apes substituted for the wolves."

"Tarzan carried a bow and employed arrows," mused Doc. "If I can locate the correct materials, I might do the same."

"You will need catgut," Stormalong pointed out. "There are no suitable animals on Skull Island from which to extract the appropriate stomach lining that I have ever encountered."

"Pterodactyls might provide a fair substitute."

"You will have to bring one down. A daunting feat."

"Remain here," Doc said suddenly.

Leaping into a tree, Doc found his way up to the top. He

poked his bronze-haired head around. Pterodactyls did not seem to be nocturnal. Therefore, they had to roost somewhere.

Peering about, Doc saw something gleaming redly in the moonlight and realized that he was staring out at the slaughtered Triceratops. That gave him an idea.

Dropping back to the ground, making so little noise that Stormalong was momentarily startled even though he was expecting the big bronze man, Doc Savage said, "I have a better idea. Come."

Doc led his grandfather through ferns and foliage to the clearing where the Triceratops lay, emitting a foul stench of death.

"Dyaks did this?" Stormalong asked.

"Evidently. They only took the horns."

Stormalong grinned. "Even Dyaks would be hard pressed to haul a Triceratops head around with them."

Removing his Bowie knife, Doc climbed the leaden beast and began carving out a felt swatch. He cut two, brought them down, and proceeded to cut out holes for their heads.

Doc donned his first, saying, "This will make us all but dart-proof against Dyak blowpipes."

"Capital idea!" Stormalong climbed into his, looked down at himself and noted, "I fear my arms and legs are exposed."

"It cannot be helped. Let's go."

"One thing more," said Old Stormy.

"Yes?"

"Should I take a Dyak dart in any limb, I must ask you to employ your knife to remove said limb before the poison reaches my heart."

"Dyak darts work too fast for that remedy to be effective," reminded Doc. "And there is no means at hand to staunch the stump, in any event. You would bleed to death."

Stormalong Savage drew himself up to his full, considerable height. "I would rather bleed to death at the hands of my own kin than suffer the indignity of dying via the sting of a Dyak dart," he pronounced firmly.

Doc said nothing. His grandfather's fatalistic talk was beginning to bother him.

They pushed on.

"Doc?"

"Yes, Grandfather?"

"No matter what happens," Stormalong said thinly, "do not let them take my head."

"I will not," promised Doc.

"And in return I solemnly promise to safeguard yours."

After that, they spoke not at all, as they threaded through the jungle while the rumbling of Kong's intermittent roars punished their ears.

Chapter XLII

THE ROARING OF Kong reached the ears of Monyet in the safety of his bamboo perch. He stifled his coughing and listened attentively.

He had been eating a grub he had discovered in a hole in the tree that supported him. He finished chewing the living thing, enjoying the squirming taste of it in his mouth, then swallowed. It reminded him of a sago worm.

"Kong..." he breathed.

A disturbance in the undergrowth caused the Dyak prince to shift his attention earthward.

"Who?" he hissed.

"It is I—Ukung," returned a soft voice.

Monyet peered downward, discerned a hairless face blackened by charcoal war paint looking up with dark eyes rimmed with ivory.

"Where are the others?" he hissed.

"Scattered. Some dead. They know to come here."

The Dyak scout wrapped his legs around the tree trunk and ascended by pulling his curled body upward by rapid movements of his strong hands. He joined Monyet there.

"Kong has returned to his lair," Ukung reported.

"Yes, I hear him. So?"

"We can lay siege to Kong there."

"Two of us?" spat Monyet.

"No! We will find the others."

"I will not leave the head I carried all this way. We will wait for the others to return."

Ukung sat down and unsheathed his curved *mandau* sword from its hardwood scabbard. He ran its iron edge against a length of bamboo, testing its sharpness.

"Where are the white devils with eyes of gold?" asked Monyet.

Ukung was slow in replying. Monyet grabbed him by the hair.

"Answer!"

"We assembled a dugout, dropped it into the water and attempted to board the big sailing ship of the golden-eyed ones."

"Attempted?"

Ukung looked shamefaced. "We no sooner slipped aboard than thorns bit into the bottoms of our feet. Everywhere we stepped, they stung like wasps. We were forced to leap into the water in retreat."

As proof, Ukung showed the naked soles of his feet. Red puncture marks peppered them. Some still bled.

"What did that?" asked Monyet.

Ukung drew from his thick hair a sharp tack, its point encrimsoned.

Examining it, Monyet hissed, "Clever."

"Painful," returned Ukung.

They sat in sullen silence while they considered their situation.

When they crossed the Indian Ocean to Skull Island, the *balla* had broken up. One group made landfall, while the others arrived later. The two groups had not yet reunited. The second group was about in the jungle, fending for themselves.

Before long, a party of their fellow warriors put in an appearance, their lean bodies darkened by charcoal.

"*Selamat siang, Penghulu* Monyet!" they hailed, calling him their chief.

"Where are the rest of you?"

"Dead, or lost."

Monyet frowned. "Our numbers are still formidable."

"The heads of the enemy will lie in a pile at our feet before the sun rises in the morning," said a warrior called Maban.

"We will carry them back to be buried with our bones so that they will be our slaves in the next life," added another, hoisting his *mandau*.

"Let us be about our business then," decided Monyet. "Two of you help take the ape head down."

Two Dyaks scrambled up in the traditional crouching climb. They began tying the head to a fat pole of bamboo with cord. This grisly object they carefully passed down to waiting men on the ground.

When that was accomplished, Monyet climbed down. He struggled with it, his lungs not yet recovered from their ordeal. Hate burned in his breast. Hate for the brazen men with eyes of gold.

Soon, every man had reached the jungle floor. The head of the dead kong was hoisted onto the bare shoulders of Ukung and Maban and, with Monyet in the lead, the long march to Skull Mountain began.

The desiccated head bounced with each step, in a macabre dance of death.

Overhead, the half-moon continued its slow majestic rise, throwing light that painted the marching Dyaks until their charcoaled skins shone eerily, like ashy ghosts.

One word burned in their brains: *"Kajai!"* Headhunt!

Chapter XLIII

CLARK SAVAGE, SENIOR, heard the mighty roars of the beast-god Kong, and feared for the worst.

Extricating himself from the mound of dirt and debris that the ape-beast had caused to crush him to the ground, he had watched his son being carried off by the big black-haired brute. His Very pistol was lost—buried in the heavy filth.

Savage had attempted to follow, but it was a useless undertaking. His legs were too tiny, his steps too small. There was no catching up with the great ape that walked in what seemed like seven-league strides.

Stubbornly, he commenced a trek to Skull Mountain regardless, Chicahua leading the way, slashing through the jungle with his machete.

It was quicker work to hack than to circle around the dense foliage. In the darkness, they had no certain sense of the surrounding terrain. In time, they found their way to the River of No Return. Walking single file, they followed its rustling banks.

"Keep a sharp watch for Dyaks," the captain warned his Mayan crewman.

Chicahua needed no such admonition. He gripped his machete with fists of hard bone, the knuckles standing out with white intensity.

In his heart was loyalty. But in his brain burned the desire to decapitate those who had removed the heads of his brother and fellow crewmen.

Now they were making their way to Skull Mountain and, after a period of silence, a thunderous roar split the night, sending unseen frightened things scattering amid the brush.

"Kong is awake," he told Chicahua.

But the Mayan had no thought of Kong. His obsidian eyes searched for humans.

Their eyes stayed focused on the looming eminence that was Skull Mountain. They were coming up on it from its blank rear flank. It didn't resemble a death's-head from this angle. It might have been an ordinary mountaintop of the stony type.

So it was that they failed to detect the Dyak outrigger canoe slipping up behind them, following the course of the river, determined oarsmen propelling it along at a brisk clip.

Their first indication of danger came when something flicked past Chicahua's right ear.

Lifting a hand, he smacked at the ear, thinking it a pesky insect. It was a natural mistake to make. Bugs had bothered them all along, and the fear of Dyak darts had grown dull after so many false alarms.

But Captain Savage, treading behind his Mayan, was not so complacent.

Whirling, he spotted the dugout, propelled by blank-faced oarsmen.

"*K'ulel!*" Captain Savage called out. Foes!

Out came his revolver. He took dead aim and knocked a warrior into the water before the man with the blowpipe could accomplish his dirty work.

The splash was followed by sharp cries of anger.

Chicahua came around with his blowgun rising to his mouth. He dropped to his haunches, just as a dart whistled over his head. His reflexes, once awakened by danger, were blinding.

The Mayan's cheeks blew out and the man with the empty blowpipe standing in the dugout bow found a feather sticking in his shoulder.

The bitter bite of curare entered the Dyak's system, made him go cold all over. He collapsed in the bow, eyes glazing. He took a while to die. By that time, it was all over.

Dyaks leaped out of the dugout and began splashing to the opposite banks. They were brandishing their iron blades. Their intent was clear. They were seeking heads.

Captain Savage accounted for two more of them. His revolver barked twice, spitefully. Each shot was true. Dyak screams caused the others to break off their attack and fall into retreat.

But it proved to be a tactical retreat. They found shelter, began crawling off.

Chicahua by this time had inserted another dart into his cane blowgun. He began seeking a target.

Only one Dyak remained in the dugout—a man with an oar. Seeing the blowgun turning toward him, he began backing up frantically. Too late.

Chicahua expelled a harsh breath and impaled the man's tongue in his open mouth.

The Dyak dropped his oar and began hacking and spitting, his mouth full of feathers, his impaled tongue already paralyzed, so that he could not cry out.

The man pitched forward in death, his paddle dropping into the rapids.

Captain Savage rapped out a curt order in the Mayan tongue.

They raced for the dugout, plunging into the tumbling river and scrambling aboard.

TAKING up the oars, they began rowing toward Skull Mountain.

It was no easy thing. The river current was against them. But it could be done.

Seeing this act of piracy, the Dyaks crouching in the weeds sprang to their feet and took off in pursuit, yelling, *"Kembali! Kembali!"* Come back! They looked comical, chasing after their own canoe. But it was no laughing matter.

Paddling hard, Captain Savage spied fresh figures lurking around a bend in the tumbling stream.

"Could that be my son?" he wondered aloud.

But that was hope speaking. The new arrivals were dark of skin and feathered and ornamented as no white men ever were.

"Dyaks!" he hissed vehemently. Mentally, he counted the bullets in his revolver and the cartridges in his belt. They were insufficient for the task at hand.

Behind them, the wildly pursuing Dyaks began yelling.

"Musuh! Musuh!"

That meant "enemy." They were between two fires now. If these were civilized men—even pirates—they might surrender and ask for terms. But the only terms the Sea Dyaks understood were head trophies.

Turning to Chicahua, Captain Savage barked in K'iche, "We will disembark and split up. They may catch us both, but they will have to work at it."

But Chicahua had other ideas.

Poling the dugout canoe to the left bank, he stepped out and drew his machete. Screaming rage, he fell upon the nearest Dyak warrior charging toward him.

It was madness. But if so, it was divine madness.

Chicahua plunged in, machete held high. The Dyak met the down-sweeping steel with his own ringing blade of iron. They clashed, separated, clashed again. And off came the Dyak's sword hand at the wrist. The power of the Mayan—and his superior blade—would not be denied.

Sweeping around, Chicahua separated the falling man's head from his neck. It was a lucky strike. The blade edge passed between two vertebrae, otherwise the results might have been less decisive.

Another Dyak came around. Chicahua inserted sharp steel into his foe's vitals, twisted hard. That brought an agonized screech.

The scream had a marked psychological effect upon the others.

White men they had battled, and vanquished, but not this coffee-skinned demon. Seeing the havoc he was wreaking, they backed away cautiously.

Out came their blowpipes. Ironwood mouthpieces found pursed lips.

"Jalk'atij," Captain Savage barked suddenly to Chicahua. Stand aside.

Up came the revolver of Captain Savage. Bullets began splitting facial bones before they could inhale. One lucky shot ran the length of a blowpipe, destroying the open mouth behind it.

It became a strange battle there amid the cattails by the cascading river.

As his captain's pistol barked and its cylinder turned with each squeeze of the trigger, Chicahua selected a fresh victim and eviscerated him, as if slaughtering a wild boar.

Soon, they had whittled down the Dyaks in the front.

The ones bringing up the rear broke, milled about, began attempting to regroup.

Methodically, Captain Savage picked them off where he had a clear shot.

Finally, the last smoking shell was expended.

Captain Savage holstered his useless revolver and glanced back at the forbidding mass of Skull Mountain.

Down came a roaring that shook the blood. But there was nothing to be done about that. It was time to face Death.

Sweeping up a fallen *mandau,* Captain Savage walked deliberately toward a Dyak who writhed in his death agonies. He relieved the dying man of his *duku* knife.

A dripping red blade in each hand, he turned to help Chicahua with his bloody work.

They could claim his head only after he had sent many of them to their Maker....

Chapter XLIV

OVER THE THUNDEROUS Kong roars, Doc Savage heard the strident sounds of struggle. The salty tang of blood came to his sensitive nostrils. Almost immediately, it assailed him in an overpowering tidal wave of hot odor.

Before he could speak the words, Stormalong Savage snapped, "Combat!"

"Coming from the river," rapped Doc.

A moon-burnished apparition, the bronze man pitched in that direction, Old Stormy sprinting hard behind him, a floppy-bearded scarecrow.

They tore through brush and ferns, oblivious to everything else.

Doc leaped over an obstacle he thought was a ground-traveling root. It was only after he passed it and heard a grunty noise that he realized he had narrowly escaped running into a slumbering sail-backed dinosaur of a type he had never encountered in any book. It was no lizard-like Dimetrodon, but rather a creature sporting a duck-like bill and a fabulous bony crest, one that walked upright when awake.

The "root" had been its recumbent tail....

After making sure that Old Stormy had maneuvered his way around it, Doc focused on the path ahead.

He broke out of the trees without regard to his own personal safety. Looking west, the bronze man spied a clot of men in hot contention.

The tall form of his father was in the center of the melee, Chicahua loyally beside him. They stood back to back, fighting off with shimmering and sparking blades a clutch of close-pressing Dyak warriors, attired only in loincloths and colorful headbands sprouting upright black-and-white feathers.

Dropping to one knee, Doc inserted a dart into his blowgun, then pushed it out with all of his formidable lungpower.

The dart struck true. It pinned a tattooed shoulder blade. A man jumped. Twisting, he went down.

Turning his attention elsewhere, Doc had released a second vicious missile.

This one, too, found a man's shoulders. A fresh yelp of surprise resounded. And another Dyak corkscrewed to the ground.

This brought redoubled fury to the defensive work of Captain Savage and the Mayan. Their blades rang and scraped opposing blade and bone. Blood spurted.

By this point in the fray, Doc Savage was rushing to the aid of his beleaguered father. He had his Bowie knife out now, and he plunged in, point-first.

The gleaming steel fang penetrated a throbbing jugular vein. Doc stepped back ahead of the inevitable jet of pumping blood.

His fist smacked a tattooed face, broke the jaw out of skew. Another dark face turned to confront him. Bronze knuckles mashed the nose flat.

The stunned Dyak never felt the Bowie blade hook in and open up his stomach wall, allowing its contents to disgorge in an unpleasant pile at his feet.

The Bowie knife was a terrible weapon, but not more terrible than a curved *mandau* sword. Yet in the Herculean bronze man's fists, it became an unstoppable thing of penetrating steel.

Dyaks fell, broken, then retreated, howling.

Coming in from another direction, Stormalong met them with his vicious slasher-claw weapon. He opened up the throats of those foolish enough to mistake his white beard for easy prey. Possibly, they thought his bearded head would look good in their longhouse back in Borneo.

If so, they made a fatal mistake.

Dayak swordsmen died with their blades not yet bloodied, their tattooed throats gaping redly.

One skulker slipped up from behind, *mandau* held two-handed, poised to take the white-haired head in the single swift sideways stroke required of the Iban headhunter.

Unfortunately, the Dyak was considerably shorter than his intended victim, who towered over all.

Hearing the beginning sweep of the curved blade, Stormalong whirled, jumping back. The blade bit, slicing off the greater portion of his whipping beard.

Howling his wrath, Stormalong snatched at the floating length of beard and flung it in his foe's eyes.

By the time the Dyak got his vision freed, his sternum had been opened by a downward swipe. He fell backward, and a second slice of the vicious claw savaged his throat.

The sight of the great wiry scarecrow with the yellow eyes of a lion standing unscathed over so many fallen had a stark psychological effect of the survivors.

The Dyak warriors who could, broke for the trees.

STANDING back-to-back with his father and Chicahua, Doc sheathed his knife and employed his multiple-barrel blowgun to send fleet darts winging after them. Two went down. Those who made it into the trees had better luck. Most escaped with their lives.

No darts came whispering back in their direction.

The three Savage men gathered together and for a long time, only their eyes communicating their unspoken feelings.

"I have seen the elephant, my boy," said Captain Savage in an emotion-thickened voice. "And I now believe."

"You are referring to Kong," returned Doc.

"I am."

"Orders, sir?"

"Back to the ship, posthaste."

"We may make it before daybreak if we hurry," advised Old Stormy.

Just then, the Earth shook. Crowns of trees trembled in sympathy. Winged things gave forth startled cries and flew off.

Their searching eyes turned in the direction of Skull Mountain, silhouetted by the brilliant tropical half moon.

A roar rippled over the grassland. It was as if the sound created a blade-disturbing wind.

"Kong is coming," warned Stormalong Savage, fumbling at the remains of his beard.

"We had best hurry," suggested Doc.

Turning, they ran for the forest. The fact that it was the same patch of jungle that had swallowed their surviving assailants mattered little now.

Kong was coming. All of them understood that the great beast-god of Skull Island owned nostrils that could sniff them out from the routine odors of the jungle.

Their best chance was to mingle with the confusion of smells created by the retreating Dyaks, even if that meant encountering those vicious warriors anew.

There was no other way. Kong was coming!

Chapter XLV

HEARING THE SHOUTS of a skirmish, interspersed with cries and calls in the Iban tongue, Monyet urged his men toward the darkling river that rolled down from Skull Mountain.

Something else was coming down from its grim summit, they knew.

His footfalls shook the ferns, made the frond-headed palm trees tremble excitedly. The very air seemed to shake. The ground quivered warningly.

"Kong!" cried Monyet, smiling darkly in anticipation.

The Dyak prince rushed ahead. His men, bearing the head of the young female kong jittering on its bamboo-pole litter, picked up their pace, struggling to keep up with their battle-eager leader.

The sounds brought other Dyaks running from where they had been creeping through the jungle, seeking the white men with the eyes of gold.

Soon, Monyet was generaling a growing column of barbaric hunters, bristling with swords, spears and blowpipes.

Slashing and hacking his way with a *duku* knife, Monyet lead them toward the juicy sound of rushing water.

When he broke out into a clearing of bamboo grass, Monyet's eyes raked his surroundings, seeking quick understanding of the situation.

He spied Dyaks lying about, groaning, dying, utterly vanquished.

Monyet's tattooed faced gathered into a savage frown.

"Where are the *musuh?*" he shrieked out.

The dead heard him not. The dying attempted to reply. But their agonized voices were drowned out by a greater noise.

A roar like a volcano blowing fury sounded close at hand. A stink like the breath of a dragon rolled down upon the Dyak prince.

Skidding to a stop, craning his head about, Monyet sought its source.

A shadow seemed to loom overhead. It was no shadow, but an awesome thing of dark substance. A black, hairy monster. Taller than any tree. Rivaling any mountain. More powerful than the most awesome volcano.

Immense golden eyes looked down at Monyet like a pair of strange full moons. For a moment, a terrible fear overtook the Dyak.

Kong!

Just then, the two warriors bearing the bouncing head charged out of the bush.

The amber eyes of Kong flicked from their stunned, upward-turning faces to the bouncing trophy hanging between them. Focusing on the familiar black skull, they congealed like ice.

From his fanged mouth issued a terrible, tree-shaking roar greater than any heard before!

Chapter XLVI

KONG'S FIERCE CRY of reverberant rage froze the blood of everyone within the sound of his voice. Myriad living things on Skull Island, from the rummaging rodents to the towering Tyrannosaurs, took notice.

Upright Hadrosaurs popped their snuffling duck-billed heads up. Long-necked sauropods broke off their laborious snoring, and opened their limpid, slumbering orbs.

Pterosaurs of all colorful configurations took flight from their rocky aeries, beating toward open water.

All of Skull Island awoke to the fury of the beast-god given voice.

A hand as large as a boulder lifted, formed a ball of bristles, bone and muscles, then came crashing down.

The Dyak who had taken the lead of the trophy-carrying pole was lucky. Ukung was simply smashed into a blob of flesh by Kong's avenging fist.

His fellow warrior at the rear was not so fortunate.

The fist sprang open and muscular fingers like black pythons wrapped around Maban. Kong lifted him high, holding the screaming Dyak to his face. Eyes met.

Maban's howls impinged themselves on Kong's small ears.

Kong quenched them by taking the man's howling head between his teeth and biting down. He pulled the headless body free, spat out the suddenly fleshless skull and crushed the limp body into a fleshy sack of broken bones.

Abruptly, Kong dropped the remains and looked around for fresh victims, black lips snarling.

Below, Monyet was screaming orders.

"Darts! Darts! Feather him with darts!"

Dropping their useless swords and spears, a dozen Dyaks began loading their blowpipes with the lethal darts that were long needles of bamboo.

The first volley shot up, peppering Kong's massive lower legs. It was as if the hairy calves had suddenly sprouted quills.

Swiping down, Kong brushed at the source of the scorpion-like stings. Knocking some loose caused momentary pain.

Plucking a splinter out between two fingers, Kong looked at the pathetic feathered thing. If he expected the feathers to twitch or flutter with life, he was mistaken.

Dropping the dart, Kong rotated his brutish head toward the source of the stinging wave.

Another wave whispered upward. More pinpricks stabbed his legs—in the back this time.

Kong roared. The throaty howl was one of annoyance.

Dyaks were sneaking up from behind, blowpipes balanced in cupped hands, mouthpieces pressed to their lips. They let fly. Quills sprouted amid bristling fur. Turning at the waist, Kong gave out a sharp bark of surprise.

More Dyaks began climbing trees, endeavoring to obtain the advantage of height.

Once up in the sheltering boughs, they began raining darts upon his hair-tangled chest. Others aimed at his broad face.

A giant hand groped out, found a blowpipe tube, and pulled it out of the owner's hands. The latter toppled from the trees, breaking his spine on the gnarled roots of its base.

Bending, Kong brought his furry fist down upon the tiny helpless human. Bones crunched. The fist lifted. Kong noticed something sticking to his hand. He peeled off the flat thing that had been a man, flung it away disdainfully.

More darts came. Dozens of them. Snarling, Kong batted at the climbing waves, like a man beset by a cloud of stinging hornets.

His forearm became quivered with the tiny things. Kong smacked at forearms, breaking the splinters, inadvertently driving the dart-points deeper into his flesh.

Their poison, although invariably fatal, was insufficiently powerful to fell the black behemoth.

But as wave after wave arrived to replace the plucked thorns, the accumulation of poisoned points began to seep into his raging system.

THROWING back his head, beating his massive chest with bristling fists, Kong howled his unholy wrath. The stars in the sky seemed to shake in sympathy. The moon actually quaked, but that was a freak effect of the hot atmosphere.

"More! More!" commanded Monyet, bringing his own blow-pipe to bear.

He blew a single dart into the lower spine of the monster.

A hairy hand reached back and swatted at the spot in vain.

Monyet sent a second dart into that paw. It flinched. Puzzled, Kong began sucking at the wound. A third missile struck a spot behind the beast's right knee.

Dart after dart flew out. Men were growing winded. They scattered before the stamping feet. They cowered in trees to escape the clutching monster hands.

Still they puffed whispering death from their ironwood tubes in unremitting streams.

Three warriors, after exhausting their darts, picked up the trio of severed Triceratops horns, which they had carried with them for just this opportunity.

They rushed up behind the monster ape, began worrying its heels with the sharp javelins, which had been slathered with fresh poison.

Kong howled, turned. The men rushed around, trying to

evade those awful crushing feet.

Kong found one with a hand, flung the warrior screaming into the trees—and certain doom.

The second perished when Kong's hairy right heel happened to lurch back and inadvertently crushed him. Kong never noticed.

The third ran away, dropping his clumsy tool of death.

Crouching amid the ferns, Monyet's hoarse voice rolled out. "Pick up those horns! Strike him again!"

And when only one brave man rushed in, Monyet burst out of concealment and picked up one of the clumsy Triceratops horns.

The sharp thing, going into the beast-god's right ankle, lodged there.

Monyet kicked it in harder, then fled as Kong stormed about, seeking the source of this new insult to his lordship.

Kong found the base of the stinging annoyance, wrenched it out.

No sooner had he brought it up to his face to examine the thing than another Dyak slashed his other ankle with the remaining horn.

New sounds began issuing from Kong's mouth. Odd grunts and grimaces. His amber eyes grew strange.

Sensing his vulnerability, but not understanding it, Kong turned toward Skull Mountain, then began to stamp in its direction, his immense shoulders rocking with his rolling gait.

Along the way, he encountered the three Savages.

They had witnessed the brief battle and were running toward the sound.

Seeing the approach of Kong, they dived into the river. With one intent, they started swimming with the current that ran toward the Plain of the Altar far downstream.

Kong's agonized eyes, fixed on the peak of Skull Mountain, had not noticed them before this.

Now those golden-colored orbs dropped. They came to rest

on the bobbing heads.

Two of the human heads Kong recognized. Both possessed the amber eyes of his forebears.

But the one that brought a grunt of surprise to his fanged lips was the one with the bushy white beard.

Veering, Kong lunged for that flailing form. Down swept a hairy hand, down and then up again.

Coming back with it was Captain Stormalong Savage.

The beast-god lifted the man to his quivering nose, sniffed the waterlogged figure carefully. A simian grimace crossed his face. Amber orbs seemed to light up when they recognized the yellow eyes of the tiny human in his paw.

Kong tucked Old Stormy to his heaving chest, and knuckle-walked on his free fist toward Skull Mountain, oblivious to the cries and shouts of protest that echoed below.

Chapter XLVII

MOVING WITH SUPERHUMAN speed, Doc Savage reached out for the hairy arm that had scooped up his grandfather, clamped fistfuls of thick black hair and attempted to ride up with him.

The speed of the great ape's reflexes proved too much. Doc was thrown off, to land back in the raging river.

Sinking, he kicked back to the surface. Looking around, Doc spied his father's transfixed face. The bronze man knifed toward his father's floating form, joined him. Almost immediately, his helmet of bronze hair began drying, a peculiar property it possessed.

"I tried," Doc said, voice twisting.

"No mortal man could have succeeded," his father assured him.

They turned to watch Kong march toward his lofty lair, like a mountain moving toward another mountain.

"His fur is quilled by Dyak darts," observed Doc.

Captain Savage nodded. "No doubt the brute is rapidly succumbing to the poison. It may or may not kill him, but the poor devil understands that his peril is great."

"We have no choice but to follow him to his aerie," said Doc grimly.

Captain Savage squared his shoulders. "As I said before, and as they used to say in my youth, I have seen the elephant. But I am not afraid of it, fearsome as the beast may be."

They climbed out of the water, which was rapidly carrying them away from Skull Mountain.

Chicahua began speaking rapidly. He pointed south.

"Dyaks coming this way," snapped Captain Savage. "To fight them now would be pointless. Let us melt into the bush."

They slipped into the jungle, began working their way toward Skull Mountain, looking in the creeping dawn like a dormant volcano holding its awful potential in reserve.

Along the way, they came upon a herd of horny-backed Ankylosaurs stampeding away from the retreating Kong, their club-headed tails beating a mad tattoo.

Scampering up a handy tree, the three men roosted there until the armored monsters had passed, like a rolling wave of thunder on blunt, pounding feet.

The entire jungle was alive now. Alive with panic. Shadows moved everywhere.

Things crawled and flashed through the ferns, dimly seen.

"We will stick to the trees," said Doc.

They did so, moving along branches, leaping the intervening spaces where they must.

Reaching a point where they needed to rest, they paused. Doc poked his head out above the jungle canopy, allowing his vision to adjust to the early light conditions.

A darksome shadow silhouetted against the low-rising sun, Kong was scaling the side of Skull Mountain. He did so one-handed, with evident difficulty.

Doc could not make out whether Stormalong Savage was still clutched in the fearful hand that hung limply, but he hoped he was. For if he was not, his grandfather's fate would be unthinkable.

Captain Savage joined him. Roosting on a lower branch, Chicahua stood guard against prowlers. They watched in silence, their faces drained of color, expressions gone flat with shock.

Soon, Kong vanished into his rocky lair via the rugged cliff that gave access to one intensely black eye socket.

"We will have to assault the brute where he dwells," said Captain Savage firmly. "With luck, he will survive his wounds before he can harm brave Stormalong."

Doc Savage said quietly, "I do not know if anything mortal could kill Kong."

"In that case," thundered the Captain of the *Orion,* "we will take our illustrious forebear from his hairy hand by force of arms, if need be!"

That, too, struck Doc Savage as an unlikely prospect. But he kept his opinion to himself.

REACHING the base of Skull Mountain took the best portion of the morning.

As they neared the grim-visaged summit, they were forced to travel on foot. They did so with as much stealth as the terrain permitted.

With the rising sun, the air became busy with pterosaurs and other flying things. A few wriggled out of the triangular nose cavity in the mountain's face, and took wing.

One cast a threatening eye upon them: a Pterodactyl, brown as a bat. It circled, its long, bony skull switching about as it attempted to keep them in sight. The beat of its membranous wings was unlike any bird they had ever seen, but its behavior brought to mind a vulture circling intended prey.

"He has us in mind for a meal," suggested Captain Savage.

"Agreed."

Doc decided that striking first was the best course of action.

Taking up his blowgun, the bronze man inserted a dart. Placing one tube to his mouth, he tracked the thing carefully, puffed sharply.

The dart struck the body in the chest—and the flapping creature gave out a long screech. It began flapping away wildly, then seemed to change its mind.

Returning on outspread wings, the pterosaur swooped lower

and lower.

Doc sent another dart at its great mass. This one struck a wing, caused the creature to fold up in midair, before getting itself organized again.

When it finally found its equilibrium, the Pterodactyl shook its agitated head in all directions, again trying to fix the three men walking along the ground.

Doc said, "It appears to be resistant to the poison."

"If only I had bullets," groaned Captain Savage.

Doc went in search of a vine and some stones, thinking a bolas might make an effective weapon for tangling up the ugly monster. But he found none and the thing was swiftly beating its harridan way toward them.

Twin blood-drop eyes focused on them, its bony head resembling a grotesque double-headed hatchet poised to strike. It swooped down.

"Hit the ground!" rapped Doc suddenly.

Captain Savage knocked Chicahua to the grass, followed suit himself.

Doc set himself, his Bowie knife jumping into his hand.

The thing abruptly curled its angular wings in a braking action and long talons jerked up, aiming for the bronze giant.

Doc was running now, running to meet the monster—head-on!

When they finally collided, the bronze man flung a clod of dirt into the red eyes. The thing emitted a fierce screech. It became a long scream of death when Doc Savage tore at it with his short steel fang, fending off clutching talons and twisting the blade point into the spot where it would do the most damage—the long thin neck.

A gurgling resulted as blood filled the Pterodactyl's torn throat. Doc hacked a hole, then slit the throat lengthwise with an abrupt downward rip.

That ended the combat. The winged thing folded up, landing

atop Doc. As its eyes slowly closed, the bronze man crawled out from under its jerking form. Motioning for the others to hurry, he resumed the long trek to Skull Mountain, now shining in the full light of morning. Clouds marching across the sky threw shadow patterns across its craggy dome, and some of these wavered in and out of its hollow eye sockets, giving the death's head countenance the same macabre semblance of life the face had possessed when they first laid eyes upon it.

BY noon, they reached the broad, rocky base, and began climbing without any discussion or planning. There was no need. To reach the lair of Kong was their only objective. Time was of the essence. Nothing else mattered.

The ascent was slow, the need for silence great. From time to time, they paused to con the terrain below.

"No sign of Dyaks," said Doc.

"But they are present," said his father. "Make no mistake about it."

They resumed their climb. It was a matter of finding trustworthy hand- and foot-holds. Loose rocks could precipitate an avalanche, which would betray their approach.

So they proceeded carefully, Doc leading the way.

Doc reached the cliff ledge first, climbing onto the stone-sheltered ledge and lying flat where he could not be seen. There he paused, listening.

The sound of Kong's breathing came, low and labored. Doc had heard it before, of course. But this time it was different. It sounded ragged, no longer strong and naturally rhythmic.

Venturing to raise his head, the bronze man dared a quick glance, then ducked back.

What he saw told him a great deal.

Kong lay recumbent, flat on his back, face upward, mouth agape. He seemed to be breathing through his open mouth, another sure sign of distress.

Doc stole another peek.

Kong was oblivious to him. He stared upward, like a man expecting death, eyes focused on eternity. His great barrel chest worked like a slow bellows.

From time to time, a hairy paw moved, feeling along its fur, questing and removing a long needle-like dart when he found one. Kong appeared to have little strength for this procedure. Each dart, he tossed away without looking at it. Doc could see that there were many more darts yet to be discovered.

Of Stormalong Savage, he had glimpsed no sign.

Withdrawing, Doc returned to the spot where his father and Chicahua crouched.

"Kong is dying," Doc reported.

"Never mind him!" snapped Captain Savage. "What news of Old Stormy?"

"I didn't see him," admitted Doc.

"We must enter the den of the devil without delay."

Doc hesitated, wanted to say that it was too dangerous, but realized that if they did not enter as a group, his father would plunge in alone. He could not blame him.

Nodding wordlessly, Doc Savage turned to lead the way. He did not bother to load a fresh dart into his blowgun. It would hardly have any effect upon Kong now....

Chapter XLVIII

DOC SAVAGE WENT over the lip of the high, jagged cliff that led into the hollow eye socket of Skull Mountain as rapidly as he could. This in order to get in before his father could catch up. His intention was to absorb the brunt of any defense by Kong.

But all that Kong did was make a sharp intake of breath. A snuffling grunt came, and the Titan ape attempted to turn its head. It appeared to have little reserve strength for that.

One amber eyeball did roll downward into the corner of its socket. It began tracking the bronze man in an unnerving way. It was larger than Doc's head.

Keeping his distance, Doc made a circuit of the prone ape, walking past the massive feet, both of which were cocked askew.

The musky smell of Kong was strong, and drowned out all other odors. Doc could detect no other persons in the lair.

Reaching Kong's opposite side, Doc came upon Old Stormy.

The incredibly tall seaman was stretched out several feet away, where he had evidently crawled in an effort to escape Kong's death clutch.

Doc detected the jerky movement of his chest, but no other action.

A groan came from the elongated giant. He was still tangled up in the Triceratops poncho Doc had made for him.

Rushing to Old Stormy's side, Doc carefully removed the cumbersome garment and felt him over. The head lifted, turned.

Cat-yellow eyes brightened.

"Doc," he groaned.

"Here."

"I am afraid...that...I am done for...."

Doc made a cursory examination. He discovered broken ribs. Many of them.

"Kong did this."

"He... did not know what he was doing. He was...lonely, without forebears or issue...the last of his breed...."

Old Stormy coughed once, and a spray of syrupy blood came, speckling what remained of his long snowy sea captain's beard.

Doc felt of the man's amazingly long arms and legs. They were intact. No broken bones. His medical knowledge was coming to the fore.

Looking up, Doc saw that Kong's other eyeball had now fallen on them. There was pain in it. Nothing more. No threat. No menace. Nothing but worry. The awesome creature never seemed more human.

Doc's hand drifted to the herbal bag around his neck. It was supposed to be a repellent, but it seemed useless now. Kong could scarcely move now.

A voice hissed out, "Clark!"

It was Captain Savage.

"Over here," called Doc.

Captain Savage rounded the feet of Kong, and his metallic gaze fell upon Stormalong lying there. His entire face winced when he saw the crimson spray of beard.

"Father!" he choked, rushing forward.

It was as if Kong was not present.

"He is in a bad way," Captain Savage said, after making his own examination.

"Broken ribs, at least one lung has collapsed. No doubt there are other injuries of an internal nature."

Doc offered, "We dare not move him in his present condition, lest his injuries become compounded."

Captain Savage turned to glower at the recumbent Kong. "That foul ape!"

"Kong is not at fault," said Doc. "Not entirely, at any rate."

Glowering, Captain Savage seemed on the verge of rebuking his son when Old Stormy hacked out, "The boy is…correct. Blame no one…but the Dyaks."

"What can we do?" Captain Savage asked his son.

"If he has any chance, it will be through proper medications," decided Doc.

"Of which we have none in this doubtful den," frowned Savage Senior.

"Penjaga," wheezed Old Stormy.

They turned toward him. "What is that?" demanded Captain Savage.

"The Keeper knows all the island herbs," explained Doc. "She could help."

"Yes," said Stormalong Savage. Suddenly, he rolled his yellow eyes up in his skull and his bearded face turned over to one side.

Kong grunted once, sharply. His nearest arm stirred. He struggled to reach out to Old Stormy, but lacked the energy. His paw fell flat, fingers curling inward.

STRIPPING off his shirt, Doc rushed to the great dark pool that occupied a corner of the lair of Kong. He soaked it, then brought the sopping article back to his grandfather's side.

Captain Savage took it from him, and began wiping Old Stormy's brow, saying, "See if you can fetch up some water."

Doc moved about the great cavern, found nothing at first, then spied a bar of light. He squeezed through a rift in an inner wall of rock.

On the other side, he discovered what appeared to be a natural warehouse. There were hardwood chests containing art objects, sealed scrolls, and other artifacts of a civilized people. Statuary predominated. The figures were coated with dust and grime, but appeared to have been worked by master artisans. The people depicted seemed of Asian origin.

Rummaging around, Doc discovered cups and goblets carved of some mineral material resembling soapstone. He took two of these back and washed them in the pool, then filled them with water from another side of the still impoundment.

Captain Savage quirked quizzical eyebrows when Doc returned with the brimming cups.

"Treasure," clipped Doc.

Captain Savage nodded, attempted to pour some of the cool liquid into his father's blood-specked lips. The waters slipped in, brought spasms to Old Stormy's chest.

Then he stopped, stood up. "I dare not make him drink too much. Every time he coughs, it risks further lung punctures."

Removing his Colt revolver from its holster, the captain asked, "Have you any bullets? My revolver is empty."

Remembering the rounds he had left behind during his first experience in Kong's lair, Doc excused himself and climbed up onto the shelf. They were still there.

"Here," offered Doc, after he had returned.

Captain Savage examined them critically. "I fear the combination of immersion and jungle humidity has done them no good," he muttered distractedly. "And I dare not test one until I have a worthy target."

Doc Savage said, "Father, you must remain here. I will fetch the old woman."

"Very well." Captain Savage set his hands on Doc's shoulders. "In you," he said thickly, "I place all my hopes. The Savage line must endure."

Doc said nothing. His eyes went to his grandfather, as if fearful of seeing him for the last time.

"I will return directly," he promised.

Guarding the entrance, Chicahua stopped him as Doc moved toward the ledge.

"*Enemigo,*" said the Mayan, pointing to the plain below.

Enemies.

Between the wall and the severe countenance of Skull Mountain, brown figures were moving through the bush. Dyaks. They were working their steady way in this direction, Doc saw.

Skirting the heaving body of Kong, Doc returned to his father's side.

"Dyak war party approaching."

"Chicahua and I will hold them off. But how to get you out of this accursed place without being seen? They will hunt you down, son."

Doc strode over to the dark pool. He peered down into its depths.

"Do you suppose that this connects to the torrent that is the source of the River of No Return?"

"If it is a natural well, it might."

"Rainwater did not make this," said Doc, kicking off his boots. "I am going to chance it."

Captain Savage nodded gravely. "If you become disoriented, return at once. I will not lose you as well. That is an order."

"Aye, aye, Captain."

Doc began charging his lungs for the plunge. He removed everything possible, starting with his boots—all except for his Bowie knife and scabbard. He took two minutes to prepare. The Pan-pipe blowgun he shoved into the small of his back, where it was unlikely to impede movement.

The last thing he did was to seal the Dyak dart sheath as tightly as he could before placing it in a back pocket. Doc wondered if the pasty poison would retain its potency after immersion.

Then the bronze giant leaped into the pool and was gone.

With pained eyes, Captain Savage watched the spreading ripples. No bubble of oxygen popped to the surface. Not a one. When five minutes had passed, he returned to minister to Stormalong Savage, his metallic features a knot of pain.

Chapter XLIX

PRINCE MONYET SURVEYED the bruised and blood-ied remnants of his Dyak forces.

They had been devastated. One had lost an eye, and another an ear. Fingers were missing from many. These were the survivors.

These men went among the mortally wounded and, in an act of Dyak mercy, with swift, downward strokes of their *mandau* blades relieved them of their heads so that they would not suffer the indignity of decapitation by enemies, and be damned to spend the rest of eternity roaming the jungle as *buan*—headless ghosts who knew no rest.

This was soon accomplished.

Calling together what remained, Monyet stood before them, moonlight glinting on his gold breastplates.

"We will hunt them down. All of them. We will take their heads. We will beard the mighty Kong in his lair. We will take his head. And when we are done, we will paddle home in triumph!"

The mere thought of how the village women and children would greet them on their arrival, hailing them as heroes, ignited their flagging spirits. Heads were like gold to them. They occupied places of honor in every longhouse fortunate enough to boast one. There, they dried, the rats eating away the outer skin until time transformed them into dried black death's heads of superhuman power.

But the thought of the many men lost on the venture tempered their ardor.

For, after all those losses, they had no heads except for the one trophy they had come with—the skull of the young kong. It was a disappointing boast.

But they were Dyaks. To question or disobey their prince was not in their nature.

So when Monyet turned to begin the dangerous march toward Skull Mountain, every man followed.

They left the kong head behind. There would be time to retrieve it later. And if they did not because they could not, it would not matter. For they would all be dead.

Marching at the head of his men, *duku* in one closed fist, blowpipe in the other, only Monyet lacked such defeatist thoughts. His dark eyes burned. His mouth formed a snarl of determination. He had no intention of failing, much less dying. He would have the heads of his enemies and they would occupy places of honor in his family longhouse. Of that, he was absolutely certain.

His firm confidence in himself, his belief in his destiny, was unswerving. It remained with him even after he witnessed at a distance the brazen giant with the lungs of iron, who had bested him in contest, beat back and defeat a flying bat-lizard—armed with no more than a short knife.

It was an impressive feat. But Monyet feared failure more than he dreaded death.

And because his warriors understood this, they followed him to his certain destiny....

Chapter L

DOC SAVAGE DESCENDED into a cold, unwelcome darkness. It was so still he began to doubt the wisdom of his plan. Very quickly, all light ceased to excite his retinas and he was moving down by feel, fingers scoring the slimy sides of the well. To a wonder, they felt slick, manmade. It was possible this was created—or at least improved—by the unknown race that had left behind those relics in the chamber of the other eye socket.

Deeper and deeper sank Doc, his lungs holding their reserve of air. He released none of it—not even when something that felt as slick and slimy as the stone sides brushed one bare forearm.

Something suddenly wrapped about his wrist. Doc felt a tug—sharp, powerful, utterly irresistible.

Free hand flashing for his blade, Doc drew it and began hacking at something both sinuous and rubbery. The coil constricted. Doc felt himself being pulled into deeper darkness.

Hooking the blade under the tightening thing, Doc sliced upward and away from his trapped wrist.

The Bowie edge cut through!

Feet kicking, arms beating, Doc drove himself further down until he felt a new tug. This was a current of water. He surrendered to it.

Banging off rocks, the bronze giant found himself helpless in the flow of water. Still, he refused to release a breath. If Doc was right, he would be carried to the safety of the open air. If not—death. There was no turning back now....

A crack of light careened into view. Doc got control of his tumbling. Just in time.

A flow of water yanked him out of the rugged flank of Skull Mountain and deposited him roughly into the foaming headwaters of the River of No Return.

Doc kept his head down and his mouth closed. He released a breath finally, but refused to surface. Taking control of his trajectory, Doc swam with the current, not sticking his head above water until he could hold his breath no longer.

When he broke up into open air, Doc peered around, ready to dive ahead of Dyak darts. But he saw none.

Climbing onto dry land, Doc looked back at the base of Skull Mountain. He saw nothing alarming. So he struck out in the direction of the tremendous great wall gleaming in the morning sun, walking along the river bank. He stopped from time to time to pluck extra thistles.

Along the way, he noticed the inflamed circular marks on his right wrist. Their significance was unmistakable. Sucker marks of an octopus tentacle....

AFTER some slow going, Doc realized that the river would carry him farther, faster, if he simply entered it. He did, began swimming.

The course became a torrent and when it became too dangerous, Doc, not knowing when he might find himself striking rocks or going over a natural falls, struck out for land and resumed his trek on foot. He went at a trot, seemingly tireless. He regretted the absence of close-packed trees, otherwise he would have taken to the branches. His lack of boots seemed not to bother him at all.

An hour of this took him to a stand of green bamboo shoots and the bronze man worked through the close-packed growth.

Doc encountered no Dyaks, failed even to scent them.

He doubted that he had been spotted coming out of Skull Mountain, but going up was another matter. They had taken care in climbing the skull-faced side, but to reach the lair, they had to walk along open space, where they were exposed. The Dyaks beating toward Skull Mountain would be chiefly interested in Kong, but would be only too happy to add the heads of his father and grandfather to their collection.

Finding Penjaga the Keeper proved not so difficult as Doc Savage first imagined. Moving through the jungle, Doc suddenly smelled a human.

Creeping around in a circle, he attempted to come up on the blind side of the lurker.

His stealth was excellent, and he made little sound.

Yet he found himself looking into a long gun barrel poking out of a clump of ferns.

It was the muzzle of his Annihilator submachine gun! Instinctually, Doc froze in place. He did some swift mental calculating. The bronze man knew the weapon had been devoid of ammunition when he abandoned it. The only other clip had been lost when Kong seized him. It was possible that a Dyak might have salvaged one, but would he possess sufficient mechanical knowledge to load it properly? Unlikely. But not impossible.

And who was to say that this was a Dyak?

Doc decided not to risk any rash move. Concern over the fate of his family tempered his usual willingness to plunge into a situation, confident in his physical powers.

"Do you want me to surrender?" asked Doc in a clear voice.

Ferns rustled. Up from the shivering greenery rose a small wizened figure clad in dinosaur skins.

It was the old woman, Penjaga, her face a quivering web of fleshy wrinkles.

"Do not make me shoot you, Gold Eyes," she warned in piping English.

"I was seeking you out," said Doc plainly.

Her wise old turtle eyes narrowed. "Why do seek me?"

"Kong lies dying yonder on Skull Mountain. As does Old Stormy. We have no medicine for either."

Penjaga lowered the weapon and hefted a pouch made of some lizard-like skin in one hand.

"Why do you think I am walking the jungle like this?"

"I do not know," admitted Doc.

"Is that what you always say? You do not know? You do not understand? What *do* you know?"

Mustering his patience, Doc asked, "Can you help?"

"Take me to Skull Mountain safely and we will both see."

"Come then," said Doc.

He left the Annihilator. There was no point in attempting to carry it back to Kong's lofty lair, given the dangerous trek ahead. As before, it seemed unimportant now.

While they crept through the amazingly verdant bamboo and fern underbrush, Penjaga noticed the pouch around Doc Savage's neck. Her nostrils wrinkled.

"Where did you get that?" she asked sharply.

"My grandfather gave it to me," Doc replied. "He said it was a charm to ward off Kong."

"Nothing can ward off the mighty Kong!" the Keeper snapped.

Doc eyed her. "Old Stormy told me you gave it to him for that purpose."

"He did not lie," she said as they pushed fan-like ferns aside to peer ahead. "I lied. The herbs within are brewed to soothe Kong. I gave Old Stormy that pouch to protect him should he fall into Kong's hands again, as I knew he would. He should have kept it about his neck."

"I see," said Doc, motioning Penjaga to follow.

"Take care to keep it about you when you stand before the mighty one."

THEY encountered only one Dyak on their march. A lone

scout. He had been perched high in a coconut palm, looking for them, when he moved suddenly. His elbow struck a heavy coconut shell. It was ripe to fall. It did.

The drupe landed with a thud, cracked, disgorging its watery milk.

Doc froze.

"Coconut," said Penjaga contemptuously.

"Dyak," corrected Doc, indicating his nostrils.

The Dyak heard them and sent a dart hissing downward.

Doc dodged it, loaded one tube of his own blowgun. He returned a dart of his own.

The Dyak was hardly in a position to evade it from his lofty perch. He tried to tuck his legs up under him and took the missile on the callused sole of one foot.

Quickly plucking out the barb, he threw it at Doc, but missed.

That was his last act on Earth. Giving a mingled cry of fear and warning, he toppled from his precarious seat. The poison had worked.

The hapless man was probably dead before he hit the ground. In any event, his body did not exhibit any outward manifestation of dying. It simply lay crumpled where it fell, head askew on his broken neck.

Doc collected the man's leather dart sheath and pushed on, Penjaga trailing him stealthily.

Chapter LI

MONYET LED HIS forces toward Skull Mountain, swimming in the midday mists.

They stopped along the way only once, where they found a cache of very large eggs. These they broke open into hastily *duku*-halved coconut shells, mixing the contents with coconut water, drinking the nutritious combination greedily.

"These are the eggs of the dragon-lizards who dwell here," said Monyet, wiping his mouth. "They will give us the strength of a dozen men."

This was their firm belief because the Iban god of hunting was a being called Gana, who had the fantastic form of a dragon. The fact that Skull Island was infested by dragon-lizards and fierce, reptilian birds the Dyaks took as a sure omen of success in their head hunt. These creatures, they reasoned, must be the children of Gana.

They were convinced on this point until a roaring two-legged reptile burst out of the foliage. The monster took the head of the nearest unwary Dyak into its massive jaws and began chewing it. The sound of the man's skull breaking under the thing's terrible teeth reminded them of the sounds of the stolen eggs breaking, which had been the creature's brood. But the irony of that was lost on the scattering Dyak band.

Darts whistled into the creature's thick hide but appeared to do no good.

Monyet ordered his men to scatter, and so they left the

dragon-lizard to his human meal. The mealy sound of human bones breaking followed them for a time.

Eventually reaching the rock-strewn base of Skull Mountain, Monyet ordered a warrior to forage ahead as a scout. The latter left rapidly.

The lone warrior began working his way up the stony side of the summit. He managed to reach a high spot when a strange warrior stepped out on the ledge jutting out from beneath the hollow, fire-blackened stone eye sockets, and sent him plunging earthward by blowing a dart into his unprotected chest.

Seeing his scout tumble to a certain fate, Monyet hissed like a snake.

"We will have to find another way up," he snapped.

Two warriors volunteered for the duty. They went up. This time, one expelled darts while the other climbed. Then, the first man paused to cover the second climber.

In this way, they managed to keep the coffee-colored guardian of Skull Mountain from firing down with impunity.

Unfortunately, they ran out of darts before they reached the formidable ledge where the lone sniper stood sentinel. Reluctantly, they returned to earth.

Monyet ordered three men up this time. He filled their pouches with fresh darts, saying, "He will run out before you do."

The three scampered up the face of Skull Mountain, seeking the broken ledge under the cavernous hollows.

This time, the coffee-skinned guard changed tactics. He began rolling rocks down the side of Skull Mountain.

One landed atop a man, bounced off. When it reached the bottom, the man it struck had landed atop the settling stone, his limp body splayed like a beached starfish.

Monyet grinned, displaying filed black teeth. That still left two men, and they now knew what to expect in the way of defenses....

Chapter LII

RUSHING BACK TO Skull Mountain, Doc Savage took in the seriousness of the situation at a golden glance.

By the time he broke out to a point where he had a clear view of the forbidding peak, a clutch of Dyaks were scaling the flanks of Skull Mountain while others were dodging stones and boulders sent crashing down by Chicahua the Mayan.

But Doc could see what Chicahua could not: That there were many more Dyaks than the ones who were obviously acting as decoys. These skulkers were creeping up, unsuspected and unseen.

It was just a matter of time....

Penjaga squeezed her wise eyes at the stark summit of Skull Mountain.

"What is good for the ant is sufficient for the beetle," she intoned.

"Meaning?"

"They climb three sides. We will climb the fourth."

It made sense. Doc knew that returning via the torrent was impossible, for the tumbling current ran the wrong way.

Or was it impossible? Doc now knew that a great natural reservoir existed under the looming mountain. From this issued the River of No Return. But what fed it? Searching his memory, he recalled other wild tributaries he had glimpsed on the faceless side of what his grandfather called Mount Skull. It stood to reason that something fed that reservoir, and its perpetual cascade on the other side.

"Can you swim?" asked Doc suddenly.

"Of course!"

"If I take you with me, can you hold your breath and not panic?"

Penjaga stiffened her spine. "I will walk through fire for Kong."

"First, I need to thin these ranks. Wait here."

"Wait!"

"If you stay low, they will not find you," Doc called back.

"No. Take these, short Savage."

From her pouch, Penjaga extracted a number of needle-like barbs.

Doc examined them. They resembled sting-ray spines, but belonging to a type he had never encountered. Dark and vicious, they undoubtedly came from an evolutionarily divergent species, similar to the giant devil ray.

"I catch them in the pools and eat them," explained Penjaga. "Their barbs are filled with a venom that strikes swiftly."

Studying them, Doc took out a milk-thistle spikelet and saw that it could be attached to the base.

WITHOUT saying a word, he removed his bamboo blowgun from his belt and began tying the downy tufts to the sting-ray spines with thread. They fit perfectly.

Doc asked, "How fast does this stuff work?"

"It causes a man to fall faster than he can take two breaths. But he does not die. He simply goes to sleep."

"Killing them would be better for our purposes," Doc said flatly. "A dead warrior does not rise to fight again."

"It is what I offer you. Would you have me take them back?"

"No," replied Doc. "Thank you."

The bronze giant melted into the bush without saying another word.

It was late afternoon now. Darkness would have been preferable. But the bronze man had to work with what he had.

Crouching as he moved closer, Doc inserted one of the spiny darts into his blowgun. He had too few to test one on an animal first. It was do or die.

Sneaking up behind one warrior, Doc sent a spine into the back of the man's neck.

A hand went to the spot reflexively. Probably the man had an inkling of what had befallen him before he dropped to the grass. But it didn't matter. He was soon on his face.

On a hunch, Doc extracted the dart from the man before moving on. Sting-ray spines were a venom reservoir, just as a wasp's sting is an injector for its venom. It was entirely possible that the darts could be reused before they lost their potency.

Sweeping around, Doc lay down on his stomach and began creeping closer.

He had spotted a Dyak warrior loitering at the rear.

Into his bamboo blowgun went the dart. Doc raised the mouthpiece to his lips. He put the entire explosive power of his indrawn breath behind it and expelled it all.

Doc had aimed the dart for the side of the man's neck, where the carotid artery could be seen pulsing. It was a tough target to strike, but the dart sped true.

The missile appeared as if by magic in the warrior's neck. This man yelled and hopped in place before collapsing. But when he fell, he stayed down.

Going to his side, Doc retrieved his dart and went in search of another picket.

This time, he filled every tube. The thick spikelets remained in place.

In this manner, the bronze giant picked off unwary Dyaks where they loitered in reserve, awaiting the struggle for control of Skull Mountain to be decided.

When he had vanquished all that he could without risking raising an alarm, the bronze man tucked the ingenious blowgun into his waistband, and returned to Penjaga's side.

"We will go to the river now," he announced.

Penjaga followed. They circled Skull Mountain, coming to the blank western side where no Dyaks lurked.

They slid into the water, began wading. Doc led the old woman to the base of the mountain. The riverbank was well-sheltered by undergrowth, so they would not be seen from the low ground. From the air was another matter.

Removing his belt, Doc tied the woman's age-withered wrists together and then ducked under the loop.

"You will ride on my back," he told her.

Penjaga said nothing. Either she was too afraid to speak, or her confidence in the bronze giant caused her to concentrate on taking air into her lungs in imitation of Doc Savage, who was charging his lungs with great, indrawn breaths.

Without warning, Doc plunged underwater, began swimming with powerful overhand strokes.

Doc raced for the mountain. He had seen that the river on this side fed into a kind of low cave. This only made sense. The water pressure of the river running under Skull Mountain kept the natural well filled. Otherwise, the constant outflow would have drained it long ago.

Soon, they were knifing through darkness.

There were only two possible outcomes now. Either the current would carry them to the interior well, where Doc could endeavor to propel himself up the great, still water shaft, or he would emerge out the other side, carried out by the torrent, as before.

As his eyes attempted to pierce the anthracite darkness, Doc felt a sharp tug.

His hands moved freely when he tested them. Kicking his legs, Doc found that they, too, moved unencumbered.

Then what—?

Astride his broad back, Penjaga the Keeper began struggling, her feet kicking in panic.

Something had hold of her!

Reaching for his Bowie blade, Doc Savage began twisting, seeking the unseen thing that had arrested their swim.

In the impenetrable darkness, he detected a vast oblate form, sensed whipping disturbances in the water, as if multiple arms were reaching for him....

Chapter LIII

CAPTAIN CLARK SAVAGE looked up from ministering to Stormalong Savage, his mustached face etched in grave lines.

"How goes it?" he asked Chicahua in his native tongue.

"I will hold them back, Captain."

"How many darts remain?"

"Six."

Captain Savage frowned. Rising to his feet, he skirted Kong, this time going around the head. The great creature's eerily human-like eyes were closed now, his scarred chest rising and falling rhythmically.

In the perilous situation, it was as if Kong was the least of their concerns. He might have been already dead, for all the attention they paid him.

About the bristle-coated creature lay myriad Dyak darts plucked from many points. These were tipped with blood, and proved to be useless. Chicahua had salvaged one, but when he attempted to expel it from his own blowgun, it became lodged in his weapon's barrel. It was like trying to load the wrong caliber bullet into a revolver.

Stepping out onto the rocky cliff ledge, the captain dared a look downward.

Dyaks were posted far back, out of range of dart and bullet. He detected one clambering up the mountain face itself, well below his position. Then another popped into view, withdraw-

342

ing suddenly from sight.

Taking up his Colt, Captain Savage risked a shot. The hammer clicked, but brought forth no result. Frowning, he tried again. Misfire.

Running through the entire cylinder convinced him that his modest ammunition store was utterly useless. Reloading from his pocket produced no more welcome results.

"If we only had a bow and arrows..." he murmured. He shook his silvery head angrily. "I might as well wish for a Winchester rifle."

Sizing up the situation, the captain of the *Orion* turned to his Mayan crewman, who had followed him so silently Savage had been unaware of him until now.

"You watch over Stormalong. I will defend the entrance."

Chicahua hesitated. The look in his obsidian eyes was reproachful.

"I do not doubt your prowess, bosun," Captain Savage reassured him. "I only wish to conserve your strength for the long siege ahead. No one could have defended us more bravely."

With that, Chicahua withdrew silently.

Captain Savage saw that the Mayan had made a pile of loose stones.

Picking up one with both hands, Savage raised it over his head, then hurled it down on the shiny black spot that he knew to be the hair of a climbing Dyak.

The climber lost his footing, fell from sight. Two others came into view, began loosing darts upward.

Captain Savage withdrew, began kicking rocks in the approximate direction of the raiders. He started one minor avalanche, but dared not poke his head over the cliff edge to ascertain what he had accomplished. The Dyaks were devils with their blowpipes.

Soon, the captain had exhausted his store of rough ammunition.

Still, the Dyaks came on.

Scrounging up another stone, he cast it downward. It started others rolling, but no Dyak landed amid the rubble that resulted.

Looking about, he found larger boulders too massive for a mere mortal to move.

Having no other choice, Captain Savage sought out Chicahua and said, "We are down to your final six darts. I regret that I will have to ask you to resume your defense, for I have no expertise in blowgun proficiency."

Chicahua accepted the Triceratops-hide poncho Doc had left for them and placed it over his person. Then he returned to his station, machete concealed beneath it.

There, he displayed cunning by not showing himself for nearly ten minutes. This emboldened the Dyaks, and they began to inch nearer, shooting upward from time to time.

Chicahua spat down five feathered darts and sent five Dyaks reeling and madly clutching stone until their fingers lost all strength. They slipped from sight. The rocks below broke them.

One slender dart remained.

SCOURING the terrain, Chicahua sought the spot where Monyet waited for the path to Skull Mountain's summit to be clear.

The look in the Mayan's eyes told all. If he could only bring down that Dyak, he would die content.

But it was not to be.

Chicahua inserted the final dart into his cane tube and caused a Dyak to howl in the knowledge of sudden inevitable death.

Then, having no other recourse, he retreated to the inner chamber of the peak whose countenance was the personification of Death.

Captain Savage read the bleak look in Chicahua's smoldering eyes.

"I fear my son may be too late," he said.

Chicahua nodded grimly. His fists clenched and unclenched with repressed emotion.

They looked around for other resources, but to no avail. They had exhausted every last one.

All that remained was the great dark pool. It lay still, untroubled as a mill pond. Dark as tar, it might have been composed of some substance mined from Hell's lowermost regions itself.

"We could brave the pool," Savage said gravely, "if it were not for Old Stormy."

Chicahua nodded. He was being given permission to escape with his life—alone.

Silently, he turned around to stand before the inevitable Dyak swarm, to lay down his life before the enemy could seize his captain and friend.

Hanging his head, Captain Savage looked at the still coppery face of his father. He saw death in it. He wondered if Old Stormy, were he to open his eyes one final time, might not see the same stark cast on his son's visage?

Then, a rattling of rock, followed by the padding of stealthy feet came from the direction of the ledge.

"Dark men come," hissed Chicahua.

Stealing a final glance at the sleeping face of his father, Captain Savage issued curt orders.

"Kill as many as you can. Sell your life dearly. Count on me to do the same."

They made fists of their fingers and waited for feathered heads to peer around from the recumbent form of Kong, who had towered over all, but was now reduced to an insignificant player in the drama to come....

Chapter LIV

THE FIRST DYAK warrior to sneak around the corner brandished a *mandau*. It flashed in the dim cavern light, wicked and wavy.

He came padding on bare feet, his teeth flashing white.

A second and third man came behind them, carrying *duku* short swords. With these, they would cut down their foes, while the first relieved them of their heads with the curved *mandau*.

Or would have, if Chicahua had not suddenly rushed forward and seized the lead Dyak in hands that were vises of vengeance.

The warrior, not expecting an attack by an unarmed man, gave out a shriek, bleating inarticulately as his blade was wrenched out of his hands.

Chicahau then unsheathed his machete and employed it to slash twice at the Dyak's muscular midriff. First, he sliced it open, and then in a back sweep, emptied the man's exposed bowels into the floor.

As the groaning Dyak died, Chicahua stepped over his crumpling form and proceeded to beat back the two *duku* blades with great downward strokes.

He bisected one Dyak's sword arm at the elbow and, grinning fiercely, went after the other.

Seeing the terrible ferocity of the Mayan and, remembering the cruel fate inflicted on his fellow *Courser* crewmen, the surviving Dyak turned tail. He collided with others filtering in through the hollow eye-socket entrance.

Chicahua pried the *duku* blade from the dead fingers of the vanquished and tossed it back to Captain Savage, who caught it readily.

Face hard, the Captain of the *Orion* leapt in to join the fray.

Together they charged, blades flying, clashing, smashing, creating brief sparks.

Soon, the Dyaks were in disarray. Chicahua made sure of that. The new arrivals had carried only short swords. The Mayan had the advantage and pressed it. Blades banged, edges skittered and rang. Blood spurted freely.

In this ferocious fashion, the first wave of Dyaks was beaten back to the ledge. But others began pouring in, yelling war whoops.

"A tactical retreat is called for," puffed Captain Savage, wiping gore off his forehead.

They withdrew to the spot by the pool where Stormalong Savage lay dying, oblivious to his peril. Captain Savage and Chicahua examined their bodies for wounds, then looked over one another. To their amazement, they discovered only freely-running cuts, none very serious. Their superior size and muscularity had won the first engagement.

It was not long before another wave of Dyak warriors resumed the assault.

This time, the blank-faced, charcoal-smeared raiders crept around Kong from his other end in a counterattack.

Chicahua leaped to meet one foe. Captain Savage took up a wide-legged stance over his father's prone and defenseless form, and prepared to kill or—if necessary—to perish bravely.

That latter possibility seemed certain now.

Chicahua fought with a fury that could not be withstood. He slashed and hacked and made a pile of arms and legs and stumpy torsos at his feet. He took care to deprive as many foes as he could of their heads, still living or otherwise. This put tremendous fear into the opposition, who believed that losing one's head in battle was as shameful as taking an enemy's head was honorable.

But the wave that he broke was only one of two.

The other came howling and screaming up on Captain Savage, who stood his ground unflinching.

Looking down at his father's bushy-bearded face one last time, the captain prepared to take as many lives as he possibly could.

The first Dyak leaped in. Blades touched, clashed, retreated.

Suddenly, the Dyaks stopped cold. They were no longer looking at Captain Savage. They were peering past him.

Captain Savage dared not turn to see what drew their amazed gazes. Then, as their dark orbs went wide, he could not resist.

For, behind him, the surface of the pool was boiling and thrashing madly.

Huge greenish tentacles flopped upward, swayed mightily. The crest of a bulbous brain-like head, its skin changing colors iridescently, emerged until the tops of two malign hooded eyes began to show themselves. A coiling tentacle relaxed, snaked out, questing in their direction, its pale suckers looking like horrid blank eyes.

Then, without warning, everything sank from sight.

It was all over in less than thirty seconds. Captain Savage stared blankly, as if he had seen a mirage. A tinge of greenish-blue began to bloom amid the disturbed waters. It spread.

A smooth bronze-haired head broke the surface. Flake-gold eyes, whirling with unleashed power, revealed themselves.

Out of the pool emerged Doc Savage, his firm mouth parted. From his lips issued a wild trilling. It was not a sound of surprise or expression of concern now, but a weird battle cry.

It filled the cavern, made every ear ring, every heart thrill.

Stepping onto dry rock, Doc reached up and snapped the leather belt that was around his muscular neck.

Penjaga the Keeper fell at his heels, eyes bugging out, breathing heavily.

Taking time only to wrest a still-flipping coil of greenish octopus tendril off his left bicep, Doc Savage waded into the Dyaks.

Hands like metal mauls made fists and wrecked faces.

Bright blades were useless against this indomitable man of living metal. With his punishing fists, he struck them from the hands of his opponents, then smashed the stunned blank faces of the disarmed ones. Mortal flesh was incapable of standing up to him.

Dyaks retreated, howling in fear.

Blowing water from his blowgun tubes to clear them for action, Doc sent sting-ray spines whispering after them, one after the other in fast succession. Those he hit, fell.

Stepping out onto the cliff ledge, the bronze giant sent more flying downward.

Dyaks dropped like flies swept clear by a fly swatter.

In an impossibly short space of time, the Dyak horde was scrambling back to the base of Skull Mountain, racing wildly for cover.

Satisfied and confident, Doc Savage turned to rejoin his father's side.

"I got here as fast as I could," he said simply.

Captain Savage's eyes shone with undisguised pride. "Your timing was impeccable," he said, thick of voice.

Their eyes met in silent understanding, then they turned to matters at hand.

Penjaga knelt at the side of Stormalong Savage, her hair dripping water in long gray strings.

"There is little more I can do here," she said sadly. Then Penjaga went to Kong's heavily heaving form, discovered bright bits of feather and balsa-wood fletching sticking out from his hairy hide. She walked around Kong's great bulk, removing the long, splintery bamboo darts, tenderly applying herbs that had been wetted by immersion to the tiny punctures.

"There are so many," she said. "I do not know if I can save him."

"Try," said Doc.

"Give me that bag about your neck, Gold Eyes," Penjaga demanded.

Doc removed the strangely-scented pouch, now sopping wet.

Taking it, the Keeper approached the head of Kong, her aged voice breaking into a song that brought to mind a barbaric lullaby. She approached cautiously at first, then threw the contents of herbal bag into the air, releasing their scent.

To the astonishment of the others, Kong roused, emitting a contented grunt. Penjaga gave one dark wrist a reassuring pat, then proceeded to climb atop the tangled-fur chest like a sailor boarding a gently-heaving sailing craft.

Otherwise, Kong did not react.

Captain Savage took Doc aside and asked quietly, "What did she give my father?"

"Something she poured into his mouth from a small vessel. I do not know what it was. We can only hope for the best."

Doc knelt and examined Old Stormy. When he regained his feet, his face was set. "We may be too late. But we will see."

Captain Savage bowed his pewter-streaked head and turned away, saying nothing, his inner turmoil held strictly in check.

THE hours drifted from day to dusk and soon darkness was again creeping over the fleshless face of Skull Mountain, throwing the stark hollows of his granite visage into greater, deeper shadow until they resembled unfathomable pits.

Doc returned from lying on the ledge outside where he had been observing Dyak activity below.

"They are regrouping," he told his father.

Captain Savage nodded. "Their numbers are greatly reduced."

"And we have few resources," countered Doc.

Captain Savage looked stricken. His clear gold eyes held a

helpless light.

"Could we escape via that well?" he asked.

"It is very possible. But Stormalong would have to be left behind."

Captain Savage looked off into space. "If we abandon him, the damned Dyaks will take his head."

"I promised him that I would not allow that," said Doc quietly.

Snapping back into focus, Captain Savage whirled. "What?"

"Earlier, he specifically requested that I prevent the Dyaks from taking it," explained Doc.

Captain Savage's golden eyes grew introspective. "A promise is a promise. If you made that vow to him, then you are honor-bound to respect it, even if it means your demise. And the same chains of honor that bind you, bind me as well. It is settled then. We will make our stand here, Dyaks be damned."

Doc Savage said nothing. He was thinking that he wished he had his Annihilator submachine gun. But it would have been impractical to bring it up the well, even if he had the ammunition to feed it.

It bothered him greatly that he felt an irrational psychological need for a now-useless hunk of machined metal when he still had his brain and his brawn—not to mention all of the training still at his command.

Chapter LV

PRINCE MONYET WAITED for the sun to go down. "Make pitch torches," he ordered his men. They found appropriate pieces of wood, and dipped them into a tar pit, one of several that dotted Skull Island.

They began reassembling, including those who had been brought down by mysterious darts fired from the jungle earlier. Darts that did not kill, but put them to sleep.

Conferring, they assembled everything they knew of the situation.

"There are three gold eyes, and one old woman," reported the Dyak scout, as if the latter did not matter.

Monyet nodded eagerly. "Good. We are many."

"They have no darts, unless the brazen devil brought his own."

"He must have," said Monyet. "For who else felled our men who slept?"

"Darts that do not kill are not so very fearsome," a warrior suggested.

"They are if you fall asleep climbing the side of a mountain," countered the Dyak leader. "And awake in the afterlife without your head."

All fell silent. To lose one's head was the ultimate disgrace. To have it removed while sleeping and defenseless was especially shameful. A sleeping warrior cannot defend himself, has no chance to take an enemy head—or to keep his own.

It was a sobering proposition. They were not afraid to die—
if they could do so fighting manfully.

Monyet questioned one man. "You saw the brazen devil arise
from the pool up in the mountain?"

"Yes. After defeating a great eight-armed devilfish that dwelt
there."

Monyet's eyes narrowed in thought. "Perhaps we have been
assaulting that peak the wrong way."

"You think there is another way up?"

Monyet's slitted eyes went to the hollow orbs of Skull Mountain, eye sockets now dark with moving shadow.

"Once before," he said, "the brazen devil bested me through
the iron in his lungs. But Monyet has mighty lungs, too. I will
prove who has the greatest lungs. Come! We will find the same
way up that the brazen devil discovered. And from the pool,
we will take him unawares. Then we will take their heads...."

Curved *mandau* swords and *duku* knives were thrust upward
to the rising tropical moon.

"Antu pata!" the Dyaks roared. "Trophy heads!"

Chapter LVI

PENJAGA THE KEEPER climbed down off the hairy breast of the once-mighty but now inert Kong.

"He may live," she croaked. "He may not. We will know in one moon. Maybe two moons."

Captain Savage growled, "We do not have two moons."

"Father," said Doc, "I can take her out safely and return."

"My work is not yet done!" snapped Penjaga. "I will stay."

"These men," reminded Doc, "collect heads."

"They want the head of Kong," Penjaga sneered. "I would like to see them try." She spat on the rock floor that had been worn flat by countless tracks.

Doc looked around. How long had Kong dwelled here? The stone floor was well-worn, as if bare feet had smoothed it over generations. Perhaps centuries.

He had investigated the treasure room, found little that was useful. The statuary were too large and heavy too be moved far, even if they could be squeezed through the intervening crack.

They could be thrown out the other eye socket, but not effectively. The Dyaks were not positioned for that defensive maneuver to work.

Deep in the night, Stormalong Savage stirred. Yellow eyes pried open.

The others moved to his side, gave him fresh water from the part of the pool still unpolluted by devilfish blood.

354

"I live," Stormalong rasped out.

Captain Savage forced a reassuring smile. "Yes, Father. We have beaten back the Dyak enemy."

Seeing Penjaga's winkled-turtle face, Old Stormy muttered darkly, "I suppose I have you to thank for this."

"I came to save Kong," sniffed the Keeper. "But I could not ignore you, you long thing of hair and narrow bones."

Old Stormy smiled. "Penjaga and I have been friendly enemies for a very long time now."

"Pah!" spat the old crone.

They made him comfortable. For the vaulted interior of the cavern remained tolerably cool, neither hot in the day, nor cold by night.

Doc and his father went out onto the ledge to watch for signs of a renewed attack.

"We may die here," said Doc quietly.

"We may."

"There are many questions I have wanted to ask you...."

"And I have so few answers," said Captain Savage, absently. Then, seeming to snap out of a reverie, he spoke up.

"I can tell you one thing now."

"Yes?"

"I was not speaking the truth when I represented to you that I could no longer afford to complete your training."

Surprise flicked in Doc's restless flake-gold eyes. He had never known his father to be careless with the truth.

"No?"

"My funds have been diminished. That much is true. But I fully expected to replenish them. I told you half the truth. The conditions of the present did not mean that the future was so clouded."

"But why?"

"During the late war, I did secret duty. The *Orion* served as an unofficial Q-ship. I presume you know what that means?"

"Yes. The *Orion* operated as a disguised schooner-of-war, designed to lure the enemy into traps and engagements."

Captain Savage nodded. "I am proud to say that the *Orion* sank three German submarines with depth charges during that period. I made no money and spent much. Hence the deplorable state of my finances at present."

DOC SAVAGE said nothing. This was a revelation. But after some thought, it was not really a surprise. It explained the hydrophones in the locked trunk, among other things.

Doc asked, "Then why did you represent to me that my training could not continue?"

"All your life, you have been a dutiful son, going where I sent you, learning what you had to. Now on the threshold of manhood, with a war behind you, I had to see what stuff you were made of. If you were to follow in my footsteps, I had to take your measure."

"I see."

"No, you do not see. I did not mean that you had every choice in the world. I fully expected you to resume your training. But in your own time and place. I had confidence that you would see the wisdom in that."

"You may have been correct," allowed Doc.

"But, first and foremost," pressed Savage Senior, "I had to cleanse you of red war, and the accompanying lust for battle. I had to set you on a new path—away from war."

Doc looked blank. "I have come to see my war experiences as an extension of my training."

"I could not do so until you were out of uniform, of course," said Captain Savage, ignoring the comment. "The fortuitous discovery of the *Courser* provided the opportunity. It was my intention to guide you through this adventure and test your mettle."

"So this was all a test?"

"You performed magnificently," said Captain Savage, a thin

trace of paternal pride warming his tone.

"Thank you."

A shadow fell over the captain's wind-burned face. "But it was all for naught, if we die here," he said harshly.

"We are honor bound," Doc reminded.

"That we are. That we are."

The two men shared a long silence. Doc Savage broke it.

"The Annihilator submachine gun lies in the jungle. Spare ammunition can be retrieved from the *Orion.* Also tools, with which I could create grenades by filling bamboo tubes with black powder and capping both ends."

"An ingenious stratagem. But to reach the *Orion* and return with all that, I do not think there is the time, much less the opportunity."

"A man is not beaten until he is dead, or has given up," said Doc. "The author of Tarzan had a saying he put into the mouth of one of his characters: 'I still live.' Father, we still live."

"Yes, we still live. But for how long? We are outnumbered, low on ammunition—such as it is—and utterly without provisions."

As if to underscore his point, Captain Savage took his empty revolver from its holster and flung it away.

"That," he said, "is of no more use than your vaunted Annihilator. For of what use are firearms without proper ammunition?"

Doc Savage watched the revolver skitter away, thinking it would make a fair club during a last stand.

"Father," he said abruptly, "you are fond of quoting Teddy Roosevelt."

"I served under him during the battle for the San Juan Heights, as you well know," returned Savage Senior with a trace of stiffness at the inappropriate use of the familiar name.

"Did Roosevelt not say, 'Do what you can, with what you have, where you are?'"

"Well put. But our situation remains unchanged."

Doc looked back into the cavernous gloom.

"I see a weapon more powerful than a thousand Dyaks."

Captain Savage stepped back. His stern gaze went to the Keeper ministering to the titanic beast-god.

"You cannot mean Penjaga?"

"No," replied Doc. "Kong."

Chapter LVII

DOC SAVAGE MOVED to the cavern pool, whose wild
ripples were only now settling down.

Penjaga stood there, a look of disgust upon her wrinkled
features.

"It has been fouled," she spat. "Fouled with devilfish blood.
Of what good is it now?"

"It could not be helped," said Doc. But his golden eyes were
whirling with a renewed animation.

Moonlight flooded in from the hollow entrance, giving the
interior of the lair a thin shine. In that wan light, the blood of
the vanquished octopus—or whatever it had been—gleamed
greenly.

"What does Kong usually eat?" asked Doc suddenly.

"Kong eats whatever he wishes to eat," snapped Penjaga.
"Slashers. Deathrunners. Devilwings. I have seen him break
their necks and devour their still-living flesh with his terrible
fangs." She hung her head. "But the great Kong cannot do that
now."

Stopping to scoop up the soapstone goblets he had earlier
discovered, Doc began filling them with verdigris-hued water.
He presented the brimming receptacles to the Keeper.

"Give him these to drink. The blood will renew his strength."

Penjaga's old eyes brightened.

"You *do* know things," she said softly.

Taking the ancient goblets in each gnarled hand, Penjaga

brought them to Kong and climbed atop his slowly heaving breast. The crackling of his ribcage cartilage sounded like the creaking of a ship's rigging.

Doc looked about, found the length of maimed tentacle he had ripped off his arm. The sucker marks still burned on his sun-bronzed skin.

Walking over to Kong, he watched Penjaga slowly pouring the greenish water into the beast-god's open mouth. The pulsing action of his hairy throat showed that Kong had begun accepting the nourishment.

Doc tossed the tentacle up.

"See if he will take that."

Penjaga picked up the limp, detestable thing and made a prune face.

"Kong eats red meat," she sniffed. "Not cold fish."

"Try. Anything that will give him strength may save his life."

Shrugging, Penjaga carried the rubbery green thing over to the great fanged mouth. She dangled it gingerly, as if fearful of falling into the awful maw that devoured slashers and pterosaurs alike.

Kong's wide nostrils flared, sniffed and sniffed again, curiously intrigued.

A tongue larger than a rubber plant lifted into view and touched the tentacle. Tasting it tentatively, Kong began licking the rubbery morsel with increasing interest.

Surprise on her age-weathered face, Penjaga lowered the length into Kong's yawning mouth.

The great creature began chewing, slowly and rhythmically.

It took a long time, but finally Kong finished his methodical masticating and swallowed the pulverized matter.

"He does not like it," Penjaga commented. "I can tell."

"But he swallowed it," Doc pointed out.

"Bring more."

Doc went to the pool and, after taking three deep breaths,

disappeared below, Bowie knife in one bronze hand.

He was back not long after, a huge freshly-severed tentacle draped over one brawny shoulder.

Methodically, he began cutting it into sections. These he carried to Penjaga.

She fed Kong only the smallest pieces first, progressing to the larger as they disappeared down the beast-god's gullet.

Guarding his father's prone form, Captain Savage had watched all this with a dull interest, the worry lines etched into his brassy features.

Chicahua padded up, began speaking in his own language. The Mayan had been a silent but absorbed observer of all that had thus far transpired.

"What is he saying?" asked Doc.

"Chicahua is saying that Kong reminds him of Hunbatz. That is a monkey god out of his people's mythology. There were two monkey gods, Hunbatz and Hunchouen. Hunbatz is the Howler Monkey God. They are very sacred to the Maya. For their holy book, the *Popul Voh*, stipulates that, in a previous age, men were made of wood. The wooden men were destroyed by the gods, but those who did not perish survived as monkeys. He thinks that Kong is one of those survivors. Mr. Darwin might possibly subscribe to that identical theory."

Doc nodded. It explained why the Mayan had been so much in control of his emotions during the difficult proceedings.

"How is your father?" asked Doc.

Captain Savage lowered his voice. "Failing. And those Dyak devils have been too quiet these last few hours. I fear the worst."

Doc went to the ledge, peered downward.

THE half moon painted the great wall in the distance, making it look both formidable and ageless. Once again, Doc wondered how long ago it had been erected and what manner of people had built it.

If Penjaga had been younger, it might have been possible to

guess at her origins. But the Keeper might have been Annamese or Javanese—or any Asian people. Discerning her origins was beyond him.

Below, the watching Dyaks brandishing pitch torches, their hairless faces wavering blankly in the shivering lights.

Doc's whirling eyes searched for Monyet, whose gold chest plates would catch and reflect the torchlight. He could not find the man.

But suddenly, his eyes discovered the man's long feather headdress lying on the ground, apparently under guard. There was no sign of the Dyak prince near it.

Under his breath, Doc emitted his low trilling.

Returning to his father's side, Doc addressed him.

"The Dyaks are watching, not acting. But there is no sign of their leader, Father."

Clark Savage, Senior's brow furrowed. "I fear they are up to some subterfuge."

"Agreed. But what?"

An electric tension came into their golden eyes. Their gazes wandered about the granite cavern, returned and locked.

A single thought passed between them like an electric spark. At first, it went unspoken. Captain Savage said, "Do you suppose that skulking devil intends to take us by surprise?"

"My thought exactly."

Their eyes shifted in the direction of the weirdly-green body of water.

"The pool…" muttered the captain.

"He will likely drown in the trying."

Captain Savage frowned darkly. "If he does not, we must be prepared."

Stationing Chicahua at the ledge, the two Savage men repaired to the pool. All thought of Kong and his failing health had fled.

"If he does survive the swim," said Doc, "he will be in no

condition to fight."

"True. Therefore, that cannot be his plan."

They were walking around the circumference of the pool as they discussed the matter, watching its darkling jade surface.

At one point, they stepped into a spot that had not been visited before.

Suddenly, Doc's whispered words echoed loudly above their heads.

Halting, they froze in place.

"My word!" exploded Captain Savage.

"There is an acoustical anomaly in this part of the chamber," decided Doc, stepping forward and back and hearing his voice rise and fall in volume in an uncanny way.

Captain Savage said, "The ancient Greeks possessed the secret of constructing their amphitheaters so that an actor could, by speaking in a normal tone of voice, be distinctly heard over a large area."

"I wonder if this is a natural phenomenon, or one made by man...?"

"There is no time for idle conjecture now," Captain Savage said impatiently. "We must—"

Suddenly, Chicahua called out to them.

"Remain here," Captain Savage advised. "I will see what he wants."

Rushing to the ledge, Captain Savage saw the situation before the agitated Mayan could describe it.

The Dyaks had built several scattered fires. These were set in the northeast, upwind of Skull Mountain's perpetually-grim face. The smoke was rising in dark columns.

The smell of smoke was already carrying to his nostrils.

As he watched, they began throwing bundles into the leaping yellow flames. The smoke took on a heavy, evil quality in the moonlight and the odor reaching upward began to sting the eyes.

"Withdraw to shelter," Savage told Chicahua.

Returning to the pool, he conversed with Doc Savage in low whispers.

"The Dyaks have a method of smoking out victims from longhouses they attack by night. They throw chilies into the fire, which produces an agonizing smoke, burning eyes and lungs, impossible to endure for very long."

Doc nodded grimly. "I smell it already."

"If they create a noxious smokescreen, we will be driven out of here, or overcome if we make a stand."

"Perhaps it is a diversion...."

"We are powerless to prevent this."

Doc Savage looked from his father's face to that of Old Stormy lying there helpless and inanimate. His gaze flicked to Kong, whose nostrils began twitching. The awful unfamiliar odor was seeping into his laboring lungs.

"Son," said Captain Savage.

"Yes, Father?"

"I ask only one thing of you." He lowered his voice. "Do not permit them to decrown me. Even deceased, I could not bear the thought of a proud Savage head decorating a Dyak longhouse, the flesh of my face being eaten by household rats until my eyeless skull is exposed."

Doc Savage looked his father straight in the eye and strange, troubled lights played there.

Captain Savage went on stiffly, "I, in turn, offer you the same provisional guarantee. If it is within my power to prevent—"

"Quiet," said Doc suddenly.

Taken aback, Captain Savage said, "What?"

"I said, please be quiet."

And without saying another word, the bronze giant strode over to the precise spot where the acoustical phenomenon was most potent.

Chapter LVIII

PRINCE MONYET SWAM through a darkness that made him believe he had fallen into a pit so deep there was no escaping it.

His lungs ached. His eyes watered. He swam blindly, feeling his way whenever he encountered stone or rock outcroppings above him.

His fingers were scraped raw by contact with these rough surfaces. His chest was tightening. Every fiber in his being screamed for an indrawn breath.

Stubbornly, Monyet refused to take one. To breathe was to die. To inhale meant choking on the bitter water of defeat.

Monyet of Skrang, son of Ramba, would not surrender to his weakness. He would stay strong, show the brazen devil that he possessed lungs as formidable as any man. He, Monyet, would prevail!

A dull sound made his ears ache. He felt like a grub impaled upon a pin. Twisting, he sought any sign of an outlet, any hope of fresh air.

Struggling through water both dark and cold, Monyet began to lose hope. In his despair, he began to pray to the Dyak gods of the Seven Heavens. But most of all, he prayed to Djata, the water god who lived in earthly rivers.

Djata, carry me on your powerful currents to my destination, bear me to the place where I can take revenge upon my enemies. Do not swallow me forever in your cold embrace, for I have yet to prove my prowess against my foes.

In the smothering cold dark, Monyet surrendered to the current. Blind to all that was around him, his wiry strength ebbing, he had no other choice....

Above his head appeared a faint shimmer of moonlight on water. He was rising now. Monyet began kicking furiously. His *duku* blade was sheathed by his side, cutting edge turned upward, horn handle within easy reach. Its iron weight dragged him. But he refused to remove it. Monyet ached to draw it. But he needed both hands, both feet, and all of his willpower to push his aching body, upward, ever upward, toward that disk of shimmering watery moonlight, where clean air and supreme victory lay....

Chapter LIX

TAKING A POSITION in a specific spot in the chamber of Kong, Doc Savage set himself. His throat pulsed, his lips parted.

And from those lips came a strange vocalization.

The sound might have been the call of some fabulous prehistoric creature of the skies over Skull Island. It could have been a lost melody out of Earth's past. It might have been the eerie voice of Circe, or the wild piping of Pan. But it wasn't.

It emerged from Doc's lips, low in the beginning, rising in cadence, then growing in volume and vocal strength.

In the weird acoustics of Skull Mountain, this trilling was magnified, echoing and reechoing until it filled the entire granite chamber.

Lying nearby, Kong gave utterance to a cheeping grunt, as if curious, or even afraid. For the beast-god did not understand what his small ears conveyed to his brain.

This was a new sound in his experience.

Penjaga peered around, puzzled.

Over in one corner, Stormalong Savage seemed to rise, and speak. But his words were lost in the overpowering music.

Out in the jungle below Skull Mountain the magnified melody careened. It wafted over the shaggy palm crowns tossing in the breeze. It caused birds and beasts alike to snap heads around and cry out in surprise.

All of Skull Island heard it, from the natives in the village who suddenly lined the great sprawling wall, rapt with wonder, to the Dyaks tending their devilish fires below.

Others heard it, too. And in the covered jungle lanes, swift, furtive things were moving, coming closer, lured by the awesome sound.

Doc Savage kept up the sound for what seemed a yawning eternity. He paused for breath only once, and when he did, he took in air so swiftly that the trilling that was his signature appeared to be uninterrupted.

On and on, it wavered, climbing, falling, rising, dying, reviving, reverberating, seemingly inexhaustible.

Inevitably, the sound ceased. It trailed away like the dying sigh of a supernatural being.

"What the devil?" blurted Captain Savage.

"If I am correct," said Doc, "it will not be long."

"What on Earth are you driving at?"

Then far below, came a chorus of screaming, followed by other noises—weird, grisly, rending.

Penjaga's sharp ears took in the noisy tumult. Her puzzled face smoothed out in shock and surprise.

"Slashers!" she hissed. "Deathrunners!"

FROM below, the sounds of slaughter carried. The smoke made it almost impossible to see what transpired far beneath them.

But the awful cacophony was unmistakable—unforgettable.

Men running, fighting, being pursued. Here and there, feral cries—cries that seemed almost human, but were not.

And mingled here and there, an uncanny whistling such as Doc had heard before. The human-like whistling of the canny deathrunners mimicking the sounds of men!

Mixed in with the terrible smarting smoke, they began to pick up the definite odor of spilled blood. A great quantity of it.

Entwined with that odor, came the crunching of bones and

teeth tearing and rending—meat being ripped asunder by remorseless jaws housing serrated teeth.

Before very long, these sounds settled down to a noisy chewing and feeding.

Captain Savage looked at his son in stunned silence.

"Brilliant," he breathed. "Simply brilliant. Tarzan himself, calling for his jungle comrades, could not have done a more credible job."

"Thank you," returned Doc modestly. "But this is far from over."

From the pool, came a gurgle and a splash, followed by the padding of stealthy feet.

"Stormalong!" rapped Doc.

A bronze flash, he rushed to his grandfather's side.

Hovering over the elongated form crouched the wiry wet figure of Monyet. His dark eyes were wide, wild with the closeness of thwarted death.

One hand seized the truncated tail—all that remained of Stormalong's white beard—yanked his head off the ground and to one side. The other was clutching his dripping *duku*. It lifted.

Doc Savage plunged in. The moon threw his leaping shadow ahead of him.

Seeing this, Monyet whirled. His filed and blackened teeth showed in a fierce grimace. It might have been a wolfish grin, or it might have been a sneering snarl. It was impossible to tell.

Doc, a mighty colossus of living metal, closed with the smaller man.

In an ordinary contest, it would have been unequal. It *was* unequal.

Monyet was winded. Even though his chest heaved with every breath, his close brush with death combined with his burning hatred enervated him. He was alive with a vitality that only a man facing personal doom knows.

Doc had out his Bowie knife. His intention was to use it to

hamstring the Dyak as he wrestled him to the ground. The Lakota Sioux had taught him this tactic.

But before he could accomplish this maneuver, the bronze man had to wrest the *duku* from his foe's fist. A weapon that was designed to lop a man's head off his shoulder with a side-wise swipe.

Doc came on straight, feinted left, right, then ducked beneath the side-swiping blade.

Seizing the Dyak about the neck and legs, he threw him to the ground, swiftly applying the sharpened edge of his Bowie knife along the back of the man's knees, severing the ligaments there.

Monyet screamed, recognizing that he had been crippled in an instant.

Stepping back, Doc held his blade ready, in case he needed to strike again.

Monyet bored hateful eyes into the bronze man's own. A sneer crawled across his hairless brown face. Then, he opened his hand, showing what lay in his palm.

A Dyak dart!

Suddenly, Doc Savage became aware of the stinging sensation in his left bicep.

Grabbing the flesh, he saw the telltale blood spot.

He had been stabbed by a poisoned dart unawares!

More swiftly than he thought it possible, the metallic giant began to feel light-headed. His knees turned watery. He staggered, sought the support of a stone wall. Cold perspiration popped out on his forehead. A deep groan emerged from him.

Behind him others reacted, not knowing what it all meant.

As they rushed toward the stricken man, Monyet began crawling toward Doc Savage, his *duku* clutched tightly, his eyes avidly staring at the bronze giant's head, and the valuable orbs of gold it contained....

Chapter LX

RUNNING FEET MADE hurried sounds. Doc Savage heard all this only dimly. There was a ringing in his ears. A blood-red curtain fell across his vision. He was succumbing to the poison of the *upas* sap.

Captain Savage and Chicahua came charging in from different directions. They moved with all of their pent-up might, yelling, howling, demanding that the Dyak cease.

But Monyet did not hear them. Even if he had, he would not stop. He had only one feverish thought in mind—to harvest the head of the bronze giant whose eyes were composed of gold dust.

It all happened in less than a minute. It would never be forgotten over a lifetime.

As Doc Savage crumpled, rapidly losing consciousness, a great hairy hand lifted with a cracking of cartilage and fell over Monyet the Dyak prince.

Monyet sensed the shadow looming over him, but in his madness, refused to acknowledge it.

And so when the powerful fingers of the beast-god of Skull Island squeezed him, Monyet did not know his peril until his body left the cold stone floor and he was being conveyed, flailing and screaming, toward the yawning and white-fanged maw of the terrible Kong.

Still clutching his blade, Monyet attempted to slash at his gigantic foe.

The blade swept once, then back, then fell from his hands when a black thumb larger than he casually stove in his chest at the sternum.

Monyet screeched. His cry of mortal pain echoed and reverberated off the uncaring granite walls of the lair of Kong, bouncing among the stalactites and stalagmites, perpetuating itself wildly.

The next he knew—and the last thing Monyet ever experienced—was having his howling head inserted into the humid, malodorous mouth of the gigantic ape.

Monster teeth came together with a harsh snap. The crunch of Monyet's fragile neck bones was hardly audible over that awful finality.

The beast-god chewed this fresh morsel experimentally, then spat it out in evident disgust. It was plainly not to his taste.

When Kong flung the headless body from him, it flew out onto the ledge, to topple over the cliff's edge, neck stump pumping arterial blood, carelessly painting the rocks all the way down to its final fate.

Below, a startled slasher looked up and decided to investigate. It ate well.

Chapter LXI

WHEN DOC SAVAGE returned to consciousness, he looked around.

His father, Chicahua and Penjaga the Keeper looked down upon him, faces mixing worry with unabashed relief.

"I still live," he said simply.

"For this boon," related Captain Savage, "you may thank Penjaga and her herbs. That, and the fortuitous fact that the poisonous dart that struck you had been diluted by the Dyak's long swim. Very little potency remained when it bit."

"Otherwise, I could not have saved you," added the Keeper.

"Monyet?" asked Doc.

"Kong took his head. He threw away the rest."

"Stormalong?"

No one answered. They all looked away.

"Dead?" asked Doc, attempting to rise.

His father replied gravely, "No, but the end is near."

"Take me to his side," requested Doc.

Both Chicahua and Captain Savage had to help the bronze man to his feet.

Together, they reached the side of Old Stormy, stretched out near the greenish pool.

His yellow eyes were open. They were cloudy and their color was dull. Stormalong Savage was staring up into the vaulted rock ceiling as if into eternity.

374 / A DOC SAVAGE ADVENTURE

"Grandfather..." said Doc.

The fading yellow eyes focused. Lips curled in a thin smile. "Doc...."

"I have so many questions to ask you."

"And I have no time left on Earth to answer them. I am so sorry."

Doc groped for words. "I... am sincerely glad to have known you at last."

"And I am justifiably proud to see what you have become. Cap, you should be proud of your son."

Doc looked to his father. "Cap?"

Clark Savage, Senior, looked sheepish. "When I was a boy, my father called me his Little Captain. Cap for short."

"You loved being called that," murmured Stormalong. "When you were very young...."

Captain Savage nodded, his eyes wet.

"As soon as I grew into long pants," he said thickly, "I put it behind me forever."

Silence fell over them all. There was only the raspy breathing of Stormalong Savage. He coughed once. His lips were flecked with a pinkish foam.

"It is better this way," he managed. "For I have no ship. I do not wish to live like the sad Karo Bataks. I only wish I could walk the warpy deck of the old *Courser* one last time."

Pain touched Clark Savage's eyes. "That, I fear, is impossible now."

"You know what my last wish is, don't you, Cap?"

Captain Savage nodded. "Burial at sea. It will be done with all due and proper ceremony. Rest assured."

Filmy yellow eyes searched the faces arrayed around. Clark Savage, Senior. Chicahua. Penjaga. Finally, they fell on the stricken face of Doc Savage.

"I have no heritage to bequeath to you, grandson. No wealth. No property. No station in life. For that, I am truly sorry."

"It does not matter," assured Doc.

"I suppose not. So I leave you with these words from the Bard of Avon: 'Love all, trust a few, do wrong to none.' May they light your path."

"I will try to live by those words," promised Doc.

Captain Savage cleared his throat. "To which I might add, 'Keep your mind, your conscience and your body clean.'"

Frowning, Doc asked, "I do not recall those lines from literature. Shakespeare?"

"Nick Carter's father spoke those very words to his own son."

"I see." But Doc's expression was faintly puzzled.

With that, a low rattle issued from the throat of Stormalong Savage and his entire elongated frame relaxed. A final exhaling breath seemed to flurry his snowy white beard. His eyes closed slowly, but not completely. A glint of dull amber remained.

Captain Savage closed them with gentle fingers that trembled. "I never imagined that I would live to see this day," he whispered.

He stood up. "And so it is done."

"There are still the slashers," warned Penjaga the Keeper.

AS if they had heard her, a rattle of rock and a scramble of hard, horny claws came from the other side of Kong, whose great amber-gold eyeball had rotated downward to witness the passing of Stormalong Savage.

The titanic ape roused, turned his head toward the ledge. From his bristling throat issued a low warning growl.

Sounds of scampering persisted. With it, came an eerie whistle. It was the whistle of Stormalong Savage, but it issued from a deathrunner's throat!

"The slashers cannot climb," said Penjaga. "But the deathrunners are more clever. That one is trying to lure us to our dooms."

Painfully, Kong reached out and wrapped a hairy hand around a boulder too large for mortal man to lift. Nor could he manage to raise it in his present condition.

But carefully, he pushed it farther and farther along toward the entrance, finally giving it a jerky push. But his great arm was too short to complete the task.

Captain Savage, assisted by Chicahua, stepped in and put their backs to the stone.

The boulder made ugly grinding noises inching onto the ledge, but they managed it.

They got it to the stony lip. With a final heave, they sent it over. The cracking sound of shattering stone striking and dragging a screaming deathrunner to its doom on the rocks below gave them all renewed hope.

Kong appeared to grunt in pleasure. Then, he slowly closed his eyes.

"There are many more," Penjaga reminded. "Some have not eaten their fill."

"How can we defeat these things?" asked Captain Savage angrily.

"We cannot wait for them to finish feeding and leave," she said. "For they know that we are here. They will hide in the brush until we show ourselves. Then they will come screaming and devour us."

Captain Savage bowed his silvery head. "Then we have no hope."

"There is one thing," said Penjaga, smiling slyly.

"Yes?"

"The sting-ray spines. The slashers are not immune to their venom. That is why I carry them."

Hearing that, Doc Savage struggled to his feet. Reaching into his waistband, he extracted the elaborate Pan-pipe blowgun and Penjaga's waterproof pouch of sting-ray spines. Loading it carefully, he moved toward the ledge, pausing only to give the sleeping Kong a reassuring pat atop his bullet head.

There, Doc lay prone on the granite shelf to conserve his strength and present a minimum target. Peering down through the thinning smoke, he saw that the unfed fires were slowly burning out.

Slashers moved through the moonlight, jaws agape, their riotous feathers iridescent. They had no interest in anything other than their raw food.

Doc loaded all six tubes of his improvised blowgun. Lifting the weapon to his mouth, he charged his powerful lungs. He felt weak—was weak.

Picking his shots with care, Doc began blowing venomous barbs at his feeding foes below. Their single-minded focus on food made them standing targets, rather resembling fantastic turkeys.

One by one, they reared, stung. Scrambling to escape, they collapsed into twitching piles of varicolored plumage, raptor feet kicking spasmodically.

Others, seeing what befell their pack members, left off their frenzied feeding and retreated into the undergrowth.

Reloading, Doc brought down as many more as he could.

The bronze man sat down heavily, saying, "I believe they are bested."

"Magnificent," said Captain Savage, his voice thick with emotion.

They left Penjaga to tend to the wounds of Kong, whose breathing was the rhythmic respiration of a recovering creature.

Doc Savage began his routine of physical exercises. This went on for some time. The activity caused his bronze physique to run with honest sweat. His dulled eyes began to clear and the brisk whirling that marked the flake-gold irises stirred again to life. His healthy color returned. There were other aspects to this daily regimen, which included apparatus for sharpening the senses, but often it was impractical to include them. So Doc always made it a point to complete this portion every day without fail. Here, the muscle-testing routine had a restorative effect.

After a while, they began making preparations to depart.

It was decided that nothing be removed from the treasure

room. It was hardly practical to do so, and Penjaga communicated her displeasure when she overheard them discussing it.

"We are going now," Doc told her.

"Do not return, Gold Eyes," warned Penjaga, shaking a finger
at him. "Skull Mountain Island does not belong to you, or your
kind. It once belonged to my people, of whom I am the last
issue. Now it belongs to Kong. Only Kong."

"Thank you for your assistance," returned Doc graciously.

"Yes, your help was very much appreciated," added Captain
Savage, bowing his head slightly. "I presume you will not stay
here any longer than is safe for you."

"When Kong is strong," she said firmly, "I will depart. Not
before."

They walked over to the body of Stormalong Savage.

Glancing back at the hairy figure of the beast-god of Skull
Island, slumbering like a dormant Krakatoa, Doc said, "Father,
I have made a decision."

"What is that, son?"

"After due consideration, I have decided to return to medical
school, after all."

"That is a very wise decision, Clark."

"From now on, call me Doc. I intend to earn the nickname."

They shook metallic hands firmly.

"It is a bargain."

CAPTAIN CLARK SAVAGE lifted the body of his father in
both arms and carried him out to the ledge. The sun was coming
up in the east, infusing the lair of Kong with a warm, rosy light.

The jungle began stirring. But they had no eye for its myriad
noises, or the sight of varicolored pterosaurs lifting skyward to
skim the treetops toward open water and fresh fish.

Doc Savage was still weak, but his incredible reserves of
energy were already beginning to return.

Together, they conveyed the body down the side of Skull

Mountain by handing it from man to man. They stumbled only once. Doc's massive arms snapped out to steady the body, and they resumed their careful way downward.

At the base, they struck out, ignoring the sleeping slashers and dismembered Dyaks until Doc Savage halted suddenly.

"What is it?" asked his father, looking around guardedly.

"Grandfather gave me a piece of sound advice about surviving in the jungle. I am going to heed it."

Going among the slashers, the bronze giant methodically cut each and every one of their bright-plumed throats.

"They will not awaken to hunt us," he said simply, wiping gore off his knife onto the wilted feathers blowing lifelessly in the breeze.

By this time, Doc was able to shoulder his grandfather's body unassisted, but he soon stopped to hack together a bamboo litter, which he lashed together with rattan and vines.

Together, they bore the body to the cliff. Employing long vines harvested from the treetops, they carefully lowered the body in stages until the three men were assembled on the deck of the *Orion*, which stood at anchor, unmolested.

At a nod from Captain Savage, Chicahua raised the anchor and they coaxed the auxiliary engine to life.

"It was good that you conserved the fuel," Doc said quietly.

Captain Savage nodded absently. He was out of words, his emotions raw.

Taking the wheel, the captain put the *Orion* about. Bleak golden eyes fixed, he piloted the schooner through the jagged rock formations to Skull Lagoon.

Doc took his father's wartime hydrophones out of storage and put them into operation. This helped them avoid submerged snags.

Carefully, they picked their way out to open water.

"Father, why did you not bring this device out upon our arrival?" wondered Doc.

Captain Savage considered his reply.

"When I saw how enamored you were of the submachine gun," he said, "I thought it wise to teach you to rely upon your wits and your courage, not devices. I still believe this."

Doc said, "I am still very interested in making a better submachine gun, but I confess that I have lost my passion for doing so. Saving lives, not taking them, will make for a better world."

"Perhaps you can find a way to do both," suggested Clark Savage, Senior.

Behind them came a volley of wild cries. They turned.

Lined atop the wall, with a few arrayed on the beach, stood groups of Atu warriors. Clutched in their upraised hands were dark, round objects that could not be made out over the ever-increasing distance.

Captain Savage trained his spyglass on the men, grunted once.

"It appears," he said, "that several Dyak stragglers sought refuge on the other side of the wall. They must have set upon the natives with their headhunting ways, incurring their wrath. A foolish move. For it has rebounded upon them."

Doc reached for the spyglass, but Captain Savage refused to surrender it, saying only, "They failed to keep their heads in the matter. I will spare you the sight of what remains."

Doc nodded.

"But if you wish," Captain Savage added, "I will make a present of this antique. It was a gift from my late father, but it is high time that I purchase something befitting a Twentieth Century schooner master."

"Thank you," said Doc, accepting the heirloom.

HOURS into their journey, Doc Savage stood at the stern, watching Skull Island and its unforgettable summit recede from sight, but not from memory.

"I will never forget this place," he said quietly.

As if in answer, a great bestial roar rolled out across the waters.

In response, pterosaurs lifted off Skull Island, began wheeling.

It was the voice of the beast-god of Skull Island, Kong.

"He sounds well," remarked Captain Savage from the helm. "In time, he will once again rule as king of his domain."

"Father," Doc said sincerely, "we must keep this place a secret."

"Done. No good can come of civilized men despoiling Skull Island. We will leave its fate to history."

Another thunderous roar rolled out, stronger than before. It sounded unreal, as if the unbelievable power of it mocked the evidence their own senses had conveyed to them of all they had experienced.

Then Skull Mountain Island was swallowed in the mists that were only now gathering across the face of the Indian Ocean. Soon it was entirely obscured.

THE *ORION* sailed another day or so, until they reached the approximate position where the *Courser* had been scuttled.

Sails were struck. The schooner began wallowing in the waves.

They prepared to consign the body of Stormalong Savage to the eternal waters.

Sailcloth of Egyptian cotton was laid out on the quarterdeck and the body reverently rolled into it. This was sewn closed with a sailor's needle, the bearded coppery face last. Finally, it was done.

"All hands bury the dead," called out Captain Savage.

Chicahua set a plank at the taffrail and the startlingly long body was carefully placed there, feet outward. Doc did the honors.

Captain Savage cleared his throat. "I feel as if some appropriate eulogy is in order, but at this precise moment words fail me." He turned to Doc. "Do you know the old sea shanty, 'Stormalong John?'"

"I do not, Father."

"Then, I will have to do my best alone. Feel free to join in the chorus, if you are so inclined."

Lifting his voice, Clark Savage, Senior, began to sing in a rolling refrain:

"Old Stormy's gone, that good old man
To me Way! Hay! Stormalong John
Oh, poor Old Stormy's dead and gone
To me aye, aye, aye, aye Mister Stormalong

"An able sailor, bold and true
To me Way! Hay! Stormalong John
A good old bosun to his crew
To me aye, aye, aye, aye Mister Stormalong"

At that point, Doc felt confident enough to join in the chorus.

"He's moored at last and furled his sail
To me Way! Hay! Stormalong John
No danger now from wreck or gale
To me aye, aye, aye, aye Mister Stormalong

"I wish I was old Stormy's son
To me Way! Hay! Stormalong John
I'd build me a ship of a thousand ton
To me aye, aye, aye, aye Mister Stormalong"

The signal was given, and Chicahua obediently tilted the plank. The shrouded body of Stormalong Savage slid downward and was immediately swallowed by the swells.

"Old Stormy's dead and gone to rest
To me Way! Hay! Stormalong John
Of all the sailors he was the best
To me aye, aye, aye, aye Mister Stormalong...."

Epilogue

THE LIGHT WAS dying outside the widows of Doc Savage's skyscraper headquarters when he concluded his account.

Monk, Ham and Renny were silent in its aftermath. They were all thinking the same thing: It was the longest they had ever heard their bronze chief speak uninterrupted.

Monk put it in his own words. "That's some yarn! Too bad Long Tom and Johnny weren't here for it."

Renny rumbled, "Johnny would get a kick out of it. But we'd better not tell him, or he'll try to pry the location of Skull Island out of Doc, then go on the biggest archaeological spree of his life."

Doc said nothing. His flake-gold eyes were strangely still and reflective.

"As you all know," he said at last, "only recently did we learn that my father had discovered a lost city built by Mayans in the Valley of the Vanished in present-day Hidalgo. Chicahua and the others belonged to that enclave, whose ancient gold mines now fund our operations. This was my father's greatest secret, which only his untimely death revealed. He refused to touch that wealth, reserving it until the time I proved myself worthy of its use."

"Did you ever discover any clue as to your father's motivation for training you as he did?" wondered Ham.

"Not directly. He was always reticent on that score, so I never pressed him. My father died before he could divulge anything more than I have recounted."

"Too bad," muttered Renny.

"But I did obtain a significant clue after his passing," added Doc, rising and striding over to the massive steel safe that dominated one corner of the reception room.

After manipulating the dial, the bronze man returned the map of Skull Island to its proper receptacle, and then removed something else.

"When I first opened my late father's safe, I discovered this."

Doc laid on the great inlaid table a thick paperbound book, now turning brown with age. The title was *The Old Detective's Pupil; or, The Mysterious Crime of Madison Square.*

"It was an old dime novel," he explained. "Starring a young sleuth named Nick Carter, it was bylined Nicholas Carter. I had read a few of these when I was a kid, but I always preferred Sherlock Holmes. This is the first of the many Nick Carter novels published by the Street & Smith concern beginning in 1886—a year before Doyle created Holmes. It recounts how the father of Nick Carter, wishing his son to follow in his professional footsteps, trained him up in all the scientific skills necessary for that purpose. Detection. Disguise. Ballistics. Languages. Every investigative science known to man. Nick Carter became a consulting detective, ultimately the greatest in the world."

Monk brightened. "I get it. Your father got the idea from that story."

"It is the identical notion," mused Ham, "but carried out to a greater degree."

Doc nodded. "My father wanted me to be versed in all scientific knowledge, a much loftier goal, in order to follow his path in roaming the world, coming to the aid of those in need, and dealing out justice to wrongdoers beyond the law."

Renny rumbled, "That explains where he got the idea, but it doesn't go very far toward revealing what motivated him to do it in the first place."

"That," said the bronze man glumly, "we may never know."

The four men fell silent as they reflected on the strange story and its sad aftermath.

Monk opened his simian mouth to offer another comment, but just then a buzzer sounded.

"Someone at the door," grunted Renny.

"Maybe it's somebody in trouble!" beamed Monk. "Ever since missin' out on that King Kong fracas, I've been itchin' after some action."

Doc directed, "Ham, show them in. Let us see what new adventure fate has brought to our doorstep this time."

About the Author
WILL MURRAY

WILL MURRAY (1953-) has written the exploits of heroes ranging from Remo Williams to Squirrel Girl, but *Skull Island* is the first time he has teamed up two legendary characters in one iconic adventure.

While the author has been long associated with Doc Savage, his connection to King Kong is less well known. He initially encountered the magnificent monkey back around 1963, but has forgotten whether he first saw Kong on TV, or read about him in *Famous Monsters of Filmland* #25. Either way, he became a lifelong fan.

Unlike most, Murray actually met the Eighth Wonder of the World. Back in 1986, as a journalist for *Starlog* magazine, he visited the set of *King Kong Lives!* at the old De Laurentiis Entertainment Group Studios in Wilmington, North Carolina. Kong was temporarily indisposed, being strapped down on a huge operating table while awaiting a mechanical heart. But he was still impressive. On the DEG backlot lay Carlo Rambaldi's forty-foot mechanical King Kong robot from the 1976 remake, sadly rusting away. So technically, Murray faced two incarnations of the fabulous ape that day.

None of this prepared him for writing *Skull Island*, but it didn't hurt.

Skull Island is the first exploration of the family history and origins of Doc Savage, and is a dramatic departure from the Doc Savage stories written by Lester Dent and the other writers who worked under the house name of Kenneth Robeson. Hence the decision to publish it under his undisguised byline.

With nearly sixty novels to his credit, Will Murray can only wonder: What next?

About the Artist
JOE DeVITO

FOR OVER THIRTY years, Joe (1957-) has specialized in SF, Fantasy and imaginative genres of all kinds. Along the way, he has painted and sculpted many of Pop Culture's most recognizable icons. He also illustrated and co-authored (with Brad Strickland) two novels. The first is *KONG: King of Skull Island* (DH Press, 2004). Over ten years in the making, it is a Cooper-endorsed prequel/sequel to the original King Kong story. The second book, *Merian C. Cooper's King Kong* (St. Martin's Griffin, 2005), is an expanded updating of the original 1932 novel credited to Edgar Wallace and Delos W. Lovelace.

The year 2012 saw the release of electronic versions of *KONG: King of Skull Island*, as well as Part 1 of an interactive iPad app. Part 2 of the app, an audiobook version from Radioarchives. com, and a Young Adult series based on the *KONG: King of Skull Island* book, are scheduled for 2013.

DeVito recently sculpted the 100th Anniversary statue of Tarzan for the Edgar Rice Burroughs, LLC, is painting covers for The Wild Adventures of Doc Savage written by Will Murray and Lester Dent, and is participating in the development of two films: *KONG: King of Skull Island*, and his newest creation, *The Primordials.*

About the Patron

GARY A. BUCKINGHAM, P.E.

IF A FASCINATION with books and reading is hereditary, it must have come only from my parents, Allen and Lynn, as there are few other traditional readers in the extended family. It seems there is a corollary in education, as we each have a college advanced degree. Although we have moved and traveled extensively around the country, our home is Wisconsin.

I met Joe DeVito at the Edgar Rice Burroughs Centennial Celebration near Los Angeles in August 2012. While I have attended a number of popular culture conventions in the past and met many artists, there was something about Joe's friendly greeting each time I passed by his table. Of course, his Tarzan art statues (three formats) on display were of primary interest. Before this, I was aware of his Wild Adventures of Doc Savage cover paintings, as well as Will Murray's excellent new and ongoing writing contribution to the Doc Savage canon. I had already read the first volume and was very positive on my outlook for the rest of the series.

However, my collection of Doc Savage previous to this was only ten of the Kenneth Robeson Bantam paperbacks and some Marvel, DC and Millennium comic books and magazines. I had none of the seven collaborations done by Joe and Will twenty years ago. My main interests of collecting had concentrated in other areas.

To quite an extent, Joe's admirable realistic art style has pulled me in to expanding my collection. The ultimate expression of this, to-date, is commissioning the cover painting for this book. I thought about it for a week after Joe mentioned the possibility to me in August, and then made the telephone call that started the three of us on the cover design and implementation.

Glad to say, Joe was right in his enthusiasm for the process, in that I feel my participation in the cover design was welcomed equally by Joe and Will. I'm pleased to mention that the autogyro on the cover was my idea, and the addition of a different frontispiece drawing from Joe as well as making the cover a wraparound conclude my contributions. Naturally, Joe DeVito deserves almost all the credit for his wonderful renditions of the ideas he, Will and I proposed.

I have been published just once in the field of popular culture. This was a seven-page, 15-illustration article entitled "Illustrations of the Canaveral Press Editions" in the (Edgar Rice) *Burroughs Bulletin* #77, Winter 2009. I hope to write more in the near future.

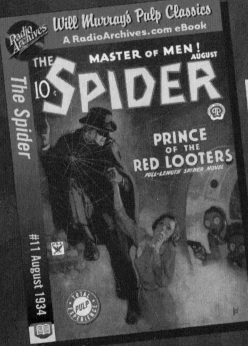

THE COMPLETE ADVENTURES OF **THIBAUT CORDAY** AND THE
FOREIGN LEGION

The greatest creation of Theodore Roscoe is collected for the first time! One of the most popular writers to ever appear in the pages of *Argosy,* Roscoe penned the adventures of Old Thibaut Corday of the French Foreign Legion, who appeared in more than twenty stories from 1929 to 1939.

Never before reprinted in a comprehensive series, it's now available in four volumes.

$19.95 ea • altuspress.com

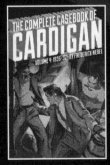

Made in the USA
Columbia, SC
28 October 2023

25111789R00224